BELVIDERE.

I

X
Sans Nom

To this special group, the spelling and grammar police, please put your pencil down; I will save you the suspense.

This novel may be a grammar and sentence structure nightmare to people who obsess about such things. The pages that follow are vaguely, or not so, reminiscent of Beat literature, which can be described, by some, as a rejection of standard narrative and linguistic values, including, but not necessarily limited to, syntax, punctuation, sentence structure and morphology. The writing style is idiosyncratic; it is how the author thinks, and how the author believes this fictional account should be told. And just as important, it's how real people speak and communicate in the real world, which is rarely textbook or *correct*. It is real, or at least how this author perceives reality, which is all that matters between these end-papers.

In any event, there **will** be mistakes. And all the mistakes in this book were purposeful, and will be defended as such, even if they weren't. After two long years of editing, this writer simply got tired of re-reading and proofing. So what you see is what you get, whether it's *right* or not.

My suggestion is to take the broader view: simply enjoy the characters and enjoy the ride they take you on. Along the way, if you feel the need to get enraged, do so at the abject violence, the graphic sex, the racism, the bigotry, the coarse language, the heathenism....but for God's sake, don't get enraged at punctuation....leave the poor periods alone.

For Earl....

Who, after forty years, somehow, found me,
and decided, with the help of some friends,
to tell me a story.
I simply listened, and wrote it down.

It took fifteen years.

I hope anyone who reads beyond this page
finds the journey as worthwhile as I have.

Earl is in my heart;
and I love him, very much;
he will never die.

C.

Novel Synopsis:

A mysterious man is sent to a dead-end town; to do what, and to whom, he simply doesn't know. It's all part of a game he neither understands, nor controls. He befriends those he will likely betray; there will certainly be trouble if he does not. A fantastical, mysterious journey; an ephemeral olla podrida of raw erotica, graphic violence, racism, heathenism, bigotry and vulgarity, all buoyed by the providence of friendship, love and kindred souls.

TABLE OF CONTENTS - I

PROLOGUE: THE DOWNHILL STONE IS ALREADY IN MOTION

It's inevitable.

A single day will quietly pass for each of us, unannounced, which reckons as the zenith, the peak of our life; the day where our lifelong achievements have crested, our potential tapped, succeeding days the downhill roll of the stone.

For the ambitious man, the one who looks at his morning reflection and convinces himself better days, more successful days, always lie ahead, no matter the means of measure, be it artistic, familial, emotional or financial, the manifestation of this fateful day represents the ultimate obstacle, for there is no cure, no recourse, for the de facto Rubicon.

For the ambitious man without faith, without a belief in some greater purpose in the before, or the after, this self-inflection assumes utmost import, for outside divine providence, one's self worth, ones image of accomplishment and legacy by the sole, is all he has in the end, when the light fades to black.

It is maddening; how can one truly know with any sense of certainty if their best day has already passed....was it yesterday, last week, last year....with future efforts unknowingly futile – left only to those who survive us to realize?

What if you sensed your day had passed? What if you somehow knew? Would you be content to bide your time, to close your term in relaxed retreat?

Perhaps your day is still on the approach; most would like to believe as much. If so, be rest assured, it marches closer, with no hint of fear, hesitation or reprisal.

So look within, dear reader – from this day forward, how do you propose to push that fateful time to the horizon, to the point it is asymptotic with your last conscious day....your last breath? To end on the highest note.

Or should you even care?

Thousands of moon jellyfish drift along the bulkhead in the harbor of Olde L'Acadie, in rhythm with the tide, slowly pulsing to and fro. There is comfort and serenity in being witness to this simple dance, in wanting to join, to embrace, that adagio, and wanting nothing more.

Maybe that is simply good enough.

Maybe not.

Back to the dawn of time, for every successful man, there have been countless also-rans, men with a hunger for success, for more of whatever it is they already have, or some of whatever it is they feel they lack. Artisans, merchants, professionals and proletariat alike....men who wake and splash their faces to greet each new day, a clamor to reach the pinnacle, not realizing their race has already been run.

For them....for many of us....the downhill stone is already in motion.

Master Cord Brin
Bayside, in the quiet midst of moon jellies
Halifax Harbor, Nova Scotia
June 24, 1906

CHAPTER 1 – ROCKING GENTLY WITH THE SWAY OF THE BUS

Fuck.

The word bounced about his brain, for no particular reason.

Typical.

The bus hummed along at a good clip; the grass median was a blur and the season's corn stalks drying in the fields passed by - an endless line of silent sentries. He stared blankly at the kinetic scene, his head lightly touching and then lifting off the glass, on and off, as the bus gently rocked along. It was a beautiful sun-splashed day; it shouldn't have been.

The destination was fast approaching.

He cracked his knuckles; half responded loudly, like oft-cracked knuckles do; the others were blanks. He stretched his legs and frowned a bit, then casually looked to the middle seat of the row; the porcelain sat beside him, safe, secure, pushed snug against the low, steady purr of the Sherpa bag, still always together, inseparable. She knew….Chicken knew. He smiled to himself at the thought...that little uptick smile that accompanied pursed lips.

The aisle seat was empty, as was the near-seat across the aisle. Both were still warm; bodies there, no longer were.

Three rows from the front.

Six months of lost weight was certainly visible, must be thirty-five to forty-odd pounds, he figured. A lot. He's not sure why it came to mind at this point, but it did. He could see it, or lack thereof, in his face, in his stomach. He was donning a new outfit, the first change in travel-wear in years, but there was no choice in that regard. His old habit: comfortable blue blazer and green, linen button-down, his faded jeans, a favorite pair, thread-worn, with the beginnings of a frayed hole in the crotch, and the tried tassel-loafers, which shined with a rich gloss, sporting remnants of white *Ammens* foot powder, which also faintly colored the tops of his feet, were, in toto, long gone, burned in the incinerator, converted to electricity, pulsing through overhead wires.

His new outfit fit well, better than his old one ever did; the shoes were shined to an even luster. Newly shined shoes usually put him in a good mood, but not today.

Certainly not today.

He felt apprehensive, tired and not particularly proud. But he knew this conte was to be expected all along.

But he never figured it would end this way, not this ending….never.

He quietly closed his eyes and extended a long exhale as he settled back in his seat, alone, rocking gently with the sway of the bus.

CHAPTER 2 – SO BEGAN THE JOURNEY

> *"Standing in the pouring rain;*
> *All alone in a world that's changed;*
> *Running scared now forced to hide;*
> *In a land where he once stood with pride;*
> *But he'll find his way;*
> *By the morning light;*
> *Will the wolf survive."*

The earworm played over and again in his head.

Los Lobos….he wondered whatever happened to them. He always thought the video should have been about the wolf, not a man – that made it a bit of a disappointment – but he always liked that little barefoot Mexican girl; he assumed she was Mexican, anyway.

She was certainly bangable.

He was the last passenger on the bus – seated solo in the last row, as far back as you could go; it was quiet, except for the sound of the tires pawing the pavement. He listened to himself breath as he stared out the window, watching the side of the road come into focus as the bus slowed.

He reached into the front left pocket of his jeans, pulled out the single slip of paper and looked at it again – as if the words might have changed.

Belvidere, New Jersey

He figured he would give it a year; then smiled sad to himself, knowing he would give it only as long as she would let him. Ultimately, it was up to her. It always was. Her call. Unless there was trouble; trouble trumped.

The dusty, off-white transport rolled to a stop onto the lonely gravel shoulder, alongside a large concrete pad – that was the extent of the depot. He slowly walked the empty aisle to the front, nodded, wordless, to the faceless driver, and exited. Throughout the long ride, they never once spoke, and their eyes never met.

He stretched and looked about as the tired, ashen carriage slowly pulled away. The diesel coughed, a small black petrol cloud appeared, then disappeared, into the atmosphere; the gears of the dingy beast ground loudly, and the pale *Greyhound* rounded a lazy bend in the highway and soon disappeared from sight.

Across the quiet two-lane highway stood *Luigi's Rancho*, an imposing two-story roadside log cabin, touting Italian-American fare and featuring a frowning fish, a longhorn and a dancing martini glass, all set on an oversized wooden sign – plucked from the 1950's and dropped into the 21st Century.

It was April 20th, Thursday, day number one; a clean slate.   The weather was gorgeous - sunny, with a cerulean sky....no hint of a cloud. He ran his hand back and forth over his shaven head; with eyes closed and skyward, he absorbed the sun.

What kind of hand had he been dealt this time?

This one didn't have a good feel or bad feel; somehow, it just felt....different. A stray dart will do that.

He wondered what she had in store.

The earworm returned.

He looked around; the concrete pad was surrounded on three sides by a weathered, split-rail fence. An opening midway led to a grass path, a wide swath cut in an overgrown field, dotted with last-year's brown thistles, hundreds of them, and the first hints of green on barberry bushes and wild roses, scattered throughout the field before him.

A sign posted to the split-rail announced:

Pequest Fishing Access

He ambled down the grass avenue, which dead-ended about fifty yards ahead. Half-way there the din of the roadway disappeared, replaced by the sound of rushing water.

He found himself standing, alone, on the grassy bank of a mid-size stream, about seventy-five feet across. The water was fast-moving, running hard, muddy and swollen from spring rains, in a heady rush to somewhere else. Across the way, spread along the far bank, hundreds of skunk cabbage were in full leaf, bright green against a landscape still largely brown – the throes of a long winter hadn't been tossed just yet. The land on the other shore was wooded, a mix of mature trees and an understory that showed the first tinge of green; a swath of leaf buds just beginning to burst, the lightest brush of color on a gray and tawny canvas. An old stone row began ten feet off the distant bank, and marched into the woods, till it curved out of sight into the brush, a farm field long-forgotten and fully reclaimed by the forest.

He turned, his back to the river, and took a half-piss behind an overgrown patch of wild rose, a mass of thorns – towering high above his head. Finished, he took a last look, and made his way back to the road, in no particular hurry.

About a hundred yards west, the direction from which the bus arrived, was a set of signs; he slowly walked that way, up a long, gradual hill, and followed their directions. That was the plan.

The first announced:

Belvidere – Keep Left

The second read:

Water Street To
Manunchunk Rd

Belvidere

U And Left Turns

This must be it.

Halfway up the long incline, he hooked a left off the highway, onto a little two-lane: Water Street. He was surprisingly relaxed, yet anxious.   He usually was, in the early stage, like this. It had been a long ride, but had he put enough miles behind him?   In a sense, the physical distance was immaterial, but it somehow seemed helpful, nonetheless.

Far away made for a better fresh start; it always starts that way anyway....fresh. But it never seemed to stay fresh very long.

The walk was quiet. Water Street ran high above that
shallow creek he just pissed beside, the Pequest, he
presumed, strewn with exposed cobbles and boulders,
steep wooded banks cropped both sides. A blue County-
route signpost hugged the right shoulder, leaning into the
road, crooked from some long-past brush-by:

South 620
Warren County

He hopped the guardrail, walking along the narrow top
of slope. At first the pavement was a good hundred feet
above the water; he was eye level with treetops rooted
on the creek bank, along with smaller trees, clinging
precarious to the side of the slate and loam precipice.
He could see the stream far below him, the water
popping and dodging the rocks and snags of dead trees
along the banks, which had long-since fallen into its
path.

The sound was muffled, but pleasant, soothing.

The walk along *620* was several hundred yards, and he
stopped now and again to just gaze down at the water,
far below him. It was mesmerizing. He saw a deer on
the opposite bank, and it saw him. Although he was half
a football field away, the deer took no chance; in three
bounds, it disappeared, dissolving into the browns and
grays of the forest.

The top of bank widened and he found himself
wandering a bit deeper into the woods, about twenty –
thirty yards off Water Street, until he stumbled onto a

clearing, to what looked like an old road, perhaps the original Water Street. It stretched before him no more than two hundred feet, plus or minus; he could see where it once ran through the woods, since a series of large century trees framed the edges. The asphalt surface was long-since covered in a thick layer of loam, but patches of old black tar and stone were visible here and there – reminders of the road that once was. Even those open patches were coated with thick carpets of moss. It looked like the end of the world.

Dozens of old trees along the way were broken and splintered in spectacular ways....some fallen across the old roadway, like a tornado ran through, or some giant had long ago ambled by, a *Gulliver* in *Lilliput*, snapping trees like twigs. He never saw such a site....so many old-growths snapped, mangled and splintered along an abandoned stretch of road, all but reclaimed by the loam, bramble and briar.

This place was acquiring a definite feel, and that feeling was.....*strange*.

He saw a slight clearing in the timber, down by the creek, far below. He carefully scaled the steep bank to the water's edge. The rocks were covered in moss, as were the bases of the trees, roots gnarled and buttressed.

Primordial....that's how it felt.

But it was tranquil. He was surrounded by the sound of the river and the calls of early spring birds, hiding in the trees. Two mallards flew by, low, twenty feet above the water, heading downstream, leading the way. They soon disappeared.

More skunk cabbage sprung in every direction; along the bank, just down-water, was a large carpet of beautiful tiny blue flowers, the first thought that came to mind were periwinkles, but that was just a guess; he wasn't sure what a periwinkle actually looked like, but he thought they looked like these.

Maybe not, probably not. They were pretty, just the same.

He walked gingerly around them, doing his best to leave them undisturbed.

With the moist soil underfoot, spring flowers and skunk cabbage came flies, and he soon found himself surrounded. The flat bank disappeared into a steep splintered shale-stone escarpment, making it impossible to track the river any further downstream. To dodge the flies, he made his way up the steep bank, slipping and falling as his footing gave way beneath loose leaves, spongy soil and flakes of shale, till he was back on Water Street, once again high above the creek.

He brushed the dirt from his jeans, and followed the street south.

As he walked along, the road grade gradually dropped, and soon enough, the creek rose to greet him.

It already felt like an old friend.

He found a path off the road, with a trout-stocking placard stapled to a tree. He followed it back to the creek, a worn footpath from many a fisherman who came before. Up ahead, he saw what appeared to be the remnants of an old concrete dam, broken in spots, and littered with a tapestry of branches, trapped and woven together along its crest. But the detritus provided only a brief pause, for the creek had found its way around and through the obstacle. Soon enough, he thought, what little was left of the dam would too, be gone....washed away.

Off to the right, in a man-made channel long-since abandoned, the river ran past, through and under an old industrial waterwheel, rusted and frozen in place, ages ago. He wondered why it had been built, for its time had long-since passed; the stream, and the wilds, once again, were slowly, methodically, in reclamation mode.

It seemed everything in this place was old, broken and forgotten.

So it seemed.

Another carpet of blue blossoms laid ahead, astride the fisherman's path. A gnarled twisted vine, with the girth of an ocean-liner chain, was visible just off the trail – he never saw anything like it….it had the look of make-believe. He tried to follow its circuitous path up the tree it clung to, but it disappeared high overhead, into the sunlight, as if it climbed infinite, into the sky. If he was a kid, he'd be convinced it was Jack's beanstalk, it looked that big, it looked that cool.

And the gnaw came again; this place was just a bit strange….just a bit off, somehow.

He picked and weaved amongst the picker bushes and worked his way clear of the woods, back into the sunlight along Water Street.

Directly across the road, partially hidden from view, stood two tall, circular river-stone pillars, twelve feet high at least, between which hung an imposing, tired wrought-iron entry gate, padlocked, the grapple fused in a thick layer of titian rust….untouched, for years. Through the wrought iron rails, he spied a long, narrow gravel drive, overgrown with weed, which carved its way through a beautiful weald and disappeared, with no hint as to its end.

Brothers of the Sacred Heart

The words were scripted on a small, neglected sign by the stone pier entry – the painted letters peeled from the weathered wood surface.

Above it stood a second, stern warning:

No Trespassing

He eyed the seven words, notably the two last, rolling them over, wondering if they were meant for him....knowing, someday, he would arrive. He would expect as much from a place such as this, barred from that chaste glen on the other side of a long-forgotten locked gate...banished from that endless narrow gravel drive, with no hint of an end, winding through a seemingly beautiful forest, now overgrown, thick with weed.

But then again, he always seemed to have a free pass; *no trespassing*, in a strange way, wherever he landed, didn't seem to apply to him....never did.

Maybe this one finally did.

He spun around, drinking in the pillars, the signs, the scene, and he sighed. On such a sunny, hopeful day, this place felt deserted, foreboding....lonely.

An *end-of-the-road* feel, that's how this place felt. That was the finger he put on it.

He left the gate in silence and continued south on Water Street, moving further from the bus depot, and closer to whatever she had in store for him, somewhere ahead, out of sight.

The river had jogged, or perhaps the road had....perhaps both, for the two came closer together; he could see the rush of water through a thin stand of still largely barren trees. A lone fly-fisherman was standing in the river, downstream of the broken dam. It was the first figure he saw. He watched voyeur as the gut line danced adagio, back and forth, just ticking the aqua surface, till the fly landed on the water's skin and waited for a taker. Several late model pick-ups scattered along the shoulder up ahead, buffed hoods reflecting the glint of the sun, hinted at other fishers, hidden somewhere along the banks of the creek, hoping to land a keeper.

Other than the first, he never saw another.

A lone, faded red truck, tired and worn, was set a good distance from the others, on a seemingly impenetrable stretch of river thick with briars and underbrush hugging the road.

He was putting his money on that guy.

Along his walk, a car on this forgotten road passed once a minute or so, maybe less; he avoided eye contact.

A large, faded metal sign – an old advertisement, was set crooked, just off the shoulder; it was overrun - engulfed by vines and undergrowth – to the point it was nearly consumed. He walked within ten feet of it and could have easily missed it.

But he didn't.

It was a welcome sign of sort, a You-*Are-Here* red dot, announcing the:

Pequest Bend Picnic Grove – Serving Ice Cold Beer and Coca-Cola

But there was no picnic grove, no beer, no *Coke*.

The *Picnic Grove*, like everything else he had witnessed on his journey so far, had long since succumbed to the advance of trees and underbrush; the rusted sign stood alone, marking only what had once been.

He stared at it, figuring that sign was set in the 1940's....1950's latest. Maybe even the 1930's.

It was old, it was long-forgotten....and the people who read it, long gone.

He was surprised it hadn't been snatched; it was an antique *Coca-Cola* advertisement....the real deal. Probably worth much more than nothing on the auction block. The fact it still stood there, for decades, marking time, made him smile. Maybe people, for the most part, were honest around here.

Or maybe there wasn't anybody really here, except for fleeting fisherman and people driving cars, on their way somewhere else.

Here too, like before, the woods along the water were littered with massive fallen trees, in advanced stages of decay, lying amongst outcrops of metamorphic rock, covered with more thick, green ethereal moss.

Nearby, a small, one-story masonry building, with a timeworn, slate roof, stood quiet; a roadside wallflower. Out front, a few feet off the white line, two lime green *National* gas pumps dispensing leaded *Flying A* petrol, announced their presence, with large glass dial gauges and chrome garniture – the last gas no doubt being sold to *Picnic Grove* patrons. The price dial was frozen at *$.709* per gallon; the pump only had three digits, all to the right of the decimal.

Dormant neon signs in the windows hawked *Ballantine*, *Schaefer* and *Schmidts* beer – he wondered if they still worked; he wondered if the building even had the power to try. He pressed his face against the front plate glass, covered in a film of dust and road grit, and panned the inside as best he could.   He had hoped the place still had legs as a bar – maybe just one leg – a true shot and beer joint for the over-seventy set.

But it didn't; the building was dead, like everything else he had seen so far.

He wiped the grit from his cheeks and looked around; a large sugar maple had long ago fallen across the back of the empty parking lot; its skeleton remained.   The lot was covered in a blanket of last year's leaves.

Where the hell had he landed?   Where the hell had she sent him?

He crossed Water Street once again, his yellow-brick road, making his way toward the Pequest, toward the water.   He walked a bit, the terrain flattened and the woods thinned to a narrow band, hugging the near bank. He ambled into a grass meadow, which looked as if it was cut, but not often, the brown stalks from last year's growth were still north of his knees.

The sun's rays filtered through a stand of birch along the bank of the creek; it speckled the ground with light, which danced as the branches swayed.   Through the framework, in a shallow eddy, stood a lone heron, perfectly still and regal.   He carefully made his way to the water's edge, fifty feet upstream of the winged fisher, and quietly sat down.

No fishermen were in this reach of the creek; a murder of crows lit in a sycamore across the way, beyond the far stream bank; a solo chow-hound ate along the roadside, pausing to sit upright and rest its paws on a too-empty spring belly and assess the scene – it ignored him, as did the heron and the crows.   He was less than one hundred feet from the road, but the lie of the creek and its narrow wooded fringe of brambles and understory effectively isolated him from passersby.   He saw several cars pass, but heard nothing; the brook drowned them out.

He laid back into the grass, damp brown sand and sedge along the bank crest, pulled off his boots and socks, and stretched his toes in an animated manner – he hated wearing socks. Then he slowly placed his heels in the cold water, submerging half his foot. The water was like ice.

He couldn't remember the last time he had done such a thing; it must have been when he was a kid. The faint smell of budding greenery and the distinct earthy aroma of running water caressing exposed soil along the bank face jettisoned him to childhood jaunts down to the far end of the lake, at the dam, where it morphed and was reborn a river.

With the aroma, thirty years rewound in a flash, parking him at a place filed away and long-forgotten.

He folded his hand behind his head, closed his eyes, and let his mind weave and wander wherever it wanted to go.

So began the journey.

CHAPTER 3 – THE LAST TRIP TO THE DAM

He would dodge the State Park rangers and scale the high wrought iron fence; the sharp spear points would impale him as he flexed over the top, leaving bits of black paint and iron oxide on his shirt. He would tighten his stomach as hard as he could to limit the indents; the points pushing on his taut skin, stretching it, while he fought against his weight on the iron, till the skin split. It hurt like hell when the points drove into his chest and stomach; they would only pilot a quarter inch or so, but it felt as if they were exiting his back.

He muscled his legs over top, and tensed as the points grazed his balls, until he dropped precipitously onto the crest of the concrete dam. That fence had to have been over eight feet high; it stung the soles of his feet when he landed flat-footed….but you had better land flat-footed and stable.

Otherwise you were in trouble….big trouble. Falling off that dam was a one-way ticket.

He would only make the jaunt when the water was redirected and the dam crest was temporarily dry, which happened periodically; some unknown hand at some unknown location would render a decision on managing lake levels and magically the overflow would trickle to a stop.

The crest would still be covered in thick films of slippery green algal growth, which thrived when the dam was topped by the rush of lake water, but gasped and slowly dried dormant when the tap was shut, only to revive at the next taste of water.

In between tastes, the dam, and the slime, preyed on kids like him.

You had to land on that crest firm and straight, smack in the middle of the three-foot wide precipice, with both feet planted at exactly the same instant, or you would slip right off and end up in the drink on the lake side, if you were lucky, or over the dam and into the rocks far below on the downstream side, which he supposed you could theoretically survive. Maybe. Likely not.

He never saw anyone go over the dam, although he read about a wooden boat that did once, the captain jettisoned right at the crest; she splintered at the bottom into a pile of kindling. He remembered keeping that article for awhile.

A three foot wide dam sounds plenty wide on paper; but not when your dropping down blind, off a spear-top fence, on the run from the rangers, onto a layer of slime as slick as ice. Plus you had to worry, halfway across, if that unknown hand, at some unknown place, would turn the dial, and the water would start again over the crest, carrying you along for the long ride down.

And even if the water spigot stayed off, even though the lake had stopped spilling over the dam crest, it still flowed through the bowels of the structure – at least some of it. The water was redirected and telescoped through one to two open sluice gates, set alongside the dam, right by the fence. Sometimes they cracked open one; sometimes they opened two. The water would cannon in a deafening roar, especially if both sluices were gunning; he remembered being showered in spray and feeling the raw power as the jets shot into the air and arched to the craggy waterway below. You couldn't hear a thing above the explosion of water next to those gates; screaming to someone nearby was useless; you might as well mime.

Thus were the obstacles on the jaunt.

And with them all in mind, he would scamper the hundred plus feet to the far end of the dam, dodging the occasional steel bolt, which protruded several inches from the concrete crest; he didn't know why those bolts were there, they served no purpose other than to hide in the slime and trip kids. If you caught your foot on one and slipped, again, you were done.

At the far end, he would hop off, shuffle down a steep, stone embankment, down past the old gristmill wheel and river fountain, to where the violent, walled waterway calmed a bit, opening into a natural stream corridor.

He never went in the drink….not once.

He must have run that gauntlet two dozen times – probably more; no other kid on the block did it more than once or twice – and even then, he never saw any of them scale the spears; they would tuck in a break in the fence fifty yards away, and scamper along the headwall and down onto the crest.

Pussies.

He was sure they had been telling the story to their own kids for years by now, and he was sure it got better, and they got braver, with age. He wondered how many stories started with them going over the spears.

But none of them ever did, just him.

And he never told his story to anyone, ever.

He remembered the park rangers would sprint to the fence and scream profanities at him, but they always seemed to reach the wrought iron and yell once he was safely to the other side of the dam – never on his way across the precipice; and they would never give chase once he was safely off the dam.

As a twelve year old, he always thought he was too smart and quick for them, but looking back, he was sure they secretly let him scale the fence, a front row seat for the half-gainer they hoped the little-shit would do off the downstream side, into the rocks.

Bastards.

He would yodel as he ran through the dark river tunnel under the road, engulfed by the echo, while hopping from rock to rock, trying to stay dry. The river beyond the dam turned shallow, strewn with cobbles and boulders, just like the Belvidere creek before him; he would hopscotch as far down river as he could, the game would end when his feet got wet.

He could go for over a mile downstream; he had the rock path memorized, tacking back and forth in a well-planned zig-zag, a puzzle solution committed to memory. Along the way, he would revisit eddies, little islands which held no more than a tree or two, sand beaches and tiny tucked-away inlets - features he gave fancy monikers, the way an explorer does. He would bury things, all sorts of treasure, along the way, to dig up the next time, or turn rocks looking for crayfish, salamanders, snakes and spiders. He wouldn't hurt them; just look at them, study them, talk to them, then let them go.

Sometimes he went downstream with friends, but that was rare - he enjoyed it better alone.

Alone was always much better. Although he wouldn't have called himself one as kid….he was a loner. He definitely was. Maybe that was one of the criteria.

His journey would always end the same way, laying along the banks with his bare feet in the water, just like he was now.

He smiled as he looked down as his forty-three year-old feet; he swayed them back and forth; they were numb from the cold creek….it felt good.

He remembered pulling his tee-shirt up, to see the new set of holes, with the trails of blood that ran vertical, pooled and congealed in his navel. It was his badge; he was proud of them. He would dip his hand in the water and rinse the red stains off his skin, swirling his fingers on his chest in circles till the blood dissolved and ran off his belly, soaking into the ground he lay on.

He liked knowing he was leaving some of himself there, along the river….spear-blood in the silty sand. The cold water would sting the punctures; he would continue to pour river water on them, over and over, till the sting turned numb.

He did all his crossings that same year, in '75, starting in the spring.

He smiled to himself; then he drifted on and his smile faded, with the last trip to the dam.

CHAPTER 4 – EVERYTHING DISSOLVED AND SLOWLY FADED TO BLACK

It was early November, the 9th, the summer park rangers were long gone and the fall ranger shifts were less frequent, with skeleton staff. They mainly stayed in the park administration building drinking coffee, rarely making the rounds, especially in the cold. The state park was open year round, but no one ever went there in the fall and winter – it was his personal estate, to do as he wished, alone.

It was a seasonably warm and sunny Sunday. Both his parents were out of town, which was quite unusual, and his siblings away – scattered at school and with friends; he, the youngest, was staying home alone, overnight, for the first time in his life. His mother trusted him implicitly; his dad somewhat did, at times, with reservation. Since his father trusted no one, such was a glowing endorsement.

He tooled around the park solo, exploring on and off the footpaths that weaved through the deep woods above the visitor center; climbing trees, scuffing his jeans and listening to the sounds of the forest; doing nothing in particular as the day wore on. He felt different today; a bit more in charge....self-sufficient....older. He wasn't a boy, not today, not anymore; he was a young man....someone to be reckoned with. It showed in his gait....to him, anyway....since there was no else to see it.

By late afternoon, the sun suddenly slipped behind a wall of leaden clouds that seemed to arrive unannounced, the wind whipping from nowhere; it got wicked-cold in a hurry, like it sometimes does in the Fall, closing in without warning. He was in a too-light tan tee-shirt, and the wind cut him quick.

He remembered deciding to head home; he was cold, hungry and bored. On his way, he walked past the sluice; a white cannon of lake shot into the waterway below – the roar seemed louder than usual. The squall caught the spray and was blowing it steady through the fence, covering his face and chest with a fine lake-water mist.

He got a deep bite from the dampness....a real bone-chill.

He walked up to the fence, without even looking for rangers nearby; he didn't care....not today. Guys like him didn't worry about things like that....he remembered talking tough to himself. He remembered how quickly it went from dusk to near dark, like someone playing with the dimmer switch.

He wasn't sure why he started climbing the wrought iron fence; it was quickly getting too dark to cross the dam, even for him. Yet he scaled the fence anyway, slower than usual, and proceeded to hoist himself over top. But today he was distracted and not as careful; not as scared as he normally was....as he should have been.

As he felt the jagged tips in their familiar spot on his chest and stomach, he decided to hesitate a bit longer than usual; to relax his stomach and feel the pain. Then he would get off and head home.

He was strong, and in control. He owned the fence, the dam, the park; was his to do as he wished, when he wished.

He spent a little too much time reminding himself how impressed he was with himself.

Holding himself aloft on the skewers for that extra moment or two, it could be counted in half-seconds, was all the ammunition the fence required. It had waited all summer, patiently, for today.

Sapped of the strength he needed to dislodge; four spears quickly took advantage of the weakness and attacked, ripped open the shirt, the skin, and drove right past the quarter inch point.

This was new territory.

As hoped, bravado quickly turned to panic, and in his panic, his right hand, wet from the mist, slipped, his tightness broke, and the points dove in deeper, laughing at him. His own weight was slowly impaling himself; he could feel the jagged, rusted spear tips at a depth he had never felt before; they felt like they were burrowing far inside him – *deep* inside.

It was becoming bitter cold; how did it get so cold so fast? Yet he was hot as an iron, he could feel liquid bead on his upper lip and forehead; his ears were beet red – and felt on fire.

He couldn't pull himself off; he was stuck like a pig, and slowing sinking on the skewers. They were relentless, slowly advancing into him, an eighth inch at a time.

They had all the time in the world.

Raw fear swept in; from nowhere a shot of adrenaline enveloped him, his entire body tingled, but not in a way he could use. He desperately tried to get a grip on the fence and work his hands north, but his palms were wet and too far down the shaft; even if he had the strength, he didn't have long enough arms to dislodge himself. His arms continued to tingle; they felt numb and useless.

His body kept pumping adrenaline into dead limbs.

His own weight was killing him.

His mind raced, searching for a solution he couldn't find. He figured he would have to just let go and try to re-grip – but to let go would drive the spears in too far, much farther than he could ever recover from.

There was no one to see him, no one to hear him, no one to help him under the cloak of darkness and the roar of the cannon-water. The park was empty; the wind mocked and howled passed his ears.

He tightened his grip on the wrought iron and clenched his teeth as he felt the steel inch deeper. He screamed as he struggled, but not a sound emerged from his lips – it simply echoed in his head.

Then, slowly, his focus shifted to the thought of dying, really dying, at twelve years old….and to his surprise, he found himself okay with that. And that wasn't just tough talk to motivate himself; and it wasn't about giving up either; it was different….it felt very different.

And he became calm.

It was then that everything dissolved and slowly faded to black.

He didn't remember feeling any more pain; he didn't remember making a noise.

He certainly didn't remember how he got off that fence.

He woke and found himself laying prone, looking up at the rusted black wrought iron posts beside him, far past the spear points, which seemed to extend a mile above him, to a thousand stars in a crystal clear night sky.

Was he dreaming? Was he dead?

His body didn't feel right; he was just kind of there....watching. He didn't know how to describe it any other way. Thirty one years later, he still didn't.

He lay on the cold gravel beside the fence and fixed his gaze on the two Dippers – they were the only constellations he knew. His shirt was damp with blood, but much less than he would have expected. He didn't raise his shirt; he was afraid to look.

The park was silent; the water had stopped running through the sluice and it wasn't running over the crest; it was silently resting against the dam – like a plate of smooth glass. He didn't hear a single noise, no rustling leaves, no cars along the distant road crossing over the river tunnel – nothing.

He never felt such deafening silence....it was peaceful and serene; he thought of going to sleep.

He slowly rolled over to his side, sat up, and rested in that position a bit, trying to remember what happened. Then he simply stopped thinking, and shuffled the ten minutes home in silence. He entered his room and lay on the made bed, fully dressed.

He felt no pain.

He cocked his head slightly; the clock radio washed half his face in a soft, green glow.

It was 1:13 am.

Time stood still....frozen at 1:13. He stared at the digits, a hazy phosphorescence in the night, waiting for the digit to flip. Minutes, hours seemingly past....nothing....1:13 just quietly stared back at him. He blinked his eyes, and blinked again, and again....waiting....waiting.

He never saw 1:14.

The next morning he woke remembering a graphic dream, a vivid nightmare about a horrible puppet, exploding crickets and orange-eyed flies. He never had that dream before....never.

But he did, more than once, since.

But none were ever as vivid as the first one that night....never so *real*.

At some point, years later, he could never remember when, but he knew he still a kid, the dreams simply stopped. But the memory of that nightmare never left him....and the puppet, the crickets and the flies....they remained in his head, traveling companions, for the last thirty-one years.

All the way to Belvidere.

The deep holes in his stomach, his chest, healed like the shallow ones normally did. No complications, no infection, no more pain than usual. He was afraid to look at them, so he didn't. He just cleaned them as best he could without getting too close, then put bandages on them, just once, and hid them from the family. The shredded shirt tossed in the trash.

They never found out.

He never told anyone what happened that night and he never climbed the fence again; he never once went back to the park.

And thirty-one years passed by.

He slowly opened his eyes, hiked his pants a bit and looked down at his tan fading on his lower legs. Then he pulled his shirt up and ran his fingers back and forth over the four linear skewer scars running down the center of his chest and stomach.

It was hard to believe that story was real, even to him.

He ran his hand across his belly; it was bigger than it should be. He must be pushing two hundred fifteen pounds; muscular, thick, but too fat. There was no getting around that fact. The scars had stretched and expanded in size, in step with his expanded gut, like pulled *Silly Putty*. He slowly pulled his shirt down over the oval, to put it out of sight.

He closed his eyes again and tried to get past the earworm from the bus ride and remember the other verses; no luck. *Los Lobos*....what ever happened to them?

He shifted his weight on the bank, and rolled over onto his right side and stretched long like a lazy man does.

He didn't have to hurry; he didn't have to be anywhere, at any time, for any reason. He sighed, stretched again for good measure and cracked a slight smile; his lips didn't part, just the right side of his mouth curved uptick, just a bit. He cracked his knuckles and closed his eyes.

It had been a long bus ride, but so far, he was content.

Inconspicuous and out of trouble.

His first taste of Belvidere, or at least the road thereto, was not nearly what he had imagined. What did the darts have in mind this time? Especially these darts, especially the fourth dart. And with that, the puppet, the crickets and the flies shuffled back into the recesses and left him alone….and he forgot about them, for awhile.

And he forgot about the time.

1:13 am.

CHAPTER 6 – HELP WANTED - NOTHING MORE, NOTHING LESS

He sat up in a start; for a moment, he had forgotten where he was.

He wasn't sure how long he dozed; he quickly looked around and realized he was still alone. He let out a slow, long exhale. The heron, crows and woodchuck were all gone; for that, he felt a bit empty.

He remembered coming home from kindergarten, early afternoon, eating egg-on-toast, always on *Wonder Bread*, cut into a dozen little squares, which soaked the yoke and ketchup, and watching *Kimba the White Lion* – no one he had ever spoken to as an adult remembered that Japanese *anime*.

It was his favorite cartoon, bar none, and he relished that no one else remembered it – he owned it; when he was a kid, he was *Kimba*.

At forty-three, he still remembered the tune:

*'Kimba....Kimba....Kimba....Kimba....Kimba....Kimba
....Kimba....Kimba;*

Who lives down in deepest darkest Africa?
Who's the one that brought the jungle fame?
Who's the king of animals in Africa?
Kimba the White Lion is his name;

When we get in trouble and were in a fight;
Who's the one who just won't turn and run?
Who believes in doing good and doing right?
Kimba the White Lion is the one.'

He would watch *Kimba* run through the jungle all alone at the start of each episode as he rocked back and forth in his bean bag chair and sang along out loud. Then he would carefully eat his egg-on-toast squares one at a time, in the same order, every day – he couldn't remember the order, but he remembered the routine - even as a five year old - routine mattered.

What ever happened to *Kimba*? He couldn't conjure how the series ended, how *Kimba* fared, but he figured it must have been well.

Afterward, he would lay with his mother for a nap on his parent's bed - always covered by his white baby blanket. He was told years later, as an adult, that the blanket was originally blue, handed down through his siblings. He was last in line; by the time it was his, it had long since been bleached white. It was the color of snow and soft as silk. To him it was never blue, it was always white....born white.

He felt content, safe under that blanket – his blanket – with his mother close by his side. He remembered her warmth lying beside him, *sui generis;* it would envelope him, protect him. Her body heat felt different, if that is somehow possible. What he remembered about those naps was the heat, the radiance; that's what made the memory stick.

He would remind her daily to awaken him if she woke first – and he would do the same – that was the deal they struck. Yet every day he would open his eyes to the orange glow of dusk and find himself alone on the bed.

He would go downstairs to find her busy in the kitchen, cooking dinner or attending to some such task, where he would promptly scold her for forgetting their pact. She would smile sweetly and apologize, assuring him she would remember the instructions better tomorrow.

And so went the cycle.

It was that same empty feeling he now felt, lying along the stream bank….the birds and gophers gone, leaving him alone, without a sound.

The sky was still brilliant; the sun hadn't really moved – a half hour at most had passed, he thought, but it felt longer.

His mind started to wander again, this time into troubled water. But he was done reminiscing for awhile; he needed to get to town before it got too late. He shook his head a few times left-to-right, a lifelong habit to clear his thoughts - a tap of the reset button, then righted himself.

He planned to walk along the bank of the creek for a bit, but it was too thick with brush, which quickly turned to a wall of thorns, hooking and biting his legs and arms; one long, curved bastard found flesh in his side and drew blood.

Fuck he mouthed under his breath as he unlatched himself hook by hook, retreated, and made his way back to safer ground along the road.

Across the way, he came upon a large white sign that plainly announced:

DSM

Set alongside a paved drive and a football field-sized rolling, manicured lawn, surrounded by a high chain link fence and automatic gate.

Contractor's Entrance

Was posted by the entry. The drive arched over a grassy knoll and disappeared; no buildings, people or activity was evident beyond the fence - the plant must be buried in the woods somewhere out of site.

He knew the Dutch pharmaceutical *DSM*; finally, something that wasn't decayed, or on its way to same.

But how is it DSM found themselves out here, in the middle of nowheresville, just a stone's throw down the street from the *Picnic Grove*?

He wasn't sure if he was happy stumbling upon a bit of familiar civilization, or unhappy he wasn't actually discovering some lost planet, at the far end of the twilight zone.

Water Street straightened and continued for another quarter mile or so; along the way, he passed floodplain, ball fields and more foraging groundhogs.

A bit further, he came upon a red, painted triptych, peeling and faded:

Welcome to Belvidere – New Jersey's Best Kept Secret

He walked over to the sign, it was covered in print and pictures much too small to see from the road – only a walker could read it, and even then, it was minute print.

I guess it *is* a secret, he thought; certainly nobody can read it.

The sign was planted a good thirty-five feet off the shoulder, set alone in a nondescript grassy area, with no accommodations, such as a bench – just the sign. He thought it a bit strange.   A listing of local businesses, important-sounding officials, and a birds-eye map of the town filled the space.   He wondered if the people listed were still alive.

He stood and carefully studied the names, the geography, the landmarks.   There was important information on that board; of that he was certain.   He just wasn't sure quite yet which pieces those were.

The creek he had visited and napped beside *was* the Pequest River.   It apparently bisected the town, before emptying into the Delaware River.   He smiled; the *rivers* to which he was accustomed were a tad larger.   A second creek, the Pophandusing, ran along the southern edge of town, also on its way to the Delaware, just downstream of the Pequest.   He carefully studied the street layout, the landmarks and the text, committing it to memory.

Belvidere was the County Seat; the Courthouse bellied up to a four-acre park in the middle of town.   A church sat mid-block on the three remaining sides of the green – the Methodists, Presbyterians and Episcopalians each took a front-row seat around the promenade.

The Catholics were apparently relegated to the backseat, situated on a side street, a full two blocks south of the park; right then he knew he would like this town.

He remembered Father Dryan - the endless incidents, insolence, confrontations....shaking his head at the memories.   What a fucking asshole.   Fucking Catholics.

He shook those thoughts and refocused.

He retook to the road; a lazy curve to the left provided a soiree into a sentry of Victorian-style residences, intermixed with other older homes of indistinct provenance – the first face of town.   The river, his chaperon thus far, quietly dog-legged to the left and flowed out of sight, traversing behind the homes on the south side of Water Street.

It was midday on a Thursday; the straight, tree-lined sidewalk before him was empty as far ahead as he could see, a good three to four long blocks. The trees were still mostly bare, a few had hints of green, with pink flowering trees dotted here and there. The houses were rooted unusually close to the walkway, the *Painted Ladies* had large, sweeping porches, with turned balustrades, meaty rails, ornate circular and square columns and wooden decks, painted in a spectrum of bright colors.

At first glance, the assemblage looked impressive, architectural gems with garniture no current builder could justify, handcrafted by artisans who no longer exist. Every third or fourth house was recently painted, neat as a pin. The fillers, however, were somewhat worse for wear, sporting not so much a fine patina, earned with age, but rather a general sense of dinge. Evidence of peeling, fading and general neglect came into focus when given more than a passing glance; like an attractive woman who's a keeper at twenty yards, only to reveal road-wear the nearer she gets, the lines of neglect coming into focus upon closer inspection. It appeared a neighborhood in transition, with tired homes rescued here and there, others in a slow state of decay, waiting, hoping, to be saved.

It was still early in the season, but porch rockers and wicker furniture were making an appearance, slowly emerging from winter storage, back into place for summer people-watching, tea-sipping and napping. He thought nothing beats a grand front porch for an afternoon nap, newspaper folded across your chest.

He happened upon a somewhat-crisp, Georgian brick, in generally good shape; his eyes ran along the balustrade ringing the wide, wraparound porch, the decking painted a light battleship gray, the porch ceiling a varnished beadboard.

As he approached, a second-story window slid open; the

frame jiggled and the dull friction of wood sounded as the sash ran inside a painted track. A white sheer escaped and lazily flapped in the warm April air, waving as he walked below. He caught a glimpse of the petite hands and wrists of an unseen women opening the window; they looked like attractive wrists.

A familiar song spilled from the window and gently wafted into the street.

Sunset Grill

He slowed his gait, put his head back and fell into the summer of 1985, like he always did when he heard that song.

My God, it had been over twenty years:

Respectable little murders pay;
They get more respectable every day;
Don't worry girl, I'm gonna stand by you;
And someday soon;
We're gonna get in that car and get outta here.

He would scorch the levee rim road in a silver Chevy, blasting the radio and trailing a rising plume of gravel dust a full half-mile behind him. He would always drag full throttle to hit the far end of the levee before the haze of dust settled at the beginning – that was the game....his game that he told no one....shared with no one. That levee was three miles long and scary steep, with the slope falling fast on either side of a mere twelve foot ribbon of road.

37

He would drive with an eye in the rear view, coaxing the dust cloud to stay aloft while trying to corral the car as he edged past ninety miles per hour. He would jerk the wheel a bit as the rubber ran along the levee rim, right before it dropped off. Going over the edge was a one-shot deal – there was no recover if you went south – you'd be done. Dead.

He came close, but he could never beat that damn dust cloud….it would settle to the ground at the beginning, before he could pass the end, three miles down-levee.

He lost every time.

Till now, he never thought of those drag runs as grown-up dam scampers, but they were. They absolutely were.

He woke one morning and drove up to the levee as the August Bootheel sun was pushing through loose-knit wisps of clouds, low on the horizon; it was already hot and humid; the air was thick, vintage late summer Mizzou.

Just as he reached the levee rim, the sun climbed above the horizon and the sky turned orphic, the cloud edges were on fire with sunlight, white hot embers, glowing across the horizon. He was sure no one else was looking at that sky right at that moment, no one had the vantage he had, and saw what he saw - it was put there just for him.

He switched on the radio the moment the Chevy turned onto the levee and gunned the car, like he always did. Right at that moment, the song was just beginning to play, as if on cue:

Sunset Grill

Right at that moment, at twenty-two years old, he knew

good times, very good times, were going to come his way – it wasn't a matter of if, it was simply a matter of when. It felt providential, not in a religious way, but rather in a sense of peculiar good fortune.

That epiphany was over twenty years ago; how should he assess that predilection? Had it already borne fruit, or was he still on a rising road?

That was a mixed bag, and loaded question, for sure. He had some good, for sure – most would certainly label it as such….but at what cost? And the good was woven in a tapestry of very bad. And there was no separating the two; they needed each other.

Was that success? Was he a success?

Tough question.

At what point does one say to himself I'm satisfied, I'm fulfilled, I'm not interested in the better times that surely await me around the next bend – for what I have already experienced *is* the *good* in the good times – more isn't necessarily better, it's just more.

He thought about it, and realized he wasn't ready to answer that question. Maybe he never would be.

His thoughts then turned to her, which they always did when he thought about the Bootheel. Peace of mind. It wasn't 3:30 pm yet….not there....so she was still asleep. He hadn't seen his little girl in over twenty years; he wondered if she'd even recognize him. He knew he'd recognize her. *Monsieur* Roy was a good man. Some day, he suspected, they would finally meet. Some day, he promised himself, he had to finally make that happen.

The music faded into the background as he left the Georgian behind and headed for what appeared to be downtown; he spied a distant traffic light, several blocks away.

A slight, disheveled man in droopy tan shorts was walking toward him at a good pace, head down, intently watching his sneakers. He was balding, with a long, unkempt salt and pepper beard and thin, stringy black hair around the perimeter of his crown, which seemed to defy gravity, extending in multiple directions, like he stuck a finger in an electric outlet. He could have been a cartoon character.

A little less than a half-block away, without hesitation or acknowledgment, the man jaywalked and passed him on the other side of the street, never looking up. He must have practiced that trick before.

When he reached the place where the man jumped the curb, a mephitic aroma hung in the air, engulfing him. He shook his head and forcefully exhaled through his nose, trying to expunge the stench he unwittingly swallowed, like one does when the recirculated air on a plane blows a nameless fart in your face from parts unknown.

That was fucking *nasty*! A combination of bad body odor and ass; it felt like his face was inside the guy's shorts when he ripped.

He shook his head again and exhaled, trying to shake the stank.

What a dirtbag – he turned to glare at the back of the little man's head; he could see his shoulders shaking and was sure he was laughing.

The gassing passed. He came upon a filling station, a Chinese restaurant, the *Good Will Firehouse* and *Wanda's Hair Salon*, along with a mix of homes. *Wanda's* had the distinct look of a salon catering to blue-hairs.

Arriving at the intersection with the traffic light, he

looked across Water Street and saw large red letters on the building facade, announcing:

Sam's Market

A tiny neighborhood grocery like you see in the city, any city. Adjacent was a tiny café, that seemed to have two names....new and old.

There was an obsidian awning, with white lettering announcing:

Nonpareil

serving

Epicurean Cuisine   Lunch and Dinner

Above it stood a second name:

Boglioli's Palace of Sweets

The building facade was polished green and black slag glass arranged in a geometric pattern, circa-1930's. The wording *"Boglioli's Palace of Sweets"* was etched in a large *Art-Deco* font in the seafoam green glass over the door, an incised, painted milk shake and ice cream sundae framed the wording.

The storefront was small, with room for just two *al fresco* tables, one of which was occupied by a smart-dressed couple, sipping coffee and eating artisanal sandwiches. The windows straddling the entry displayed small two-seater bistro tables, each set with fancy earthen dishware and a single maroon candlestick. On the right side bistro, a man was finishing lunch, eating alone, engrossed in a newspaper. The cafe could have been plucked from mid-town Manhattan; it seemed out-of-sorts, dropped in this place.

Especially given its neighbor to the right.

Sharing a common wall with the *Palace* was *Sam's Market*, which was as tired as *Nonpareil* was chic. The window displays were circa-1960. The smudged plate glass was jammed with over-sized paper banners hawking the weeks' specials on ham shanks, thin-sliced veal cutlets, chicken tenders, *Delmonico* steaks, stuffed pork chops, green cabbage and *Mrs. Vaughn's Shoo-Fly-Pie*. The banner corners were loose, tattered and missing, the white background dingy from hundreds of fingers changing prices and re-taping the torn paper to the plate glass over and again.

Amidst the advertising cacophony, he caught sight of a small hand-written sign, scrawled sloppily with a black marker on a piece of ripped, spiral-bound notebook paper, taped to the right of the entry door; it simply said:

Help Wanted

Nothing more, nothing less.

He didn't go right in; he simply stood across the street and observed.

The intersection was fairly busy; the light changed every twenty-five seconds.   Customers entered the market every few minutes, reappearing on the sidewalk carrying one to two small plastic satchels of *Sam's* quarry. There was no real parking to speak of – just two spots in front of the store – most seemed to be walkers, or they parked in a paved town lot, half a block away.

He didn't wear a watch or have a cell phone, so he didn't know the time. He was probably on the bus an hour and a half ago, of that he was reasonably sure. He guessed the walk into town was two to three miles, stretched by his meander and creek-side nap.

He crossed the street and entered *Sam's* – a tinny bell rang announcing his presence. It was dimly lit; his eyes took a moment to adjust.

He would come to realize, much later, there was no going back.

He surveyed the scene – four short rows of groceries and two mini-checkout stations, with food belts and cash registers they don't make anymore. The aisles were empty; a lone employee stood at one of the checkout registers, a somewhat thin teenage girl, with a small, pouty potbelly, picking her nails and breathing heavily through a partially opened mouth – her profile was that of a codfish. With the angle of her head tilted toward the floor, and with the tip of her tongue slightly exposed, he was sure he would see her drool – she disappointed him; she somehow managed to keep the saliva in her mouth.

He purposely stared at the side of her head for a full fifteen seconds – he stood no more than ten feet from her, yet, like the woodchuck along the road, she was oblivious to his presence.

A queue of five older women was visible at the end of Aisle No. 2, facing a glass deli case filled with meats, on and off the shank....an *olla podrida* of lamb, venison, beef, pork and spiced sausages. Tucked in one corner of the case was a small cache of seafood – large firm scallops, cherrystones, mussels and jumbo shrimp. Clearly, this was where things happened at *Sam's* – the deli counter.

He walked past the codfish picking her nails, past shelves lined with dusty cans and boxes of macaroni and cheese mix, stove-top stuffing and egg pastina to settle into the end of the queue, an imposter listening in on the banter between patrons and the butcher – a barrel-bodied middle-aged man of average height, behind the glass. He had dark hair, with a forehead which extended over the top of his head, and was working its way down the back of his neck. His nose was patchy-red, oversized and somewhat mangled, the result of too much alcohol, for far too long.

The butcher attended to the demands of the senior women in line, but was visibly annoyed by the process. He worked quicker than his facial expressions belied – yet the pace was still measured, operating at half-speed, just because he felt like it. He tuned out all but the specific body he faced at the front of the line, with cryptic, rude responses to the orders placed on the other side of the glass.

The next batter stepped to the plate.

"Hello Frank, may I have a half-dozen pork chops
    please; I would like the kind…."

He quickly interrupted her.

"Lean or Regular?"

"Lean, please, with…."

"Center Cut?"

Frank asked, with a classic eye-roll, knowing full well
the answer before he asked – this client was predictable,
like all the regulars.

"Yes, that would be nice; I'm, having a…."

"Chicken breast too, is that right?"

He assumed the standard Thursday afternoon chicken
order.

"Oh yes…and be sure it's your Grade A *[she was fairly
certain there was nothing but Grade A sold in the shop,
even though she didn't know what Grade A actually
meant, nor how to tell if that's what she actually got –
but the other ladies needed to know she only purchased
A Grade]*."

"On the bone? On the bone!?"

Frank demanded a second time in a louder, annoyed
tone, when the answer didn't return fast enough.

"Yes please."

Frank was being especially rude today, even for Frank.

He went to work filling the order, never looking up or
feigning attention as the woman spoke excitedly at him
about a progressive dinner party she was planning for

her friends and neighbors. She prattled on.

After a minute or so, she realized Frank had walked to the far end of the deli case to work, purposely out of earshot; she realized she had been talking busily to no one.   Embarrassed, her voice tailed off and she finished her sentence so only she heard the outcome of her story.

He felt bad for her.

While Frank finished the rest of the order, she just stood at the glass case in silence, with her hands anxiously squeezing her purse and her eyes down, wondering what the other ladies behind her in line thought about her treatment by Frank. She felt like the poor sap picked on by a stand-up comic, with nowhere to hide – the others thankful they remained in the shadows.

Frank wrapped the stock, oblivious to her embarrassment.

"Next!"

Was all he said, without nary an effort at eye contact.

She smiled and feebly said thank you to the back of Frank's head as he turned to wipe his hands on a bloody cotton towel.

The next victim stepped to the glass.

He waited patiently and soaked in the scene; he was in no hurry.

When he was one away from the stage, he leaned over to the slight, attractive older woman ahead of him and asked if she minded if he were to interrupt Frank and inquire about the position available in the window. He placed his hand on her tiny forearm, sheathed in a gray designer blazer, and squeezed it ever so slightly, holding it gently as he spoke to her. He looked intently into her eyes; she looked into his hazel eyes and turned to butter.

She was the first person he had spoken to in Belvidere – he would remember that.

Mrs. Mae Edna Bastet (no, he didn't hear wrong, she assured him, is was *Mae* Edna, and not the more common Edna Mae) told him he could certainly speak to Frank, but the owner was Sam, who had vanished into the back storeroom about fifteen minutes ago.

"Ah, so Sam left Frank solo to handle the Thursday afternoon rush – no wonder he's so cranky."

He smiled as he spoke to Mae.

"No."

She said matter-of-fact.

"Frank is pretty cranky *all* the time, but he has been here forever, and Sam has such good *meats*!"

Mae's voice inflected on the last word; Sam's meat was legendary.

She seemed resigned to deal with Frank's antics, since the deli produce was so good, but Mae was visibly annoyed, like one who tolerates a friend's child who is underfoot and misbehaves terribly, but has to be dealt with, begrudgingly, if one wants to spend time with a good friend.

He sensed that was the general consensus of the group of women in queue.

She stood there in silence for a bit, then leaned into him and whispered:

"Last week, Frank smiled and said *Thank you* to me when I left."

She said with a not-so-slight air of sarcasm.

She then put her hand on *his* arm – he responded to the gesture by leaning over toward her and placing his hand gently, but firmly, on her upper back while she spoke. He could feel her slightly lean back into his hand; it was clear she favored his touch.

She again confided, in a hushed tone:

"I think he likes me more than the other women from Brookfield."

With that, she tilted her head ever so slightly toward him and smiled warm. It was the beam of a friend, and it had the look of a smile from someone who wanted to be more than a friend. He smiled back as he lightly rubbed her back in a single circle, before gently removing his hand.

"I'm sure he does."

Mae was a surprisingly attractive older woman, probably in her late fifties, but fit and smartly dressed in classic couture – she wore a light, herringbone slate-gray jacket with a matching skirt which extended to an inch or two above her knees, showing off a pair of tan and toned legs that belonged on a forty-something year old. In fact, most thirty year- old's didn't have legs that looked that good. Some women keep shapely legs late in life; Mae was one of them. He figured she must have been an amazing looker in the day.

As Mae Edna stepped up, he politely, in a loud and clear voice, asked Frank if Sam was available to speak to him about the *Help-Wanted* position.

In response....nothing happened.

Frank continued to clean his knives and wipe his hands in a slow, deliberate manner, with his back to the deli case.

It had been about fifteen seconds....fifteen long seconds of silence. Frank had clearly staked his position in this parry.

He felt a familiar flush of blood in the skin of his forearms and the fingers on his hands involuntarily opened and shut – a shot of heat found the back of his neck. Suddenly, he didn't feel so patient.

Mrs. Bastet did not see his reaction; she stood beside her new friend, without comment.

He restated his question; this time a bit louder. Again, Frank attended to his knives, ignoring the request and extending the cleaning process to an uncomfortable length of time. He never turned to face the deli case.

One's threshold for insult is directly proportional to one's intelligence and sense of self worth he silently repeated it to himself; it was Steinbeck, one of his favorites. Yet somehow, although he liked the quote, and he appreciated the sentiment, he never seemed to be able to make it stick. He closed his eyes, set his jaw and breathed hard once through his nostrils. His hands were hot and started to tingle.

For once, the moment of reflection seemed to help.

He slowly turned, thanked Mae and walked away, toward the front door of the store and the street beyond. She found herself immediately sad that her new friend left her side, and gave up the fight. She wasn't sure which bothered her more.

The tinny bell rang on the front door; Frank heard the sweet sound of success and grinned a cheese-dog smile as he turned to Mrs. Bastet.

"Now what can I do for you ma'am!"

He belted in a boastful tone, flush with his win.

Just as Mae began to speak, Frank felt something cold and hard pelt him in the left ear – whatever it was actually stuck in his ear canal for a moment, and then fell out. It felt like a large bumblebee had flown smack into the side of his head, but he didn't hear the buzz.

Stunned, he bent down and saw a red seedless grape lying on the floor.

"What the….?"

Confused, he slowly stood up and turned to his left; just as he did, a second projectile hit him square in the front teeth; if he had been the codfish in the front of the store and parted his lips *just* a slight bit more, that grape would have sailed straight into his mouth, a bulls-eye from its launch a good twenty-five feet away.

The grape stuck to his lower lip for a moment, then unpeeled, fell to the floor and slowly rolled away from his feet.

Frank was speechless; he stood there staring straight ahead; a deer in headlights.

Mrs. Bastet, on the other hand, had no such trouble.

She and the remaining ladies in line let out a simultaneous screech of laughter that was a bit scary; Frank actually let out a little yelp, dropped his butcher's knife and stumbled back a step in a reflex response to the high-pitched cackle.

Mae then loudly shouted.

"Sale on Seedless Grapes – Two For The Price Of One!"

With that the ladies howled again, a chorus of pent up frustration set free.

Impromptu, diminutive Mrs. Ackerman at the back of the line, put her hands straight up, signaling a touchdown and yelled in the best Spanish accent a little Jewish woman from Leonia could muster:

"Goooaal!"

Like the Spanish soccer announcers did till they ran out of air on the cable channel her husband watched; but couldn't understand a single word, except for the rebel yell when the *futbol* hit the back of the net.

Like the donkey's first taste of daylight after spending a life in the mines, there was no turning back. The women were freed; the Philistine butcher had been slain, by a grape.

Frank was frozen, mortified, stunned by the sudden turn of events.

He didn't know what to do, so he bent down to pick up his knife, and then simply stood there while the ladies all laughed and yelled over one another, recounting how they remembered the action – their own version of an instant reply. By the second iteration, the story had morphed into Frank actually swallowing the second grape; God knows what the story would be by days end, back at the Brookfield Community Center.

Sam emerged from the back room to investigate the commotion; he was a butcher's butcher, a full half-foot taller than Frank and twice the size; his arms looked as if he wrestled and butchered the livestock himself in the back room. His belly looked as if he ate the livestock whole.

The stranger walked toward Sam, extending his hand in greeting. On the way, he deliberately stepped on the evidence, which had come to rest behind the deli case, in the area off limits to customers. With that, he slipped and fell sideways into the end of the glass case, knocking over a stand of beef jerky and making more of a ruckus than was really necessary. Sam tried to catch him, but the big man just couldn't move that fast.

He was up in a minute, brushed himself off and signaled he was okay, although he put his hand on his lower back and grimaced, for emphasis.

He proceeded to check the bottom of his boot, and, like an investigative reporter astounded at his discovery, he slowly scraped the remnants of a large grape off the sole, turning his boot as he did it toward the crowd, like own opens a present, so all could see the culprit firsthand. A partially eaten bunch of grapes was clearly, conveniently, sitting behind the end of the deli case, on Frank's side of the glass. No one saw the stranger slide them back there.

Sam's face was vermilion; he turned to Frank with a

look of utter disgust;

"Are you kidding me?"

He bellowed in astonishment.

"How many times have I talked to you about eating behind the counter? This man could have really hurt himself!"

When Sam spoke loudly, his booming voice stopped people in their tracks.

Frank recoiled, wincing at the inculcation, pulling his shoulders a bit toward his ears.

Sam turned to the recovering victim.

"Are you sure you're okay?"

Sam was trying to speak softly, as much as his baritone would allow.

"Can I get you a glass of water?"

Sam made the second statement slowly, as if he was still pondering the sentence as the words spilled from his mouth. He wasn't sure what a glass of water would actually accomplish in this specific situation, but it came to mind, and he thought it was the proper thing to say.

Mae stood defiantly at the front of the line, her hands firmly planted on her hips. Her cohorts grouped closely behind her in a show of unity.

She piped in.

"Frank has been eating those grapes *all* afternoon – we can't get him to stop stuffing his face long enough to give us some *meat*!"

Mae emphasized the sentence-end for dramatic effect.

She was proud how easily she grabbed the canard and ran with it – a former politician cum-lobbyist, she was comfortable and quick at deftly aligning and weaving bits of data, suppositions and quasi-facts to secure an intended result….lying was pretty easy.

In this case, it was also just fun. The girls nodded in agreement, conspirators, all of them – Frank was getting a taste of what he deserved.

Mae proceeded to add a little fuel to the fire.

"There is a divorced personal injury attorney out at Brookfield that owes me a favor….or two….we could see what he has to say about these grapes."

She paused, raising both eyebrows for effect; apparently Mae was still a hottie.

My good friend here looks like he could have easily pulled his back slipping on that little fella – God knows how that poor grape escaped Frank's feeding frenzy!"

Sam, sensing the situation was getting a bit out of hand, stated in a calm manner:

"Now Mae, I certainly don't think *that* kind of talk is necessary, let's get you ladies taken care of, on the house of course, while this young man rests a bit and gathers himself."

With that, Sam quickly grabbed a stool from the dais behind the deli counter and put his hand on the gentleman's shoulder, guiding him onto the stool. He obliged, and tilted his head in acknowledgment, signaling his appreciation of the offer.

This was going along much better than he could have ever imagined.

During the banter, Frank stood silent; he had assumed the role of the codfish, mouth agape. It was unclear if he even realized his mouth was open. He didn't protest, he just stood there glumly; mob rule was against him.

"Go on home Frank, I'll finish out the afternoon."

Sam said matter-of-fact; with that, Frank silently took off his apron and made his way toward the storeroom. As he passed Sam, he said feebly:

"I wasn't eating any grapes."

Sam's response indicated his thoughts on the matter:

"The least you should do, Frank, is fess up, and apologize to our friend here."

Frank looked at Sam, then his gaze slowly swung to his nemesis, sitting comfortably on the stool and discretely smiling, with that same uptick on the right side of his closed mouth. Frank was a beaten man, there was no fight in him. As Frank looked at him, the instigator discretely lifted his right hand ever-so-slightly off his lap and waved to Frank in several short strokes, while silently mouthing *bye-bye* in a mocking manner.

With that final indignation, Frank slowly shuffled into the back room and out of sight.

He got off the stool and walked over to the deli case; Sam had already assumed a position behind the glass and was quickly dishing out the bribery meat he promised to the girls.

"Sam, my name is Cord Brin, but people call me Ay [*like*

the letter A]."

He turned to look at Ay, who had roughly the same build as Sam, just much shorter, and without the Buddha belly.

"What can I do for ya?"

Sam asked; without waiting for an answer, he continued

"Are you in the military? Or are you a trooper?"

Ay got that a lot, with the bald head and fireplug build, people figured he was a Marine or a State Trooper. He was short....five foot eight inches at best; if he had been Sam's height, he would have been pushing three hundred pounds. How he wished all his life for an extra six inches; if there were a way to buy the height, he would own it.

He was still in decent shape, especially for forty-three, but not great shape; his arms and legs were bigger when he was lifting regularly, which hadn't happened in too long, and there was the matter of the extra 'skin' around his waist – it always went there first for him. Not a lot, but enough for him to be annoyed about it, but not annoyed enough, apparently, to do anything about it.

"No and no; actually, I was inquiring about the job, in the window *[Cord thumbed toward the front of the store]*; is it still available? And if so, what *help* are you looking for?"

Sam skeptically eyed him; he figured a high school kid was filling that position, not some guy who looked to be in his forties. Add to that the fact that Sam, who was in his sixties and lived his entire life in Belvidere, had never seen Cord before today. What was this guy's story?

Sam told Ay, in a not-too-enthusiastic tone, that yes, it was still available, and to come back tomorrow and they could talk about it more. However, with Frank gone, and a Thursday afternoon rush in progress – the deli line would queue up for another couple of hours, until it died down, right before closing.

With that Cord donned Frank's apron and stepped behind the glass.

"Hey, I can't have you back here; have you ever worked in a deli before?"

With that, Cord told Sam his dad worked in a supermarket as a kid, stocking shelves and running errands; he figured it was in the blood. That was pretty lame, but before Sam could whisk him away, Mae, once again, came to his aide.

"Sam, I want Cord to service….uhh….serve me."

And with that, she turned to Ay and said:

"Young man, I would like two pounds of choice rump roast; I would also like a dozen cherrystones, the smaller the better – please give them a good rinse and pat them dry before you put them in the bag. Once you get it packed up, if you wouldn't mind, dear, please be a good boy and carry the bags to my car."

He leaned over the glass to Mae and motioned with his finger for her to come close, so he could whisper something to her:

"You are a good little *bad* girl, Mae, and a pretty good fibber; thanks."

He smiled at her and put his hand gently on her tiny

shoulder. For being such a muscular guy, he had small hands, she thought – but they were beautiful-looking, tan, and they were so warm.

What do small hands mean again? My God, I hope that truly *is* an old wives tale, she thought to herself.

She returned the smile, stepped back from the counter and told him out loud, for all to hear, that that was one of the best compliments she had received in quite some time.

She turned to Sam.

"You could certainly use a man like Cord around here, Sam; I know the girls here would be happy with the executive decision".

Mae pulled out her checkbook. Sam told her that wasn't necessary, the order was on him; but she put up her hand mid-sentence to stop him and said, again, with added emphasis:

"It would certainly be nice to see a young man like Cord around here. Now, how much do I owe you, Sam?"

With that, she laid the check on the deli case and patiently waited for her order to be filled. The other girls followed suit, pulling out their checkbooks in preparation to pay for their upcoming orders. Sam thanked Mae and the girls with a nod and a wry smile.

With that, Cord's job interview was over.

Her order filled, and bags packed, Cord escorted Mae out the door, and across the street, to where she was parked. She walked with her arm comfortably tucked into his, ostensibly for assistance, but Mae needed no such help. She was a fine specimen; frailty was not a trait. She just wanted to show off the new toy she bought. She looked good, dressed to the nines.

They entered the lot and Mae pointed to a new, metallic-blue *Mini Cooper* convertible; a very cool, hip, little car.

"There's my little girl!"

"Very nice; you got it going-on, Mae; the car, the couture."

Cord smiled at her as she popped open a miniature rear trunk; the tiny door opened like a tailgate.

"And how about you, what have you got going on?"

"What do you mean?"

She exhaled in a matter-of-fact manner, annoyed at having to explain the obvious.

"Young man, I spent my life in politics, first being one - a successful one, I might add - and then building a pretty good career in the private sector as a lobbyist, sucking up to people just like me.

With all that practice, one of the things I'm *pretty* good at, besides embellishing the facts to help my new friends get a job *[she raised her eyebrows at Cord]* is reading people, sizing them up. I've met some pretty interesting characters in my day, and I think I just met another one. What do you think?"

"I think the story of an errand boy isn't all that interesting, Mae; sorry to disappoint you."

"You've been an errand boy for the last, what, fifteen minutes? I got you the job, remember?"

With that she smiled at him; he returned the smile,

without retort, as he placed the last bag in her trunk.

"And the errand boys I've run into typically don't use the word *couture*."

A doubting expression accompanied the statement.

"Errand boys can still use fancy words Mae, it just means they paid attention in school…at least during vocabulary."

She wasn't buying it.

"Be that as it may, I'm interested in the whole package, the entire….thirty….how many is it….years?"

She waited for him to finish the number.

"Thanks, Mae, but it's forty-three."

She smiled; he knew she figured he was in his forties, and threw him a little bone.

"Ah, I remember forty-three. Those were good times."

"When was that, last year?"

Cord inquired.

Mae smiled at him.

"*Touché*; very good; you're a good boy."

"I don't feel like a good boy; what's a good boy feel like?"

"*Exactly!* That's what I want to hear about; something tells me you are a bit more interesting than bag-hauling and shelf-stocking."

She opened her purse and fumbled around, looking for

something; while her head was down, she asked him the question no man wants to hear.

"So, how old am I?"

Cord didn't answer; he wasn't touching that one.

With that, she looked up at him.

"Okay, okay….smart not to answer. Let's just say forty-three was some twenty-odd years ago and leave it at that."

She immediately saw the surprise in his face, and she was happy – she could tell his reaction was genuine.

"Mae, you look *great*; I honestly thought you were in your *early* fifties….very early."

Okay, maybe the 'early' part of that sentence was the natural lobbyist coming out in *him*; late 40's would definitely have been insincere. Early fifties was as far back as he could credibly go. But it clearly worked; she soaked it up.

"And those legs….*very*, nice."

Cord threw that in for icing, and it was true. A bonus.

"It doesn't stop at the legs, my friend….it just keeps getting better from there….you should see the *whole* package. My personal trainer and basic good genes have worked wonders; being pampered by men most of my life hasn't hurt, either."

She was quick to add:

"But *no* physician-assisted help with a scalpel, suction tube, or syringe…. *none*! What you see is what you get."

She emphasized that last part. Mae was proud she wasn't surgically altered; very few of her friends on the old circuit back east could make that statement. There were a lot of happy surgeons in her former neck of the woods, which certainly wasn't Brookfield.

And with that, she slowly slipped her hand deep into Cord's front pocket, to deposit a not-so-thin wad of folded bills. She kept her hand in his pocket longer than she had to, as she kissed him gently on the cheek and whispered in his ear.

"What a nice surprise at Sam's today; you made my day Cord; thank you."

With that, she slipped behind the wheel and hit the sunroof switch.

"I'm sure I'll be visiting Sam more often to shop, as will all my friends at Brookfield – although I expect you to show them significantly less attention than I get."

She smiled and waited for him to nod in acknowledgment, which he did.

"And be sure to tell Sam the increase in business is due to his executive decision to hire you….don't forget. We aren't a bunch of social security retirees up there, you know; it's actually an impressive group of professionals, doctors, lawyers, bankers, land barons, you name it….even some boring engineers."

He looked at her a bit puzzled, on cue, and waited for the explanation she wanted to give.

"My ex-husband was a boring, albeit successful,

engineer.   Boring being the operative term; having money doesn't necessarily make someone interesting."

"His loss Mae."

"He couldn't keep up with me anyway."

She smiled as she turned the key and the engine rumbled under the hood.

"I just *love* this little car!"

She said as she started to back out.

"When you settle your work schedule with Sam, let me know; I want to know when you're working....and when your off."

And with that, she handed him a business card she previously fetched from her purse.

"Mae, the only women who have given me personal business cards weren't in the lobbying business....well, maybe they were."

She laughed.

"Don't worry, I'm good, but I don't charge – maybe I should.   Anyway, I lobbied under my own name for years. If you were from New Jersey, which you clearly aren't, you would know my name; those cards are gold, young man. Feel free to use it if you get in trouble – but I'll warn you, payback will be expected – we can settle on the terms and conditions later. By the way, I don't see a ring on your finger; no Mrs. Cord waiting back home?"

He smiled and tipped the card at her before he slipped it into his pocket.

"Nope. Thank you for the card, young lady."

"Just *nope* huh? Sounds a bit mysterious. And something is telling me you might need that *Get-Out-Of-Jail-Free* card more than most, Mr. Cord Brin, am I right?"

He didn't answer; he just kept smiling.

"Seriously, I want you to come see me….soon; I know you just enough to know I want to get to know you better. And believe me, all joking aside, I don't have this conversation with every grocery clerk I meet."

With that, Mae Edna pulled out, waving lazily out the drop top and leaving him standing in a puff of gravel dust she kicked up, with his first tip in his pocket, and, to his surprise, a semi in his drawers.

Mae would have liked knowing that; she wouldn't mind being his little Maggie Mae.

It was an unusually busy afternoon.

For the next several hours, until closing, Sam and Cord worked in tandem, with Ay taking orders and bantering with customers, and Sam preparing the goods for Cord to bag.

In addition to Mae, Cord walked about twenty orders to people's cars, or in front of the store, peppering clientele at the deli counter and during the delivery with incessant questions – where they lived, why they came to Sam's, where they worked and their culinary desires. He weaved the questions effortlessly; he listened intently and, surprisingly, every one answered him, in great detail. Not surprising, most people like to talk about themselves; they take great and inexhaustible interest in the subject matter – the slightest catalyst can start the process. Ay was the catalyst; and they all, bar none, took an immediate liking to him. He wrote his thoughts and observations on a piece of paper behind the deli case as he interviewed the customers. He was busy; he felt good.

By 4:30 pm, the queue ended quickly; Sam's patrons were well trained.

The butcher walked to the front of the store and flipped the *Open* sign to *Closed* and made his way back to the deli case, up onto the dais and sat down next to Ay as he sighed deeply, signaling joy in the respite from a hectic afternoon. Ay wouldn't have sat down so hard on that little stool; Sam was a big man.

The clock behind the deli case ticked to exactly 4:45 pm; on cue, the young girl at the register yelled back to Sam in a guttural voice she was leaving; that was the first time he actually heard her speak. Cord was certain she wouldn't recognize him on the street five minutes from now, despite him walking by her over forty times that afternoon.

Sam said goodbye, and then quickly yelled after her.

"Sue, on your way out, take that sign out of the window you made."

Too late. Sue's ass was through the door and out of sight in the brief instant between Sam's comments – greased lightning.

"You certainly got the A-team going here, eh Sam."

Sam frowned, slowly shaking his head in acknowledgment.

"It's tough to get anyone to work anymore, especially kids. I have Sue and her sister…."

Cord cut him off.

"There's a second one of them swimming around here? Good God, that's scary."

Sam got off the stool, straightened and stretched as he walked toward the front of the store in a slow, creaky gait….bad knees.

"You were awful busy writing all afternoon; what was that about?"

"Nothing much; just asking questions about the store, what they like, dislike, why they come here, mostly. Simple stuff. I figured we could sit down and go over it when you come back from your stroll. You probably know most of it, but some answers might surprise you.

People like to talk, and they have lots of opinions. Hey, on a separate note, I gotta run home for a bit to take care of some matters; do you happen to know...."

In Cord's mid-sentence, Sam had arrived at the front plate window and began to peel the *Help Wanted* sign off the glass. As he did, something piqued his curiosity down the sidewalk, off to the right of the store, out of sight.

Whatever it was, it was coming quick and Sam wanted no part of it.

"Uh-oh."

Was all he said.

With that, the big man turned tail and did a quick two-step toward the deli case, trying to act calm and composed as he skated toward, and past, Ay. The knee didn't look so bum anymore. Cord would bet money the man was pinching, so he didn't drop a wet loaf in his shorts.

Sam was talking a steady stream as he passed by:

"Listen, Cord, let's talk about that list in the morning, okay? I forgot I have some paperwork at the house to go over....important stuff. The front door is locked, no need to let anyone in or answer the door; I'm parked out back, so I'm going out that way. If you want to wash up, go ahead; then you can go out the back and pull the door shut when....

The door slammed shut as he was finishing his sentence; the big man was gone.

"*That* was fucking strange."

Cord said aloud to himself.

What the hell is coming down the sidewalk, he thought, and why wasn't he running too?

He remembered the old joke about the guy who was quickly lacing his sneakers as a hungry bear was running toward their campsite. His buddy says why bother putting on your shoes, you can't outrun a bear. As the guy finishes tying his laces and gets up to run, he simply says*: I don't have to run faster than the bear, I just have to run faster than you.*

Sam had the sneakers; Cord was still sitting barefoot by the campfire.

Then it dawned on him; it was Frank!

Holy shit, guess he picked on the wrong guy. *Jesus Christ, how many hours was he in this fucking Town and he was already in deep?*

He looked around for a weapon….anything; he picked up the closest butchers knife, then quickly put it down; that outcome had nothing but bad written all over it. But he kept the blade handle right by his hand, just in case, and waited for the barrage at the door.

His heart was racing in his chest.

But nothing happened; nobody came to the door.

It seemed like forever, but probably only half a minute passed. Given Sam's reaction, thirty seconds seemed like plenty of time for the *tourbillon* to hit the front door, whatever it was.

Holy Shit, he thought to himself, *the guy is going for the back door*!

He turned to run into the back room, for what he wasn't quite sure, for Frank surely must have a key, even if Sam had locked the door.

He would have to jump him as he opened the door, and hope Frank didn't have a weapon. His blood was pumping hard, adrenaline kicking in.

Fuck it, he went for the knife; but just as he grasped the handle, he heard a light rap on the front glass door. He slowly turned, his hand still on the blade as it lay on the counter.

Oh my God.

CHAPTER 9 – OUT OF THE WAY, ASSHOLE

The sun was slipping in the sky toward the free bridge over the Delaware, at the far end of Water Street, which spilled into Pennsylvania, on the far shore. The light was intense across the storefront; it baked the sidewalk and whitewashed the street side of the glass.

In the midst of that fiery glow stood a slender, female figure, gently rapping on the door. She pressed her delicate face against the glass; from her vantage, the store looked dark, gray and empty. She reached down and tried the handle; it resisted her initial push, as it did her gentle, but rapid, front and back motion, as she repeatedly depressed the thumb plate on the latch. He realized she couldn't see him in the back of the store, eyeing her.

He was frozen in a voyeur's stare; she was absolutely beautiful….stunning. One of the most beautiful women he had seen. *Ever*.

She was about to turn away when he slowly started toward the door; she detected the movement in the pitch and again pressed her face against the glass. She placed her hand around her eyes to shield the light; her other hand was on the door handle. She simply stared, expressionless, as he slowly approached the door; she didn't move, she didn't blink.

My God, she was perfect.

Most men, when they spy a woman, quickly size the physical features, the important ones anyway….sort of a Rorschach, which determines:

- if they'll bother to develop a plan of pursuit; or,
- the more likely scenario (since men tend to be gifted pursuers in their own minds, but are lazy sacks when it comes to actually implementing anything), if they will remember key features to

jerk-off to later, or fantasize about when they're banging whomever it is they're banging at the time. Transference during sex - guys use it more than most women will ever know. Count Cord among them.

To most men, this first blush is relatively qualitative and short on specifics. Some focus on breast size or the shape of the ass; some like a woman who is generally thin, or generally curvaceous, or generally fat; others focus on height or ethnicity; still others the face – with little regard to the body attached.

Some simply don't care about the woman's physical features – personality and the *beauty inside* is all that matters. C was always wary of that group….defective.

Cord's initial assessment and criteria were well beyond the norm – he recognized this, but performed the task nonetheless. He didn't have a choice, it just happened, and had been the case since he was a kid. And it's not that he wouldn't befriend a woman who didn't pass; however, to have a relationship, or even to just fuck, she had to muster.

He knew plenty of guys over the years who would shag any woman, regardless of weight, looks or physical impairment of any sort. She undressed, they got rock hard and banged away – simple as that. Cord was dumbfounded by that prospect; it would have been physically impossible for him to have sex with a woman that did not meet the majority of his criteria, like fucking with a string.

Other guys had different standards for having actual sex, versus simply a blow-job; namely, fat or ugly chicks could blow them, but keep your clothes on….please.

On the other hand, Cord had only one set of criteria for all sexual acts; and it had changed little to none over the past thirty years.

The criteria, in order:

<u>No. 1 – The Upper Arm</u>:

The first and foremost criterion was the arm, especially the upper arm, between the elbow and the shoulder. Sinewy and rail thin, definition in the muscle, especially in the tricep and deltoid. The armpit – distinctively concave, with no hair.　Not overtly masculine, just definition….a ballet dancer, or a gymnast or a distance runner.

Where the arm connected to the armpit, right at the back, had to be crisp and tight, no excess skin or fat; if a woman is out of shape, you can tell-all by the upper arms – the rest of the body follows its lead.

This was, by far, the most telling feature, and it's where his eyes went first.

<u>No. 2 – The Lower Abdomen</u>:

If the arm passed, the lower abdomen, from navel to crotch, had to be ironing-board flat, no Venus-belly allowed.　If the hip bones protruded, even just a bit, mark it a bonus.

<u>No. 3 – Chin/Neck/Collarbone</u>:

This was a critical area. The profile from the tip of the chin to the neck had to be arrow straight, no jowl, loose skin or *slope*; a ninety-degree angle from the chin bottom to the neck was the ideal.

The muscles in the neck should show with the slightest movement of the head, with the collarbones slightly pronounced.

Perfect.

<u>No. 4 – Legs</u>:

The legs would be thin, of course, but especially so the calves and upper thighs. If she stood feet together (side-by-side), there should be clear daylight….right to the crotch.

<u>No 5 – Nose</u>:

Diminutive, with a slight upward turn. This was key.

<u>No. 6 – Breasts</u>:

Small breasts preferred, but cup size didn't matter. Given the prior criteria, small breasts typically came with the package, unless augmented. He wasn't a fan of surgery, but could live with the results, if not cartoonish.

But small, and real, was definitely better.

<u>No. 7 – Hair</u>:

Hair color and length were not that important, but he did favor blondes and brunettes; he liked a fair-skinned girl with a noticeable, but not dark, tan, since that usually came with freckles.

Freckles were preferred to be numerous enough to notice, but light, not overpowering. He could live without freckles.

He liked fine, light-colored hair on the forearms, not a lot, just enough to notice.

<u>No. 8 – Hirsute</u>:

Last, but certainly not least, she had to have a significant amount hair....he disliked a shaved snatch or a token strip; but he was turned off by an unkempt, excess look. It seemed for a lot of women, there was no middle ground; they either shaved or sported a forest.

The perfect mat had crisp, trimmed edges, fully covered the lips, extended a bit above the clit, into a decent-sized triangle or oval, and faintly extending between the legs….a little hair just up to the ass was a plus. Clean shave lines along the crotch/leg intersection was essential.

Obsessive? He certainly was. Shallow? Absolutely. Hypocrite? Without a doubt. And Cord made no apologies for same.

Back to the girl in the window.

He sized her up in seconds; all the criteria - from the time it took to walk from the deli case to the cash register, just inside the door.

She wore a white, tight-fitting, short-sleeve dress tee, with a slight V-cut in the front, extending just below her collarbone, tucked into a pair of tawny Capris. It was early in the season to be wearing such a top, but the day had been unseasonably warm. She wore heelless flats; her hair was straight, with a slight wave, just past her shoulder. A slight breeze, ever so slight, caused a handful of strands to slowly dance away from her face. The sunlight accentuated the fine, fair hair on her forearms.

She had high cheekbones and dark, defined eyebrows, which framed a set of beautiful, piercing eyes. He couldn't tell the color, but the color didn't matter.

My God, her eyes were intense; the kind that grab a man and convince him to do things he knows he shouldn't do.

Beauty is power; a smile is its sword

He was right. And this woman's sword was that set of eyes....scorchers.

It took the course of less than half a dozen steps toward the door to realize she was a solid pass on Nos. 1-6; he assumed she would have air at the top of her legs, since she wasn't standing in that manner. She wasn't wearing a bra; her small breasts pressed against her t-shirt, exposing the outline of her nipples in a way that was erotic, not cheap. Her hair was lighter, either blonde or light brown; it was difficult to tell in the bright sunlight.

Number 8 was obviously a mystery....hopefully not for long.

She seemed to be eyeing him up as well, as he got closer to the door, she seemed to focus on his apron; damn, why hadn't he taken that off, it looked a bit nerdy to be answering the door in a silly, white smock. Yet she seemed to be fascinated by the garment. Then she looked to her right and saw the *Help Wanted* sign, dangling by a single piece of tape, just where Sam had abruptly left it.

She looked back and gave him a mischievous pirate smile, realizing she wasn't laying her eyes on the regular butcher....rotund Frank.

Sword number two – her smile. She was a killer, for sure.

Men make it so easy.

Say hellooo to the new butcher, young lady he thought to himself. And Mae was already a distant memory.

She seemed enamored; her lips parted slightly as he reached the door. She stared laser into his eyes, like she was scanning his brain, while that quirky smile massaged it at the same time.

And the two stood silent on opposite sides of the plate glass door, eyes locked, waiting for the other to do something, whatever that may be.

She spoke first, almost a whisper through the glass.

"My goodness, I was expecting Frank; what a pleasant surprise."

She purred the words….velvet.

"Frank had to leave early, I'm the new butcher, Cord; but people call me Ay."

He delivered the line rather clumsily; nice job, he thought – couldn't he think of a better line than that?

Actually, he wasn't the new butcher; he didn't really know *what* he was; Sam and he never discussed what specific *help* the sign in the window actually wanted.

But for the purposes of this conversation, butcher it was – that seemed to be the ticket for this young lady.

"I called in an order earlier this afternoon to pick up at closing, but I got delayed."

She lightly pouted, as she extended her lower lip just a fraction past her upper lip and gave him the saddest cat eyes he'd ever seen.

"A friend had a bit of a problem and called me….I just couldn't pull myself away; I'm so sorry for the inconvenience. Frank said he would leave the order in the refrigerator in the back room. Can I please come in, pick it up and pay for it; it would mean the world to me and I would certainly tell Sam how his *new* butcher went out of his way to be *so* kind to a total stranger."

For the record, he would have probably opened that door for her if she had declared she was going to rob the place and stab him in the heart, but still, she *was* laying it on a bit thick. He knew it, but he drank it anyway; vanity is a sweet elixir. In fact, if he wasn't mistaken, he sensed a bit of foreplay going on; he seriously started thinking about the opportunity to bang this girl – and soon.

"No problem; I was just about to leave, but it would be a pleasure to take care of you; come on back to the deli case and I'll find your package. I don't know how to ring you up on the cash register – I haven't used it yet, but I'm sure we can figure something out."

He smiled at her; the kind of smile new friends share.

With that, he reached down and grabbed the thumb knob on the door to unlock the deadbolt. It clicked open cleanly, yet when she went to open the door, it didn't move; it seemed to be hung up on something. She rattled the latch and attempted to open the door, but no luck.

"Why won't it open?"

She fretted.

What was holding that damn door shut? He thought. All he could focus on was how quickly he could get her inside that store and continue their *introduction.*

"Sometimes it sticks; you need to stick your pinkie finger in the keyhole and jiggle the little thing in there. Look in the keyhole; you'll see what I mean."

She said plainly, as if she'd been through this drill more than once. No problem, he thought, he was here to help. He bent down to inspect the keyhole, starting to squint as he got closer to the door latch.

His face was about eight inches from the door; any closer would have been too close, any farther would have given him a fair chance to react.

No….eight inches was *just* the right distance. And she knew it, having been through this drill much more than once.

Bam!

In one lightning quick move, she muscled open the huge front door open and clocked him but good – the sharp metal edge of the door smacked squarely against his temple, down across the corner of his eye, to the tip of his nose. It felt like a bomb exploded against his face.

Now Cord had rarely been put down; maybe a half-dozen times in his *entire* life, usually after heavy drinking, followed by a heavy beating, and usually by more than one set of fists.

Never, *never,* had he gone down sober, with one shot….till now.

And by a girl to boot.

The picture tube went fuzzy white; he tingled all over, down to his fingertips and toes, as he tipped away from her in slow motion, like a felled tree that picks up momentum as it descends to the forest floor. The back of his head rapped sharply against the tile floor, adding insult.

The last thing he remembered, the last memory before the lights went out, was her saying, with disgusted contempt, as she started to step over him.

"Out of the way, asshole."

CHAPTER 10 – SO….I HEAR YOU MET LILLIAN

Dusk was approaching.

The sun must have crossed the horizon, but just barely, for he could still see the streetscape pretty clearly. As his eyes focused, he began to remember what happened and realized he was now laying on his right side. The store was dark, empty and quiet.

My God, she really did rob the place! Sam *told* him not to open the door.   Fuck, now what was he going to do?

He slowly sat up.

Oddly, the first thing he noticed was the *Help Wanted* sign….it was re-taped to the window. He looked down and saw his blue tee-shirt, no apron. She *rolled* him and then *took* his apron?   As he sat up, he noticed bits of stale bread crumbs stuck to his shirt; the larger pieces rolled off onto the floor.

What the hell was going on?

A dull throb pulsed across his face, along the line of the door's impact….he had a killer headache.

He slowly fumbled to see if she took anything else; he had ten, neatly folded, crisp $100 bills in his front right pocket – he knew they would be gone.

Nope, still there.

She took the apron but not the cash? He didn't get it. The only other article on his body was the *Belvidere* note in his left pocket. That was gone.

What the fuck?

He wondered how many people had walked by the storefront with him lying there in the dark, like a sack of potatoes, less than ten feet away.

He took a bit to stand up….wobbly. He felt the back of his head and his face for evidence of blood or welts, and tried to find a mirror to see how bad he was cut. He walked slowly; each step produced a pronounced throb in the back of his brain.

Mother-fucker….his head hurt bad.

He made it to the deli counter and decided to check out his hunch. He entered the rear storeroom, which he never went in all day – no reason to. As he suspected, there was no package in the refrigerator for the little Beelzebub – in fact, there wasn't even a fucking refrigerator in the storeroom.

What a little bitch, he thought; she was *him*, but without the dick….*maybe*.

He turned on the light and looked for some aspirin, anything to soothe his headache. He found some *Excedrin* in a desk drawer and took two, dry.

On Sam's desk he saw this month's copy of some business magazine, alongside a series of four photocopied pages of queries, with the heading:

Effective Hiring: Finding Staff With The Right Stuff!

I guess Sam forgot to bring that little questionnaire behind the deli counter this afternoon before he hired Cord, he thought cynically. Maybe that will be the topic of tomorrow's meeting, along with a discussion about the beating he took at the hands of a ninety-five pound psychopath he let into the store after hours, right before he throws him out on his ear.

So much for a career in meats.

He found a small bathroom, with a face-sized mirror over the sink. How he didn't have a deep red crevice in his face was beyond belief; but aside from some puffiness in his face and a pinkish tinge along the impact line, it didn't look all that bad. It would probably shine like a red highlighter in the morning. He splashed water across his face a couple times and sighed, then gently patted it dry and headed back to the store.

His head was still pounding like a mother.

As he left the storeroom and entered the dais area behind the deli counter, he was stopped in his tracks; there, on the butcher's block, with a serious, six-inch carving knife stuck through it, was his *Belvidere* note; the knife stood vertical, harpooned into the wood.

Next to it was a neat, handwritten note, in a thick black marker used to label the wrapped meat:

Sam:

I stopped by to talk to you, but I must have <u>just</u> missed you – I saw your car in the back lot five minutes before I arrived. Were you in a hurry?

I met your new butcher – very nice guy who seemed to go out of his way to faun over me, he must have thought I was a 'special' customer, he couldn't possibly be that nice to everyone! He should also be a big help with store security, a strong, smart guy like that. He is pretty mechanical too, he helped me un-

**jam the front door, which you know sticks
from time to time.**

**There must be a mistake in the uniform he
was issued, however, because he was wearing
Uncle Frank's apron; remember the new one
I just bought him?**

**Actually, I saw Uncle Frank this afternoon –
odd, he was sitting on his front porch
drinking when he should have been at work –
did he get sick? He said something about
eating too many grapes? It all seems a bit
confusing.**

**I'll stop by tomorrow, late morning and say
Hi to Frank behind the deli counter, his usual
spot, before we have our own little talk. Oh,
and I re-taped up the Help-Wanted
sign....just in case you still need it.**

Have a Good Morning!

Love,

Lillian

She actually put a little heart where the dot on the first *i*
in her name was meant to be. Holy shit, where was the
pot with the boiling rabbit?

He pulled the knife out of the wood counter, collected
his note, and walked back to the front of the store.
That's when he noticed the next-to-last prop.

A partially eaten roast beef and provolone sandwich was
sitting on the cash register checkout belt, right above
where he was dozing on the floor; two distinctive bites
were taken out of the sandwich, and then it was left
there, to be found by him.

He couldn't believe it; this skinny little girl:

- knocked him out and shook him down;
- rolled him around enough to get off the smock;
- wrote a long, neat note to Sam, with enough sarcasm to choke a horse;
- harpooned his *Belvidere* note into the counter;
- took the time to make a sandwich; and then
- stood right over him while she ate it, dropping crumbs on his shirt.

All the while he was out cold, and didn't remember a bit of it.

He didn't know if he should be mad….or very, very scared.

To this point he had been carrying his *Belvidere* note in his hand. He went to put it back in his left pocket when he felt something tucked inside, all the way at the bottom. He immediately knew what it was by the size and the soft oval shape – he could feel his face start to flush as he fingered it and rolled it around in his hand.

The last message from the little lady.

He left the goddamn thing in his pocket – he refused to look at it or acknowledge it any further.

That was it.

He re-locked the front door, ripped off, and ripped up, the *Help Wanted* sign and took the sandwich – he hadn't eaten all day and was starved – ripping off the roast beef and throwing it on the check-out counter. As he walked to the back of the store, he thought better of trusting that sandwich; he could only imagine what booby trap she set between the slices of bread. Disgusted, he flipped it into the trash can behind the deli case. Then he took the knife and stabbed it violently back into the counter, off to the far side of the chopping block; it swayed back and forth from the force of his stroke. He left Sam's note next to it.

He walked out the back door, ensured it was secure, and made his way around the building to the front of the *Palace*, which was still humming with early evening patrons.

From his vantage point in front of *Nonpareil*, he looked over at the front door of the *Sam's*, just twenty feet away, at most. He shook his head in disbelief; he had been laid out on that floor so close to where he was now standing, with these oblivious people dining al fresco, laughing and joking the whole time. He shook his head in disgust....his brain still throbbing, the aspirin hadn't done shit.

He pushed the *Sweet Shop* door open and stepped in.

The old *Palace of Sweets* sported a long ice cream bar to the right, with seltzer taps and a dozen different sundae topping containers; a line of stools invited patrons to belly up to the bar. To the left were a series of glass display cases, holding various nostalgic candies, all from the days when he was a kid: *Atomic Fire Balls*, *Wonka Bars*, candy cigarettes, *Mary Janes*, *Sugar Daddys*, ruby-red wax lips, chocolate coins, shoe laces of grape licorice, and a dozen other classics. There were seven booths in the back, along with one central table. All the booths and the table were occupied; others sat at the ice cream bar. The place was humming.

The entire space was decorated with retro memorabilia and an eclectic mix of original art hanging on the walls, from all corners of the globe....quality stuff. Overhead, at the far end of the restaurant, a large movie screen spooled classic cinema. When Cord walked in, *Casablanca* was playing, black and white....1942. The audio was off, and C found himself standing and watching for a bit, reading the subtitles. Rick, Humphrey Bogart, sat despondent in his *American Cafe*, drinking and smoking heavy, having just witnessed his stunning lost love, Ilsa, Ingrid Bergman, mistaken stumble into his gin joint, and back into his life. Rick sat shell-shocked head-in-hand, pondering next moves. It was one of C's favorite movies. Over speakers he did not see, the soft lilting vocals of Patsy Kline singing *Crazy* backfilled amongst the din of patrons chatting away.

The place had a feel of comfort; like home should feel.

There were two customers waiting for service on the ice cream bar; the candy counter, where the register sat, was empty. He walked up to the left-side counter and was greeted by a bubbly teen, who seemed too eager to help.

"Welcome to *Nonpareil*! How can I help you?"

"What's your name, young lady?"

"Um, my name is Linda."

She answered apprehensively; she usually wasn't asked her name by someone placing an order.

"Hi Linda, I was wondering if you could help me. I'm kinda new in Town, in fact I just got in today, and I haven't made any arrangements for where to stay for the night – do you happen to know anywhere, or anyone, I could talk to about that? Is there a hotel, or bed and breakfast, in Town?" He figured he would bed down for a day or two till he could find a more permanent place to stay, if he stuck around at all. Maybe it was best just to get the fuck out.

She just stood and stared at him for a moment – her brain was expecting a request for a bowl of soup, a sandwich or possibly a piece of pie; a room wasn't on the regular menu.

"Umm, I don't really think I can help with that…."

She said, extending the sentence while she thought about it, and looked around the room for help.

Suddenly, the perkiness returned to her face; it was clear that little brain had formulated a solution.

"But you can talk to Elwood; he is the tall, thin guy over in the second booth on the right."

She pointed as she talked.

'He might be able to help you!"

With that, she hoped the stranger would move along, so she could get back to the regular menu.

Elwood? Cord thought to himself; there can't be anyone alive under eighty with the name Elwood, unless he was living in Appalachia. He figured he would soon meet what had to be the only Elwood in the state of New Jersey.

"Thank you very much; listen, while I go talk to Elwood, could I trouble you to make me up a lettuce, tomato, hot pepper and provolone sandwich on ciabatta bread, extra provolone – and how about a sarsaparilla soda – do you have that flavor?"

Linda smiled

"Sarsaparilla at the old *Palace Of Sweets*? Of course!"

And with that, she took the slip and started work on the order in earnest. She was happy again.

He made his way over to the second booth to meet with Elwood. The booth was occupied by a tall thin man who looked to be about his age, and a second gentleman who looked like an older, shorter and slightly heavier version of Elwood. They were both working on vanilla sundaes, covered in too many maraschino cherries and hot fudge sauce. He wasn't sure what a homegrown Belviderean looked like, but he was pretty sure he just found two of them.

"Elwood?"

He asked.

"That depends; you looking for money?"

With that the two gentlemen guffawed, much louder than was really necessary. Oh, boy, he thought; homegrown it is, straight out of Mayberry. He was waiting for Goober to pop his head up from the next booth and start chuckling along.

Cord responded to Elwood's joke with neither a laugh nor a smile; his head still was pounding, his face hurt, and he certainly wasn't in the mood for jokes.

Elwood took note.

"You can call me Woody, or Wood....or W; any will do."

Cord didn't acknowledge that statement either.

"My name is Cord; Linda over at the register said you might be able to help me out. I just got into Town today and haven't made any arrangements for lodging; I know it's kinda late, but the day kind of got away from me and I am in a bit of a bind. Do you know of any hotels or B&Bs close by, preferably in Town?"

Elwood answered with a question.

"How long you staying in Town?"

"Could be a week; could be a year."

Woody hesitated for only a second.

"Well, I know a place which might be of interest. One of my good clients owns a building in Town with a fully furnished two-bedroom apartment – it's available right now, in fact. The furnishings are a bit sparse, but nice, but it only has one bedroom set; I don't know if that's a problem...."

Elwood waited a second for a retort....hearing none from Cord, he continued.

"It's completely renovated; central air, washer/dryer in the unit, hardwood floors, high ceilings, new kitchen and bath, cedar closets. The downside is that it has no yard and it's a third floor walk-up, so that puts off some folks. The good thing is there are only two apartments in the whole building; one on the second floor and one on the third floor. The second floor tenants are quiet, no kids and no pets. Do you have kids....or pets?"

Cord shook his head no.

"Hell, it even has some food in the pantry; I was storing some canned soups and vegetables and stuff in there for the Boy Scouts food drive; I'm sure if you ate a bit of it till you stocked the place yourself no one would mind; especially, since I'm in charge of it."

He said with a chuckle.

Cord didn't answer or respond to the statement, but he did return a small smile, which Woody noticed.

"I could get you in there now, tonight, I got the key, and you can pay weekly, prorated based on the monthly rent, which is nine-hundred seventy-five bucks; we'll switch over the utilities after a week, if you decide to stay. Electric is on you; heat is on the landlord. Then you can go month to month for the balance of the year, but I'll have to get you to sign a lease first – the owner is a bit of a stickler and she'll insist on the lease being signed. Fair enough?"

Cord was impressed. Here was a bumpkin, he thought, who could have easily told him where the nearest B&B or hotel was, and finished his sundae in peace – he didn't have to ask how long he was staying in town, he could have assumed it was just overnight. Instead, the guy rattles off all the particulars of an available apartment without missing a beat, throws in food collected by the Scouts, gets a small commission on the rental, he assumed, and more importantly, makes one of his good clients happy by filling a less-than-desirable third floor walk-up flat. All this off hours on a Thursday night, while he is eating ice cream. Impressive he thought, especially for an Elwood.

"Sounds fine; but I'll need to see the lease first."

Cord said matter-of-fact.

Woody stood up and eagerly extended his hand to seal the deal; Ay shook it firmly. Woody quickly shuffled over to the nearby table and grabbed one of the unused chairs, while joking with the young couple sitting there – it was clear he knew them. He set it at the end of the booth and gestured for Cord to sit, which he did.

At this point, he turned to the older gentleman, who extended his hand to introduce himself as Woody's pop. Cord had figured as much.

The man only had stubs for two of his five fingers, making shaking his hand a bit odd, especially since Ay wasn't expecting it. Cord didn't ask about the fingers – maybe the old man had a run-in with that psycho from Sam's.

"The name's Elmer; but it's Moe to my friends."

With that, the man eyed Cord with a wink and a look begging to be asked about the story behind the moniker.

Cord didn't know how Moe was short for Elmer, but he also didn't really care – he turned his attention away from the old man, his lack of interest evident.

With that, Elmer got up, announced he would run up to the office, pick up the lease and keys and bring both back to the *Palace*. Cord asked if he knew where he could pick up some basic toiletries, such as a bar of soap, toothpaste, a toothbrush and the like. Woody interjected and said everything he would likely need tonight was in the apartment, except probably a toothbrush; he told his dad to pick up a brush and Cord could get whatever food he needed at *Sam's* next door in the morning.

"Did you happen to notice *Sam's Market* next door?"

Elwood asked.

"Yeah, I did happen to notice that place."

Cord said sarcastically, as he shook his head in the affirmative. Woody didn't pick up on the sarcasm.

Linda brought over the sarsaparilla and the sandwich, along with a big smile; Cord, anticipating her coming, stood up and handed her a C-note, whispering discretely in her ear to take the sandwich and soda out of it, bring him the change, and keep twenty-five dollars for herself as a tip, since she was nice enough to introduce him to Elwood and she was *such* a pleasant person that she made his day. She stepped back with her mouth open in an oval and wide-eyed, like someone had just slipped a cock in her ass; then she smiled broadly – Cord knew from that point on that he owned her.

It was funny, he thought; a minor, unanticipated gesture like that, for no favor expected in response, would pay for itself ten times over. If ever he needed a future favor from Linda, he was sure she would oblige. For young attractive girls, Linda was no more than eighteen he suspected, it was unexpected money or gifts; for older woman, it was attention or affection, even in light doses. The formula worked – it always did.

The sandwich and soda hit the spot.

A guy in his twenties walked by on his way out of the *Palace*; he stopped and talked to Woody about upcoming Little-League teams and coaching topics; Elwood engaged him for a bit and traded tired one-liners while Cord ate and relaxed. It was clear Woody played to the skill set of his audience. Cord noticed his headache had subsided, and the door imprint on his face was apparently not noticeable enough for anyone to fixate on.

"So, why is it you're in Town?"

Woody asked innocently, as the Little-League dad made his way to the front door and onto the street. Cord followed him with his eyes.

It was dark by this time, with the street lights outside *Nonpareil* illuminating the al fresco tables in a soft amber glow. Cord eyed two younger couples sharing a nearby booth; one with what looked like a four-year old who just wouldn't sit. The tawpie repeatedly crawled under the table, tangling in the feet of the childless couple, who tried their best to ignore the urchin, but their efforts were otiose – like trying to politely ignore a dog humping your leg. The parents smiled at how cute their son was, commenting to the other couple that he was a *just a little rug rat*. They then summarily ignored him, enjoying their coffee in peace.

Cord had just taken his last bite of the sandwich, so he held his finger up to Elwood as he slowly chewed, making him wait, and wait some more, for an answer to his question that Cord wouldn't provide. Woody looked at him for a bit, then, when he got bored watching Ay chew, looked about the room, waiting for Cord to clear his mouth.

"Let me ask you something."

Cord finally said, purposely deflecting W's question.

"How many people in this place do you know?"

Woody looked about the room and answered matter-of-fact.

"All of them."

"That doesn't surprise me."

Cord continued.

"Tell me a little about them. For instance, how about that older gentleman, sitting alone in the far booth."

With that, Elwood went on for a good twenty minutes, telling life stories about the various people sitting around the café that Cord didn't give a shit about. Woody was a good storyteller; mixing facts with humorous anecdotes. He quickly forgot that Cord never answered his question.

A sarsaparilla refill and a big smile greeted Ay about halfway through W's narrative.

"It's on me."

Linda lightly whispered in Cord's ear. Her warm breath on his skin was pleasant; he wasn't sure, but it seemed she let out a bit more breath than necessary for those three small words. Woody eyed him, his head cocked a bit, with a puzzled look, then, with a mix of amazement and a sense that an explanation was in order, said:

"I guess you made a fast friend."

"Guess so."

Was all Cord said, without looking at Woody or offering any further information on the matter.

With that, Moe opened the door and made his way back to the booth, greeting people along the way.

He handed Cord the lease, a red pen and a bare toothbrush, out of the box.

"Sorry it took a bit, I filled out what I could and left the rest blank. The toothbrush is new, I swear….just don't have the box for it."

Cord quickly started to scan the document; with the pen in his left hand.

"A lefty!"

Moe remarked. Cord was always amazed at how many people would notice that he was a lefty and comment on it, as if it was something special. He never noticed other lefties, nor did he care.

After about a minute or so, the document was marked up and initialed like he was grading a term paper; he was still on page 1 of 6, excluding the *Security Deposit Agreement* attached to the end of the lease. There were sections for past addresses, a social security number, personal references, bank account numbers; all problematic….and all left blank.

He turned to Woody.

"Listen, I have to read this document a little more carefully; there are a bunch of clauses that need to be slightly modified, nothing crazy, even though it might only be a short-term stint. How about I pay two-hundred, fifty dollars to the landlord now for the first week, plus pay you fifty dollars for helping me out in a pinch, which is only fair – I'm sure we'll clear up the lease in the next day or so, or, we can just forego the matter and maybe you can point me to a nearby hotel or B&B."

With that, Cord peeled off three crisp hundreds and handed them to Elmer; he knew Elwood wasn't go to let this fish off the hook.

"No problem, if you are prepaying the week and you might not stay anyway, I'm sure I can get a delay in the lease. You seem like a decent guy, right Pop?"

His dad nodded in acknowledgment as he quickly tucked the money in his shirt pocket.

"Besides, it looks like Linda would cover for you anyway."

With that, the two men laughed heartily; Cord smiled along with them, a slight lip uptick.

"Listen, do you want to see the place now, or relax a bit?"

Before Cord could answer, Woody's cell phone rang, the ring-tone set to an annoying marching tune; he reached into his zip-up jacket pocket and looked at the number, before he flipped the handset open.
"Hey Sambo, what's up? Yeah, there *is* some new guy in here. What does he look like and I'll tell you if it is him."

With that, Elwood looked straight at Cord.

"Say again….uh huh, uh huh….he's short and stocky, no hair, bit of a tan, pretty serious demeanor, probably alone? Yeah, I think I see him, yeah; in fact, I think he's sitting right here in the booth with me and Pop. No I'm not kidding."

With that, Woody laughed and Moe smiled and let out a single chuckle.

Woody then listened intently, his mouth opening in a smile like someone being told juicy news and who can't wait to pass it on.

"Get out! Are you kidding? This afternoon! Funny, he failed to mention that! I heard about Frankie getting sent home from Larry, but didn't know the details; figured I would catch up with you in the morning."

Cord leaned forward; this wasn't good.

"No, no way!"

With that, Elwood leaned forward and looked right at Cord's face; he knew he was looking for the door tattoo; Moe was leaning halfway across the table, trying to get an ear on the conversation.

Cord was getting annoyed and reached for the phone.

'Give me the God damn phone!"

He barked at Elwood.

Woody responded by quickly leaning back in the booth, like a boxer eluding a jab, just beyond Cord's outstretched arm. Ay started to stand and was about to grab the phone when Woody ended the call.

"Okay, okay, I'll tell him to sit tight, you'll be here in five minutes."

Elwood flipped the phone shut, smiled wry and said.

"So....I hear you met Lillian."

CHAPTER 11 – BROTHERS IN ARMS

Cord didn't answer Woody, and Woody didn't wait for an answer. Elwood chuckled to himself; Elmer was also smiling, as they both rose from the table and gathered their belongings.

"How did Sam know you were here?"

Cord finally asked, as the men were about to exit the booth.

"It's Thursday night at 7:15 pm; this is where I always am on Thursday night at 7:15 pm….me and pop."

"By the way, it would be nice to know where the apartment I just rented actually is."

Cord said sarcastically.

"249 Water Street; and don't forget, it's all the way at the top, the *third floor*, not the second; that's an important tidbit to remember."

With that, Elwood held up three fingers on his left hand; both he and his dad smiled like clams and looked at each other subrosa as they made their way to the register, where they paid Linda and exited the *Palace*.

Cord sat there in silence and drank his sarsaparilla, waiting for Sam. *Nonpareil* was abuzz around him, but he didn't pay a lick of attention to any of it.

The big man came through the front door in five minutes, as promised. He headed straight for Cord, making eye contact with Linda, waving to her and quietly saying hi sweetie as he walked by the register area.

Sam didn't greet Ay formally, he just slid right into the booth, a fluid move that apparently had been practiced over the years. The booths were made for the 1930's gentlemen, svelte frames, not 21st century butchers. The tables were fixed-in-place, and the space to squeeze into the bench seat was not designed for the stomach volume Sam had to move – much like shoving two pounds of bologna in a one pound sack. However, in one smooth motion, Sam bent at the knees, somehow sucked in his gut just enough to fill the daylight and slid in – mission accomplished. The edge of the table deeply creased his belly, but Sam didn't seem to mind, or even notice.

Cord looked at him with half-interest; he wasn't particularly happy with the butcher.

Sam just started in.

"Listen, sorry about leaving so abruptly this afternoon; that wasn't right and I wanted to apologize. But I did tell you not to answer the door."

Sam threw in that weak dangler.

"I don't mean to insult you, Sam, but that pretty much qualifies for the understatement of the fucking year."

Cord continued.

"Hey, here's a suggestion; how about if you had said *this* as you were running past me like a little girl, sneaking out the back door: *Cord run! Run for your fucking life! And whatever you do, don't answer the fucking door! A psycho's on the loose!* How about that, Sam? You know, that might have saved me a griddle mark across my face and a fucking afternoon nap on the shop floor."

"Listen, I saw Lilly coming down the walk; I knew she must have seen Frank and was not happy; she can be a hothead, you know *[Cord looked at him in mock disbelief as he said that, but Sam ignored him and continued]*. But she usually cools down after a bit and then you can talk to her reasonably, somewhat....sometimes. But right then, I knew she'd be all riled up, and it would be confrontational and I didn't want to subject you, or me for that matter, to her wrath right then. I figured I would call her when I got home and explain what happened....that was the plan anyway."

"Bad plan."

Cord said sarcastically.

"Did you stop at the store? Did you see what she did?"

Cord asked.

"Yeah, that's where I called Woody from; I was checking out the carnage. Lillian told me on the phone what happened and what she did. Let me tell you pal, I have to hand it to you, her buttons are not hard to push by any stretch, but you were pretty successful at pushing a bunch of good ones all at the same time – congratulations."

With that, Sam smiled and took his big paw, reached across the table and patted Ay on the shoulder.

Cord wasn't ready to laugh about it just yet.

"Did you see she made a fucking *sandwich* and ate it while she stood over me – for all I know she was dancing and chanting while she undressed me....fucking kook."

"She undressed you?"

Sam asked in disbelief.

"Yeah! She took off my apron and...."

"But it wasn't your apron, now was it, Mister: *Hi, I'm the new butcher?*"

Sam's riposte.

"I *know* it wasn't my apron and the butcher thing just kind of came out."

Cord said angrily.

"That's not the point."

"What is your point?"

Asked Sam, in mock concern.

"Did you know she rifled through my pockets, and put a….she put a…."

Cord hesitated at finishing the sentence while he shoved his hand in his pocket and wrestled around, looking for the warm, red seedless.

"….a fucking grape in my pocket!"

Sam was smiling broadly now, rather enjoying the rant.

Cord continued angrily:

"Glad you think it's funny. Did you happen see the note she left you? Did you at least see that?"

"That note wasn't for me, pal; Lilly left it for *you*."

Sam stated matter-of-fact.

"And it apparently worked; you read it and it got you steamed – she's a pro at that, let me tell you. I also saw the carving knife…."

With that, Sam chuckled.

"I'm glad you're fucking amused; I'm surprised I didn't get it in the gullet."

"Lillian could have really hurt you if she wanted; she was just trying to make a point."

"That's your explanation? Are you fucking kidding me?"

Sam leaned forward and rubbed in a bit of salt – he whispered in a serious tone.

"You're right; it really wasn't fair her tricking you like that. You know, she only weighs ninety-something pounds, you might be able to take her in a rematch."

Cord finally smiled a bit, but just a bit.

"You know, I've never been put down in one shot, ever, not sober anyway; that door stunt was pretty impressive."

With that, he seemed to relax a bit.

Sam leaned further forward and pushed his big bulldog face toward Cord, while pointing at his bushy left eyebrow; when Cord looked closer, he saw the faint remnants of a two-inch long scar, which cut across his eyebrow and extended into his forehead.

"Lilly has the door thing down pretty good."

Sam whispered.

Cord smiled in disbelief, acknowledging he apparently had been initiated into a special club – he wondered how many brothers in arms had been branded with her tattoo over the years.

"Perhaps now would be a good time to give you some background on Lillian."

Sam suggested.

He called Linda over and ordered himself a decaffeinated coffee; Cord ordered a double espresso. They both said for her to keep them topped off with refills.

And Cord looked at Sam, and shook his head.

Brothers in arms.

Sam resettled himself in the booth and began.

'I've known Lilly since she was born, I was there that day, held her in my arms; that will be forty-two years ago this December 25th. Some Christmas present, eh Cord?"

Damn, Cord thought to himself, she's forty-one? He would have guessed she was ten years younger.

He didn't answer Sam, he just let the big man continue.

And with that, Sam went on a ramble.

"Lillian is as true a *Belviderean* as you can get; she was born here and has never left. I'm not sure, but I don't think she has ever really traveled anywhere beyond fifteen to twenty miles from Town; maybe as far as Hackettstown, or Easton, or maybe East Stroudsburg. If she's gone further than that, I've never heard about it."

Maybe when she ran in high school she traveled more – but that would have been on a school bus. She was a gifted distance runner – cross-country, simply phenomenal. The best Belvidere ever produced, bar none, even to today. I remember her getting a bunch of scholarship offers, from colleges all over the country – Division I programs, big time, free ride-type deals, full tuition…the whole nut. The letters used to come in by the bunch. But she never pursued them, I don't even think she opened all of them; she didn't want to leave her brother, or her uncle, your pal Frank. She and her brother Earl live together; they've been together all their lives – Earl's her little brother….well, not so little. He's thirty-nine."

"She lives with her brother, *all her life*?"

That seemed a bit strange. He continued without waiting for an answer from Sam.

"Where are her parents, dead?"

"Her mom died in '81, when Lilly was....I guess she was sixteen. Her mom was a *stunner* – the spitting image of Lillian. She had Lilly when she was only nineteen; they were real close, super close - they looked like, acted like, sisters. Her name was Carol....Carol Liddell.

Sam continued slowly, in a reflective tone; he didn't look at Ay as he spoke, but rather stared blankly toward the back of the café.

He was somewhere else.

"They rented a neat little house out on Fourth Street, a block off the Park. It was April 7th 1981; Lilly had just come home from school. For some reason, Earl wasn't home – good thing.

Anyway, Lilly went calling for her, but Carol, her mom, didn't answer. Lilly went up to her room, which was next to Carol's bedroom and got changed – she was going to go out and meet some friends for something, whatever sixteen year-olds do after school, when she heard someone in the next room – shuffling around – nothing in particular, just noises, like someone walking around and moving things about. She went over to the bedroom door, but it was locked, which was strange. That door was never locked. She got scared and called out for her mom....loud.

The noise inside the bedroom stopped.

With Lillian frozen in the hallway, after what seemed like eternity, just an instant before Lilly was about to run away, Carol quietly answered.

'I didn't hear you come in honey – I'll be there in a minute.'

But it didn't sound like her mom, the voice was hollow, distant. Lilly was confused and apprehensive – but she just stood there, still frozen at the door, until she heard it unlatch - it seemed to take forever.

The door opened slowly; Lilly couldn't see her mother standing there at first, she was tucked behind the opening, out of sight.

Carol leaned from behind the door and stood facing Lilly, but she seemed to look right past her – right through her.   She was wearing Lilly's clothes – which she did on occasion, but it was usually just when they went out shopping together – kind of like a goof. She looked tired, very tired.

She slowly stepped forward and gave Lilly a long, tight hug…an extra long hug. She didn't say a word, she just took long, slow breaths, as she ran the fingers of her right hand gently through Lilly's blonde hair. Lilly didn't know what to do – she was scared to move or even speak.

Carol slowly pushed a small sealed envelope into Lilly's pocket, note-card size, and whispered in her ear:

'Just a little note I want you to open when you are ready....okay?'

Then she just stood and held Lilly in her arms.

'I'm so sorry honey....I love you....bye sweetie.'

She could feel her breathes against her chest, but they were getting shorter, shallow…her hand went limp and ran out of Lillian's hair, slowly falling to her side as she slumped into Lilly.

Frank found her hours later, curled up on the floor alongside Carol. Lilly was kind of asleep; I guess she was in shock.

Sleeping pills, an overdose. No one ever knew why; Carol wasn't like that, she didn't do things like that, ever. She was strong, stable – she was anything but weak; it just made no sense. A mystery, still is, I guess. Lilly never really recovered from that day; not really; that was twenty-five years ago."

Cord sat there, stunned; he didn't say a word, he just stared at Sam. He felt small and petty for complaining about Lillian earlier – he was embarrassed for himself.

He also got a chill; the hair on his arms stood up when Sam recounted what Carol said to Lilly about the note, right before she died.

Open When You Are Ready

That quote had meaning, to Cord anyway. But he didn't say a word about that, aloud.

'Sam, how do you know Carol said *that* to Lilly, when she handed her the note? Is that what she really said, or just what you *think* Carol said?"

Sam looked at Cord and didn't say anything at first, puzzled by the question.

"What's that suppose to mean?"

"I'm just curious, how do you *know* Carol said that?"

"I don't know, that's what Lilly told Frank right after it happened, even before the police were there and stuff. She told him the whole story just once, according to Frank, and nobody else. She told him when she was

105

kind of out of it, and she never talked about it again; she might not even remember she told Frank, I don't know, as I said, she was in shock, and only sixteen, for Christ sake. I assume Frank got it right, but who knows, maybe he didn't....why?"

Just a strange coincidence, Cord thought to himself, that's all.

Cord didn't answer Sam; he changed the subject. He wanted Sam to understand he truly felt for Lillian, because he did.

"What about her dad?"

Ay said quietly, respectfully.

Sam let his question to Cord drop, and continued the back story.

"Carol was a bit of a free spirit; she never really settled down."

Cord understood, but Sam expanded anyway.

"Carol was a decent woman, more than decent; she was also pretty sophisticated for Belvidere – always well dressed, well spoken; I don't want you to get the impression she was loose, or easy, in any way. She just never felt the need to be tied down. As far as anyone knows, or is telling, anyway, Carol never revealed to anyone, even the kids, who the fathers were; I don't think it could have been one father, not sure it's possible, you know, but maybe; I don't really know about all these things.

Anyway, it was never really clear whom she was intimate with – she didn't act differently to any of her male friends – and she had quite a few. And they apparently weren't all locals, she would leave town alone at times for a short spell, and leave the kids with Frank, or a friend, then come back.

Man, was she a looker."

Sam made the last sentence stand alone as he closed his eyes and shook his head; he was talking to himself.

Cord didn't ask if Sam was one of Carol's *male friends*....he didn't have to.

Sam continued.

"People would talk about it when the kids were young, especially about Earl; at some point in time, people stopped wondering; it never really seemed to matter that much to Lilly, and Earl I don't think really ever understood. I'm sure Lilly and Carol had talks, but Lilly never said anything about it. Carol always had enough money to get by, and then some; it was never clear where it all came from – honestly, it was no one's business, and it stayed that way. We're a small town, and over time, people became fiercely protective of Carol and the kids privacy, even more so when Carol was gone."

"What is the connection to Frank; is he really her uncle?"

"Frank was Carol's only sibling – he was her only family, her kid brother, seven years younger. I don't know anything about Carol's parents, no one in Town does; Carol and Frank just kind of showed up on their own one day, when Carol was sixteen. Out of nowhere....no backstory that anyone knows, or admits to know.

They stayed up at the convent outside of Town for awhile, the *Brothers of the Sacred Heart,* for a couple years, then Carol somehow moved into the house on Fourth, a little Cape; it was a rental, and that's where she stayed. Not sure how that all worked, how it got paid for; it just happened. You didn't ask Carol things like that. Frank shuffled around Town, place to place; wherever he could find a bed. Sometimes he would crash at Carol's for periods of time, then he would leave again. When Carol died, Frank moved into the house permanently; he ultimately adopted the two kids.

Frank adored his older sister; she was glue, the decision maker – he deferred everything, all decisions, to her. He wasn't really prepared to cope with her death. She was only thirty-six and the two teenagers she left behind, especially a sixteen-year old Lilly, with every boy in Town after her, and the issues with Earl, made it tough. Frank was….how old was he? God, he must have been around twenty-nine when he moved in with the kids. But he was really still just a kid himself. Frank wasn't, still isn't, very sophisticated.

He was a quiet, shy man, who wasn't much with the ladies – about as far away from Carol in terms of looks and social skills as you can get. He always longed to get married and have someone take care of him, like his sister took care of him, I think, but with the two kids, it kind of put a damper on it, at least in his mind. I think he used the kids as an excuse, actually; Frank was never much of a catch. And he used booze as a crutch. Still does.

He never ended up getting married – truth be told, it's more like Lilly adopted and took care of him since he moved in twenty-five years ago; she was always mature and street-smart for her age.

Lilly also took care of Earl….the two of them.

Frank always had menial jobs that he shuffled between, trying to make ends meet, and to keep in hooch. I hired him at the store in 1983, mainly out of respect for Carol and the kids, and he's been with me ever since. For the most part, he's been sober, or at least a functioning drunk, a couple of falls off the wagon here and there. In the store, I try to keep him to the butchering, which he's very good at – but communicating with the customers is always a challenge; he is a bit lacking in the social skills, as you know."

Sam took a couple sips from a fresh cup of coffee Linda just brewed, and resettled in the booth. And switched gears.

"You know, Lilly never ran competitively, or ever joined any type of team, until after Carol passed away.

She went out for cross-country the Fall after she died, in '81, when Lilly was a junior. The guidance counselor suggested it; and surprisingly, Lilly listened. She never really listened to anyone; I don't know why she even did it.

And just like that, the odyssey began.

[Sam shook his head, as if he still couldn't believe the story he was about to tell]

You know, she never lost a race – not one – from the very first race she was in. It was uncanny. Coaches never saw anything like it....a brand new runner, no experience, nothing. She wouldn't stretch, or prep in any way, she would just walk over and stand on the starting line waiting for the gun to go off – just staring straight ahead, off into space, in her own world, never talking to anyone. And she always looked angry, and scared-to-death; I remember her face was always the same.

Angry....and scared-to-death.

Earl and I went to all her meets – we never missed one, so I know – and the other girls, even her teammates, would be afraid to stand near her; her eyes were so intense, like they were looking beyond whatever everyone else saw, deep into the woods.

And she was relentless; no one came close to her when she ran. She would sprint like it was a hundred yard dash in the beginning of every race, to get far ahead of everyone; it didn't matter if the course was easy in the beginning, or easy in the end; she just put distance between her and everyone else right from the start. Everyone said it was her strategy, you know, to psyche the other runners out.

But I don't think so.

I don't think she cared a lick about the other runners, or even the race; it was like she was running for her life every race....scared-to-death....I know I keep saying it, but that was the look. She would cross the finish line and you could literally see her heart pumping in her chest. She would usually be red and puffy around her eyes, like she'd been crying. But I never saw her cry – well, just once. The only one she would talk to before or after the race was Earl; I don't know what they would talk about, but she went through the same ritual every time.   You don't ask Lilly questions like that....not Lilly.

I remember her very first meet, the very first time she ever ran in a real race.

For some reason, Belvidere had scheduled North Hunterdon, which was a big, regional school, a real cross-country powerhouse, a national caliber team....impressive.

North had one of the top girls cross-country teams in the State every year; in '81, they were nationally ranked in the top ten; they had Division I scholarship-quality girls five deep on the team *[Sam held up his open hand, five fingers stretched wide apart]*; their best runner was a senior – she had won last year's *Meet of Champions* race as a junior; she was *the* top girl in New Jersey that year – and ranked nationally....high....like top five, in the country, she was in the paper all the time – no one ever beat her, a real star, and real pretty too. If you followed the sport, you knew her – knew her name – everyone did.

Everyone.

Funny, but I can't remember her name any longer *[Sam scrunched his forehead, deep in thought]*.

Anyway, North Hunterdon decided to come up here to run their first meet of the season, which they must have agreed to since they knew Belvidere would be an easy, early season tune-up to prep their girls for harder teams to come along later in the season – kind of like a glorified practice....a trounce. Belvidere was never very good.

I remember the North parents, in their BMW's and Mercedes – there are some pretty wealthy people down that way – complaining having to drive *all* the way up to Podunk Belvidere – half didn't even know how to spell it, or where it was, even though it's only thirty minutes up the river, for God's sake. But it was like this big sacrifice of their precious time, just so they could slaughter this little no-name school.

They all were joking about it.

Their five fastest girls would all line up in a bunch; each one of them would be the top runner if they went to any other school. They ran in a pack and just overwhelmed you....ate you alive; it was their strategy.

And it worked.

I remember the five of them stretched as a group and talked as a group, before the race, preening like their own little rock band, coddled by their parents, milling about, and fawned over by trainers; the team had coaches *and* a whole separate set of personal trainers. These girls had an air about them - it was pretty impressive to watch, actually; they were a heady, confident group of skinny teenage girls. Good-looking, too. They had the whole package going on *[Sam took another sip of coffee and stretched his big arms over his head, and resettled in the booth]*.

Anyway, I remember Lilly being oblivious to the whole pre-show; she was standing right on the starting line, all alone, like usual - a good ten minutes before the race even began, she just stood there – so anxious to start the race.   I'll never forget her eyes, like they were on fire….intense….looking out at nothing.

She was *focused,* to put it mildly.

Soon enough, the rest of the Belvidere team, and the *second-tier* North runners shuffled over to the starting line to join her, about a minute or two before the gun.

Then, fashionably late, the *entourage* came over and planted themselves right in the middle of the pack. They intimidated all the Belvidere and secondary North girls, who moved out of their way, to the periphery.

All except Lilly.

Now, remember, they had never seen Lilly before, no one had. They figured she was this little, skinny blonde newcomer, a nobody, who should give way to the celebrities, you know, something like that. So, when Lilly didn't move, they tried to elbow and shoulder her out of the way, all the while ignoring her, talking amongst themselves.

I think you can guess how Lilly took to that *[Sam chuckled, and Cord smiled]*.

Lilly didn't say a word; she just hauled off and leveled the closest girl – two stiff arms to the chest – that girl went down like a sack of potatoes, and hard, right on her ass. She didn't even have time to put her arms out to brace herself before she hit the ground. Turned out the girl she decked was *the* star runner; the best of the best in that bunch – last year's state champion.

Pandemonium broke loose.

The North coaches and visiting parents went ballistic, running like a pack of mad dogs over to the start area, charging that Lilly should be disqualified and demanding she apologize to the queen who landed on her rump.

Yeah, Lilly apologize, like that would have ever happened *[Sam chuckled when he said that]*.

Sam remembered the girl's mother screaming at Lilly, asking her if she had *any idea* who she just *touched*; not just *anyone* gets to stand next to her daughter. She warned Lilly if her daughter was *damaged* in any way she would live to *rue* the day. She actually used those words, *damaged* and *rue*. Who uses the word *rue* in a real conversation?

Earl just stood by and watched; he knew Lilly could take care of herself.

At this point, the Belvidere coaches didn't know anything about Lilly's true ability; she never pushed herself in practice – she didn't even like to practice, and tried to get out of it any way she could. They figured she was a newbie, middle-of-the-pack type of runner, at best. It she brought up the rear, it wouldn't have been a surprise.

Anyway, while the melee is going on, Lilly just stood there, with fists clenched and wild eyes, ready to clock anyone else who came too close to her.

No one did, not a one. This little skinny blonde girl - she scared the shit out of all of them....with those wild eyes.

So the dust finally settles, the Belvidere coaches fall all over themselves apologizing to this 'superior' team on behalf of Lilly *[Sam made air quotes]*; Lilly never apologizes to anyone – she never even opened her mouth.

The other team decided to *allow* Lilly to run after the elite girls convinced their parents and coaches that they want the new girl in the race; they collectively *forgave* her.

The group of five girls had actually huddled during the commotion and concocted some sort of payback plan....I was watching them. They figured they would crush and belittle the Belvidere girls on the course, worse than normal; but they had special plans for Lilly.

They were whispering amongst themselves, probably figuring they would steamroll her in the woods, or run her off the course, some kind of payback like that, you know, to put her in her place. Make the new little-girl cry.

So they line up....no one stands near Lillian....and the gun goes off, and before the North girls can even think, Lilly sprints, and I mean an all-out sprint, out front. The pack of five, who didn't know what to do, at first gave chase as a unit, then quickly backed off and chuckled amongst themselves, figuring she's playing rabbit, and they would slam her when she dogged it in the woods.

But the first two football fields of distance on the Belvidere course were through an open, cut hay field, and they just saw Lilly get farther and farther ahead in a full sprint, with no sign of slowing....*none.*

Then it happened; it was beautiful.

Panic set in.

You could hear the pack of North girls start yelling at each other as they ran through the field; you couldn't hear what they were saying, but it was clear they were coming unglued.

Then, they disintegrated into utter chaos – it was a beautiful thing. Each girl was looking out for herself, starting to run hard, figuring Lilly was getting too much distance – even if she did run out of gas later on – it still might be too much for them to make up.

The North Hunterdon coaches were screaming at the girls to stick to the plan, to stick together; but there was no plan – this was a free-for-all.

Despite their efforts to catch up, Lilly entered the woods a full fifty yards ahead of the splintered pack, who were spread out in an extended line – I could still hear the girls yelling in the distance, expending precious energy fighting amongst themselves. The rest of the Belvidere and North Hunterdon second-tier runners were back in the dust.

This was a race of five….against Lilly.

All the runners disappeared into the distant wood-line, then it was quiet, and everyone waited. It was a beautiful, fall day; Indian-summer weather, one of the nicest days of the year, I remember.

A little more than seventeen minutes later, a sole runner emerged from the woods; she was a good football field away. All the North Hunterdon parents stood up to see which of their girls was out front.

But, of course, it wasn't one of them; it was Lilly, all alone, and sprinting, still sprinting, toward the finish line.

The starting area was dead silent, even the Belvidere coaches didn't make a noise; they just stood there, mouths open, and watched this skinny little girl sprint, all alone, straight through the finish line.

Then she stopped dead, and walked away, and never said a word, never made eye contact, with anyone.

Cord, she crossed the finish line a full minute ahead of the next girl, who later turned out to be an All-American four straight years in college – a *minute*! That just doesn't happen. And in her first race, ever. It was unbelievable – no one said a word; they all just stood there, in silence.

They slaughtered us, of course; but that elite group of girls from North, who straggled in at numbers two through six, were all crying and heaving for air. Two fell down just past the line in exhaustion; the star bent at the waist and puked, her hands planted on her knees.

Amidst the sobs and tears, they were all bickering and fighting with each other; it was classic *[Sam smiled broadly and closed his eyes, savoring the memory; he was so proud of Lilly]*.

The one Lilly had pushed down called her a cheater – another called her a *fucking freak*; but they all stayed a good distance from Lilly – they were afraid of her.

Smart girls.

But Lilly never paid them a stitch of attention; she just sat down by herself, a good ways away from everyone, with her head down, looking at the ground. Belvidere's assistant coach, in a daze himself over what happened, trotted over to congratulate her, but she waved him off. Earl went over and sat with her. He said something to her, she slowly shook her head no, and started to cry. That's the only time I saw her cry. Earl put his arm around her and they both just sat in silence.

She had just ran the race of a lifetime, anyone's lifetime, and she was crying….and it wasn't a good cry. I never asked her why.

The coaches from both teams huddled, all talking at the same time as they shook their heads – they looked like bobble-heads. They simply didn't know what to make of it; it must have been some sort of fluke. Did she cut the course? She must have. The parents consoled their stars, making up their own set of excuses.

Of course, as the meets went on, they realized Lilly was no fluke.

Both years she ran in high school, she would have beaten all but the most elite boys in the State….one or two were better….but that's it; her time as a senior would have placed her second in the State….for the **boys** *Meet of Champions*. That is simply unheard of in girl's cross-country; it just doesn't happen.

Except it did.

But some races, not often, but sometimes, she would just decide not to run, and no amount of coaxing or punishment would change her mind. When she decided not to run seemed completely random; it was something she decided on her own – it had nothing to do with who she was running against, or the weather, nothing that seemed tangible. If the coaches scolded her, she would just threaten to quit. They only tried that tactic once; she was simply too good to let go.

Lilly didn't care a bit about her times, or medals, or ribbons, or anything like that, she wouldn't take them, or just turn around and throw them in the trash, right then and there. She would never talk to the newspapers, or even her teammates or the girls on the other teams. She was there, but not really, you know what I mean?

People didn't like her for how she acted; they thought she was some sort of Prima-Dona; but it was nothing like that – she wasn't there for them; I don't even think she was there for her. I'm not really sure why she ran; whatever the reason, she kept it to herself, or maybe she told Earl.

And she only ran cross-country. The cross-country coach in Belvidere was also the track coach; he was beside himself trying to convince Lilly to run, but she would have no part of it. She ran in the woods, that was it.

And then, after high school was over, after just two seasons, she stopped. I never saw her run again, even for fun, since she was seventeen years old.

And that was that."

Cord didn't even know where to begin; he had so many questions.

What did that note say from Carol?

Why did Lilly start running?

Why'd she stop?

But he decided to start with Earl.

"What are the *issues [Ay gestured with his right hand]* with Earl and where is he?"

Earl and Lilly have an apartment in town together, actually, what time is it?"

Sam inquired, as he looked at Cord.

"I don't have a watch."

Ay said. With that, Sam pulled out a pocket watch and noted the time.

"Right about now, Lilly has already made dinner – some red meat and potatoes and some vegetables, because that's what Earl likes and it's all he ever really eats – she'll have some pasta. They are probably done with dinner and Earl cleaned up the dishes; that's his job. Lilly is probably reading or surfing the web in her living room – she's a smart girl and a big reader – and Earl is close by, probably listening to oldies rock and roll music with his *Walkman*, or whatever they call those things these days, or watching classic TV shows or movies on DVD, with earphones on – Lilly won't let him watch anything if she has to hear it. If you cut a hole in the ceiling, they'd probably both fall on your head right about now."

It took a bit for that last statement to register.

But when it did, Cord pulled back in disbelief, as he looked up at the ornate tin ceiling and gumdrop shaped, candy-colored glass chandeliers in the *Palace.*

'What did you say? Do you mean they literally live in *this* building, *right upstairs?*"

He got a tinge of anxiety and excitement at the same time, knowing Lilly was so close – the ceiling height in the café was thirteen feet he figured, so she was, *literally,* about fifteen feet away from him.

That fact felt strange.

He was completely confused as to how to feel about her – angry, scared, sympathetic, lustful – all the above, maybe more. He didn't like feeling enamored with her, knowing every guy who saw her likely felt the same way – he would rather have been able to see past her looks and be indifferent about it.

But that wasn't the case.

'Wait a minute!"

Cord said aloud.

"What's the address of the *Palace*?"

"251 Water Street, why?"

"Are you fucking kidding me? What's the address upstairs – is it 251 Water Street too?"

"No, it's 249 Water Street, there is one apartment on the second floor, that's Lilly and Earl, and one on the third floor, which I think is…."

"It's not empty anymore!"

Cord said sarcastically.

"Oh, so *that's* why you were meeting with Woody – I was wondering what that was all about – congratulations on your new place, and I see you have met the neighbors, at least one of them."

Sam said as he smirked at Cord.

"Great! Am I going to have to scope the hall before I leave my place to see if it's safe?"

"Listen, and I'm not joking, okay, Lilly is a great girl with a heart of gold. She's just very protective of Frank and Earl, especially Earl – you just found the wrong guy to pick on."

Sam continued, trying to drive home the point.

"Let me ask you a question, Cord; it's a simple question, but I want you to really think about it before you answer, okay? Be honest."

'Sure."

"You're standing in the middle of the road, on a bad curve, and, out of nowhere, a bus suddenly barrels around the bend, much too fast for you to get out of the way – the only way for you to live would be for someone to quickly shove you out of the way, but in doing so, they would be now in the path of the bus. They would only have a split second to make a decision; not long enough to really think about it – they would have to just do it – instinctively. Who would do that for you? Who would really, honestly, sacrifice their life for yours?"

Sam stared at Cord intently and waited for him to reflect on the answer.

It didn't take long.

"No one."

Was all he said.

Sam was taken aback by the swift, resigned answer.

"Oh, okay….then who would you save? Who would you die for?"

For this second query, Cord reflected for an uncomfortable length of time, given the brevity of his first response.

"No one."

He finally whispered, as he slowly shook his head in the negative and shrugged his shoulders, sitting back in the booth.

Sam looked at Cord with sad, disbelieving eyes; it wasn't his intent to get such an answer from Ay, but rather to make a point about Lilly.

He let Cord's answers drop, without comment.

"Well, I can honestly say there would be a line of people fighting to be the one to save Lilly, and I would fight to be first in line. And that's the God's honest truth. Those same people would be saved by Lilly – no question – even if she *had* put some of those same people down over the years."

As he said that, Sam pointed to the scar on his brow and smiled.

"Listen, I suspect you are a pretty tough guy Cord, I can see it by your looks and I can see it in your eyes – I don't suspect many people would get the better of you. Me, on the other hand, I'm a pretty mild-mannered, even-tempered guy, and I don't like confrontation. But, with that said, I'm also much bigger than you, and I can assure you, if you ever did anything to hurt or upset Lilly, or exact some sort of revenge, I want you to know that I would hurt you….do you understand that?"

"I have no intention of hurting or upsetting Lilly, or getting even, in any way Sam; I am over the frontal attack, really. I just want to keep to myself and stay out of the limelight – really."

"Good."

Was all Sam said, relieved that he didn't have to play tough any longer it made him uncomfortable. He liked Cord, and he wanted him to get along and for him to work out over at the market.

"You never finished explaining about Earl; what's his story."

Sam continued.

"Earl's a big man, physically, much bigger than me [*Cord found that a bit unnerving*], but in many ways, he's a kid.   He's just a very gentle and kind person; you'll never meet anyone like Earl.

I'm a shade under six-three; Earl is a good four to five inches taller than me. Easy.

When he was a teenager, he must have been seventeen, he was helping out over at the feed mill just outside of Town. Tossing around hundred pound sacks of grain like they were nothing. They have a big old grain scale there. For the hell of it, the boys told Earl to hop on; they were taking bets on his weight. He topped out at three hundred sixty, as a seventeen year old! And the boy didn't have much fat on him, certainly less than you *[Cord sarcastically smiled and mouthed a thank you to Sam for that one]*.

He was, he still is, a monster of a man.

Just like Lilly, he was never into any sports, and despite arm-twisting like you wouldn't believe by the football, basketball and track coaches, he never played. Just to put him in a uniform would have intimidated any other team. The football coaches asked him just to stand on the sideline, or walk up for the coin toss, anything to get him in front of the other team, but he wouldn't have any part of it. He was afraid of most people, and preferred to be alone, or with Lilly, or his mom.

He was fourteen when Carol died, in what, eighth grade.

Even if he wanted to, Lilly would never have let him play anything in high school.   Carol would have, but not Lilly, too protective.

But man, despite how big he is, can that kid run fast, especially when he gets excited about something.   I can't imagine getting run over by him, especially if he had a full set of pads and a helmet on; that's pretty God-damn scary.

Earl doesn't really talk to anyone, except Lilly – he calls her Bibby sometimes. He couldn't say her name when he was a little kid, that's what came out – and it stuck. No one else calls her Bibby, just Earl – no one would dare to – she is **very** protective about that.

When he talks to Lilly, he can talk up a storm, like he stores it up – she can't get him to be quiet sometimes, but it is usually only when they're alone. Everyone else he'll pretty much ignore, or, if he knows you, you can get him to say a word or two, usually only to answer a question you ask though. He'll usually never talk to you first. He does to me, and Frank sometimes....but God, we knew him as a baby.

Despite his strength and size, Earl really has no idea how strong he is compared to other people, he would never knowingly hurt a thing, he is very gentle...except, I guess, if someone ever tried to hurt Lilly – not that Lilly can't take care of herself, as you know all too well.

Earl was very close to his mom – she truly understood him.

The two of them would sit together for hours side by side on a bench in the Park up by the Courthouse, with their heads gently leaning against each other, holding hands – they wouldn't talk, but they were talking, if you know what I mean.

She would rub Earl's back and he would run his fingers through her hair – he loved to comb her hair. Earl was truly happy when he spent time with his mom. He still talks about her, even though Lilly doesn't like when he does.

I'll tell you this, Earl is listening, even if you think he's in another world. And he has a memory like no one I know, he can remember the smallest details on things you and I wouldn't even notice – and he doesn't ever forget, *ever*."

"Christ, I've been prattling on like a little girl; well, have you heard enough about Earl and Lilly?"

Sam asked, tired and still stretching after his third cup of coffee. He looked at his watch and saw the time had crept to 8 pm.

"I suppose."

Said Cord, but he really did want to hear more; he had more questions than answers.

"Wait, what did the note say that Lilly's mom gave her?"

Cord couldn't believe he almost forgot to ask that question.

"I don't know….no one does. Lilly apparently never told anyone what it said, even Earl. I don't think Earl even knows there *was* a note. As far as Lilly remembers, no one even knows about that note but Frank, if she even remembers telling him. Only Lilly has the answer to that question. I don't know what happened to it….she might not even have it anymore."

Sam excused himself and went to the men's room, at the back of the restaurant, flipping open his cell phone on the way. He came back a few moments later and stood at the booth, as Cord sat, finishing his third double-espresso, not that he couldn't fall asleep drinking the fourth – caffeine had no real effect on him.

"Listen, we spent all this time talking, but never discussed work – you know, you really aren't the new butcher, or any butcher, right?"

Cord responded with an expression depicting how annoyed he was that Sam felt it necessary to restate the obvious.

"What I'm looking for, what the sign was for, was a helper to unload the trucks, you know, the produce, sweep, stock shelves, carry groceries, help with inventory control and ordering, stuff like that – a whole mix of things….stuff Frank and the girls won't, or can't, do."

"Sam, I kind of figured that one out on my own – you don't need a butcher – but your butcher needs some people skills – and you have the front covered – if you want to call it that. But listen, I think there are some material changes you can make, things I noticed in just half a day in the store, changes your customers want to see. We should talk about it – I'm willing to be your errand boy, as you described, if you let me run with some ideas to improve the store. I know you've been there thirty-eight years, but sometimes you can't see the forest, my friend."

"Fair enough; we can talk about that tomorrow. Now there's the matter of hours and pay, which we didn't discuss. I would like you to work six days a week, if you can, and as for salary, I know it is not a lot, but I can start you…."

Cord interrupted:

"Sam, six days is fine; whatever pay you think is fair is okay with me – it's not that important to me. However, I will need to come in late tomorrow, probably some time after lunch; I need to take care of some personal matters."

Sam nodded in agreement; that was easy, he thought.

With that, Cord started to stand up to leave, but Sam motioned him to stay put.

"Listen, why don't you stay just a bit longer, I have someone I want you to talk to."

Cord didn't even have time to react, when, on cue, the front door of the *Palace* swung open.

And in walked Bibby.

CHAPTER 13 – A DEEP PEACEFUL SLEEP

From nowhere, he felt butterflies in his gut; what was up with that?

Sam leaned down and whispered to Ay quickly, with a sense of urgency.

"Now listen, don't tell Lilly about our discussion, especially about the history, okay, and for God's sake, don't call her Bibby, even for fun, 'cause she won't think it's funny, and it *will* be a carving knife in the gullet….got it?"

With that, Sam patted him on the back and walked toward Lilly, where he gave her a big hug and whispered in her ear. She pecked him on the cheek and told him she would behave herself. She asked Linda to bring her a bottle of sparkling water and a *crème brulee.*

As she approached the booth, he couldn't stop thinking about the story Sam told him about her mom, he looked at her with sadness, feeling bad knowing the story, even though it was so long ago. She saw his sullen face and hers immediately turned annoyed. As she got to the booth, she stood over him while she spoke. She declined to sit down.

"Let me take one big guess, Sam told you the *tragic* story of my mother; that fucking pity-face gives it away every time."

So much for the sympathy and sadness – and second introductions.

"What story are you talking about?"

He said weakly; Cord was a good liar, but he got caught off guard, and he was dealing with a pro.

Liars know when liars are lying.

"Don't give me that shit, I know exactly what Sam told you; that stupid story gets more pathetic with every retelling."

"Out of the way asshole; do you remember saying that after slamming me in the face, *in the face!* With the door? Of course you do. Now it's: *that fucking face* and *don't give me that shit;* what's your problem? Do you even know my name? Why don't you try this on for size: *Hi, I'm so sorry for hitting you in the face with the door, that was awfully rude of me. By the way, what's your name? My name is...."*

He *almost* said it. He wanted to, it was on the tip of his tongue, but some involuntary form of restraint, tucked in the back corner of his brain, in a spot he didn't control, stalled the syllables from spilling….Bibby.

Good thing.

Still, she wasn't impressed with his plea for reason.

"Look *Mr. Butcher*, I don't care what your name is and I'm certainly not sorry for knocking you out – you shouldn't be fishing for apologies; I'd be hiding from the embarrassment, if I was you. Regardless, you deserved worse."

"For what? For wearing Frank's faggy apron – sooo sorry."

He said sarcastically.

"I finished the day out, you know, and helped Sam, when your fucking uncle got sent home."

"And why'd he get sent home? Because you were playing games with grapes and got him in trouble!"

Lillian's voice was loud and confrontational, and people in *Nonpareil* started to take notice of the kerfuffle. Man, she had the shortest of short fuses. Cord tried some damage control; he put up his hand in a stop gesture.

"Whoa, whoa, listen, Lillian; Sam told me your name was Lillian."

He figured he should clarify that point, so she knew how he got her name. He forgot she signed it on his note, stuck to the counter with a butcher's knife.

"I'm sorry for wearing your uncle's apron, it was an honest mistake – I forgot to take it off after I finished helping Sam; I'm also sorry for the grape issue. Oh, and I'm sorry for saying I was the new butcher - I'm not sure why I said that, I guess I was just a little nervous."

With that, Cord chuckled a bit, hoping his mea culpa (actually three) would break the tension and help her calm down a bit. He flashed his trademark smile, the self-deprecating look that usually got him out of hot water with women.

She hesitated before she began to speak; maybe it did the trick - it works every time.

Then, in a whisper, as if she was letting him in on a secret, she bent over, leaning into his personal space.

"You wore the apron to the door and said you were the new butcher because you were attracted to me, and you thought, somehow, it may help you get into my pants. You're pathetic."

That was her conciliatory retort, presented calmly and smugly, right in his face.

Cord was speechless; he was busted! She was dead-on right, and she *knew* it!

This girl was unbelievable.

But there was no way he was going to let that statement hang unanswered, not after he made a peace offering and got squashed for it.

"Sorry, honey, to burst your bubble, but you aren't my type; skinny, no tits, you look a little boyish to me. Plus, I like women a little younger – like in their thirties. I was just being polite by opening the door; sounds like a little wishful thinking on your part."

That's the ticket, he thought to himself; the perfect retort, delivered deadpan, without hesitation. A perfect skewer to put that bitch in her place. Of course, none of it was true, but he delivered it with such a look of indignation and embarrassment for her that you could take it to the bank. He set the hook and was ready to reel her in. He could see it in her face – she bought it. This girl was an open book.

"Oh, I guess I misunderstand….sorry. I actually don't think much of my looks and I overcompensate, sometimes, for how I feel about my looks by acting tough….kinda. I didn't mean to hurt your feeling by suggesting you liked me….sorry."

She frowned sad, put her head down and slowly slid into the booth across from him in a demure, submissive way.

At first he figured this is another game she's playing, he wasn't going to buy in; he's not that stupid. But then he thought about the stories Sam told, and he started to feel bad, to doubt, what he said….why couldn't he just be nice to her? She raised her head slowly and her eyes were starting to get a little red and puffy.

What a fucking ass he was, he thought to himself.

She continued.

"Listen, the reason Sam asked me to come down was to apologize for hitting you with the door and taking your

Belvidere note – you know, the whole knife thing. I'm sorry I did that to your note; I didn't mean any harm, I was just mad about my Uncle, sometimes my temper gets the better of me – I'm sure Sam told you about that little problem of mine. Anyway, I really am sorry. Are you sure you're okay? That line is getting a bit red on your face."

With that, she reached over and put her tiny hand on his forehead; it was soft and warm, and gently, slowly ran her thumb back and forth along the line where the door creased him, barely touching his skin.

He felt a familiar tingle in his crotch, right at the exact moment she touched his forehead – there wasn't even a second of delay. Man, how did that happen so fast?

"You don't need to do that; it's…."

Cord said lightly.

But before he could finish his sentence she cut him off.

"Shh. Just close your eyes a second and relax, you've had a long, hard day, and part of that was due to me. So, let me make it up to you, just a bit. I promised Sam I would be nice and that's what I am trying to do – please let me do this little thing."

With that he obliged, closed his eyes and just felt her hand gently running along his face.

My God, just the light touch of her fingertips on his face was erotic. In less than ten seconds, he could feel his cock pushing against his jeans.   And the more he thought about trying to make it go away, the harder he got….typical.

Thankfully, she couldn't see his lap, since they were both sitting in the booth.

He finally gave in, and starting fantasizing about what he been subconsciously thinking….undressing her, standing behind her and unbuttoning her Capris, sliding them down past that firm little ass, and slowly peeling off her panties – he figured they would be black lace – to see that pussy, God, he could picture it just the way he liked….and her loving every minute of it.

He's not sure how long it took to realize her hand was no longer on his forehead. He cracked open his eyes and looked across the booth….no Lillian.

Oh shit.

He slowly looked to his right; and there she was, crouching next to him, outside the booth, with her gaze fixed squarely on his crotch, on his stiff dick, straining against his jeans.

No hiding that puppy.

Are you kidding me? She did it to him again. Why can't a guy control his dick?

He didn't even try to hide it; the cat was well out of the bag. He just sat there, like a mope, not knowing really what to do. He was so busted.

Lilly, on the other hand, knew exactly what to do.

"Let me ask you a question. As I was gently rubbing your head, the big *stupid* one on top of your shoulders, that is, were you thinking about slowly undressing me, or are you one of those guys who gets right to the part where you slip it in, without all that silly foreplay? Oh, I'm sorry, that's right, you couldn't have been thinking about me, I'm too skinny, and boyish….and old."

With that, Lillian laughed condescendingly, stood up and breathed a single word into his ear.

"Schmuck."

She grabbed her untouched bottle of sparkling water and *crème brulee*; as she started to walked away, she said.

"Listen, just leave Frank alone and try to keep your eyes in your head, and your head in your pants, when you happen to see me, which is hopefully never, and we'll be just fine."

Fuck he whispered allowed to himself; he didn't have a retort.

Lilly yelled over to Linda and told her to put the sparkling water and dessert on *his* bill *[pointing over her shoulder at Cord, without bothering to turn around]*.

She had only gotten a few steps away, when he mustered a response worthy of her attention.

"Oh, by the way, it's the former....you know, the foreplay option. And try not to make too much noise tonight fantasizing about what I would do, and you *will*; the ones who like to talk about it always do. I don't want you to disturb your new neighbor upstairs."

Lillian quickly spun around and returned the ten steps to the table, putting the water and dessert back down loudly for effect.

"What's *that* suppose to mean?"

She demanded.

"What part?"

"The fucking neighbor part."

He motioned for her to come close to him, but she wouldn't close the gap. She had her arms crossed in front of her stomach; she was wearing a jet-black lightweight merino wool sweater with three-quarter sleeves and a crew neck; she had on the same tawny Capris as this afternoon. He couldn't tell, but he was sure she still wasn't wearing a bra. She could have stepped right out of a magazine shoot, short of the puss on her face, as she stared at him.

"I'm waiting!"

She demanded.

"Do you want to hear what I have to say or not? If so, then you've got to come a *little* bit closer *[he extended the word 'little']*. Let me whisper my little secret in your ear. Don't tell me you're afraid?"

"Hardly."

She answered indignantly. And with that, she reluctantly lent the side of her face toward his, and waited.

He whispered slowly.

"I think it is pretty self-explanatory, don't you, *neighbor*. Listen, I might be in Town for awhile, so I'm happy we had a chance to meet, it's been a real eye-opener. And let me tell you something else, young lady, and you can bet the bank on this one. When you're lying in bed tonight, I want you to know I'll be in the bedroom right above you, literally on top of you, thinking long and hard about you and me. If you're lucky, and you start behaving like a good little girl, I'll tell you in the morning how you were a *bad little girl* all night long.

I think you're the kind of girl who likes it when a guy's in control; this daytime act....it's a scam. I think I'll stand behind you, bend you over, put you on all fours and bang you doggie-style, figuratively, of course. Maybe you can fantasize about that tonight to get yourself off; don't forget to say my name when you finish, because I'll be getting off on it too, that's for sure. *Have a good one.*"

As he finished, he realized that may not have been the smartest yarn to weave with this psycho; but so far, he didn't have a knife sticking out of his chest – that was a good sign.

Surprisingly, she just stood up and stared at him, not in an evil way, or an offended way; not in any way at all, really.

Maybe she was processing.

He felt it probably wasn't too safe to wait around for a reaction. Cord quickly slid out of the booth and headed toward the register to pay the tab, including Lillian's untouched fare.

She ultimately didn't give him the satisfaction of any reaction or response to that little story; she simply grabbed her dessert and bottle of water and beat him to the door, getting onto the sidewalk first. She turned right and went into the adjoining apartment stairwell door.

Cord was close behind, walking right behind her, focusing on that beautiful little ass. She sensed he was getting too close to her for comfort, but she wouldn't be pushed – she kept her pace the same; she could feel him right behind her, so close, but not touching her. She stopped at her landing and he continued by her, without stopping or saying anything.

"I can call the police."

She said as she opened her door, but didn't go in; she just stood there and watched him head up to the third floor landing. She didn't believe he really rented that room….no fucking way.

She kept her finger lightly on her cell phone....speed dial No. 13 – Marty; he would wet himself to sprint over there and make life miserable for this asshole - all she had to do was ask.

Cord didn't give her the satisfaction of a response.

She let out a little gasp of disgust when he fished a key from his pocket, slid it into the lock and it clicked smoothly, opening the door. He looked down the staircase and waved with a shit-eating grin.

"Goodnight, sweet dreams."

With that, he gently closed the door.

Woody rented that fucking apartment to that guy without telling me first? I'll deal with him in the morning she said to herself, as she slammed the door shut.

'What's the matter; what are you mad about *now*?"

Earl asked as he sat in the front room, overlooking the street.

"Nothing....don't talk to me."

Was all she said.

Later that night, as Lilly lay in bed, she could hear Cord walking around upstairs; she heard the water run in the bathroom and then, hearing him shut the bedroom door, it was clear the bastard happened to pick the bedroom *right above hers* – good fucking guess, she thought.

She lay there in the darkness, staring at the ceiling; all she could hear was the ticking of the clock on the dresser and the occasional car idling at the light. It had to be after midnight, but she couldn't sleep. He had her wound tight and fucking lit up, but good.

She was fighting the urge, but the more she tried to ignore it, the more she obsessed about it. In the end, she just couldn't help herself. She reluctantly gave in, and slowly slid her hand up to, and under, the elastic on her panties.

She closed her eyes, and lightly ran her fingers through her pubic hair, and then down to the top of her pussy, right on the bone. She pulled her lips apart and rubbed the right side of her clit, running her finger down between her lips to get it wet, and then back up again….the full length….back and forth.

After a few minutes, she slid off her panties and rolled onto her belly; with one finger rubbing each side of her clit, she ground her cunt into the bed and fantasized about being dogged hard, over and over again. She came quickly, then a second and third time as she fantasized about being held down and pumped against her will.

She whimpered when she came, so Earl wouldn't hear from the next room, but she wanted to be loud. She was still louder than she should have been. She even said his name when she came, just like he said to, just to feel extra dirty.

They were the best orgasms she had in a while, in spite of herself....in spite of that asshole upstairs. But he would never be the wiser. She smiled at her little secret.

Afterward, she was annoyed for actually doing what he told her to do, even though that was part of the thrill – and why the orgasms felt so good. The stupid bastard had that part of her pegged. It's was always easy to be mad about something like that after she came – but when she was in the act, the thought was always lasered on how to make it last….and to make it intense. Calling his name, even if it annoyed her now, did the trick.

Besides, she reminded herself again, it was her little secret.

She could have come more, but she was satisfied and tired. She rolled onto her side, kicked her panties onto the floor and fell into a deep, peaceful sleep.

CHAPTER 14 – WHY HADN'T HE JUST LOOKED?

April 21st; day two. Friday morning.

He opened his eyes slowly, rolled off his side onto his back and stared at the ceiling; he slept remarkably well.

It was light out, but he didn't know the time – he saw a clock in the kitchen last night, but it wasn't visible from the bedroom. His face didn't hurt and there was no remnant of a headache. He ran his finger across the imaginary door line; no raised welt – unbelievable, he thought to himself. But then again, maybe not; no matter the injury, he always healed quickly, and better than expected. Seemed to be part of the rules.

He tightened and stretched his legs hard, as he simultaneously bent and raised his right arm over his head; he let out a loud grunt, like a yawn, but not quite – it felt good. He awakened with a hard-on, no surprise there; but he wasn't thinking about her – that was a surprise.

He let it go limp, unused.

He didn't remember jerking off to her last night as he promised. Come to think of it, he didn't remember jerking off at all; he must have just fallen asleep. He had no recollection of any dreams, but that was expected; he used to dream often as a kid, vivid, but they stopped many years ago....decades ago.

Now it was just empty, black, no memory. Nothing.

At least he assumed they stopped; if he was dreaming, his mind kept it a secret – he never recalled a single one; not even bits of dreams right when he awoke, like most people. He never gave it much thought over the years; he wasn't sure why he was thinking about it now.

The thought of her masturbating to his story last night made him smile with a sense of control, although he knew she didn't – she wouldn't have even if she wanted to – she would never give him the satisfaction. He knew her enough to be certain of that.

He wondered how she liked to be fucked, how often she fucked, if she even had a boyfriend.

He could imagine the sap she would *allow* to have sex with her – he bet the guy would have to be completely submissive for her to grace him with open legs. Better yet, she probably would don a strap-on and do him.

Jumping out of bed and stomping on the floor to annoy her was appealing for a fleeting moment, until he realized it would be just a bit juvenile. But the thought made him smile some more.

He just lay in bed for a while, staring at the hair on his arms and picking his nose half-hearted; he wondered how many people would actually admit how often their fingers end up in their nostrils on a regular basis – and what do they do with the pickings? He rolled his between fingertips till it was dry enough to flick on the floor – he didn't know where the tissues were in the apartment, if there were any at all. The floor would do for now.

He closed his eyes and thought about the pelicans. How he transitioned from nose-picking to birds, he had no idea. It made no sense, other than minds wander for no reason, they just do. That was as good an answer as any.

He loved pelicans.

They would work up and down the shoreline, usually solo, although sometimes two or three, sometimes more, would glide on the air currents together and fish the same stretch of beach at any one time. Even then, they worked alone. He liked that. Loners.

He usually saw them at dawn or dusk, and he wondered how they passed the remains of the day, probably drying their wings outstretch, then napping on some beachfront *palapa*. When he saw them, they would usually ply a stretch of sand, scanning the shallow waters no more than twenty-five yards off shore; you wouldn't think a pelican would be a graceful flier, but they were, gliding effortlessly, till they suddenly dove break-neck and pierced the water surface, submerging their entire upper body.

They would dive once a minute or so, on average; he couldn't believe how hard they hit the water, over and over. He was never close enough to see the actual fish, but he guessed by the throat action they were successful three out of four dives. Not a bad living, and usually prime real estate to boot.

He would watch them for hours, frequently smoking a cigar, drinking neat bourbon or port and thinking. He had to stop thinking so much; thinking leads to doing, doing leads to trouble. He needed to blend in, be a normal Joe; nothing fancy, nothing to draw attention or create situations. It always sounded like a good plan.

He did a real good job with that plan so far in this bum-fuck Town, he thought to himself – anything on the agenda today would have to be an improvement over yesterday.

He shook his head in disgust. Maybe he should just figure out why he was even here to begin with, that would be a start. But he knew that was futile; she would reveal the purpose in good time – she was never in a rush.

He slowly rolled out of bed, making his way to the bathroom. He stopped himself before reaching the bedroom door and decided to drop for a set of push-ups, sit-ups and leg-lifts. Might as well start now, if he had any real intention of getting back in shape. He did a set of fifty each and held his legs up for fifty seconds. The push-ups were cake – they always were; for the leg lifts and sit-ups, however, that roll of stomach fat fought him on every rep – it wasn't going to give up quite so easy.

Fucking sit-ups, he hated them.

He was out of breath as he shuffled down the hall, jumped in the shower and thought about the day ahead.

As he stood there, eyes closed and water cascading over his head, he felt a well of annoyance build regarding yesterday's events and how he handled himself.

Why did he take notes at the store? And why was he bothering with Lillian?   What did he care about her story, and her life?

He'd been in town less than twenty-four hours and already he felt as if he was veering off the plan, even though he wasn't sure what that plan was.

He aroused from the rant and realized the sound he heard was himself knocking his head against the shower stall wall in a steady drum; he didn't know how long he had been rapping.

It wasn't unusual.

He got dressed in yesterday's clothes; the customer comment list was in his pocket. He crumpled it into a ball, threw it in the kitchen garbage and turned to take a quick inventory of what apartment edibles and supplies he needed to buy. He slid the draft lease into the back of the kitchen drawer.

It was 7:40 am.

He hadn't gone through the apartment like he normally would; he wasn't going to either – as-is is fine, he thought. At least for now. He just grabbed his key and was on his way.

He opened the apartment door and spied a small metal cylinder lying on the floor, along with a note.

Great – here we go again – thinking it was from her.

It wasn't.

He picked up the tube and realized it was a cigar, a *DeMuth*, along with a note from Woody welcoming him to town and giving him his business card if he needed anything else, anything at all.

The bumpkin was continuing to impress, even though he fucked with him on the Lilly front.

He looked down again and noticed a bottle of wine was placed against the wall, to the right of the door.

He had never heard of a *DeMuth*; he put the note on the counter just inside the apartment door and put the cylinder in his pocket. It was already cut, and Woody provided a box of matches from the *Belvidere Hotel* – Cord smiled at the intended irony – he was starting to like W.

He bent over and picked up the bottle of wine; it was a red – a French Burgundy *Pinot Noir*. Not typical, and certainly not shabby; C was impressed. If it had been a Bordeaux *Pomerol*, he would have been much-more-than-impressed, but it was a nice gesture nonetheless. He leaned into the apartment again and placed the bottle in the lower kitchen cabinet and shut the door. He didn't bother to lock it; no matter where he landed, he never did.

He passed the second floor apartment landing without hesitating. As he walked by, he could hear a television, but it was muffled and incoherent. He was trying his best to both avoid her, and not meet him. No sign of either this morning – good. Come to think of it, he should stay away from Frank too – that advice from Lillian he *would* take. They all spelled trouble.

He smiled….new day….fresh start.

Nonpareil was pretty crowded. A different crew worked the morning shift; no Linda. He ordered a black coffee and an *everything* bagel – raw and dry; he didn't make small talk with the waitstaff – he wasn't in the mood.

He parked in an empty booth across from last night's seat to people-watch. He sat for a good hour or so; surprisingly, few people from Sam's yesterday came through the café this morning, a couple at most. They did not see him in the booth and he did not seek them out.

As often happened, without warning, he had quietly slipped into an angry, stormy mood; what happened to that fresh day he was smiling about an hour ago?

It was about 9 am and he tired of the *Palace*.

He rose, bought a short seedless baguette, another black coffee to-go, along with the local daily rag and headed out the door. It was another beautiful day, but it didn't brighten his mood.

The Town was bustling at the light, which was the intersection of Water and Greenwich Streets; he headed south on Greenwich, toward the Courthouse – he remembered the route from that ridiculous sign yesterday, on his amble in.

One half block from *Nonpareil*, Greenwich crossed the Pequest River, which was dammed just upstream. The banks on either side of the bridge were walled by old buildings partially extending over the waterway. A greasy spoon on one side was packed with patrons, shoveling in bacon, eggs and home fries at aluminum tables, with plastic tablecloths.

The turbid spoondrift cascading over the dam smelled earthy. A father and son, no more than ten, playing birthday hookie, stood silently on the bridge, side by side; their fishing lines were taught and disappeared into the fast flowing creek, red and white bobbers fighting the current.

It reminded him of fishing with his dad, when he was the same age. He should have smiled at the thought, but he didn't.

He made his way three blocks up Greenwich to Second Street, hooked a left and walked past a series of mostly-neat Victorian homes. A three foot high, rusted chain-link fence, probably fifty years old and once straight, now ran a bent, drunken-curve, demarking the edge of one yard from a narrow paved alley, that weaved behind a series of homes. All these old towns had back alleys, the places where the garages, and horse barns hid. They were colloquial, and he liked them, he always did.

Alongside the wobbly eyesore, lay a thick bed of daffodils and early tulips, all a golden hue, each in a slightly different shade; that alone made the tired fence anything but ugly.

Second Street ran but a single block, till it magically opened upon a beautiful square, a public green, it must be three to four acres, he figured, somewhere around that size; each side was about two hundred feet long.

The Park was carpeted in bright spring-green grass, the kind that bursts to life again, overnight, after soakings of April rain. It was a bit messy, like it had a hint of bed-head, sporting overgrown tufts here and there. It needed that first-of-the-year mow….then, it would be regal.

Spread amongst the Park had to be a hundred or more stately trees, doyennes, all of them, and variety by the score. The buds were starting to swell on some, others still winter-slept.

Someone had planted a mixed bag of pearly white and yellow daffodils – the color of butter; it was a large patch, along a stone-grit path entering the Park...a welcome sign of Spring. While most of the flower stalks still stood, some, closest to the footpath, were randomly broken or uprooted – the remains trampled and disfigured; purposely crushed under heel into the gravel and mud alongside the grit.   A few were pulverized, just for emphasis, he guessed, by kids.

He shook his head and became angry that someone would do such a thing. Dirtbag kids, for sure.

He turned his attention to an imposing, red-brick Courthouse flanking him to the left, with four, immense, Doric columns supporting a massive entry pediment, stretching three tall stories into the sky.   The edifice faced the Park; a soaring eagle vane topped a majestic central clock tower, looking west.

It seemed beautiful, at first glance.

The raptor reminded him of his father, who loved eagles; paintings and sculpture filled the house when he was a kid.   A similar vane, atop the chimney, adorned that childhood home. He wondered if that eagle still flew; he hadn't been back there in years. He was sure it did....at least he hoped it still did.

From his vantage, he could see two of the four tower clock faces – each belied the other. To the west it was 6:25; to the south, the hands were frozen at 5:05. It was neither accurate, nor precise; for that, he was disappointed.

As he stared silently at the clock tower, his eyes began to notice the peeling, weather-worn paint, some here, more there....along with splintered, rotten clapboard; the more he stared, the more decay, and neglect, he noticed.

The majestic clock tower was not so majestic. He looked away, eyeing the balance of the Park; he saw the three churches, just as depicted on the triptych coming into Town; each bisected the three remaining Park fronts.

By far the most beautiful, the Presbyterian Church, flanked his right. A soaring, bone white structure, with a towering spire and intricate stained glass, fitting of its place alongside the Park. Postcard picturesque and prominent.

The Belvidere Presbyterians must be a proud lot.

The houses here were more impressive than those along Water Street, set further back from the street and exhibiting better manicured lawns and more formal landscaping. They were still tinged with neglect, but much less so, and a regal feel prevailed, owing less to the imposing edifices, and more to the surprisingly simple beauty of the park setting. It seemed a wonderful place to sit, relax and enjoy some longed-for solitude and anonymity on a quiet Friday morning.

Perfect.

Two gravel footpaths connected the far corners of the Park in a large X; four benches were set in the center of the Park, where the gravel paths crossed. Benches, sponsored by the local Rotary, were set along the perimeter sidewalk, at the midpoint of each side. A half-dozen non-descript picnic benches were scattered throughout the Park, that was the extent of the garniture. It was a passive, understated walking park, a genteel venue for strollers, dog-walkers, bicyclers, picnickers....and for now, newcomers.

He stood in silence, boxed inside quintessential small town; a New England storybook scene set in the rolling Highlands – who would have guessed such a place existed in this corner of the world….northwest New Jersey.

It was a Town that tricked time….by about fifty years.

He made his way along one of the gravel legs to the center of the X – it was still somewhat early and no one was sitting in the Park interior, although there were two sets of power-walkers and a young, coffee-toting woman with her dog lapping the perimeter sidewalk.

He was pleasantly surprised at the solitude in this central forum on a Friday morning; there were plenty of parked cars closer to the Courthouse, but whomever parked had long since made their way to wherever they were headed, likely lost in the maze of the court building. All he heard was a medley of birds, an occasional passing car and the slight breeze that weaved through the network of trees. Squirrels were all about the Park, chasing up and down tree trunks; starlings strutted the grounds, looking for food, darting amongst a litter of sweet gum seeds, dry, the pods the color of rust. He heard the distant buzz of a prop plane overhead….unseen.

He planted himself on a bench, unfolded the newspaper and pulled off pieces of the baguette as he drank his coffee. This was what he enjoyed doing most - reading and relaxing in a public venue. He came an awfully long way just to sit here, in this tiny midtown Park, and read a paper about a place he knew nothing about. But the sun warmed his cheek, and for now, it seemed worth it. He felt content.

The storm clouds in his head earlier had passed and life seemed good; well, maybe just okay, but that was still better than most days.

Across the way, he eyed a tall, Italianate-style Victorian, white with black and sage accents - oversized double doors at the entry. The main structure was three stories, with a fourth floor cupola overlooking the Park – the gilded roof sparkled in the early morning sunshine.

The end-to-end porch was guarded by two, life-size bronze lions, with open mouths and gnashing teeth. The grounds were manicured, the porch decorated with dark green wicker furniture and floral cushions; there were four huge ferns set in plant stands, even this early in the season. There didn't appear to be any activity at the house; it seemed quiet….asleep.

The dog walker had left; a mother-daughter tandem passed by on old-fashioned pedal- pusher bicycles. The Town was pretty flat, so the two glided by without much fuss or effort. He liked seeing clunker bikes.

Cord had been soaking the scene, so he didn't hear the heavy footsteps from behind, kicking up the gravel, till they were just about upon him.

This guy was big, and got bigger as he approached; six foot six, or more, and half again as wide. Wide enough to question if he could fit through a door without a twist.

Holy shit he thought to himself; those were the first words that came to mind, seeing this monster of a man approach dead-on.

The gentleman didn't say a word or so much as acknowledge Cord's presence – he just planted himself on C's bench, his massive thigh brushing hard against Cord's and pinning the fabric of Ay's jeans between the man's leg and the wooden slat seat – C was pinched in place, unable to move his leg.

There were three empty benches only a few feet away.

If the stranger had been sitting alone on the bench it would have been crowded, but with Cord next to him, it was sardine-tight, and certainly odd, and certainly uncomfortable; two grown men sitting tight on a bench, who had never met, or even made eye contact.

C was worried the bench wouldn't survive the weight; the wood seemed to groan under the strain.

The big man just put his oversized hands gently on his own knees and stared at the Lion House. He carefully, deliberately and gently set down on the gravel at his feet an overstuffed, foot-long hoagie-style sandwich, at least that's what it looked like, since it was encased in wax paper, a bag of spicy barbecue chips and a bottle of *Vernors* soda.

Ay couldn't believe it....this guy had a bottle of *Vernors*!

He hadn't seen that ginger soda since he was a kid. It was Cord's absolute favorite, and he had completely forgotten about it till he saw the bottle sitting on the ground next to him. He couldn't believe they still made that stuff.

It wasn't like regular ginger ale; it had vanilla in it, and a bunch of spices and extra carbonation that gave it a kick. He always remembered drinking *Vernors* with his dad, mostly fishing or reading the newspaper on a Sunday afternoon at the dining room table. Although Cord was sure he must have drank plenty of bottles alone, or with friends, when he thought of *Vernors,* he thought of his dad.

His father also drank it as a kid; it was his favorite pop running around Detroit. It was a real treat back then – not something his dad got to drink every day.

He doesn't remember when his dad stopped buying it, or when he last had his last bottle; it had to be thirty years ago, at least thirty years ago.

But enough of that; this seating situation was a bit too weird, and needed to be addressed.

'Excuse me, do you want me to move?"

Cord said sarcastically; possibly the gentleman didn't see him. Considering that happened to him more than once so far in this Town, he figured anything was possible.

But there was no response from the stranger; he just continued to stare blankly at the Lion House. His food sat neatly at his feet, untouched.

Cord was feeling mighty conspicuous and uncomfortable, as any normal guy would, even though no one was in the Park.

Why would some guy sit right next to him like that?

Although he was the size of a house, the man had an unmistakable, gentle air about him.

Cord thought a little more, looking at his bench-mate. But no, it couldn't be this guy, it didn't make any sense.

But, in a tentative voice, he asked anyway, since he certainly seemed to otherwise fit the bill.

"Are you….Earl?"

Again, no response, the stranger did not pretend to give even the slightest acknowledgment to Cord, the man he had sandwiched on the bench.

Cord tried to lightly, inconspicuously move his leg; no luck - his jeans were pinched tight between that tree trunk leg and the bench top.

This guy *had* to be Earl; he was certainly how Sam described him....most of it anyway. Otherwise, there were two enormous, quiet, childlike men walking around Belvidere. But did he forget anything Sam said? He didn't think so, but, maybe he did. He must have; surely Sam would have mentioned this skin *condition*.

Well, if it was Earl, and he assumed it was, he apparently had the pleasure of meeting the whole dysfunctional family - Frank, Lilly and now, the not-so-little little brother.

Didn't he just decide about an hour ago to avoid this bunch?

Cord was about to wrest his leg free, get up and move to another bench when he suddenly heard a sonorous boomlet, a thunderous crack, like something striking metal.

Ay hated sudden loud noises; it caused extreme, instant, agitation – which had gotten worse as he got older. Certain loud noises, like the one he just heard, immediately set him off. His mood turned foul and his eyes darted to identify the source.

Traversing one of the gravel paths, heading toward the Park center, toward him, was a group of three older teenage boys, along with three young girls. Trouble....that was his first impression.

Just as Cord eyed them, the nymphets peeled off; each was wearing a short jean skirt and a halter top, one in maroon, one teal and one violet, as if they dressed in tandem. There was a lot of April paleness showing; the clothes were inappropriate so early in the season - it certainly wasn't hot enough to warrant the display of skin.

One of the boys barked loudly, appearing to gesture for the girls to stay; they ignored him and walked away.

The boy ended his pleading, yelled sex-profanity at the girls and continued with his mates toward Cord and his bench-friend. They were all talking much louder than necessary, making histrionic hand and facial gestures as they spoke, the way punks looking for attention usually do.

Cord didn't like how this was unfolding; inimical delinquents. He could feel his face start to flush.

The thunderclap he heard before resulted from one of them smacking a metal stop sign at the corner of the Park with a wooden baseball bat he was now swinging like a pendulum, in a deliberate, exaggerated manner. The metal sign was still lightly vibrating from the blow — he didn't know how it was still standing - that's how hard the jag-off smashed it with the club.

The cudgel-bearer was the smallest of the three, they usually are; sporting black canvas sneakers and black jeans, a purple tee-shirt with some illegible mix of graphic pictures and wording, likely a concert souvenir, and a reversed baseball cap; he stood five and a half feet tall, if he stood on his toes.

A true little-shit, and clearly the instigator.

The second was tall, well over six foot, lean and muscular, wearing a plain black muscle tee and two-sizes-too-big baggy jeans, falling off his ass, exposing blue patterned boxer shorts. A white kid who so wanted to be a nigger.

He was silent and walking at the rear of the pack, but he was clearly the leader.

The third, the muscle-head in the group, was lazily straddling a bike, walking it with one foot scuffling along the ground and carrying an open cardboard quart container of milk. This kid was big; six foot plus and thick through the chest and gut – a combination of muscle and fat – the kind of kid born oversized....farm-boy strong, but lazy, coupled with a dim bulb between the ears. You could see it in his face, in his eyes.

The thug had a shit-eating grin on his face, as did the little-shit. The tall one, bringing up the rear, was expressionless.

Up the diagonal grit path they came, slow....deliberate. The three were clearly focused on Cord and the big man sitting next to one another in the middle of the Park; there was no mistake, C's bench was the destination.

It was too late to switch seats now; to do so would have been more obvious, and would have suggested that something was awry, even though there really was – Cord still didn't know why the big guy sat next to him in the first place.

The trio was just about upon them, and they weren't going to simply pass by.

Cord didn't think anyone else had come into the Park, but he didn't look about to see; at this point, it was too late to care – he was laser-focused on the big farm-boy, straddling the bike.

The kid had half-dry milk residue around his upper lip that he was either too lazy or stupid to wipe off. The little punk was holding the bat loosely, with the barrel end pointing at the ground, still swinging it like a pendulum and ticking the footpath grit here and there, laughing aloud as he was walked.

The bike-rider was still smirking; the leader walking slightly behind, still expressionless – his mouth a thin, horizontal line. He had a series of Chinese characters tattooed on his deltoid, which trailed down his tricep; a large dragon tattoo wrapped his neck and shoulders, seeming to disappear down his back. Two thick silver rings pierced his left eyebrow.

There were going to be no door tricks this time; in the span it took the boys to reach the center of the Park, Cord had become agitated – agitated in a reckless way, in a way that got him in leave-town-fast sort of trouble. The anger boiled and his jaw set hard.

He slowly, methodically stood up, but he didn't clench his fists, he just let his arms rest by his side. With his thumb on each hand, he methodically pushed down on the second joint of the remaining eight fingers and cracked each individual knuckle; first on the right, then the left – six out of eight cracked – half loudly. He put his left foot slightly ahead of his right and cocked his neck back and tightened it. His stare was blank, looking at the bike, but with a peripheral ken, waiting for one of the other two to talk.

The big man just sat on the bench, oblivious to the unfolding scene, still staring intently at the Lion House.

Cord had a real bad feeling; he knew he should have looked around the Park first, but he didn't.

Why hadn't he just looked?

The bike rolled to a stop in the gravel, with the front tire just about touching the behemoth's knees; the bat-boy stood closer to Cord, but it was clear both kids were focused on the big man. The ring leader stood back and watched, his arms folded across his chest.

They all looked to be about eighteen, or close to it, probably high school seniors; the troublemakers others avoid. But the two men they confronted were both muscular and clearly capable of crushing them – at least that's what they should have thought.

"Hey Earl, what's hanging bro?"

The little one yapped as he reached down and snagged the virgin bottle of *Vernors* off the ground, and in one motion, popped the cap and took an oversized swig. He held the bottle up to the sky, spying it like an icon, while he gulped down the soda in an exaggerated, loud chug. He forced a wet belch into Earl's face and laughed, relishing the role of unlikely bully to such an imposing man.

Earl couldn't see the Lion House anymore, the two troublemakers were standing in his way, so he just lowered his head quietly and gazed at the ground. He didn't say a word; his hands stayed on his knees....he remained passive.

It was clear Earl was frightened, and just wanted them to go away.

The biker bent down, grabbed the bag of chips and popped the top open by giving the bag a violent squeeze, all while holding his milk carton. He raised the bag and poured a mouthful of chips into his mouth. He chewed the quid like a cow, loudly, and with an open mouth, partly for effect, mostly due to white trash habits learned at home.

This initial volley happened in a matter of seconds. The boys figured Cord was another Earl; a dopey playmate, which they summarily ignored – to this point. This dance with Earl was clearly ritual.

Cord had slipped into a different place.

His eyes glazed, yet wild, partly focused on some distant point, like a deranged dog. His skin quickly became fever-hot and a broken monotone hum, like a moan of a man in pain, slipped lightly from barely parted lips.

The hum tone was low at first, but quickly got louder. A pool of saliva welled in Cord's mouth, which topped his lower lip. A tiny filiform slowly began to dangle from the corner of his mouth.

The smallest boy turned toward the creepy moan and saw Cord in a sort of daze, head cocked, drool just beginning to spool, and laughed in disbelief as he stepped back from the spectacle.

"What the fuck? Holy shit Earl, what's up with your fucking girlfriend?"

He turned to the dragon and chuckled.

"Dude, step back, I think he's fucking rabid."

As he uttered the words, while he had briefly turned his attention, Cord slowly corkscrewed his body, leaning back as his left hand swung in front of this body.

In a lightning move, he shifted all his weight to his right leg, took a big step forward with his left, past the talker, and unleashed a brutal shot with his right fist into the bottom on the biker's jaw, while yelling incoherently, something that sounded like *Hoofah.*

The biker's body, in toto, tensed rigor mortis; his hands contracted instantly, violently, exploding the bag of chips and carton of milk. His tongue was slightly extended at the moment of impact; the full tip was severed clean and disappeared in the melee. Atomized blood and milk coated the impact zone.

The biker's body slowly fell to the side, rigid as a board, still straddling the cycle. He hit the ground cold, no brace of his fall, and lay motionless, unnaturally stiff, his face had already turned an ashen pallor.

He was surely dead.

A steady stream of fresh blood, like a cracked faucet, ran from the corner of his mouth, bit tongues bleed like a bitch, pooling on the ground. It was unnerving, the amount of blood beside the fallen body.

Cord was covered in a mist of milk and blood, stark white and crimson, which mixed as it ran down his face. He didn't wipe it off.

He slowly turned and inched his face closer to the bat-bearer; his not-right eyes burned a hole in the boy's forehead. The little punk, also soaked, stood motionless with mouth open, staring blank at his lifeless friend.

There was no laughing, or mocking, or anything; the bat dropped involuntary from his hand, but he still tightly gripped the bottle of soda – he didn't realize it was still in his grasp. His whole body was trembling, like a little girl; the boy closed his eyes and winced as he felt Ay's hot breath on his cheek – Cord was that close.

C took his right hand and quickly, violently, gripped the kid's throat like a vice; the little boy yelped a high-pitched wheeze, as Cord slowly squeezed shut the arteries in his neck.

Ay quietly whispered at him.

"Qu'est-ce que vous avez dit?" *[What did you say?]*

A mere moment passed in silence; no answer. He couldn't respond if he wanted; Cord had closed his throat.

Then C, with lips almost touching the boy's face, screamed in pent anger, his neck muscled flexed and his face flushed red. The volume could be heard well beyond the border of the Park; he sprayed spit over the boys eyes, nose and mouth.

"Qu'est-ce que vous avez dit?!" *[What did you say?!]*

Cord clamped down harder on his throat; he could feel the lactic acid burning in his bicep as he slowly crushed the slender, pencil neck. The kid, trembling violently, with eyes bulged from their sockets and face beet red, parted his lips, but there were no words, just a faint wheeze; he saw the little legs rattle uncontrollably, then quickly go limp, from fear and the lack of blood to the brain. Cord was holding him erect by the neck, like a puppet.

His eyes rolled back in his head and the all-white underside, crackled with bulging, red spider veins, filled his sockets; in a moment or so, he would pass out.

Cord again whispered at his face.

"Qu'est-ce que vous avez dit? *[What did you say?]*

He loosened his grip and the boy fell in a heap on the ground. After a second or two delay, he violently coughed and heaved, gasping for air. In a few more moments, he was reduced to a quiet whimper, curled fetal; a bright red hand tattoo cinched his scrawny neck. Cord figured he'd live, and redirected his attention to the dragon.

C methodically bent over, picked the bat at the barrel end and slowly walked over to the last boy standing, who to this point had stood and watched the events unfold without moving or speaking; at some point he had unfolded his arms from across his chest.

The assault happened and ended in less than a minute, but it seemed much longer.

Cord figured he didn't have much time.

"You, I'm going to hurt."

Is all Ay said, as he gently pointed the bat handle at the dragon, with the knob no more than an inch from the middle of the kid's chest.

No response and no movement; no attempt to grab the bat, which is what Cord wanted him to do.

"He's stupid and slow, and this one tries to compensate for being small and weak."

Cord said, motioning with his head to the two prone casualties.

"But you, on the other hand, don't appear to have an excuse. And for that, you're going to pay."

Cord was greeted by silence; the boy stood there, frozen.

"What is a Rubicon? And you'd better answer the fucking question."

C whispered to the dragon.

The boy didn't speak, he simply shook his head once in the negative, trying not to do anything which might prompt an attack.

"It's kind of like a line in the sand; once you cross it, there's no going back – and there will be consequences. You and your friends crossed that line."

Cord slowly, gently, pushed the handle of the bat into the boy's chest until it stopped against his rib cage.

"Take the bat and do with it as you wish. I won't move. With a good swing, you could probably just about take my head off.

My bet is you're a chicken-shit, and don't have the balls to do it.

But I'll tell you this, if you step up and take the chance, you'd better kill me with that one swing, because that's all you'll get. And you won't be the first that's tried.

And when I get up, and I *will* get up….I always do….I won't kill you, I'll just snap your spine within two steps, and you'll spend the rest of your life drooling and shitting in a diaper, looking up from a fucking wheelchair. I can promise you that.

Now pay attention son, because this is very important.

You had better grab this bat and make a decision….you had better not let it hit the ground, or you'll never walk again."

Petrified, he grabbed the handle just as Cord released it, but the weight of the bat in his limp arm swung it down and the end hit the gravel; the boy still held the handle touching his ribs with a death-grip.

He instinctively recoiled, and let out a frightened yelp as Cord began to move.

But Cord didn't attack.

He peeled off his blue tee-shirt, and, in a slow, deliberate manner, wiped clean the spray of milk and blood which hadn't already dried on his face. His chest and arms were big, from years of lifting and the pump of the assault.

He held his arms horizontal, to the sides, palms up, like he was nailed to the cross. But that's not what the frightened boy noticed.

It was the fucking scars.

The countless scars, some incarnadine, others faded to flesh. A two-inch raised line across his right pectoral, a large horizontal jagged line in the middle of his stomach, followed by three more; a four inch raised red scar down his right lateral, and at least a dozen circular scars, both linear and random, throughout his torso.   Then he noticed the three inch line across his right bicep, at the elbow, like a knife had sliced his arm in half.

And they were just the ones he could see; it was like C had been dissected and sewn back together.

Cord stood in front of him and stepped closer, arms now bent at the elbow and palms up – ready for the dragon to tee up.

"Adversity introduces a man to himself."

Cord whispered. And with that, Ay slowly closed his eyes….and waited.

Nothing happened.

The boy dropped the bat and took a half step back.

"Please….don't."

Was all he said, his lower lip quivering involuntarily as he raised his open hands toward Cord in a *stop* gesture.

Cord took a step toward the dragon and motioned him with his hand to stand still; the boy yelped again in fear.

It was then that he wet himself.

In a deliberate manner, Cord hooked his hand around the boy's neck, jerked it violent toward him and whispered quickly in his ear....instructions; he jerked his head once or twice again, pulling it toward him for emphasis while he was jawing at him. The boy was limp and submissive.

Cord finished and shoved the kid away in disgust.

The boy pulled out his wallet, trembling, and started to finger through it clumsily; Cord violently grabbed and butterflied it, pulled out two twenty dollar bills, then threw the wallet back at the boy, who had since turned and bent to tend to his small friend, urine-wet pants stuck to his leg.

The little-shit appeared recovered, but was still lying fetal and immobile; he breathed slowly, covering his face with his forearm. He was like the bug that plays dead, hoping the danger will pass.

The biker wasn't dead. He starting to move a bit, but was still incoherent. The dragon whispered into the ear of the small kid, who listened intently and slowly shook his head in agreement. Cord watched the exchange.

Ay stepped toward Earl and offered his shirt, so big man could wipe his face and clothes; Earl didn't respond; he had sat quietly throughout the entire ordeal, without comment or movement, still staring blank at the Lion House. The milk and blood was drying on his face and had soaked into his light blue button-down Oxford.

"I'm sorry about all this nonsense Earl; these shit-heads won't bother you again, ever."

Cord lifted his gaze to the dragon when he uttered the word *ever*; as instructed, the boy apologized to Earl on behalf of the three; the other two were in no condition to proffer confessions.

"They want you to have this forty dollars to pay for the food they took, and to clean your clothes."

With that, Cord folded the bills and stuck them in Earl's front shirt pocket. Then he gently put his hand on Earl's broad shoulder and squeezed it as he bent down to whisper in his ear.

"I know you're too good a person to hurt them, but I'm *not,* and now I think they understand that. Some day, if I'm lucky, I'll be more like you."

Earl didn't say a word, but for the first time he raised his head, looked at Cord and offered a faint smile….acknowledgment. Cord had never seen eyes like that on a man –completely innocent, completely trusting….completely good.

But that snippet was all he revealed; Earl again went expressionless and looked ahead at the Lion House – like a dog staring at the door, waiting patient for something to happen.

Cord took his tee-shirt and gently, but quickly, wiped Earl's face and arms, to remove the majority of the still-wet milk and blood spittle.

He then put on his wet shirt, grabbed his paper and what was left of his baguette and coffee, now cold, and sat down on the next nearest bench to Earl and waited for the inevitable.

He didn't have to wait long.

CHAPTER 16 – WHEREVER EARL WAS GOING, HE WAS GOING TOO

The Park perimeter was empty; no one occupied the Park interior but the five of them.

He couldn't say who was around during the altercation; if there had been anyone, they were, by now, long gone. No one was visible in the yards of the buildings around the Park either; it was eerily quiet for a beautiful Friday morning. Scattered cars still traversed the perimeter roads, oblivious to the goings-on in the Park.

But Cord wasn't going to kid himself; that melee was not lost upon the small town quidnunc that always seem to be watching – of that he was sure.

Right he was.

Soon enough, a police utility cruiser quickly came upon the Park, then slowed until the occupant noticed the group in the center, at which time it activated its lights and siren, jumped the curb and drove right into the Park center, along the same gravel path the kids traversed. The lights were spinning and gravel sprayed like buckshot behind the squad car as it sped up and fishtailed toward them, faster than necessary.

Cord sat silently and watched the scene unfold; he had to be *very* careful.

Less than five minutes had passed since the assault ended; Cord sat alone, on his own bench.

Earl continued his intense watch of the Lion House, as if the whole incident had been a mere distraction of his view. The two walkers were huddled on one of the other benches; the biker was sitting on the ground, a ripped piece of white tee-shirt protruding from his mouth, pink and wet with blood and saliva. His head was cast down in a blank stare, memory still fogged. A pool of vomit marked where he had been lying; swallowing too much tongue-blood soured his stomach. Remnants of yellow blow had dried on his face and shirt.

Cord sat quietly, waiting for the interrogation to begin.

The policeman exited his car in a deliberate, somewhat exaggerated manner, noticeably shifted his billy-club on his waist and unsnapped the holster for his gun. He walked like he had the billy-club shoved halfway up his ass.

He was a shade over six foot and in his thirties, probably late thirties, with a short, flat-top, which was a week past a needed trim. At first glance, he looked to be in good shape, with broad shoulders and a thick chest; but a uniform can hide a lot. Cord saw a midsized tire around his waist, and a small jowel growing under the chin. In another couple years, Cord figured, he would be a fully ripe, middle-aged couch potato, wearing the home-team jersey top and eating nachos and dip, ass sunk deep in the couch, during a Sunday afternoon sports marathon on the tube.

The officer visually assessed the scene and called out to Earl from the side of the car in a booming voice.

"Earl, you okay?"

Earl didn't answer, but the officer saw that he clearly wasn't hurt. He walked slowly over to the group, keeping his eye on Cord and calling out to the boys.

"Buck, are you okay? What about you other two?"

With that, he looked to the two sitting on the bench.

Cord did not move a muscle or say a word. He did not make eye contact with the officer.

"Everying is fine, Mar....*[he was about to say Marty, but thought better of it]* Officer Brewer; Tommy and Vinny were just fucking around with each other and it got a little out of control."

Is all Buck offered. He didn't look at or mention Cord or Earl.

"Why is Earl in the middle of this mess? And why are his chips and pop, the same stuff he eats every time he sits on that bench, all over the ground around your friend, who has a God-damn bloody rag shoved in his mouth and puke on his face. And don't tell me Earl has anything to do with this, Buck....don't even go there."

Buck sat still, not sure how to retell the same lie, but he tried to fumble through it, knowing what would happen to him if he screwed this up. He didn't dare look, but he could feel Cord staring at him.

"Listen, Tommy and Vinny were fucking around, pushing each other and stuff, and it got out of hand; I don't know how Earl's stuff got on the ground. I'm sorry, all right, sorry they were screwing around."

Now that last part was actually the truth, Ay thought to himself.

The officer exhaled in exasperation and put his hands on his hips; he was ready to make a speech.

"Nice try. Now let's see if you can follow this *alternate theory*, Buck.

Earl was waiting here to see Carol, like he always does, every month....same drill. Minding his own business, like he always does.

You and your punk friends come into the Park and see Earl, like you usually do, if your smart enough to remember what day of the month it is, and you aren't too lazy, drunk or high to actually walk over here and give him a hard time.

Given those substantial hurdles, you make about one in four times.

The punk sidekicks change from time to time, but you, Buck, you always stay the same. Usually the bunch of you pick on Earl a bit, take his food, and go on your way, feeling tough.

But you, Buck, you're too much of a chicken-shit or embarrassed to do it yourself, since it's Earl, so you have your loser friends do it - and never when anyone is around and can call me, or worse for you, call Lillian.

Now all that's all pretty standard, simple stuff….but the unknown in this equation is *you*."

And with that Officer Martin Brewer turned and looked directly at Cord, pointing his billy-club directly at C's forehead.

He walked slowly over to Cord, never taking his eyes off him; as he did, he barked at Buck to sit down and keep his mouth shut, along with the other two. He never even feigned interest in administering first aid to the oaf on the bike; Cord didn't know if he was a Vinny or a Tommy; he looked like a Tommy. Tommy sounded right for a dolt; Vinny sounded like a little-shit name; that was his guess.

The officer stood about five feet from Cord and stared him down. At this point, Ay made direct eye contact, but tried to act respectful and obedient. This was too important to fuck up.

"Who are you….and what are you doing in Belvidere?"

I'm looking for better days; but as to why I'm really here, for that, you'll have to ask Jenny Cord sighed silently to himself.   That was the truth, but Cord couldn't, and wouldn't, dare say that.

"My name is Cord Brin; I was visiting my good friend, Mae Edna Bastet, who lives out in *Brookfield;* I'm sure you know her *[Officer Brewer looked at Cord with no hint of knowing Mae any more than he knew Cord – either he was good at hiding his hand – doubtful; Mae was pulling Cord's leg about her clout – doubtful; or lobbyist influence didn't trickle to the Mayberry police force....C placed his bet on Door No. 3].* Anyway, she and I were chatting yesterday and she told me of this lovely Park by the Courthouse, so I came up here to have a cup of coffee and enjoy the morning."

"A *lovely* Park?"

The officer mocked; he made no mention of being impressed with Mae, or even remembering Cord dropping her name.

Cord sat in silence, so Martin continued.

"What I'd like to know is how this young man came to find himself full of puke and blood, and that one with a red ring around his neck? And why is his blood all over you and your shirt?"

C answered in a calm monotone.

"Officer, I was sitting on the bench minding my own business, when this other gentleman sat down *[Cord pointed at Earl],* who was also minding his own business. Then these kids came along; I wasn't paying attention – I was reading my paper – all of a sudden there was shouting and next thing I knew these two kids were on the ground. I'm not the only one who got sprayed, we all did."

The officer wasn't impressed.

"I'm only going to ask you this once, and you had better tell me the truth – did you have anything to do with these boys finding themselves on the ground and in harm's way? If I inspected your hands, would they fit the ring around that kid's neck? Listen, I know you probably saw these kids picking on Earl and got steamed; I don't blame you, actually I admire you, most people would look the other way, afraid to get involved. But I just want to clear this thing up."

Good one; nice good cop/bad cop in the same soliloquy Cord thought to himself; they must teach that at the Belvidere Police Academy.

"Sorry officer, I can't help you. Listen, I don't know these kids; they told you it was amongst themselves. If I did anything, don't you think they'd serve me up?"

"Not if they thought you would hurt them worse if they did. Now, a little more about you, Mr. Brin. Where are you from, because it sure as hell isn't Belvidere."

With that, Cord caught a much-needed reprieve from the unlikeliest of sources; a bike rider was heading full speed toward the center of the Park, kicking up the gravel along the path.

The officer followed Cord's eyes and saw the bike, and its rider; a look of resignation flashed his face, and his authority melted away, puddling in his boots.

The rider skidded to a stop in the middle of the cabal. Martin sighed.

"Lilly, I'm handling this. Earl is fine; I don't know who called you, but it really wasn't necessary."

It was a weak attempt at remaining in control. He knew it was futile.

Lillian ignored him completely; she dropped the bike and turned to Earl. She cradled his head into her chest and kissed him long and gently on the side of his temple, just above his ear. She wrapped her arms as best she could around his broad shoulders and squeezed him as one who can't love someone enough does. Then she whispered in his ear; he nodded and whispered back. No one heard the short exchange, outside the two. Then Earl flicked his head ever so subtly toward Cord; she followed it with her eyes.

Lilly let out a long, indignant breath and directed her gaze at Buck; she never even looked at the policeman as she spoke. Buck looked at the ground; he didn't dare stare down Lillian. And he was scared shitless; C could see his left hand shaking.

"Who do you think called *you*, Marty."

She said sarcastically.

Now, it was a known fact about Town that Officer Martin Brewer *hated* to be called Marty, especially when he was in uniform, and especially by Lilly. If Buck had finished his '*Mar…*' earlier and called the Officer 'Marty', he would presently be handcuffed and sitting in the back of the squad car….no question.

Only a select few really got away with it: the Chief, Frank, Sam, Earl, and, of course, Lilly.

Martin just stood there and took it from Lilly, like a big mope. He was no match, not by a long-shot.

"The call about Earl in the Park came from Gail to *me*, not *you*. I'm the one who called down to you guys, rather than dealing with Buck myself. I thought you'd be happy I did that – I know Buck should be. Isn't that right *Buck*? You *mother-fucker!* You're lucky I don't kick your fucking teeth in, or fucking…."

She didn't finish the sentence, spit left her lips as she yelled in his direction. She simply stared him down in silence. That was even scarier.

Buck didn't say a word, and he didn't take his eyes off the gravel by his shoes. His heart was pounding, wondering what Lilly was going to do and thanking God Marty was there to stop her….maybe.

Then Lillian, realizing Earl was fine, and the situation was hers to control, simply flipped her hair, and her mood changed instantly; with a perky snap in her voice and a plastic smile, she turned her gaze to Officer Marty and chirped.

"Hi Cord, how'd you sleep last night?"

"Oh no; Lillian, please tell me this guy's *not* another loser boyfriend."

Martin's words dripped with disgust – it came out of his mouth just as he thought it; by her face, how quickly he realized it was an improvident comment to make, aloud anyway.

"Christ, I'm sorry; Lilly, I didn't mean it."

Marty did a quick back-pedal; time to do some quick damage control.

"I'll take care of all of this, and your friend isn't in any trouble, don't you worry."

She looked at him, incredulous.

He stepped closer to her and began, yet again, his pursuit of that elusive date.

Apparently, the three-alarm mystery laying in front of him, and Lillian's new boyfriend, could wait just a bit while he tried to line up his dream date to the *Officer's*

Ball next Saturday; it was *the* annual County social for the men in blue, and what a coup it would be to have Lilly by his side.

Marty moved seamless from interrogation to grovel. And the reason was simple.

Martin had loved Lilly from the very first time he laid eyes upon her….he was just five years old. In fact, his earliest childhood memory, the very start of what he remembered as *his* life, was the day he met Lilly.

Now, Marty was aware most five year olds don't care about girls, in fact, they hate girls; they care about *Tonka* trucks. Well Marty liked *Tonka* trucks too, but he loved Lilly – and he knew it, he knew it that first day.

He remembered the small, saucer-shaped depression in his front lawn; it was just the right size for him to maneuver around in – it was his Martian space ship and he had just landed. There was a rope-sized tree root that stuck from the ground – that was the steering wheel; the tips of a couple big rocks amongst the grass – they were his gauges. It was October, and the lawn was blanketed in leaves and maple tree helicopter seeds. He would gather and toss them in the air over his head; meteor showers he was flying through as he maneuvered his flying saucer around the stars.

That's when he first saw her.

Lilly was walking down the Mansfield Street sidewalk, her long, blonde ponytail flipping carelessly side to side, surrounded by an entourage of four older boys, twelve and thirteen year-olds, all vying for her attention. Lilly was nine, going on eighteen.

Marty was mesmerized.

Without thinking, he exited his spaceship and walked toward the sidewalk to invite her for a ride, not really thinking about what he was doing. He was five.

As he tried to get a closer look at her, he accidentally bumped into one of the boys.

Now, Martin actually never got pushed down; he tripped over his own feet and fell into one of the kids. But that's not how the story had been told, retold and morphed for the past thirty-odd years....and to this day, no one in Town believed Marty's version of events, which just so happened to be true.

One of the kids starts laughing and tells everyone he pushed the pudgy little kid down because he was rubbing on the kid's pant leg, like a dog in heat; that's the story that stuck - the story that Marty the policeman had to live with for the past thirty-three years.

Marty, the little dog in heat.

When Martin tried to get up, one of the other twelve year-olds pushed him back down. At first, Martin didn't realize the kid pushed him on purpose; so up he goes again, and down he goes for a third time.

Everyone is laughing, except Marty.

At this point, he realizes what's happening, and starts to cry, which makes all the boys laugh even louder, which makes Marty bawl even more. He just sits there, a pathetic five year-old lump on the sidewalk.

One of the thirteen year-olds, the clear leader of the pack of dogs, steps up and announces enough is enough, and tells his peers to leave the poor little fella alone.

Martin looks up with big sad eyes, welled with tears, and sees his new friend come to his rescue. The boy gently puts his arms under Marty's and lifts him to his feet. He squats down, face to face with Martin, and, in a soft, comforting voice, asks if he's okay, as he lightly brushed off his rump, pudgy legs and arms.

Marty slowly, coyly, shakes his head yes, and he starts to smile; everything seems to be okay.

He reached out to hug his big, new friend.

"Well, if you're okay...."

And with that, the thirteen year-old violently shoved Marty back onto the sidewalk in a heap of defeat. Then he laughed his ass off, as did all the other kids.

Marty was stunned for a second, then the gusher opened. He cried because his rear-end hurt; he cried even more just because.

Marty, who was thirty-eight years-old last week, Tax Day, could never forget what happened next....never forget the words uttered by the beautiful, blonde-haired girl.

"Oh, Button, would you leave the little *baby* alone; this is so *boring*."

Button Pierce....Martin's nemesis for the rest of his life.

Now Lilly wasn't trying to be mean, but with Marty crying like he was, a short, chubby little kid....he kind of looked like a baby.   Not that she was really paying much attention anyway.

"I'm not a baby!"

Martin yelled, and started crying even harder – like....a baby.

Lilly just looked at him, shook her head, scrunching her face in a pitiful manner, and walked away.

Martin jumped up, still crying, and ran toward his house. As he ran, he turned back and yelled:

"Stupid-heads!"

To them all, even Lilly.

Martin just happened to pick the wrong time to turn his head.

As he finished his rebel cry, in full stride, running as fast as those chubby little legs could go, he ran over, and into, the Martian ship depression, which threw him off kilter. He turned to look where he was going, and just as he did, he ran face first into a tree – dead stop. He never had time to put up his hands; his face provided the brakes on the smooth gray bark.

Unfortunately for Martin, his *stupid-head* comment had everyone looking at him when he hit the tree, including Lilly.

The impact knocked the cry right out of him.

He stood there in silence for a moment or two, then he started to wobble, like a punch drunk fighter.

"He's going down!"

Button yelled.

"No way, the kid's gonna make it!"

Another one yelled.

"Five bucks he hits the dirt!"

Button called out, as he started to laugh.

Before the other kid could answer, Martin swayed one last time, rocked onto his heels and went down like a rock onto the seat of his pants.

"Yes!"

Button yelled, hands extended over his head - touchdown.

Martin stumbled to his feet, then half-ran, half-wobbled up the porch steps and straight into his house, never looking back.

Once the door shut, the group on the sidewalk let out a collective howl of laughter. Button motioned for them to all be quiet and said:

"Sh, wait….guaranteed."

Button held up his pointer finger as he spoke; then he opened his hand and started folding in his fingers as he counted out loud.

"Five, four, three…."

He only got to three, then they heard the muffled wail inside the house; Martin must have found his mother and started crying all over again.

They all hooted and hollered on the sidewalk for a bit, then continued on their way.

Button turned to his friend and demanded the proceeds from his five-dollar wager; the kid protested – saying he never made the bet.

That wasn't the right answer.

In a flash, he found himself choked in a tight headlock – not a friendly one – the kind that cuts the blood flow to the brain. He felt himself choking, starting to pass out.

Despite his protests, and the protests of the group, Button did not loosen his grip.

"Cough it up, asshole, or out you go."

A throaty gasp was all he got in response.

Button shoved his free hand in the kid's pocket and pulled out three crumpled singles, two pennies and a gum wrapper; he released him, slapping the kid hard in the head as he did so.

While the kid fell to one knee, Button warned him he'd better cough up the other two tomorrow – he told him he would either have two bucks, or walk away with two less teeth, and he meant it – Button always meant it – he was a tough, no-nonsense kid, and to dismiss what he said had consequences; there were *always* consequences when you dealt with Button.

The kid grudgingly paid up the next day for a bet he never made, and kept his teeth.

Lilly smiled and slid her arm into Button's as they walked down the sidewalk. Lilly loved Button, she always had. He was the boy all the others looked up to, or were afraid of, or both….and he was the best-looking boy in Town….the boy all the other girls wanted to be with. And he chose Lilly. Because she was the best looking girl in Town; the girl all the other boys wanted to be with.

A perfect match.

Marty watched them from behind the drapes in the dining room window; his puffy cheeks still pink from the cry - his forehead still raspberry from the tree.

As much as a five year old can hate, Martin hated Button.

But he forgave Lilly immediately; he had no choice, he simply couldn't help it.

And that was Marty's introduction to Lilly; and to this day, Lilly never let him forget the story.   And poor Marty was still waiting for his first date....thirty-three years later.

Over the years, Marty exacted revenge on three of the boys; he had arrested them as adults multiple times for drunk and disorderly, traffic violations, delinquent child support, and anything else he could conjure, not that they made it very hard.

But not once could he get Button; even though he was the worst of the lot, he also happened to be smart; at least smart enough for Belvidere. Marty was gonna get that guy some day - he made that promise to himself a long, long time ago.

While Martin had been trying in vain for years to get Lilly to go out with him, he had the added insult of enduring a parade of delinquents date her instead.

Button Pierce was the worst of the lot by far, but the others were all basically cut from the same cloth, and they all muscled in front of him, every one. If only Lilly could see what a decent, respectful guy with a career was like, one with a steady paycheck, a future Police Chief no less, he knew she wouldn't stray. If only Lilly could just see what she was missing in good old Martin Brewer.

Back to the present, with Marty trying to seize the moment.

"You didn't return my call this week, or last week, I just wanted to ask you...."

"I *know* what you wanted to ask, so I didn't call back – simple as that."

"But...."

Annoyed, she cut him off.

"Cord, dear, would you be terribly upset if I were to accompany Officer Brewer here to the *Officers Ball* next weekend? I know how jealous you can get Sweetie, with that awful short temper of yours, but I know Marty would be much obliged if you were to see to it that I might be able to put on that little black cocktail dress I've been dying to wear and offer some arm candy to the man in blue."

Marty, who was ready to interrogate and arrest Cord a moment ago, looked at him with flushed cheeks and the saddest eyes of a dog begging for scraps; it was both pathetic and comic. He then came to realize just how big a fish Lilly was in this little pond called Belvidere; she could be queen if she simply declared it so.

"I assume we're done here....Officer Brewer?"

C said, in an extended drawl.

Marty slowly nodded his head to Cord in acknowledgment, realizing he was about to peel open the *Wonka* bar with the golden ticket, the one he had been waiting for all his life.

"Then I suppose....okay."

Cord stated dryly.

"Really?"

Was all Marty could say, in a too-high pitch; he was in shock.

"Really?"

He said it again, purposely lowering his voice an octave to act more manly, this time looking at Lilly for approval.

"Thank you."

Lilly said as she faced Cord, with a look as sincere as he had seen on her.

He knew what she meant – that was for Earl. He returned the look.

"Likewise."

Was all he quietly said.

With that Ay stood up, threw his coffee and baguette in the trash and gathered his unread newspaper.

"Be sure to bring your handcuffs to the Ball, Officer; she really likes handcuffs."

Marty stared at Cord with an embarrassed look, his cheeks still flushed.

But you could bet the farm those handcuffs would be in the back seat of the squad car next Saturday night, just in case. Any decent, respectful guy with a steady paycheck would do the same, he thought.

At that moment, Earl abruptly stood up – on Hardwick Street, which ran in front of the lion house, a candy-apple red Ferrari, an *F430 Spider*, sped a bit too fast down the road, top down, with a raven-haired woman at the wheel, her long, straight mane lazily dancing from the wind cascading over the windshield.

Earl was in a trance; drawn like a moth to a flame.

"Come on!"

Was all he said as he grabbed Cord by the shirt sleeve and tugged at him to follow.

Lilly saw what Earl had done and was dumbfounded; Earl never talked to strangers, and he would never, ever, do what he just did. She lowered her eyebrows.

"Earl, what are you doing?"

He ignored her, and with a sense of urgency, said a second time.

"Come on!"

"It'll be fine."

Cord said, looking back at Lilly.

But she didn't think it was fine – she was clearly disturbed by the whole incident; why, he didn't know.

She went to step away from Martin, to go after Earl, but the officer grabbed her arm gently and started to talk excitedly about preparing for the upcoming Ball; Marty could hardly contain himself, grinning ear to ear. Cord couldn't hear the details, but it was clear Lilly was only half-listening, while staring at the two of them walking away.

Cord raised his hand in a reassuring way, motioning Lilly to stay put. She frowned but inexplicably stayed, resigning herself to listen to Marty prattle about their 'date'.

The Ferrari turned the corner and pulled into a side driveway at the lion house; the woman got out, grabbed a too-small handbag and disappeared behind the white edifice. He was a good 150 feet away, but from what he could see, she was a looker – Earl had good taste.

Cord liked Earl.

He didn't know why, it was just a feeling you sometimes get when you first meet someone….it felt right; the chemistry mixes….the sum is better than the parts. He certainly couldn't remember the last time he felt that way. Had he ever really felt that way? Felt this way?

Cord didn't know why he was going along with Earl, or what they were up to; but he was sure of one thing….wherever Earl was going, he was going too.

CHAPTER 17 – IT WAS CLEAR SHE HAD FUCKING QUESTIONS

The twosome made their way to the Park edge, across Hardwick Street, and up the wide bluestone walkway, gazing up at the house, flanked by two life-size roaring bronze lions, mouths agape baring razor teeth, sitting upright on hind legs.

The homestead was extremely tall, an imposing white edifice.

Extending from the porch roof pediment were two twisted bronze *Medusa,* her mouth agape in menace; a trio of writhing snakes emerging from her skull. The evil twins gazed ominous from the edge of the porch roof, scoping anyone who dared approach the house, taunting them to meet her hollow eyes with the threat of stone. Below the hideous masks hung a gilded, wooden banner:

L'antre du Lion

The Lion's Den.

Snarling lions, Medusa's glare, the Lion's Den….downright homey, Cord thought to himself. He couldn't imagine what cuddly surprise awaited inside.

They passed the bellowing guard lions and climbed the steps to the red mahogany porch deck and black, oversized double entry doors. Two small bronze cherubs were set beside the doors, on the right-side surround. As Cord looked at it, trying to figure out what it was, Earl leaned in front of him and, with a meaty finger, gently pushed the head of one cherub till it leaned forward and *kissed* the cheek of the other cherub; somewhere beyond the closed doors, deep inside the house, Cord heard the faint chime of a doorbell.

Suddenly, Cord felt a bit foolish.

What was he going to say? He was standing on the porch of a woman's house he didn't know, beside a man he didn't know, for a reason he didn't know.

He turned to walk away; he figured he would stand down on the sidewalk and wait for Earl to do whatever he was doing. But before he could turn, he heard a set of doors open, not the ones in front of them, but others….unseen, interior doors.

The oversized bronze, lion-head entry knob turned and the right side door swung open, revealing a beautiful woman, probably in her early forties. She wore a polite smile, one borne of familiarity, not friendship. She sported smooth china skin, with deep green eyes and long, thick eyelashes. Her features were classical, her jaw line and cheekbones pronounced….sharp. She had a northern European look, although he doubted she was, especially when she spoke – she sounded distinctly American. But surely she must be a transplant; this one wasn't home grown in Belvidere.

Cord figured he had to have met the two most attractive women in Belvidere, or if this was the status quo, he was never, ever, going to leave this Town.

"Hi Earl; you're early again this month. Where's your soda and chips? What happened to your shirt?"

Earl didn't answer any of the above; he just smiled and pulled a creased envelope from his pocket, carefully unfolded it and handed it to her.

It simply said:

Carol – May

in neat block print letters – it looked as if a child wrote it for a penmanship test. It was off-center and a little crooked.

So, now Cord had met his landlord – not too shabby he thought – he might have to deliver his rent in person too. Although he did remember Elwood saying the landlord would insist on a lease; *she was particular*, or something to that effect. She seemed nice enough, so far. He was sure he could get the lease waived with a little cajoling; Cord smiled to himself. Ay wondered how to best introduce himself and advise her that he was the new tenant Woody had told her about.

Earl hadn't said a word, but he was beaming, with a big smile on his face. He turned to leave when Carol called to him.

"Earl, who's your little friend?"

As she looked indifferently at Ay.

She said it not because she had any particular interest in Cord, but for the fact that Earl had been coming onto her porch to deliver the rent every month for the past three years and never once had his routine changed. He was always early; he usually stared, head down, at his shoes; he rarely spoke – sometimes a *hi*, sometimes a *bye* – usually, however, she would catch a glimpse of a too-shy smile as he handed her the sealed, handwritten envelope; and he had was always delivered the envelope alone. Until today.

Little friend? Cord thought to himself; what a condescending little bitch. Actually, if he thought about it objectively, standing next to Earl, he was quite little, but that wasn't the point, now, was it? Before Cord could answer for himself, Earl stated proudly:

"This is Cord Brin, my sister's boyfriend!"

That was the first sentence Earl had spoken to Carol....ever.

"Really!"

Carol was as surprised at the dialogue from Earl as to the content of the statement.

Then she reflected for a moment, and continued.

"Ah, Lillian, and she let you come along to deliver the mail....interesting; what's the not-so-hidden message in that?"

She said slowly, in a reflective tone, as she looked again at Cord, this time, with a bit more interest. It was clear the two knew each other, and more than in just a way a landlord knows their tenant.

Cord didn't like the look.

"I'm just a friend of the family."

Cord said, trying to correct the record; even though that statement wasn't accurate either. How would Cord describe his *relationship* with the Lillian/Earl family? He didn't know the answer to that one – it seemed to change by the minute.

Cord continued, answering her question about the milk and blood spittle on Earl's light blue shirt.

"About his shirt, there was a little alterca....."

She cut him off, not being the least bit interested in what Cord was saying.

"Seems like Lillian has *lots* of friends."

Carol stated deadpan to Earl, then she continued.

"Well Earl, please tell Lillian I said hi and it was a pleasure to meet her new *friend.*"

With that, she turned her head and smiled mockingly at Cord, ducked behind the black door and gently shut it, leaving the two alone on the porch.

Yeah, it's safe to say that bitch is going to want a signed lease Cord thought to himself.

Well, on the plus side, he finally met someone who probably wouldn't stand in front of the bus for Queen Lillian.

What was up between those two?

There might be more to it, but he figured it probably had to do with Earl's obsession with Carol, who was every bit as attractive as Lilly. If Lilly was 9.8, Carol was a 9.5, which maybe was a threat to Lilly and her protection of Earl.

She was also named Carol, same as their mom; a problem in and of itself, especially with Earl's feelings. Also, Carol obviously had dough, and she was the landlord, and she was definitely not a homegrown, a good-looking outsider treading on Lilly's home turf.

All good enough reasons alone for someone as quicksilver as Lilly to get bent over. But the combination? That was a fucking powder keg. He wouldn't want to be alone in a room with those two, for sure.

There was one thing Cord *was* sure about – it wasn't Carol's money. She definitely married into it – he just felt it, which meant her husband was the big fish in Belvidere – or her ex-husband was paying for her to play the role.

He ambled across the street with Earl, heading back into the Park. By this time, Lilly had left the side of Officer Brewer and was heading toward them in a quick stride; Martin was talking to the boys, all of whom were standing together in a small group.

As Lilly approached, it was clear she wasn't happy, and it was clear she had fucking questions.

CHAPTER 18 – HEAD DOWN, SHIFTING HER SHOES IN THE GRAVEL

"That really wasn't necessary; you've done enough for Earl, thanks."

Lillian stated firm, a nail to put this little uprising to rest.

"Wow, she must be a model, couldn't ask for a better looking landlord; Earl has good taste, that's for sure. Wheels aren't too shabby either."

Cord waited to see which bait worked best.

"Please, that look was bought by crow on the surgery table, from the tits up, to the tits down."

"Isn't that a bit childish….crow….why don't you call her by her right name; like she did when she talked so highly about *you*."

Cord figured Carol's jet black hair was the crow nexus – he couldn't believe Lilly was resorting to name-calling. What a juvenile.

"That *is* her name, dipshit; Carol *Crowe*."

"Oh."

Was all he said, feeling the idiot.

She hesitated a bit, then continued.

"What'd she say about me?"

She tried to ask in an offhand, indignant tone, which was clearly contrived; she was dying to know what Carol said.

"Well, Earl told her about you and I, you know, our relationship; she seemed genuinely interested, and commented on the many boy *friends* you seem to have."

Cord fingered quote signs for emphasis; clearly, Lilly was not amused.

"Oh, she also said to say *hi*".

Cord delivered it with a finger point at Lilly, topped with a dollop of sarcasm.

"That fucking bitch, who does she think she is? Earl, you're not delivering the rent to her anymore. And why do you keep bringing it so early? No more, from now on, it goes in on the *day* it's due, no sooner. That's it, we're done with that fucking place, we're finding another place to live! What did you say to her, Earl, about me and *him*?"

Earl was only half paying attention to the rant; he answered nonchalantly.

"I said Cord Brin was your boyfriend."

"**What**?! Why did you say that?"

"Because that's what Marty said, and that's what you said when you were with Marty, and you haven't stopped talking about him all morning and you were saying his name in your bedroom last night, with the door closed, when you were...."

*"Hey, Hey, **Hey!**"*

Lilly cut him off, getting louder with each hey.

"That's not nice Earl, listening to me at night; I don't do that to you."

"I don't do what you do; and you were doing it a lot last night – this morning too."

"Earl! Cut it out! Just stop talking!"

Cord stood there and drank it in with a salacious smile. What a fucking coup.

"Hey, don't yell at him – I can't blame the guy for complaining with all that moaning going on all night….all morning too? Me, I slept like a baby; apparently I couldn't think of anything to keep my interest."

"Shut up….asshole."

She said with disgust.

"Earl didn't hear what he thought he heard anyway."

She said the second part with her head down, in a whisper. Apparently she didn't speak soft enough; Earl didn't let it go unnoticed.

"Yes I did."

"Oh give it up girl, you're busted; just sit there and take it like you've made me do in the last twenty-four hours, more than once."

And she finally did; she just sat down on the bench and put her face in her hands.

"How embarrassing."

Is all she said, followed by:

"Thanks Earl."

"You're welcome."

He quickly replied, without emotion.

She looked up at him with a scowl, but he was looking at the Lion House again; she got up and went over, put her hands on the sides of his cheeks and kissed him on the forehead.

Just as swift as that, like turning on a light switch, her mood changed again; she was chipper, the unpleasant confessional kissed away, the slate clean, not to be talked about, or thought about, again.

She is very, very scary C thought to himself.

The center of the Park had cleared and Cord hadn't noticed same till now. Officer Brewer was gone, as were the kids; the puke and blood on the gravel was even kicked away, like the whole incident was nothing but a fleeting dream.

Cord started to walk away; he called goodbye to Earl, who didn't answer, but not Lilly, just to be obnoxious.

"Come on Earl, let's go feed the ducks; I got some stale bread from Sam this morning when I went in to see how Uncle Frank was doing."

She said the last fragment loud, so Cord could hear it as he walked away. He didn't acknowledge the jab, he kept walking.

Earl got up and trotted away from Lilly, toward Cord.

"Hey, where are you going?"

"I gotta go find the Post Office; I'm expecting some packages."

Cord answered, figuring Lilly was talking to him for some strange reason. But just as he finished his sentence, he saw Earl walking by his side, looking straight ahead, and realized her words were directed at him.

"Hey Earl, can you show me where the Post Office is?"

Earl smiled, nodded and kept walking.

When you're a kid, there's always a de facto leader of the pack, the kid who usually dictated where the group went and what the group did. After a while, that kid expected to always be the leader of the pack. But packs change leaders; sometimes it just happens.

Lilly's pack was heading away from the ducks.

Lilly was in a quandary. Does she let Earl go? Yet another embarrassment in front of this annoying jerk-off she can't seem to shake. Or does she plead for the play date with the ducks? That hardly seemed like a winning, or cool, proposition. Or does she skulk along and join them – the ultimate embarrassment.

"Fine Earl, go ahead and visit the Post Office – wow, that seems pretty exciting!"

Was all she could think to say quickly – she knew it was pretty lame. The two boys never even turned around, they kept walking toward Mansfield Street, heading into the center of Town.

That quick, Lilly felt alone, and hurt.

She sat on the bench in the middle of the empty park and watched the two get smaller as they walked into the distance; she just sat and eyed them, until they were out of sight.

Hey Earl, do ya wanna go feed the ducks Lilly whispered, head down, shifting her shoes in the gravel.

CHAPTER 19 – WE WILL, WHEN SHE TELLS ME TO

Everyone knew Earl, and everyone greeted him, but he didn't return the gestures; no one seemed to mind. The fact that Earl was walking along with Cord didn't attract the attention Cord thought it would; then again, most people probably thought Earl was walking alone, and happened to be in step with Cord, since the two weren't talking.

The walk from the center of the Park to the Post Office was a mere one and a half blocks; in that span, six people greeted Earl. Of them, Cord recognized half; Woody emerged from a side alley across from the Post Office, just a block from his realty business; the other two were women C met working in the grocery yesterday – he didn't remember their names.

For a moment, he even forgot he had a job; in fact, he forgot he was suppose to be at work *today* – he was only going to take time off in the morning to run some errands, like going to the Post Office – he was suppose to be at work in the afternoon.

The whole Park incident, besides being close to a disaster, ate up a chunk of time. He really wasn't in the mood to go to work, and he felt good about that. Maybe he should quit.

"Man, I've got to go to work Earl; that blows….forgot all about it. I've got to hustle and get the boxes to the apartment."

With that, Cord picked up the pace a bit. Cord was a slow walker; some people are just a bit pokey by nature and he was one of them. Earl, who had a much longer stride, constantly altered his gait to keep in exact lock step with Ay – he was concentrating on it intently, head down, like a little kid imitating, mimicking, a grown-up's gait.

The Post Office was small, a single story, white stucco structure, with both plate glass and a section of curved, dated glass-block windows flanking the entryway. It was bustling, people in and out, like a revolving door – the noon closing time was fast approaching.

Inside, the walls of individual mailboxes and the worn, nicked customer counter were jammed into one small room, with a center table for filling out labels and licking stamps. A montage of faded government posters covered every square inch of wall space; it looked at if some had been hung before Cord was born.

He settled into the four-person queue somewhat impatiently, thinking about the grocery store. Earl stayed outside – he sat on the front stoop and began whistling a tune. Cord could only hear a few bars when the door opened, then it was muffled when the door shut, and sounded again when it opened. It was so damn familiar, but he couldn't hear enough of it at one time to place it. What was that tune? It was driving him crazy.

He turned to look through the front plate glass and spied a squirrely guy with blue maintenance pants, too-short floods and a gray tee-shirt, talking to Earl; the whistling continued while the man jawed away, no doubt some hot gossip on the local front. He had a paunch for a belly and was five foot-four inch at best, with thinning brown hair in a classic comb-over and a demeanor which screamed civil servant. As he spoke, the munchkin, looking intensely at Earl, slowly rocked side to side, wearing work boots too clean to have ever seen work. His little hands were shoved half-way into his pant pockets; he couldn't squeeze them in any further, since the pants were a full-size too tight.

It mattered little that Earl was oblivious to his yammering; Earl was the perfect captive for a guy who was really talking to himself.   Everyone knows this guy, the one you hope to see with a block to spare, to allow time to discretely cross the street.

The door opened again; a slight, gray-haired man wrestled with an oversized box, which propped the door open for a bit. The whistling continued uninterrupted for a good twenty notes.

Oh my God, Cord thought, that's the theme song from *Neighbors*!

He looked Earl's way, smiled, and shook his head in disbelief. Of all the tunes Earl could pick, he not only knew, but chose, that obscure jingle.

No other snippet could have caught Cord's attention the way that one did. It tickled his brain, flooding it with memories long forgotten. He closed his eyes and sighed.

Neighbors was released twenty-five years ago, December, 1981, he remembered it was during the holidays. He saw it in on the big screen with his girlfriend, his older brother and Joy, his brother's longtime squeeze.

Joy and Cord's brother had been together for years, from their early teens. Cord always liked Joy and never understood what she saw in his brother.

Neighbors....my God; Cord just shook his head and smiled.

It was a dark, low-budget comedy about a dysfunctional, tired and bored middle-aged couple, living at the end of a lonely cul-de-sac in stereotypical Jersey suburbia. On a same-old Friday evening, they meet their new neighbors, a swinging couple with a zest for life, who also happen to be dysfunctional, in other ways.

The entire storyline ran from a Friday evening to Saturday morning, less than twenty-four hours, with a series of ever-more-bizarre encounters between the staid, unhappy couple and the eccentric new neighbors.

Cord loved it, but *Neighbors* was panned as a failure at the time; a sad, last tribute to its main character, John Belushi, who died of an overdose a couple months after its release. To this day, most people never heard of the movie, save a few rabid Internet fans, but you can find die-hard Internet fans for just about anything.

Even *Neighbors*.

Cord ran hot and cold with his next-older brother; growing up, they would be friendly, not best-of-friends, but close, for short periods of time, followed by months of indifference and utter lack of interaction. Their age difference had a lot to do with that – an eight year old and thirteen year old simply have divergent wants and needs; the same holds true for a thirteen year old and an eighteen year old.

As adults, the periods of indifference got progressively longer; when their parents died, the interaction ended altogether; Ay hadn't seen or spoken to his brother in years; he didn't know how many years, it was at least ten, more than ten. He was married and had kids; he wasn't sure how many.

There was no specific reason why they didn't speak or interact; he didn't particularly dislike his brother in any sense – conversely, he wasn't sure if he loved his brother in a familial sense; he didn't think so. If he had to say *I love my brother* out loud, it would feel disingenuous, uncomfortable. It was a general sense of not caring – not borne of anger or hurt or incident, but rather from abject indifference. Apathy.

That *Neighbors* double date in 1981 was one of the few times, in fact the only time he could recall, where he socialized with his brother in such a manner; he couldn't remember who arranged the double-date or why, it was certainly an oddity. And Earl whistling it now, odder yet.

Actually, as he stood there in line and thought about it
some more, he did double date, in a sense, with his
brother one other time, five years later, in a drunken
orgy with two blow-pig hookers in St. Charles, Missouri,
in '86.

His brother was married; Cord was with someone at the
time, wasn't he? He likely was, probably was, assuredly
was, but couldn't remember her name.

And that was nothing unusual; he was always a dog.

It started with a night of barhopping and heavy drinking
in St. Louis, at Lacledes Landing on the Mississippi
waterfront, just north of the Arch. Although they tried to
hook up, it never happened; he didn't remember even
getting close, neither one of them. They got thrown out
as drunks at the last bar early morning, onto the
cobblestone street below Eads Bridge.

God, he remembered it well.

It was a crystal clear night; the moon wasn't full, but
bright enough for him to notice. It was a vertiginous
amble; he remembered falling at least once as they
searched for the car; it felt good lying on the cool
cobbles, the rounded, worn edges which sloped and
extended to the water's edge, slipping under the surface
of the Mississippi's blackness. He rolled over onto his
side and caught the seeming endless stretch of stainless
steel on one of the Arch legs in the distance, glowing
from reflected moonlight – a wynd that gracefully
curved into the night sky, out of sight.

He could have easily stayed down and slept, he thought;
there were at least three others he could make out in the
distance sleeping on the street, tatterdemalions on the
sidewalk below the Arch.

He closed his eyes, relaxed, and felt the space in his head
slowly spin in a counter-clockwise direction.

Sleep felt good right about now.

A sharp boot kick into his side altered those plans.

"Come on, dickhead, wake up."

Cord's brother was taller, but C was stronger – and mercurial – more so when he was drunk. Ay wasn't one to take shit from anyone, but it was his older brother, somehow, for some reason, that meant something to Cord at the time, which prevented Ay from popping him right then and there.

"Give me the fucking keys."

He said, as he wrested them from Cord's hand – in a night of trying to top each other on a variety of topics, including alcohol consumption, he wasn't going to let his little brother drive, the fact that it was *actually* Cord's car was merely a formality.

Cord sat up slowly, his head spinning from a night of screwdrivers, his drink *du jour* at the time, and tried to focus on his shirt, which didn't look right. As he pulled it away from his chest to look closer and bring his eyes into focus, he noticed his hands were smeared with blood, his shirt was sprayed red as well. Cord stared blankly at the cloth, trying to recall something, anything, about how it got there.

He must have blacked out again.

"Don't worry, it's not yours."

His brother said.

With that, he hooked C under the arm and hoisted him to his feet.

He isn't sure how, but they managed to find Cord's car; he was alert enough to know they were both too drunk to drive, but drunk enough to ignore it.

Cord didn't remember talking anymore until they were in the car and he was navigating his brother out of downtown St. Louis, onto Interstate 70, for the twenty-odd minute ride to the apartment in St. Charles.

His brother was drunk too, more so than he thought. He was driving too fast, but luckily the roads were empty; it had to be after two in the morning. Once onto 70, Cord told him the exit to take, which was a straight shot. Cord's eyelids were heavy; his head tilted back and he was quickly out. He remembered hearing the dim hum of tires on the road, and nothing else.

To this day he didn't know how or why he awoke from his stupor, he shouldn't have; the radio was off, his brother wasn't talking, the road expansion joints clicked like a metronome. And he was wasted.

But for some reason he woke up, and did so in a start.

They were going eighty-five mph and quickly picking up speed, his brother hammering the throttle with a leaden foot.

Just as Cord's eyes began to focus, the tires left the paved shoulder of the road. A cold gray wall of concrete, growing fast, was swallowing the windshield, gravel kicking the underbelly like buckshot.

Fogged from the booze, he managed to turn to his brother and saw he was out cold – eyes closed, head cocked back and tilted to the side, mouth partially open. His whole head was wobbling back and forth in tandem with the rocking of the car.

Cord let out a guttural scream; they were seconds from hitting that concrete bridge abutment head on – at ninety-five mph.

And that's when it happened.

His brother didn't open his eyes, yet he somehow jerked the wheel to the left and the car careened back onto the shoulder and across two empty paved traffic lanes – no one was on the road in either direction. The turn of the wheel to the left was a fateful fluke; to the right would have turned them headlong into the concrete wall – neither was wearing a seat belt.

Five seconds longer and the story ends twenty years ago, in St. Louis in 1986; five seconds longer and it's over. Both of them are over.

But for some odd reason, even though the story should have ended there, it didn't. In hindsight, not so old.

Back on the road, his brother sat up a bit, nonchalant, readjusted himself behind the wheel, slowly blinked the buzz from his eyes, several times, and kept driving; he never uttered a word or sound throughout the ordeal. He's not sure his brother ever realized what almost happened. As quickly as it unfolded, it was over – as if it never happened at all.

The whole thing didn't have the feel of real; but that was the story of Cord's life, over and over again.

They rode in silence, Cord wide-eyed, for the next ten minutes and never once spoke of the incident....that night, or ever. Ever.

Immediately upon entering the apartment, his brother bum-stumbled around the flat, rummaged through some drawers looking for a phone book to dial up an escort service, which he did, and promptly ordered two young, thin lookers, preferably Russian, one with larger cans for him – like ordering a late night snack from room service.

Cord was laid out on the bed, eyes closed, trying to stop the spin, listening to his brother rattle off the specific criteria for each showgirl; it seemed clear the dispatcher was writing down the particulars and had the goods in stock to deliver.

He yelled over to Ay.

"Two hundred each to stick our dicks in any hole we want; you in?"

Cord barely lifted his head off the bed and nodded once in the affirmative, with closed eyes. His brother hung up and looked at Cord with particular self-satisfaction.

"Done."

Was all he said, as he smiled and nodded affirmatively to himself.

They waited, for how long he didn't know, passing in and out of consciousness, until the doorbell interrupted the stupor.

Needless to say, the *packages* delivered to the door were, to put it mildly, a bit off spec.

Now, in a sober state, such an outcome would certainly be expected – the local hooker pool is what it is, especially an on-demand order at three in the morning. In such a situation, the voice at the other end of the line will describe whatever horse is waiting in the stable as exactly what you are looking for, be it *Russian, thin and young* or *Oriental, hairy, with curves* – whatever you want is what he's got.

But to the reasoning drunken mind, the presumed mistake was nothing short of heresy. Cord remembered being more upset with this predicament than the aborted slam into the highway overpass.

They both cried foul as the girls stood astride the entryway, with the door open, as their ride idled curbside. The two boys huddled to discuss the situation, as best two drunks can, and decided to take the dishes offered – maybe they really weren't that bad. They negotiated the fee down to a hundred dollars each, which was about a hundred and ten more per girl than they should have paid.

His brother quickly grabbed the better of the lot, figuring he had seniority. She was thin all right, and in her twenties, but a road-worn gutter-slut equipped with a set of the saggiest cowbells he'd ever seen - they were simply too long, stretched like *Silly-Putty*. when she unstrapped her soiled bra, they laid flat on her stomach, the nipples pointing north, toward the ceiling. Cord wasn't sure how that was even possible, physically; he somehow remembered pondering that fact.

His attention left her chest when she opened her mouth, exposing a single, oversized, gold front tooth, which caught the glint of light from the ceiling fan and sparkled each time the bare bulb emerged from behind a revolving fan blade.

Nice touch.

She didn't waste time and stripped down naked; his brother followed suit, threw her on the bed and mounted her doggie-style. His brother's cock looked semi-rigid, bendable….hard enough to fuck, but barely. Cord doubted he was even touching the sides; he swore his brother was pumping a big open air hole - the only noise being his balls slapping her hairy lips and flat ass.

God, it was pathetic, but aces compared to what Cord was about to be dealt.

Before him hunched a gammer; in reality probably in her forties, but with an ashen and pocked face that added a good twenty years. It was the complexion of a corpse.

She had coarse matted, shoulder-length hair, an oily mix of brown and gray. As she undressed, to Cord's horror, the beach ball he thought was shoved in her tight skirt morphed into a tightly stretched, gravid belly; but this prize wasn't pregnant.   To make matters worse, that bulb of a lower belly was covered in a layer of thin, brown hair – he swore it looked combed. The hirsute extended halfway up her distended belly, to just below a protruding, herniated navel. He never saw anything like it - he swore it must be straight from the primate house at the zoo. That Venus gut belonged on an orangutan, an ugly orangutan.

He closed his eyes and violently shook the webs from his head, hoping to shake the primate away, convinced it was all a drunken dream. When the image failed to chase, he tried a second time. No luck, and no remote to click away the scary story.

Cord didn't know what to do; he really didn't want to undress and his cock agreed; he felt it shrivel, recoiling with each unbutton of his jeans. But strip he did, and stood there eyeing the freak show, like a dolt.

She saw he was drunk and grabbed him by the wrist, leading him, like a child, into the bathroom. She ran the water in the sink, wet her right hand and started slowly rubbing his cock. He felt the immediate sting of sharp grit; she was slathering his head and shaft with what looked like an abrasive mix of black charcoal and beach sand.

"Ow! What the fuck!"

He slapped her hand away.

"Just cleaning you up."

Was all she said; as she walked away, her oversized ass, the color and texture of a bowl of cottage cheese, jiggled side to side.

He was about to vomit.

He choked back the bile, wiped the black grit from his cock and slowly walked in the bedroom, trying to buy time, to figure an escape plan.

Now, had he been a bit older, and a bit more sober, he would have thrown the slut out; but at twenty-three and out his half of the cash, he made the unfortunate decision to stay in the game.

She lay on the bed, on her side, and halfheartedly played with his dick, trying to get it hard. That was simply not happening. If he had a cock-shaft at one time, it got smart and ran; his dickhead was a nothing more than a mushroom cap glued directly to his ball-sack. He looked down and couldn't believe that was actually his dick – where did it go?

"Are you doing coke? They shrivel up like that when you're drunk and a coke-head."

He should have said they shrivel up like that when you try to have sex with an ape, but he didn't; he didn't say a word. He just looked at her, like a deer in headlights.

She just laid there, playing with what used to be his dick, while he fixated on her belly. It was getting embarrassing, even for a drunk, so he reached between her legs and tried to run his finger into her snatch, which surprisingly, didn't have much hair on it. It was as if the pubic hair left and moved north, to her belly.

He parted her large legs just a bit with his left hand and quickly ran his finger to her cunt, right to the front door, and tried to get inside. He figured he would get something going for his money.

Nothing doing; she snapped her legs shut like a bear trap.

He pushed his hand in a little more forcefully, the trap spring tightened. If his head were between those thunder thighs, she surely would have cut the blood to his brain.

That was a thought worth trying.

"Open up! What the fuck am I paying for?!"

Cord demanded.

"You paid to fuck, honey, not finger."

And with that, she grabbed his hand and tossed it aside indignant.

"Now, if you want to just look till you're ready, I'll let you have a peak."

And with that, she parted her white, spongy legs. Cord swore he heard a long, slow sniff of air escape, like cracking the valve on a tire stem.

Did she just fart on him?

That was about all he could take, even drunk.

As he tried to roll away and escape, he was engulfed by a waft of orange blossoms, jasmine, and gardenias, mixed with hints of Bergamot and patchouli. That fart was the best part of this sex so far.

But that release didn't leak from her ass, but rather her crotch; it was overpowering, like she uncorked a perfume bottle shoved up her twat.

The thought of the real aroma in that hole being masked by a piquant bouquet entered his mind. When was the last time that cavity saw real soap? And how many less discriminating guys tonight had left their signature inside? A pool of jizz, slowly fermenting in that crusty cheese-melter.

For God's sake, he said to himself, push that thought out of your head, *way out*. Another involuntary retch, thankfully a dry heave.

She ignored his convulsion and continued to pull-toy his pud halfhearted, eyeing it like some sort of science project.

"Give it up."

Cord finally said flatly, with disgust.

It was only then the blow-pig surmised that it might have been *her* that was the problem. No, she quickly dismissed that fleeting thought. She was fine; *he* was the problem.

She rose from the bed and dressed slowly, purposely taking her time. She wasn't the problem, with her hairy belly and cottage cheese ass, of that she was sure. No, he was the problem, the drunk coke-head, that was the message she was sending, that was the story she was taking home with her, laughing and recounting her escapades with the other sluts come morning.

By this time, his brother had already blown into the air pocket. Gold-tooth was already dressed and sitting by the front door. His brother was slumped over on the can, half-asleep, farting through a sloppy shit.

What a fucking nightmare.

Cord rolled off the bed and quickly found his clothes. If he could have peeled off his skin, he would have; the feeling of skeeve was thick and itchy. He'll never forget the plus-size dirty-white, old-lady underwear she pulled on, covering half her hairy belly, the other half sticking out, a joey in a pouch. She never looked at him or uttered a word as she finished dressing. She preened herself in the mirror, deliberately coiffing her matted hair as she stuck her chin high in the air; he wondered how she didn't recoil at the reflection. Slowly, with exaggerated dignity, she walked to the front door, joining her cohort. The two slipped quietly into the night; the front door deliberately left ajar. The odyssey had ended, but the nightmare remained. For years, even in a drunken stupor, he couldn't get the face of that gutter-slut out of his mind; it was seared in his brain, the thought could make the stiffest hard-on wilt.

He shuddered at the memory, and found himself drifting back to *Neighbors*.

The audience was strangely silent throughout the movie, except Cord and Joy, both of whom could not stop laughing at the sarcastic banter between the two main characters, Earl Keese, the boring, straight suburbanite played by Belushi, and Captain Vic, the sex-crazed, eccentric new neighbor played by Dan Akroyd. He remembered people turning to look at him in the theater with disbelief on their faces – what could possibly be so funny? Several people left mid-movie in disgust, at both the movie, and them.

His brother was not pleased Joy and Cord were sharing some private comedic moments he and the rest of the theater simply didn't get.

Cord didn't recall ever seeing a movie with the two of them again; his brother and Joy broke up soon thereafter, and that was that.

Cord never really talked to anyone about the movie, even though he had watched it alone dozens of times over the years and had memorized most of the dialogue. He could make himself laugh just reciting lines in his mind; the sarcastic and pathetic banter between unhappy people and the double entendre between new neighbors of the opposite sex.

He stood in the Post Office line, eyes still closed, and chuckled out loud, reliving the script; people turned to see what was so funny, and slowly stepped away from the stranger laughing to himself.

As he reminisced, he realized that was the first time he'd really thought about his brother in years. He wondered what ever happened to Joy and if she was happy. And were those two hookers still working St. Charles? My God; that was all he could say to such a thought.

He drifted to thoughts of Lilly; Sam said her mom died in April, 1981, just months before he was sitting and laughing in that theater; he wondered what Lilly had been doing in Belvidere the night he was watching *Neighbors* for the first time – if she thought the movie was funny – if she ever saw it with Earl.

He wondered what he was doing on April 7th that year, when Carol died; he wished he had some way of remembering – he didn't know why, but it would make him feel a little closer to Lilly if he did.

Lilly was twenty-two years old in 1986, when he and his brother ordered up the escorts, the girl he was hoping would walk through the door that night was a girl who looked just like Lillian, and was about her age, a year younger than him.

He didn't feel good about that, about thinking of her in those terms, as a hooker; he slipped to melancholy and stopped smiling.

"Next!"

The postal clerk's bark brought him back to Belvidere.

Cord bellied to the counter and advised the thick, middle-aged woman that two parcels for a Cord Brin should have arrived yesterday; he was there to claim them. She eyed him hard and didn't utter a word; he figured she clearly had been involved in trying to maneuver the unwieldy boxes, at least the one. She disappeared into the back; while he waited, Cord turned to look out the window.

The squirrely guy was still yapping away, when Earl suddenly stood up and reached into his pocket; he fumbled around a bit and finally pulled out a cellphone.

He flipped it open and tried to listen over the drone of the little man talking at him; Cord could see Earl was getting frustrated not being able to hear, when he suddenly and quickly extended his left arm with an open hand, not trying to hurt the little man, just to get him to go away, like swatting a fly.

The big open palm hit the talker square in the chest; down he went on the sidewalk like a sack of potatoes. Just as he went down, a teenager was walking by, who impromptu bent down and made an exaggerated "safe" call, like an umpire – Cord could see his lips mouth the word in an exaggerated tone:

"SAAAFE!"

The kid laughed and kept walking.

The little man rose in a huff, brushed himself off, and grimaced at the teenager, mumbling something to himself as he walked away. Earl ignored the whole exchange; he was listening intently to the phone, and his smile was widening.

The clerk reappeared with two packages stacked precarious on a handcart; her forehead had tiny beads of sweat. Cord was convinced she didn't wipe them away, for effect.

The one parcel was large and heavy; the second was smaller and relatively light. The latter was sealed with what appeared to be an excess amount of packing tape.

She never asked Cord for identification; he guessed she knew everyone in Town, and she didn't know a *Cord Brin*, and she didn't know him, so that seemed good enough for her.

You gotta love Belvidere.

At that moment, Earl strolled in and made his way to the counter; he didn't say a word, but he was still smiling. He saw the two boxes by Cord's feet, squatted and grabbed the big box with two hands, hoisting it onto his shoulder in one fluid motion; Cord figured that box was at least two hundred pounds.

The woman behind the counter froze; there would be casualties if that big box were to topple off Earl's broad shoulder.

"For goodness sake, Earl, put that down! It's much too dangerous! Take the hand cart; you can bring it back when you're done with it."

With that, she scowled and grunted at Cord, as if he was in some way responsible for Earl's actions.

Earl eased the box down, without effort really, and placed it on the handcart. Cord grabbed the smaller box and placed it atop the heavy parcel; as he did, he spun it around, so Earl could easily see it – on the back, in large, bold print, it read:

Open When You Are Ready

"Are we gonna open it?"

Earl asked excited.

"Not yet, Earl, but we will, when she tells me to."

214

CHAPTER 20 – WATCHING HIS BIRD WORKING THE RIVER

C regretted the statement as soon as the words left his lips.

But thankfully, Earl didn't ask who *she* was, or when she would tell him to open the box. C was happy about that; it was certainly not a discussion he was ready to have with Earl now, or probably ever. That was a discussion best left between her and Cord; it was just easier.

And Earl didn't say anything else about the phrase on the box – *Open When You Are Ready* - it apparently didn't elicit the reaction Cord thought it might, since it said the same thing, according to Sam, according to Frank, according to Lilly, that Carol said, in her last moments, before she died.

Maybe Earl didn't know his mom said that; maybe the story was wrong and she never did.

And why Cord wrote that on his box obviously had nothing to do with any of that anyway; it was stupid to even show it to Earl to begin with.

So Cord let it drop.

The two walked out of the Post Office and headed downtown; Earl looked like a kid ready to burst, wanting to spill a big secret. He just kept looking at Cord and smiling.

"Okay, I give up, who was on the phone and what do you want to tell me?"

"It was Lilly; she said you don't have to go to work today!"

"Why, did she get me fired?"

Cord said bluntly.

"I want to show you something! *Come on*, I want to show you something!"

Earl started to take the handcart and turn to the west, away from the apartment building.

"Earl, hey, I got to get these boxes to my apartment; there's some important stuff in here, come on, help me bring this stuff up and then you can show me, okay?"

Earl looked like a kid who couldn't wait to open presents on Christmas morning; he didn't want to go to the apartment. Not now; certainly not now.

Then he grimaced, put his head down and started to push that cart faster and faster toward *Nonpareil* – if they had to go to the apartment, then they were going fast.

"Whoa, Whoa, slow down!"

Cord said, but it was futile.

Earl was a man on a mission. Cord wasn't trotting, he was running, trying to keep up with Earl and the handcart, which looked like it was going to lose a wheel – it was careening left and right, with Earl trying to control it. Finally, Earl just picked the whole contraption up and ran with it under his arm; it was scary how strong Earl must be. Cord couldn't believe it; he was getting a stitch in his side trying to catch up to a three hundred-sixty pound man with more than two hundred pounds of boxes and a hand truck tucked under his arm.

Cord was running with a newspaper in his hand, and he was out of breath and falling behind.

Down Mill Street to Greenwich to Water Street they went, in a flat-out sprint across the busy intersection at

Sam's – Earl didn't even bother to look. He stopped at the sidewalk entrance to the hallway, pushed it open with his foot and lunged up the steps, two at a time, with the handcart still under his arm. It was a steep, long staircase, thirty-eight steps to the top landing.

By the time Cord got to the sidewalk entry door, chest heaving for air, he saw Earl at the top, impatiently two-step pacing back and forth on the little landing.

"Come on!"

"Okay, okay."

Cord hoped a half-jog up the steps would appease Earl. It didn't.

"Cord, open the door! We gotta go!"

Cord joined him on the landing, still out of breath – Earl was breathing fine, Ay noticed. He started to fish for the key in his pocket when he remembered he had never locked it.

"It's already open."

Earl heard the news, quickly pushed past him and deposited the boxes in the front room, down the hall. Cord threw the newspaper on the kitchen counter. Earl ran back down the hall, grabbed the hand truck and started down the stairs.

"Earl, leave the hand truck here - the Post Office is closed; we'll bring it back tomorrow. Now, where are we going?"

Earl just smiled, and they were on their way.

The big man bounded down the stairs, with Cord in pursuit; two grown men sprinting in daylight through Town in street clothes. That didn't look good; usually when that happened, some delinquent was getting chased by Marty.

Across the street, over the bridge again and down to South Water Street, where they hooked a right, went two blocks, made a dog-leg left and ran another block, cutting into the gravel drive and trailer turnaround area for the Delaware boat ramp.

Cord was about to pass out, his hands on his knees, looking down at his shoes and gulping air; Earl was not even breathing heavy – the bastard, Cord thought to himself. He'd better start exercising again; morning push-ups were just not going to cut it.

It was about half past noon on a Friday, and the boat ramp was empty, with no cars nor trailers scattered about the lot; that was unusual. Ever since the State bought the boat ramp property a couple years prior, it had gotten a ton more use as a river access point by out-of-towners; before that, the guy who owned it leased it to the Town for a buck, and just the locals really used it – it was much quieter then.

But today, it was like the old times; not a soul was around.

Except Lillian.

She was at the bottom of the ramp, crouched by the water's edge. She heard Earl coming in a noisy rush and turned around, smiled and put her fingers up to her lips to be quiet, but still motioning for him to come down to the water's edge, quickly.

Earl moved down to the water in as slow a motion as he was capable in his excited state; he moved in an exaggerated, cartoon gait, with Cord in tow.

Cord wished he could see the world through Earl's eyes; it must be a wonderful place.

Earl reached her side and crouched as best he could; she handed him the binoculars and pointed to a large rock half submerged in the river, directly across the Delaware, on the far bank.

Earl scanned the far side and then stopped, whispering to himself through a wide grin, like a kid.

"Aloysius!"

Lilly smiled and put her hand around Earl's waist and gave him a long hug.

"I *told* you; you should have listened and come with me to feed the ducks."

She had to get that dig in, for Cord's benefit.

Lilly turned her self-satisfied gaze to Cord, who looked a bit perplexed; an explanation was in order.

"Aloysius is a double-crested cormorant, like a big black goose. He's been stopping here for years every Spring and Fall, on his way south and north. He doesn't stay long, a couple days, sometimes a bit more, sometimes just a day. Earl didn't see him last year at all, for the first time in many years, and he was sad, we both were; we thought he might have….passed away."

"Don't say that Lilly."

"I'm sorry, Earl, but we both thought it may have happened; Al's been around a long time, and you know how much he loves to come see you."

"I didn't think that, I *never* thought that; I knew Al wouldn't go away and leave us."

Lilly paused a bit before she spoke.

"Well he didn't, he would miss you too much; he loves you, Earl."

And with that, Lilly smiled at Earl and then just gazed across the river at the lone black bird. It opened its wings for a minute, a good four feet across, then folded them back in.

Lilly folded her arms across her chest; she looked content.

"Al first stopped here, or at least the first time Earl saw him, was in April of '81, when Earl was only fourteen, in eighth grade. He was on his way home from school, taking the long way, a *long-cut* he would call it, like he always did; it was a Tuesday, and he stopped to see if the ducks were here – like he always did on his way home.

The mallards, wood ducks and Canadian geese would usually hang around the boat ramp, especially in the late afternoon, and Earl would feed them bread, with my mom. They weren't there every day, but most days you would get some, especially if the boat ramp was quiet. It was a lot quieter back then. Kind of like it is today *[Lilly kicked nervous at the sand as she spoke]*.

If there were a handful, he would run home as fast as he could and get her, my mom, and they would both run down together, holding hands, laughing….it was *their* thing, together, just the two of them. They hid two folding beach chairs in the woods right over there *[Lilly pointed a bit downstream]*, leaned against that big tree, hanging over the water; actually they didn't hide them, everyone in Town knew they were for Earl and my mom and didn't touch them.

Anyway, they would pull them out, set them right on the water's edge, pull off their shoes and socks, and feed the ducks and geese. Earl always put his chair a little bit in the water, just the front legs – he wanted to be *in* the water with the ducks.

The two of them would sit down there and just talk to each other and feed the ducks for hours, till it got dark. The ducks would come right up and sit with them, in front of the chairs, under the chairs, behind the chairs. Earl would put the bread between his toes so they would nip at them; it would always make him laugh.

I wasn't allowed to come along when they fed the ducks, my mom would always say that it was her *special time* with Earl, just for the two of them, down at the ramp; this was their special place."

Lillian paused a bit, her eyes were starting to water; she turned her head and tried to discretely wipe them. Cord looked away, trying not to embarrass her, and focused on Aloysius, who was standing tall across the river.

"Well, that day, that Tuesday, when Earl came down, it was like no other....ever. The boat ramp was empty; there were no swimmers, or fishermen or boaters, no one was around.

Earl quietly walked down to the water and saw something special, *really* special. There were more ducks and geese than he had ever seen, *ever*; mallards of all different shades of red, green, yellow and brown, and white geese, and brown geese and Canadians; there were hundreds of them, *hundreds,* like they were waiting for him. Right Earl?

[Earl just smiled and nodded yes, as if it was yesterday]

It had never happened like that before, and it has never happened like that since. Earl stood awestruck – he was beside himself; he would have to bring down loaves and loaves of bread, a truck-load, and he still wouldn't be able to feed them all.

He was so excited and was just about to run home and get my mom when he heard this deep grunt echo from across the river, up by the piers of the bridge, by that far one, the first one in the river, just off the Pennsylvania side. *[Lilly pointed across the river as she spoke]*

Earl looked over and saw this strange black bird, he had never seen one before, standing on a rock along the shore, with its wings stretched out, wide open, like a cape. It stopped him in his tracks. And just as Earl saw it, the bird flew off the rock and came right toward Earl, *right at him.* He landed in the water about fifty feet off the shore and just stared at Earl as he floated there. He had a long beak which curved at the end, he had two tufts of feathers, like ears, on his crown and a deep orange throat, like he was wearing some kind of fancy scarf.

Earl was mesmerized; he couldn't take his eyes off that beautiful, black bird; and the bird was locked in a gaze, eye-to-eye, with Earl. Then, just as quickly as he got there, the bird disappeared under the water, just like that *[Lillian snapped her finger once].*

Earl waited for a minute or more for him to come up, but nothing happened. Earl got scared for the bird and was ready to run in and try to save him, but he was too far out, and Earl can't swim; he sinks like a rock. The big bird was gone, just gone, like he drowned.

Earl tilted his head down a bit and started to cry, looking at the river where the big black bird, his new friend, had disappeared.

Then, all of a sudden, only twenty feet in front of him, the bird popped out of the water, and threw a fish in the air, which slowly flipped around and landed head first, right in the bird's mouth – he gulped it down in one shot.

Earl went from devastated to delighted, just like that. *[Lilly snapped her finger again]*

He forgot about running home, he just ran up and got his chair and sat there watching the new black bird dive and catch a fish, flip it, eat it, and do it again and again and again. Between fish he would grunt at Earl, which made Earl laugh; he was so happy….a fourteen year-old in his glory.

He called him Aloysius right then and there; Earl doesn't know why he called him that, he had never heard that name before, but he said it just popped into his head. Every time Al grunted; Earl would yell *Aloysius*! and grunt back at him.

Earl spent the whole afternoon with Al; Al never stopped catching and tossing fish for Earl, he fished more that time than he ever has since – it was like Al didn't want Earl to leave.

Earl never did make it home that day till it was well after dark; he was happy all afternoon."

Lillian stopped talking and Cord looked over at her; tears were streaming down her face, running off her cheeks onto the ground, her eyes were closed, but it didn't stop the tears from flowing. She made no attempt to wipe them, no attempt to stop them. Her head was bowed and her shoulders were heaving, but she didn't make a sound.

Cord knew that day was April 7th.

He wanted to go over and console Lilly, but he wasn't sure if she would be mad at him for doing it – he didn't know what to do.

So he just quietly stepped over to her and gently put his hand on her shoulder – he didn't say a word. Lilly slowly spun into him and put her head on his chest and sobbed; she kept her arms limp by her sides. Cord loosely wrapped his around her shoulders and just stood there with her, with his cheek pressed gently against her soft hair. She sobbed for a bit longer, then she stopped and breathed heavily, quietly, on his chest. She was warm, and she felt good against his body – he wished she wasn't so sad and he wished he knew what to do to make her feel better. This, what he was doing, which was nothing, was all he could think of. He was afraid to say anything wrong, so he didn't say anything at all. He would have stood there forever with her, if that's what she wanted.

Earl just couldn't wait for Al to see him any longer; he called out his name and followed it with a low, guttural grunt, which echoed across the river.

Al heard him.

A low, loud grunt followed Earl's and the bird took flight from the rock and flew over toward the Jersey side. Earl was jumping up and down; he was so excited to see his friend – it had been so long. Al landed a little closer than mid-river, looked at Earl and disappeared under the surface of the water – fetching fish.

Lilly lifted herself off Cord's chest and wiped her eyes with her sleeve, and sniffled.

"You know, if you look it up, they say cormorants only live about fifteen years in the wild, typically, maybe a little longer. The oldest one known, ever, was only twenty-three. But Al was already at least a year old when he found Earl in '81; that would make him at least twenty-six.

People say that this isn't the same cormorant, it can't be, but they're wrong; it's Al, it's always been Al."

Lilly said that last sentence like one who knows, without question, that what they are saying is true.

As Earl was standing there, he started randomly reciting facts out loud, just because he was so excited to see Aloysius again, after two long years.

"They eat a pound of fish a day, at least, which is a quarter of their body weight; they like perch and bass the best, right Lilly? His orange neck is called a gular. *[Earl extended the pronunciation goo-lurr, for emphasis]*

They're called sea crows and have black webbed feet; they fly in large, V-shaped flocks and travel together, except for Aloysius, he travels all alone when he comes to see us, right Bibby?"

"That's right; Al doesn't want to share you with anybody, Earl - he wants you all to himself."

Earl just smiled and looked through the binoculars at the cormorant fishing. After downing a half dozen fish, Al flew over to a dead tree, just about fifty feet upstream, to relax and let his wings dry; they aren't waterproof and need to be aired out after fishing for a bit. He went back to work a little later and continued the routine throughout the day.

"I hope Al stays for awhile this time, Bibby, he's been gone so long. I'm so happy he's back."

Earl was talking as much to Al as he was to Lilly.

"Me too."

She said.

"I love you Lilly."

Earl said, as he stared out at the water, watching Al work up and down a stretch of river.

"I love you too, Earl."

Lilly had brought down three loafs of yesterday's bread from *Sam*, which they all fed to the mallards, ducks and geese lounging around the boat ramp. Al never ate the bread; he was strictly a fish-guy.

The mallards were particularly voracious when it came to day old bread; the smarter ones quickly learned it was best to stay on the periphery of the mob. The birds in the middle had to fight off peers from all sides, a low success rate, when scraps were tossed into the fray. The outsiders, however, snapped stray bits with little challenge.

You would think they hadn't eaten in days; Cord never knew a duck could grab bread with other bread stuffed in its beak, like a chipmunk. They came right up to Lilly and Earl, but they kept their distance from Ay; they would get close, but if he tried to lure them from the water, they wouldn't go for it till he retreated a step or two. Then they would lunge, grab the morsel, and fall back beyond the safety of the waterline.

A scatter of people showed up at the ramp and dropped boats in the water; they quickly made their way upstream, past the Belvidere-Riverton bridge and beyond, out of sight to find the sweet spot that fishermen never reveal. There were no jet-skiers or swimmers, it was early in the year and the water was still too cold, except for the diehards, who must have stayed home. It was just the three of them sharing the river with Al and the rest of the birds.

"What'd you tell Sam?"

"I told him that Al was back; he was so happy for Earl. Everyone knows about Al. Earl insisted that you meet Al; he was afraid Al would leave before you saw him. I have no idea what he sees in you; in thirty-nine years he's never has acted this way with anybody, except my mother. So I...."

"It must be the irresistible charm."

Lilly ignored him and continued as if she hadn't been interrupted.

"So I told him I would take care of it; I called Sam and said you would be back in on Monday. I hope that was okay."

"Well, what if it wasn't?"

Cord asked playfully.

"Too bad."

Was all Lilly said, deadpan.

Cord smiled; that was the smart-ass answer he expected, and that was the answer he wanted from her.

"Why were you involved in that mess in the Park? What were you doing there?"

She asked, but she didn't wait for C to answer.

"You know, I had no idea that bullshit with Buck was still going on. I guess Marty was afraid to tell me, and Earl would never say anything – he wouldn't have wanted me to hurt Buck. And he's right; I would have killed that fucker had I known."

Cord wasn't sure if that was an idle threat, but he wouldn't want to be the one at the other end, testing the theory.

She continued.

"You know that little fuck used to be in my house a couple times a week when he was about six years old. His real name is Bill, like his father, but no one ever called him that, or Junior either. Not sure where *Buck* came from....stupid name. He was the only kid they had, which was a good thing.

They lived two doors down from us, out on Fourth Street, a block off the Park. His mom did shift work, multiple jobs, the dad was long gone, that dirtbag left when Buck was two, maybe three.

[Lilly had crouched and was writing her name in the sand with a short, bent stick she found along the shore. She wrote in neat, careful script, as she recounted the story – she would write it, cross it out, and write it again, each time in a slightly different way or size , over and over.]

Anyway, she was nice enough, she worked hard and tried to be responsible. I liked her, and she trusted me, and she especially trusted Earl, so she would throw us babysitting money to watch the little monkey.

The kid got the dad's genes, that's for sure; he was always a troublemaker. But he loved Earl, like a father figure I guess, or maybe just a big brother, and never acted up for him. For *me,* now that was a whole different story; that little shit would get under my skin like you wouldn't believe.

He used to eat with his mouth wide open. God, I could have ripped his tongue out; the sound of slapping food would drive me fucking nuts.

Now, when he was alone with Earl and I, he never would do it; he actually wouldn't even speak when he was around me alone – he was too afraid. He would just sit quietly and try not to move or do anything to piss me off. Then, he was actually tolerable.

But the minute his mother came through the door to pick him up, he would shove some food in his mouth, anything he could quickly find, and start chewing with his mouth wide open, exaggerated chewing, so I could see right down his fucking throat. All the while hugging his mother's leg for protection and smiling at me with a shit-eating grin, mocking me. I swear that kid must have hidden stashes of food all over the house, so it would be nearby, no matter where he was, just so he could get it into his mouth in front of me as quick as possible when his mom came through the front door.

Little fucker, I wanted to throttle him; man, did that kid get under my skin. *[Cord thought to himself that getting under Lilly's skin didn't take much doing by anyone – case in point – although he had to agree about the open mouth thing]*

I could never believe his mother would allow him to do that; but honestly, she was so frazzled all the time, it wasn't high on the list, so to speak.

[Lilly was shaking her head as she spoke, getting herself annoyed all over again thinking about that kid chewing with an open mouth – that was over ten years ago – this girl just never let go, never].

Why I didn't beat that kid to a pulp the next time I watched him I don't know; I guess I'm too good a person. *[Lilly looked up to the sky in a reflective manner and sighed, pondering the rhetorical question. Cord looked at her in disbelief – waiting for her to smile, to give him the wink and nod that confirmed the obvious joke – it never came. My God, now that was truly scary].*

I put up with it because we needed the money, and Earl loved Buck, why I have no idea *[she shook her head slowly side-to-side in disbelief as she said it].* He used to play all sorts of games with him, hide-n-seek and shit. It was hard to tell who was more excited when they got together.

After about a year of watching the brat, she got a boyfriend with a good job and decent money and didn't need the babysitting anymore. And that was the end of that *[Lilly stood up, tossed the stick in the water and rubbed out her names with the front part of her shoe]*.

You know, years later, long after he stopped being friendly to Earl, Buck used the get the shit kicked out of him in middle school by bigger troublemakers; then he would tell them Earl was his best friend and would pound them if they didn't stop. Now Earl would never do any such thing, and most of them knew it, but just in case they were wrong, and that little shit was pretty convincing, they would stop picking on him, just in case.

And now he does this shit to Earl. You know, Earl would have never told me something happened in the Park today, he would still protect him, because he knows I would kill him. I bet if you asked Earl, he would still say he loves Billy; he would call him Billy, never Buck, just Billy, like when he was a little kid *[Lilly shook her head in disgust]*."

Cord picked up a rock and skipped it across the water; shitty throw, only three skips.

Swarms of gnats hovered just above the surface, moving en masse to and fro. Dimples on the water surface, like raindrops falling, sprouted from below; unseen fish picking off low-flyers. Occasionally, a fish would arch and breach the surface; some looked to be pretty God-damn big.

By this time, Earl had taken off his boots and socks, rolled up his pant legs as far as he could, which wasn't very far due to the size of his calves, and had waded into the water to the bottom of his pants, to get a little closer to Al.

Lilly told him to be careful; the river bottom drops off quick. Earl shot her an annoyed look, making it obvious he knew that.

"Well, you never answered my question?"

Lilly declared, from nowhere.

Cord smirked and shook his head; he hadn't answered because she hadn't taken a breath for the past ten minutes, griping about Buck.

He spoke before she changed her mind.

"I'd seen the Park, on a sign, on the way into Town, and went looking for it this morning. I'd planned on having a quiet morning reading the paper and drinking a cup of coffee. So, I found the Park, found a bench, sat down and started reading my paper. Pretty boring stuff, and the Park was empty."

Cord laughed to himself at that thought of having a quiet morning as he tossed another stone; this one was a nice flat disk and skipped a good five times, his best so far.

"Then this big guy comes out of nowhere and plants his ass right next to me on my bench."

Cord pointed over to Earl as he said it; Earl wasn't paying a bit of attention to either of them.

"That's Earl's bench; Earl always sits on *that* bench."

Lilly added, as if Cord needed the clarification.

"Thanks for the input. Anyway, I didn't know it was *Earl's bench*; I didn't even know it was Earl, but by Sam's description, I figured that's who it must be. I found out I was right when the three dipshits came into the Park."

"What'd they do to Earl?"

Lilly knew the general answer, and didn't really want to hear the details, but she asked anyway, in a somewhat hesitant manner.

"According to Marty, they did the same thing they always apparently did; they took Earl's food, and he just sat there with his head down *[Cord shook his head to himself]*. Earl is such a good person; you only need to know him for a minute to figure that out. Anyway, it wasn't about the food, it was about three losers trying to make themselves feel like they matter. I just did what you would have done, although it was probably a bit mild to your taste."

"It didn't look mild."

And with that, Lilly smiled at him.

Cord was amazed how a simple affirmation, how a small smile from Lilly could make him feel so good. He moved the conversation forward, trying to change gears.

"What's up between you and Carol, the landlord?"

Cord knew he was treading on potentially dangerous turf; surprisingly, Lilly answered in a civil manner.

"She moved into Town in the early '90's; that house had been empty for a couple years, it was the old Beaumont place, he was the local vet – had his pet office in the basement.

We always thought that house was haunted growing up, all sorts of animal ghosts in there, the ones who never made it out of old Doc Beaumont's basement alive. He was creepy. Earl and my mom used to sit on their bench, the one you sat on, and look at the house telling each other cat, dog and hamster ghost stories, Earl had hamsters and gerbils as a kid, so he wanted to tell scary stories about them too. Some of the stories were pretty good, my mom's, and some were pretty corny – Earl's; I mean how scary can a fucking hamster story really be, for Christ's sake? And then there was Earl's famous dinosaur dream story; he got a lot of mileage from that one. I bet Earl remembers every one of them to this day. He loves telling ghost stories and being scared.

The Beaumont's retired to Naples, down in Florida, or maybe Marco Island, some stupid place down there that all the old, wrinkly people go to get warm, before they croak.

I don't know where *she* came from, but she came alone, and has been alone in that house ever since. For what, fourteen years now, I can't believe I've put up with her for that long.

I never see any guys, or girls for that matter, ever come there to see her, not that I pay any fucking attention to it *[Lilly spit the words with such distaste, Cord figured she paid a great deal of attention to it]*.

She's not there a lot, she supposedly has another house somewhere else, but who knows, she certainly doesn't talk to anyone in this Town. I'm not sure why she's even here; I wish she would just go."

"Why, what has she ever done to you?"

Lilly didn't answer right away, she was thinking about that one; the facial didn't look good.

"What, are you, her fucking buddy now, because she fawned all over you on her porch? Give me a break."

"She didn't fawn over me; in fact, she belittled me, kind of like you; two peas in a pod."

"Don't compare me to that bitch."

Cord looked at her incredulously and raised his right hand.

"You're right, how could anyone call you a bitch?"

"I don't like how she treats Earl."

Lilly said emphatically, kicking at the sand; that was the best answer she was going to give him.

Cord wouldn't let her get away with that.

"She actually treats Earl fine; she's nice to him, and you should see the smile on his face when she…"

"Oh, for Christ's sake, give me a break; like she's so good-looking. She thinks every guy in Town wants to get her in the sack because she has money and a fancy car."

Ah, now Cord was getting to the heart of the matter, and he was right on his first guess – competition.

"Well, yeah, that helps, but the fact is she *is* pretty hot. And I bet she likes boys, but if she likes girls too, that's even better. You know, while we were standing there on her porch, your brother and I both couldn't keep our eyes off that chest of hers; we talked about it at length and we both think your wrong, they're definitely the real thing."

Cord was shaking the soda bottle; she was about ready to pop. Why he felt the need to tweak Lilly was beyond him, but he did it anyway. Stupid move.

"You….were talking about her *tits*….with **my** brother, on her porch? Forget it, you are **not** hanging out with Earl any more; *you're fucking done*….cut off."

Cord turned to look at Earl.

"Hey Earl, can I come with you next month to see Carol and drop off the rent?"

Earl quickly turned around, sporting a huge smile.

"Yeah! You can bring your rent too; we can do it together! Maybe she'll ask me more about you and Bibby!"

"Earl, I don't think it's a good idea to drop the rent off like that; we should just mail it when it's due, like everyone else."

Lilly said it half-hearted, hoping she might get a longshot okay from Earl.

Earl didn't say a word; his smile vanished and he looked at Lilly like he lost his best friend in the world. He started to put his head down.

Lilly couldn't take that sad-sack look for more than a few seconds.

"Okay, okay, just deliver the rent. But why do you have to go with *him*?"

And with that, she fingered Cord hard in the chest; that actually hurt, he thought to himself, as he let out a little reflex grunt.

"Because he's my friend."

Cord smiled, not at Lilly, but at Earl.

Earl didn't see him; he had turned back to watch Al. Now that he was still going to deliver the monthly rent, he was content again.

"Earl, how can he be your *friend*; you've known him, for what, two hours?"

Earl turned around again and looked at Lilly with sad eyes.

"How long do I hafta wait till I can call him my friend?"

Lilly just stared at Earl for a moment, then she turned her eyes to Cord and frowned.

"Just forget the whole thing."

"Hey Earl, what do you want to do tomorrow? I don't have to work."

Flush with victory, Cord went on the offensive.

Earl turned to face them.

"Let's see if Al is still here!"

"Okay, you got it; we'll bring down some tunes, some bread for the ducks and hang out together! Maybe we can see if Carol will give us a ride in that *Spider* of hers, so we can go out to dinner; after hanging with Al all day, we'll be so hungry, *we could eat a baby's butt through a park bench!*"

"Hey, that's from *Neighbors*!!"

Earl shouted.

Cord smiled and said.

"There aren't too many people walking around who know that, Earl, besides you and me, that's for sure."

Lilly looked at him with astonishment; she was too shocked to be angry – yet.

"You are *so* gay; how *old* are you?"

Cord just looked at her with a goofy, shit-eating grin. He was winning the battle, and he knew it.

She turned to Earl and launched a counter.

"Hey, you got stuff to do around the house Earl; you got to help me with the dishes, the laundry. I'm not doing all that by myself while you're running around with nerd-boy here."

"Right, the dishes, the laundry; hey Earl, how bout I come over tonight and we'll do whatever you need to do, so we can *go out and play* tomorrow – what do you say?"

"You aren't coming into *my* place."

Lilly said indignantly.

"Earl, can I come over tonight?"

"Sure."

"I got some good ghost stories to tell."

"Really?"

"You bet."

"What are you doing?"

Lilly barked at Cord.

"What are y*ou* doing?"

Cord retorted.

She didn't respond, she just folded her arms across her chest and looked out at the water and stewed.

They both stood in silence for a couple minutes.

"What are you mad at me for? Just because Earl likes Carol and wants to be friends with me? Things could be worse."

"Hardly."

"Why did you move into that apartment anyway, if you don't…."

And with that, the soda bottle blew.

"What is this, twenty fucking questions? How about this: it's none of your God-damn business! And don't go asking Earl; it's none of your *fucking* business, period. You saw the bird, now get the fuck out of here and leave *us* alone; that's right, **us**, this isn't a threesome."

She looked at him with a truly angry face; man, she could turn on a dime. This wasn't playful banter anymore, she was pissed and wasn't kidding around.

He pushed it a bit too far, like usual; looks like he was back to square one. *Fuck.*

Wasn't he winning this debate? How did he go from victory to road kill in less than ten seconds?

Now what should he do?

He felt awkward standing there, in the middle of their bird feeding session, knowing Lilly wanted him gone, and Earl not really paying attention to the whole kerfuffle. But he wasn't going to run away either, just because she said he had to.

He stood there for what seemed like eternity, just looking out at the water, trying to figure out what to do next, how to exit with some self-respect, some dignity.

The remaining duck bread was nearby, but the mallards had moved seventy-five feet upstream, to where the Pequest River dumps into the Delaware. The water churns there, and the ducks were bobbing in the choppy white water, looking for food and enjoying the turbulence.

Earl was in another world, engaged with Al; he could apparently watch him for hours. Just then, Al popped up with a baby river eel, writhing in his bill; he tossed it up a bit and down the gullet it went.

"Hey, guys, did you see that! Al caught an eel!"

Earl didn't turn around as he spoke, afraid he might miss some of the action. It broke the tension a bit, so Cord tried to regain lost ground.

"I'm sorry, none of my business."

C said, belated, and sheepish; no response from Lilly.

Lilly still had her arms folded across her chest, looking out over the river, at nothing. Inside she seethed; why did she say *anything* about her mother; she never spoke about her mother to anyone, even Earl, and here she was babbling about her and the rest of her stupid life to this idiot she didn't even know. She was pissed about that more than anything else.

She only half-heard what Cord said, not that she would have answered him anyway.

How many times was he going to be shellacked by her, he thought to himself; then he got mad at her being mad at him.

"Whatever…."

He said, loud enough for her to hear.

Still no response.

He took off his boots and socks, and walked down to the water's edge and stepped in – damn, that water was cold.

He stood there for a minute or so, just looking up and down the stream, feeling pretty conspicuous, and foolish.

Why was he hanging around?

Because he liked being around her, that was the real answer, although only someone with a lobotomy would want to continue to be belittled by her – someone like him, apparently.   And he liked being around Earl too. But, if he had to be honest with himself, at this stage in the game, she was the stronger draw.

"Hey Earl, I'm gonna go unpack; thanks for helping me with the boxes. I'm glad Al came back."

"Okay. Hey, what time are you coming over tonight?"

Cord looked at Lilly and coyly responded, through a frown.

"I don't know Earl, we'll see about that later."

"Tonight's not a good night, Earl, we've got a lot of stuff to do."

She said, arms still folded across her stomach as she was looking out at the water. There was no *we'll-see-about-that-later* in her look.

"Okay."

Was all Earl said, his back still turned; he didn't put up a fight for Cord.

Well, I guess that's that, Cord thought to himself. I got to get the fuck out of here; this is embarrassing, and a waste of time.

He walked over to put on his shoes. He pulled off his tee-shirt to dry his feet; he didn't want to keep it off long, he didn't like the shape his stomach was in, and he didn't need to give her more ammunition.

Then, out of nowhere, as he was bent over, his bowels started to grumble.

Oh no, he remembered he hadn't taken a dump this morning; he was *way* past due, and the coffee he drank was a natural laxative – he was actually surprised he made it this long without soiling himself.

Ohh, there it went again; this was quickly becoming an emergency. He started to cramp and his butthole was quivering. No way he was holding this one in for the five block walk back to the apartment.

He quickly dried his feet, stood up and turned away from her. As he was putting on his socks and boots, he could feel those dagger eyes on him, he just knew it.

He quickly turned around, and was right as rain; she was looking, but it was at the countless scars on his sides and back, similar to the ones on his chest. Normally she would have turned away when he spun around – God forbid him catching her looking at him, but the voyeur in her couldn't stop looking at all those scars. She said nothing and made no eye contact with him.

What the hell was that all about, she thought to herself; it was like the guy was cut up and sewn back together. She never saw anything quite like that; but rather than turning her off, it made her wildly curious. What's this guy's story?

He put his shirt back on, but was a bit hunched over; he couldn't stand up straight – the cramps were debilitating. No way was he going to make it back to the apartment in this condition….no way.

Jesus, how did he continue to get himself in these ridiculous situations with her?

He stood about fifteen feet from her; he tried to move nonchalant further away from her, without making it look too obvious. Extra space was a good thing.

He figured he needed to let go a bit of pressure, a little fart, and hope to God it wasn't wet; if he soiled himself in front of her he was getting right back on the bus.

He figured he'd try to let out a little test gas, to see if it would be:

- wet;
- loud; and/or
- foul.

He knew everyone did it – everyone. On a date, in the theater, on the plane, at work (you want some companionship in your office – let one rip – someone will immediately walk in, guaranteed), in the car, in bed; there should be a formal term for the test-fart process, it shouldn't be nameless.

Even Lilly must have done it at one time or another, he rationalized to himself. But, unfortunately, now it was time for him to do it. Why couldn't it be her, and not him, not now.

His mind was racing; it's really not that easy to do. He had to unclench his cheeks just enough, but not too much – too much would be disastrous. And there are no take-backs in this game; once she hears it, smells it or sees it, she might as well scrawl loser, weirdo, whatever, on his forehead; he would be done….just crawl in a hole and never come out.

He hoped to God she still wasn't looking at him. As he stood there, he pretended to readjust his boots on his feet and fix his shirt, when he was really in pretest mode.

Here it goes; he relaxed the buttocks and gingerly made a small, gentle push.

Please, please, don't be a loser….please.

It appeared to be a success! No wet residue in his briefs, only a slight muffled sound that was far too low for her to hear, and most important, no odor.

Bingo, relief was in sight.   At least something went right; but when you have to count a safe fart as a success, the bar is set pretty low.

If he could just relieve a little more pressure, he could walk upright, and should be able to hoof it back to the apartment and unload on the can; that was the plan.

But, unfortunately, he didn't wait long enough for the waft to reach his nose on that test run, and he proceeded prematurely – his cramps hurt too badly to delay any longer.

Still, the next one was not wet shot and only a muffled noise ensued, but the third criteria was a big, mephitic failure. He had never smelled anything come out of his ass quite like this; it was absolutely rank. Jesus, that was *really* bad, he thought, as he tried to discretely get away from himself.

Thank goodness Lilly was now a good thirty feet away and not speaking to him; the last place she would want to be is anywhere near him.

He hoped the stink would quickly dissipate and travel downstream, away from her, and him, for that matter. He turned to start up the boat ramp, when, with horror, he saw Lilly coming right at him.

Holy shit, what was she doing? He had to think fast. Why was she coming at him?

He looked down; the remaining loaf of bread for the ducks was sitting by his feet. He quickly grabbed it and went to throw it to her.

"Here, stay there – catch!"

He yelled loud; she was getting too close, too quick.

She was in no mood to play catch voluntarily, so he forced the issue, and lobbed the loaf of bread at her, awkwardly hitting her in the upper chest and neck with it.

It annoyed her, but it didn't stop her.

"What the hell are you doing?"

Just as she said it, he knew it was too late.

As if in slow motion, he saw her nostrils flare, like an enraged bull; it wasn't a happy look. Her whole face contorted in utter disgust – just like he did when that short, Jesus-looking guy farted in his face yesterday on the way into Town.

His fingers and toes started to tingle, like they do when you're a kid, nervous, not knowing how to get out of whatever mess you're in. He frantically looked around for someone, something, anything to blame; but he was alone. A dead duck.

"I told you to stay over there!"

Was all he come up with.

She shook her head violently and uttered an unintelligible sound, quickly shuffling away to find fresh air.

"That smells just like chicken shit! You are a **pig!**"

"Actually, wouldn't I be a chicken?"

It just came into his head; she didn't think it was funny.

"Earl, you remember going to Bobby Gill's farm as kids and he had that long, chicken coop; remember how that place smelled? Do you remember when you fell down in a big chicken-shit pile; you couldn't get the stink off for days."

"Yuck!"

Earl yelled from the river, remembering the incident vividly.

"Yeah, that's right, *yuck*; it was disgusting – just like your new friend's *ass!* You better not stink up the apartment buddy, or I'm getting your ass thrown out – no pun intended. Man, that's fucking nasty, I can't believe you smell just like Gill's chicken farm; I haven't smelled that stench in twenty-five years."

"Well come on over here and I'll give you another shot of the memory."

Cord said as he started to walk away. He was beyond embarrassment; there was nothing to do but walk away. He wasn't going to apologize again; time to check the bus schedule.

"I didn't fall in the poop pile, Lilly, you pushed me."

Earl added, after he thought about it a bit.

"I don't remember that, Earl, you're making it up."

"Am not, you did it on purpose too, you were laughing."

Lilly didn't answer Earl; she wasn't done with Cord.

"I can't believe you did that!"

She said as he started to walk away.

"I didn't plan it – I *told* you to stay away, and of course you listened, just like you always do to anything I say. Serves you right."

With that he headed up the boat ramp and back to the apartment.

"See you later Earl."

Cord said, without turning around.

"Bye."

Was all Earl said, as he continued watching his bird working the river.

CHAPTER 21 – BUTTON PIERCE

Cord was out of sight.

Lilly picked up the bread, but she didn't feed the ducks; she was only going for it in the first place to see if Cord would try to talk to her again. She certainly wasn't going to talk to him first, but she would be nice enough to give him another chance to talk to her.

She wasn't expecting that kind of greeting.

Part of her wanted to believe he somehow did that on purpose; but she knew he really didn't. She felt bad for him, actually; she knew how embarrassed he must have been.

She guessed she could have been a bit nicer; she decided to give him another chance to forgive himself.

Lilly turned to look at Earl standing in the water. The ice cold water didn't bother him in the least.

"Hey Earl, what did he tell you about himself?"

"Who?"

"You know who, stop playing games; what did he say?"

"Nothing."

"We'll he had to say something. What did he say when you walked over to drop off the rent."

"Nothing."

"What did he say to Carol?"

"He said he was a friend of the family."

"Really? What is that suppose to mean? Does he *know* us? Is that all?"

"Yep."

"What did you do at the Post Office?

"We picked up two boxes and brought them back to his apartment; we ran the whole way, because you called."

"He wanted to see me?"

Lilly said high-pitched, anticipating the response.

"No, I wanted him to meet Al."

"Oh, right."

"Did he say anything about how he got all those scars?"

"What scars?"

"What scars! Are you kidding me? You didn't see the scars all over his body?"

"Nope."

"Well, did you notice if he had a cell phone, a watch, a wallet, *anything*; did he pick up any mail at the Post Office?"

"I already told ya, just two boxes; the one he said we could open when she tells him to."

"What do ya mean? When who tells him to? Who's she?"

Earl raised his shoulders once; an *I don't know* shrug to all three questions. Then he answered.

"It said on it, on the box, he writes very neat, in big black letters:

Open When You Are Ready

[Earl moved his pointer finger across the sky as he said it, like the bouncing ball following the words in a sentence]

So I asked him if we could open it now, and he said not yet, but soon, when she tells him to."

Lilly froze.

That same stanza haunted her for the past twenty-five years, since she was just sixteen years old, standing in the hallway, listening to those whispered words leave her mother's lips, as she died in Lillian's arms. That fateful phrase defined Lilly to this day....who she was....and who she wasn't.

"What did you say?"

Earl looked quick at Lilly; he knew that tone, and it usually meant trouble.

"Am I in trouble?"

He breathed, afraid of her answer.

She just looked at him blank, trying to process.

Earl put his head down, waiting to get yelled at; he knew too well the instant anger that followed that tone.

And he was scared.

Lilly just stood motionless, staring at Earl; she was breathing quickly, in short breathes, trying to think.

She thought about those words *every* day of her life; they haunted her. But now it was out in the open, in discussion, rather than crouching quietly, hidden behind a curtain in the back of her brain.

And she was scared.

"Earl, what does that mean – *Open When You Are Ready*? What does that **mean**? **Why** did his box say that? Did it say **exactly** that? Who is *she* Earl? **Who is she**?! **Answer me!**"

Lilly was flailing her arms wild as she spoke, and had no idea she was doing so.

Earl didn't answer, he just put his head up to look at her. He was crying.

"I'm sorry the box said that Bibby."

Tears were streaming down Earl's cheeks; he was trembling.

Lilly ran into the shallows, shoes and all, hugging Earl hard.

"I'm sorry I scared you Sweetie; I didn't mean to yell at you, you didn't do anything wrong."

She stood for a minute in silence holding him; she was hugging him for her as much as for him, until he stopped crying, stopped shaking. When she was sure he was okay, she quietly whispered to him.

"Earl, my feet are freezing."

With that, he put his arm around her waist, picked her straight up, as if she was air, and walked her out of the water on his hip.

"Why are you so mad at that box, Bibby?"

"I'm not mad, I just got caught off guard a bit; those words kinda mean something to me, but it isn't important, don't worry about it."

Lilly stood silent, thinking hard while she dried her shoes and pant legs with a towel she brought for Earl; she knew he would end up in the water at some point trying to get closer to Al – he always did. She didn't think *she* would.

Lillian started mumbling as she dried herself, the words getting louder and the toweling more vigorous, as the thoughts progressed.

"What kind of guy says he's a friend of the family, when he isn't, and walks around without a wallet, or a phone or anything, just some big bills in his pocket and a stupid note? And why does he have those scars all over his body, like Frankenstein? And *why would someone write that on a box?*"

Now Earl figured she was angry at the towel, whipping it around in a frenzy, trying unsuccessful to dry river-soaked shoes and pant cuffs.

She stopped, threw the towel to the sand and placed a hand on each hip. She was agitated.

"What did the box look like, Earl?"

"A box."

"I *know* that, how big was it? What did it look like? Did he say what was in it?"

 As Lilly spoke, the words came ever faster and louder.

Earl started getting scared again, and answered her in a timid voice.

"I don't know, I don't know, it was just a brown box, kinda big, but not real big, but not small; it had lots of tape on it."

Lilly stopped when she saw Earl getting flustered again. She thought for a bit, and tried a different tact.

"Earl, where did you put the key to Mr. Boeman's apartment, when you used to watch his cats?"

"Why?"

"Just where is it, Earl."

"You weren't allowed to watch his cats, just me; he didn't like you."

"That's because he was a dirty old man, always trying to look down my blouse or up my skirt, and I told him so. Now, where are the keys?"

"You aren't going snooping in Cord's apartment looking for that box Lilly – I'm telling!"

"Earl, I'm not going snooping….the keys?"

"No!"

"**Earl**, we don't know *anything* about him; he was asking all sorts of questions about you and me, but we don't know *anything* about him. All we know is his name, if that's even his real name; what kind of name is Cord, or Ay, whatever….those aren't real names. And where does he live?"

"Upstairs."

She looked at Earl annoyed; a frown framed her face.

"I *know* that, I mean before; and why is he here? And what's in that box? And why is he working at Sam's?

And why did he help you in the Park and say he was a friend of the family? And what's in that box? And why does he have all those scars?   And who is *she*? Something is going on, and I am going to find out what – I don't trust that guy - **and what's in that *fucking* box**?"

Lilly told herself to just breathe, take it easy and stop thinking so much. She wasn't sure she even completely believed there was some grand conspiracy, but she was getting herself all worked up thinking about it. The note on that box scared up issues she would rather forget, and intoxicated her at the same time; maybe it was some sort of sign.

The wording couldn't be just a coincidence, could it? Not that wording, it couldn't be, that's not regular wording. And who would ever write that on a box? Nobody would, unless it was some sort of sign, some sort of message.

"Well, we'll just see what the Internet has to say about Mr. Brin."

She said under her breath.

Intoxication won.

"Where's the key, Earl?"

"I'm not telling! Stop asking, 'cause I'm not telling!"

She let it drop; she knew just where he hid the stuff he didn't want her to find, including the *Kama Sutra* how-to book and all those old girlie magazines, circa-1980, Earl found in the dumpster when the Saunders house burned down out on Sixth Street, back in the Fall of the same year.

Earl had been looking at, and hiding, that Hindu sex position book (sixty-four positions, explained in entirely too much detail, in eight different categories) and those same old *Oui*, *Swank*, *Playboy* and *Penthouse* magazines for the past twenty-six years, thinking Lilly didn't know a lick about them. Little did he know she found them all the very first day he brought them home in 1980; she smelled something smoky in the house, and followed her nose to the little crawlspace under the old second floor bathtub in the house on Fourth Street. Now, in the apartment, Earl hid them in the back of his armoire.

She bet the third floor key was right there with them.

"Earl, I'm cold; I'm going back home. Are you going to stay with Al for awhile?"

"Yeah, I want to stay. What are we having for dinner?"

"What do you want?"

"How 'bout flank steak, lots of steak, with the yellow rice and mushrooms, and mashed potatoes, and corn, and rolls, and string beans, and peanut butter cup ice cream?"

Earl said smiling; that's all he could think of, for now.

"Are you done? Are you sure that's enough?"

Lilly said sarcastically.

Earl just smiled at her.

"Okay, I'll stop and see Sam on my way home."

"Is Cord coming over tonight, Bibby?"

"Not tonight Earl, I want to do a little homework first, okay, and clean up the apartment, then maybe we can have him over, okay?"

"Okay."

Lilly asked him to walk into the shoreline, the water was too cold, which he did. She gave him a big hug and a kiss on the cheek and told him to stay close to the shore. Even though the water was running smooth and low, the current was tricky.

Earl shook his head in the affirmative to let her know he listened. He knew from his mom not to go in passed his knees; it got deep quick, with lots of hidden rocks and snags - roots and sunken tree limbs – and the underwater currents were strong, even when the river looked tranquil.

Al kept working – he wasn't tired; neither was Earl. Lilly fished a folding chair out of the woods and sat it on the water's edge – the front two legs submerged in the water, just as Earl liked it, just as her mom used to do for him. She kept two chairs in the same spot, leaned against the same tree that their mother did.

A bass boat was slowly tracking down the ramp to launch, its back-up horn bleating at Lilly; Al flew over to a dead tree river-side and waited for the imposter to pass. Earl sat in the chair and ate some of the semi-stale duck bread right out of the bag; he was hungry.

Lilly went on her way; she had some research to do.

Cord got back to the apartment, clicked the door open and went in. He kicked off his boots and socks and shook his head as he walked down the hall; how did he forever find himself in these situations - that was beyond embarrassing.

When you go out with a new someone, what's the last thing you can't do, because it's embarrassing? Fart – it's a universal fact. You could be having anal sex, or ass-to-mouth sex for that matter, but God forbid, don't fart – too embarrassing. It made no sense, but it was true. He didn't know why, but it was usually the last rite of passage in a relationship; if you could blow in front of your partner without shame or embarrassment, regardless of the stank, you could do just about anything….the relationship had reached maturity.

And here it was, he launched the nastiest bomb he could remember, and a hot girl he likes walked right into it; the timing couldn't have been better if he tried. How come stuff like that never happens to girls?

He fell onto the bed and stared at the ceiling; good God, has it only been two days in paradise?

He heard the hallway door open; someone was coming up the steps. Too light a tread for Earl. He quickly ran to the door and cracked it, just in time to see her standing at the second floor landing with two white plastic bags of *Sam's* groceries in her hand; she slipped in the key and stepped into the apartment.

As much as he wanted to hate her, or just ignore her, he couldn't.

He tried to follow her sound as she walked around; if she kept her shoes on, he figured, he might be able to track her through the apartment. He felt embarrassed, like a little kid spying; but that didn't stop him from laying down and pressing his ear on the wood floorboards, frozen in place, straining to pick up any stray sound.

"How *old* are you?"

He replayed her question in his head; right about now, he felt like he was all of fourteen, but he couldn't help himself.

She went into the back room; he assumed it was the kitchen (it was directly below his kitchen) and he heard the water run. Then she went into the front bedroom – toward the road. Damn, he was in the rear bedroom; he guessed he was sleeping above Earl. He would have to move his bedroom to the front, above her, he thought.

Lilly went over to the armoire, parted the doors and slowly drew open the lower drawer. There, all the way in the back left, nestled under a couple of shirts Earl never wore, was the *Kama Sutra* book and the nudie mags, six of them, vintage 1980.

The magazines each had a mix of individual woman spreads, some twosomes and group sex shoots, especially in the *Penthouse, Swank* and *Oui* magazines; she remembered liking *Oui* the best. *Playboy* was lame; *Swank* was a bit gross at times, even for her.

When she used to be in a studious mood, she would crack the Indian how-to book; it was pretty thorough, explaining in excruciating step-by-step the do's and don'ts of the eight major positions, each with eight variations, hence the sixty-four count. It also explained forty different ways to kiss, all from the 4th Century to boot. Crazy. To this day, she never figured where that book came from or how Earl first got his hands on it, snookering it into hiding all these years.

The sex positions had cool names like *butterfly*, the *congress of a cow* (doggie-style); *leapfrog, congress of the crow* (69), *black bee, stag, Medusa, clinging creeper, thunderbolt, tigress*, and her three personal favorites – the *cowgirl, 21* and *tossing the salad*. She had done all the acrobatics over the years, her own little checklist, though she could never remember the names.

But when she got to the two-page, step-by-step for *coital alignment*, her eyes would glaze. Lilly was a visual person; she did much better with the pictures.

She used to smile when she saw little pencil marks next to the positions, with some sort of coding: stars, checks, numbers and letters – some secret Earl-language. Why he took notes over the past twenty-plus years she wasn't sure. Earl was thirty-nine and never had a girlfriend; he would just assume die than talk to a pretty girl, except for Carol, that is *[Carol wasn't really that pretty, Lilly reasoned to herself].* And with her, it was only a handful of words in the last three years.

However, with Cord around, who knows what Earl would do; she frowned at the thought. Cord was going to be a bad influence; he already was.

Lilly had used Earl's magazines to masturbate countless times over the years; ever since the advent of the Internet, however, the rags were passé; she used the free porn sites with teaser videos to get off. She hadn't looked at Earl's magazines in the last five, maybe seven years, she thought; Jesus, it had been a long time since she came to this pile of paper.

She wasn't sure if Earl actually ever jerked-off to the pictures; she never caught him. God, she couldn't say the same thing for herself; Earl nabbed her, directly and indirectly, countless times, last night included.

She remembers whenever he parked in the second floor bathroom out on Fourth Street, and the *visit* passed the fifteen-minute mark, he knew he invariably had fished the magazines or *Kama Sutra* out from the crawlspace beneath the bathtub.

But when she tried to listen through the door, which she did more than she would admit over the years, she only ever heard him flipping the pages; there was never any heavy breathing or hand-on-shaft friction. Occasionally she would hear him snicker under his breath, but that was it. When he eventually came out of the john, he never had a hard-on. Lilly couldn't figure it out. If she had ever asked him, she was sure Earl would have died of embarrassment, so she let it go.

Lilly, temporarily distracted from her pursuit of Cord's apartment key, picked up the February, 1980 *Oui* and flipped to her favorite spread; a girl-girl-guy threesome….but it wasn't really a threesome.

The girl was positioned on her back at the end of the bed, spread-eagle, her legs held wide apart at the ankles, while the guy stood at the foot of the bed and pumped her *[a modified butterfly perhaps? She smiled to herself]*.

All the while, the other girl was hiding in a nearby bedroom closet, watching the two through a slightly opened folding door and rubbing her pussy, masturbating *[there was no name in Kama Sutra for that one, she smirked]*.

Lilly always liked that bedroom setup; she had a few lesbian flings years ago and would have liked doing a threesome, girl-girl-guy. But the situation never arose. Not that she wouldn't jump at the chance if the table was set; when it came to sex, Lilly wasn't shy.

The *Oui* article never explained the setup of the scene, so Lilly made up her own liaisons over the years to help her come:

- The little sister was in the closet, sneaking a peak at her older sister and boyfriend balling;
- The girlfriend was in the closet, watching her best friend and her best friend's boyfriend fuck;
- The girlfriend watching from the closet, while she *lets* her best friend do her boyfriend – and the boyfriend knows he is being given a freebie – *lucky dog*; or
- Same scenario, but the boyfriend *doesn't* know he is being watched and fucks the best friend anyway – *cheating bastard.*

When Lilly fantasized about that last scenario, her favorite, it usually ended with the two girls *punishing* the boyfriend - sometimes tying him up and making him face the wall, so he couldn't watch while the girls went at it - other times making him watch, a helpless cuckold, while they both balled another guy, or some other variation on that theme.

Lilly spent a lot of time thinking about sex.

And now, Lilly focuses on that last variation; she smiled thinking about it while she dropped her hand down to her crotch and used her middle finger to put pressure on her clit. She decided to stop thinking about Cord's box for a bit.

There were other fantasies she concocted for that bedroom threesome, including several versions of who the guy and girls were, people that Lilly knew, that she would never admit to. But when it came time to daydream, the unspoken, darker, versions were the ones that ultimately surfaced. She came to them almost immediately, felt ashamed about it and vowed to never think of them again, until the next time, when she invariably would use it to come again. They were a taboo elixir; irresistible.

She must have looked at that set of threesome photos a hundred-plus times over the years, but she still could get excited thinking she was in that scene. It felt more exciting now, "rediscovering" it after so many years; it brought back a flood of memories.

She closed her eyes and felt her pussy throb below her finger. She pushed a little harder, and slowly moved her finger up and down, caressing the side of her clit. God, that felt good.

Cord was falling asleep lying on the floor, waiting for something, anything, to happen; what the hell was she doing? What the hell was *he* doing?

With that, he realized just how ridiculous it was for him to be lying on the floor like a kid, listening, for something; what that something was, he wasn't quite sure.

He got up in a huff, brushed himself off, and headed for the kitchen to snag a knife. Then he turned for the front room, to unpack. Time to give his brain a bit of a rest from analyzing and re-analyzing the nutty girl downstairs.

He sliced open the box, unfolded the cardboard and stared at the contents.

This is it – should he unpack? Was he going to stick around? Or should he just reseal the box and head back west.

As if it was his call to make. Somewhere, Jenny must be smiling.

He stared blankly at the open box for a minute or so, and thought about Lilly, and then about Earl.

He shook himself out of his trance and got to work.

He would stay, of course, until she said it was time to go. Those were the rules and that was the game.

Lilly had always been a horny girl; she liked sex, but she liked to masturbate just as much, if not more; the masturbation was almost always more satisfying. Lilly had been masturbating as early as she had memories, and almost daily for most of her adult life.

Lilly would come when she was horny, but she would also come when she was stressed; it was the ultimate stress reliever, for her anyway.

She couldn't count the number of times in grade school, that nervous, anxious time just before taking a test, that she would orgasm right in her chair; those were some of the most intense Lilly had; she could feel her eyes roll back as she muffled herself at climax.

When she was done, she would breathe easy, feel relaxed, and start the test.

When she was younger, up until the third grade, she would stretch across her desk, grab the far top edge with both hands and grind her pubic bone back and forth on her chair; pretty God-damn obvious, the whole desk would shake-right in the middle of class. Yet somehow, amazingly, she never got caught.

Until the sixth grade, that is.

By then, she was more reserved, but no less prolific. She had long forgone the desk-shake routine and now rather inconspicuously squeezed and rubbed her thighs together, working her clit via friction till she came. She got very good at it; fast and efficient.

That worked for a long while, until she finally got caught, nabbed by that creepy kid Darrell, in sixth grade.

She was particularly nervous about a big math test, and was vigorously rubbing her thighs together, not being particularly discrete, and oblivious to the kids around her. Just as she started to orgasm, she heard his high-pitched whine whisper over to her from the next desk. She couldn't, and wouldn't, stop herself, so she kept going till the spasms stopped, coming right through his commentary.

"Hey, I know what you're doing! *I know what you're doing*! Hey! **Hey!**"

She never even looked in his direction.

Only after she finished did she daintily resettle in her chair, pick up her pencil and turn to him, trying to be as polite and diplomatic as she could be, to nip the incident in the bud, Lilly-style.

She slowly leaned over and whispered at him in a courteous tone, maintaining a smile.

"Go fuck yourself you little pervert. You say *anything* and I'll kick your teeth in."

"**Hey!** There's no talking Darrell Parker! Stop talking to Lillian; this is a test! Now move yourself to the other side of the room young man! You should know better, now **move it!**"

And with that, Mrs. Webber stood up from behind her desk, all four foot eleven and a half inches of her. And she never rounded it up to five feet; she never gave herself the half inch, to make it a respectable five-foot even. Not Mrs. Webber.

She was the senior math teacher and the doyenne of the faculty; it seemed kids great grandparents had Mrs. Webber in school; parents would tell their kids she started teaching before electricity. Yet one thing you didn't do, no matter who you were, was disobey Mrs. Webber; no one, not even the football players who towered over her, wanted to endure her wrath. There was a whole lot of attitude packed into that sub-five foot frame. When she spoke, you listened, but good.

The entire class looked up from their papers to stare at creepy Darrell, the culprit. He turned beet red. Lillian smiled at him with the best shit-eating grin you could imagine.

"Yeah, stop bugging me, dough-boy."

She said out loud, which caused the two closest rows to snicker at the slovenly kid, with wrinkled, too-big clothes, always-messed hair and bad breath.

And with that, Darrell, the smartest kid in the class, the kid who never got in trouble, a teacher's dream, was forced to skulk to the other side of the room. He purposely shuffled over, head down, to a desk as far away from Lilly as he could possibly get.

The next day, Darrell quietly entered Mrs. Webber's room and sat at his new, far-away desk and never spoke a single word to Lillian in class again. Actually, that was the last time she had *ever* spoken to that creepy kid, come to think of it.

Six years later, Darrell was valedictorian in her senior graduating class; he spoke eloquently of future goals to achieve, lifelong dreams to fulfill, of better days ahead for all. He didn't speak at all about high school.

And she remembered none of her classmates paid much attention to what he said.

Ten days later, anxious to put the bad memories of a childhood filled with teasing and torment behind him, to start fresh, far away from Belvidere, the fat sap got run over in the rain by a dairy truck crossing the highway.

Dead at eighteen.

The poor kid didn't even die quick; he somehow got caught up in the undercarriage and was dragged head first, screaming, under the tanker a couple hundred feet down the road before the driver even realized what happened.

He was pretty pulpy by then.

He was the first kid her age, in her class, the class of 1982, to die. All the kids talked about it, the dead kid. And for a short time, Darrell became the most popular kid in Belvidere.

A bunch even went out to the County road north of the blinking light at the Hazen crossroad, to see if they could find where his face peeled off on the pavement. Yet no kids from school went to the funeral, not a one. Lilly heard it was a closed casket; not much left of his noggin. His parents moved away years ago, to where, she had no idea.

The buzz in Belvidere lasted clear through the summer; creepy Darrell, the first kid in their class, out of all 169 of them, to die. He won the lottery no one wants to win.

"Remember that fat kid, the one under the truck...."

Followed by a belly laugh by all; that was how classmates introduced the subject years later, even his name got dropped, forgotten. There was no more Darrell, just the *fat kid*. And all the guys would swear they were the one who found pieces of his face on the road.

And that was how creepy, valedictorian Darrell Parker was forever remembered by his fellow classmates from Belvidere High School.

But enough digression; Lilly got back to thinking about the good stuff....the sex.

Lilly always came multiple times on her own; but during sex with guys, she rarely came, even if it felt good. She didn't know why; it was just the way it was. It didn't help that the guys she had been with over the years didn't focus all that much on her orgasms, or lack thereof; it never made their radar screen.

As she got older, into her late thirties, she became much more sexually aroused, as if she needed any help to stoke that fire.

Like a lot of women, she also became more cognizant of the slut factor.

Most woman's magazines she read put the slut cut-off at twenty guys, more than that and you earned the moniker, less and you generally did not.

However, most guys, that is most guys a woman would *want* to be with when she got older, put that factor at a much lower figure, usually less than ten. Single digits. Wishful thinkers.

Now some guys simply don't care about such things, true, and others don't want to know any prior details. But some do, they really do. And this was a bit of a dilemma for women in a new relationship, where the guy happens to be one of *those* guys who wants to know where he is in the queue.

In response, women were always trying to find a way to rationalize a lower number, by redefining, massaging, the definition of what sex really is.

For instance:

Was anal sex really sex?

Lilly was indifferent to this one. Most girls don't have just anal sex with a guy anyway, so the credit factor is low, Lilly included - she got no credit;

What if it was a quickie and no one came? How many strokes really constitutes sex anyway? One? Ten? How many seconds does it have to be in?

Lilly rules say quickies don't count; she never really quantified in her own mind what a quickie was, but in any event, she used it to drop a few stragglers off her queue;

What if it was a drunken one-nighter that you weren't one hundred percent sure really happened?

Lilly felt that if a tree falls in the forest and no one saw it, then she didn't have sex – this dropped out the one-night stand she thinks she probably had with that wedding reception bartender;

What if you didn't know his name and couldn't pick him out of a lineup?

Refer to the bartender above;

What about oral, digit, toy and machine sex didn't count – no matter how far along and kinky it got?

Lilly never added up the count in this subgroup, nor did she want to – one hundred percent credit due and owing;

Did lesbian sex count?

This count stood at three – one hundred percent credit (although all guys would increase the slut factor to one hundred if it applied to lesbian sex – one thousand if they could watch lesbian sex);

What about sex with the same guy – did it count only once, no matter how many times he came back to the trough, in-between relationships with other guys?

Lilly had this scenario with two separate guys – full credit on the repeats;

What about group sex – does it only count for the guy(s) who actually finish in/on you – do short-timers who just stop in on their way to someone else get a pass.

Lilly could actually hopscotch this scenario – multiple man sex didn't apply to her – not yet anyway;

And so on.

For the guys who care about this numbers game, most figure that whatever number a girl tells them, it is fudged on the low side, sometimes by as much as half. The number of girls a guy chalks up, on the other hand, can generally be cut in half, or more, but that's a whole separate discussion.

Lilly's number, using the criteria listed above, settled in at about eleven by her count; that number was a bit blurry and more than a bit fudged. And they all happened, except one, in a twelve-month flurry, between 1997 and 1998, when she was thirty-three years old. It was a busy year.

She counted them again as she stood there with the *Oui* in her hand, partly to reconfirm, and partly to reminisce.

For Lilly, it was a never-ending process to rationalize, hypothesize and generally finagle a way to get it down to the single digits. She needed to find a new magazine article with more exception scenarios; she made a mental note to herself.

The thought of past rendezvous got Lilly juiced; she sat on the edge of Earl's bed, laid back and closed her eyes, folding the magazine on her chest.

None of the guys Lilly was with, except one, the most important one, asked about the total number of cocks she let in – it went with the territory, considering the type of guy she bedded. Lilly had been pretty spontaneous that year, and she was not known for making tempered choices with regard to sex; she went on impulse, and she liked bad boys – a potent combination.

She ran the list in her mind; they were typically lean, muscular and on the taller side of average - *road crew* types that women steal a second look at in the rear-view mirror.

Most were into guns and cars and not terribly bright or ambitious. A mixed bag of wicked looks, hard bodies and dim bulbs – good to look at, selfish in sex and not much else to offer. But they usually had good stamina, would fuck hard, and most important, would fawn over Lilly, especially in the beginning, trying every trick in their bag to get her legs to spread....the prize at the end of the prowl.

All the '97/'98 studs were locals, Belvidere and the outlier Townships of Harmony, Hope and White, who knew each other as friends or acquaintances; and they all knew they were members of Lilly's exclusive little club. Fucking Lilly was a major trophy to be bragged about, especially by this reckless lot. Unlike her mother, Lilly's liaisons were not so discrete. But they all, save none, were smart enough to keep their mouths shut when the guy who truly ruled was around. That would have been very dangerous for one, and all; and they each understood that - even dumb guys are smart enough to understand that.

The lesbian liaisons numbered three, and all were infinitely more satisfying. Each happened with sisters of the various guys she was dating at the time. All three were attractive (Lilly simply wouldn't have sex with an unattractive woman), and they all pursued the relationship with Lilly, not that Lilly played all that hard to get. And Lillian clearly set the table.

Two of the three were straight; Lilly was the first foray for both of them.

As far as Lilly knew, none of the brothers ever figured out the family tryst; the sisters, and girls in general, were much more discrete about such things. Lilly let it go on as long as she dated the particular brother. Lilly never pursued; the sisters always came back for more. Lilly liked it that way; it made the foreplay that much better.

As she laid on Earl's bed, she smiled, remembering all her *rules*. God, remember the rules.

Lilly would only have sex with them in their brother's bedroom; and it had to be in the brother's bed. That was such a turn-on to Lilly, especially doing both the brother and sister in the same day.

Lillian pushed hard on her pubic bone.

Lilly would ask the sister if she wanted to be first or last; invariably they wanted to be first – they derived a sense of pleasure, knowing their brothers would be second in line. One of the three, however, almost always desired to follow her sibling, for reasons best left to the imagination.

Many times, Lilly would be peremptory and make them submit to exactly the opposite of their request; simply to contradict, and control. Then the issue of order became a game in and of itself....a game within the game. Was what the sister requested *really* what she wanted, or was it in anticipation of a switch by Lilly?

God, she missed those days as she rubbed the cotton fabric on the crotch of her pants.

Lillian would usually make the sister stand in front of her and slowly undress, frustratingly slow, in a specific order that Lilly dictated. When they were done undressing, they would be either fully or partially naked; Lilly liked it best when she made the sister keep on a piece or two of clothing, usually a buttoned blouse – white or black preferred. It would be mostly undone and barely hang open, partially exposing a breast, or her pussy, depending on how the fabric hung. The girls learned what clothes Lilly liked and dressed to please her when they knew she was coming over, increasing the odds of a potential liaison.

Lilly loved the control....she inhaled it.

It was funny; the girls would suggest, or encourage, their brothers to call Lilly for a *date* to hang out at the house, watch a movie, or some such thing; the brothers were clueless, never figuring the motives of their dirty little sisters.

Invariably, the brother would be sent for a pizza run; that was the most common ploy. But it had to be to the *really good* pizza place down in Harmony Township; the round trip ride was a little more than thirty to forty-five minutes – not long enough, but it would do; much

further and the boys would balk and get the pie in Town.
And that simply wouldn't do.

Little side trips (cigarettes, or to the pharmacy out on
Route 46) would be tacked on as much as possible, but
not so many that the gopher would revolt and cancel the
trip altogether. Games within games.

The lesbian liaison would start before the front door
clicked shut, on the brother's way out of the house.
Sometimes Lillian would make them stand in the
window and watch their brothers get into the car, while
Lilly undressed them from behind, so they were standing
naked in the window as the brother drove away. She
would whisper in their ear as she disrobed them, telling
them what she was going to do to them, and them to her.

Lilly was a bad little girl.

After they were naked, or largely so, they would have to
undress Lillian, slowly, no matter how juiced they were.

Lilly directed every aspect of the adagio, from the
undressing to the sex, from beginning to end; they
always had to obey – or Lilly would cut them off. No
second chances. She would always tell them beforehand
how many times she would let them orgasm; sometimes
only once, sometimes more. Lilly always had to have
more orgasms than the other girl, no matter what the
number. And they had better deliver the goods.

That was the rule.

Yet despite all the rules, the domination, the control, the
girls always came back for more, because in the end, for
them, it was worth it. Lilly simply gave good sex,
better than any guy ever had, or ever would.

Come to think of it, Lilly came pretty easily with the
girls, and frequently; maybe she was really a lesbian

who also happened to like cock, rather than the other way around.

She thought about it as she lay on Earl's bed, still rubbing her clit, so-good friction, through the fabric.

No….if she *had* to make a choice - give up one for the other, she could give up pussy, she thought, but she definitely couldn't give up cock. She just needed to find a dick that acted like a pussy.

Cord had half the big, heavy box spread on the living room floor, neatly grouped by category: clothes – by type and color, select kitchen utensils, a couple bathroom items, various memorabilia, including the lone herring gull feather – a *memento mori*, and a few books.

He slowly ran his finger along the gull feather from base to tip and carefully set it aside; New Year's day, an end, and a new beginning. That was one of the most important items in the box, maybe the most.

Cord turned his focus to the stack of books; he was especially excited about the neat little tower of classics he had been meaning to read, and others to reread, for some time.

He took a break, sat on the couch, and cracked open his favorite; the book he cherished more than any other he had ever owned, or ever read….*1984.*

He began again, for a countless time, to read about his friends, Winston and Julia. He became both excited and melancholy to visit them; he always did. It was a tortured feel.

By fluke, he flipped open to the tail of Chapter 17, the scene which made his stomach drop. He thought it strange that a random crack of the book in this new place would bring him here.

They were lying on the bed, naked, in their secret apartment above Mr. Charrington's antique shop. It was peaceful, private, and for the first time in his life, in memory anyway, Winston was relaxed….content.

Cord wanted to stop reading before the next line; why couldn't that be the last line of the book? Why couldn't it just end there?

But he knew the answer; it never does, his own life a sad case-in-point.

He wanted to save Winston and Julia and let them live out a quiet, ordinary, and wonderfully boring life in that tired, second floor studio amongst, and lost within, the proletariat. He wanted to save the glass paperweight that suspended the tiny fragment of pink coral. He wanted ordinary, safe and secure.

He hated reading on; but Cord knew he could not shut the book, not now, not ever.

We are the Dead.

Said Winston.

We are the Dead.

Julia dutifully replied.

You are the Dead.

Came the dreadful voice from behind the tired oil on the wall.

The painting fell to the floor, revealing a hidden telescreen. The Thought Police, led by little old Mr. Charrington, suddenly not so bent and feeble, burst into their room. The glass paperweight was smashed to the floor by a nameless, faceless boot-heeled soldier.

I suppose we may as well say goodbye.

Julia whispered, as they stood back to back, naked and exposed, hands above their heads; waiting to be transferred to the Ministry of Love, where they would be systematically tortured till they betrayed one another and learned to love Big Brother – only then would they be set free, and soon thereafter, terminated.

For Winston and Julia, in that one sentence at the end of Chapter 17, life was over.

Any happiness they shared was done, any joy they felt was gone; the short balance of their lives would be spent in a downward corkscrew of fear, pain, betrayal, isolation and utter defeat; death was the best ticket left.

At forty-three years old, Cord felt an adrenaline stab spread through his chest as he finished that line; even though he had read that fateful fragment countless times before, he couldn't stop the helpless, lonely reflex it engendered. Cord hung his head.

He didn't want to read any more, to revisit the slow, spiral descent into submission; to relive Winston's *Room 101*, and to revisit his own, but he knew he would….he had to.

He stretched prone on the couch, put the soft cover on his chest and closed his eyes sad, thinking of Julia. He loved her, he always had, and he always would.

He wished he knew her, could meet her, could talk to her….could save her. He thought of what he would have done differently than Winston to alter the outcome - to survive. To throw himself at the Thought Police, push her out the window; maybe she would have made it, maybe she could have run and hid forever amongst the proles. Maybe she could have simply lived. He didn't care what happened to him, Julia was all that mattered.

But he knew there was no alternate ending, there couldn't be; what was to happen, would happen in the end. It always did. He knew that ending all too well. Those were the rules.

His nose flared and his eyes reddened, welled with tears, but none fell.

For a brief time, Cord thought, a mere snapshot in his miserable life, Winston was happy; and for that, he was a very lucky man. Maybe Cord could be so lucky some day.

He righted the book on his chest, exhaled deeply, and read on, reliving once again the slow, sad spiral. He had to; he had no choice.

Lillian's mind continued its sexual troll.

Lilly's last boyfriend, the last one she slept with at the end of the flurry in '98, and the only one she had been with for the last eight years, was the only one who even asked about the queue; he made Lilly recount her previous escapades over the past year in detail, including the lesbian trysts. She had no choice but to comply, so absolute was his control over her, and so blind her love for him. But he didn't ask out of jealousy or a sense of comparison, or any feeling of inadequacy; he knew he was the best she ever had. Rather, it excited him, which in turn excited her, which in turn excited him.

But there was another reason for him to ask, which was far more important; the issue of alpha dog.

To that end, he sought out the lot who bedded Lillian in his absence, and summarily beat the living shit out of each one who dared take a taste of what he owned, of what was his, and his alone. As word spread like lightning through Belvidere and beyond, the assaults on the interlopers became increasing more brutal, each a step above the one prior. Yet not a one attempted to evade the inevitable. To do so would have invited a fate much worse; that was no joke, and they all knew it. So for the pleasure of a taste of Lillian, they all paid, and paid dearly. And none would ever dare to try and taste again.

And through the entire ordeal, the hunt, the beatings, the increasing violence, their sex got better and better; he ate it alive, and she wholly submitted to him, to whatever he wanted, no matter what he asked her to do, no matter how depraved he got, without limit, without question.

He was, and always would be, the alpha dog.

Lillian would never question him about his escapades, because she knew there were many, and any answer he gave would likely be a lie. And more important, she wasn't sure how he'd react, even to her, about such a question, which he considered to be none of her business. Even though she thought he'd react calm, the question wasn't without risk, if he somehow took offense to her query. And his taking offense to anything, even the most minor of issues, which this clearly wasn't, was always a crapshoot, and rarely worth the risk of his violence. To that end, she wouldn't poke this issue.

But unlike him, the number and variety of pussies he had taken bothered her, so she just didn't think about it, and it went away....magic. That was Lillian's solution to many a problem. Quick and easy.

He had a younger sister, two years younger, her name was Rose. The name, sadly, was misplaced. Rose clearly inherited genes from a remote branch of the family tree; she looked best at a distance, with clothes on – the more clothes and the further the distance the better. A bag over her head would have capped the ensemble. It was that bad.

If only Rose had been a female version of her handsome brother, Lilly surely would have tilted lesbian full-time, and married her.

Lilly didn't give a hoot about the whole lot of prior boys she had fucked; none were the pick of the litter. It was simply about sex and control, two powerful drugs.

But the last one, the alpha above, was different; she had loved him unconditionally all her life, and still did. She had no choice; she couldn't turn it off even if she had wanted.

But he was more than a handful, who presented his own set of problems.

His name was Button Pierce.

CHAPTER 22 – WAY TOO MUCH SEX

Button was Lilly's last fuck, but he was also Lilly's very first, and Lilly's only, save the year-long string with the motley crew between '97 and '98.

Many women, if they had the chance, would like a take-back on that first one, giving that most important chit to the right guy, or at least a better guy, who came along later, when they got older, and smarter.

But not Lilly; if she had to do it all over again, Button would still be the first to get a taste of her; he'd always be the first one she fucked.

Button was a friend from grade school; he was four years older and the two grew up together. They liked each other one day, and weren't on speaking terms the next. They cared about each other, cursed each other, looked out for each other, shared secrets that they only told the other, and invariably each would do or say things to hurt the other – only to quickly move to another topic and act as if the misdeed, whatever it may have been, never happened. Apologies weren't necessary, or given.

In other words, they were best friends.

Button was born in '60, on a dairy farm in White Township, the sprawling, rural farming community that encapsulated Belvidere, like the doughnut to the doughnut hole, as the locals would say. White had no town of its own per se; it was a checkerboard of dairy and crop farms, mainly soybeans and corn, separated by wide, wooded stream corridors and steep, rocky terrain. It was beautiful farm country.

In White, to go to Town, meant to go to Belvidere.

More recently, the crop *de jour* in the Township was ever expanding fields of houses; *Brookfield* was the latest; five hundred-plus age-restricted homes and condominiums on several hundred acres of used-to-be corn, built for upper-middle class empty nesters from more urban northeasterly counties, closer to Manhattan. The land of Mae Edna Bastet, and her retired friends. Lilly used to play in those fields with Button as a kid, alongside herds of grazing *Holsteins* and seas of *Silver Queen* sweet corn.

Button was a hunter; he hunted with his father from the time he was old enough to carry a gun. Sometimes his uncle would come along. He hunted with bows, cross-bows, shotguns, muzzle-loaders, rimfire and centerfire rifles and any other weapon he could get his hands on.

Button loved the pursuit, and he loved the thrill of the kill. He was a master huntsman, adept at the art of the chase, and the finish.

When trapping, Button couldn't describe the feeling of anticipation, the rush of adrenaline in first seeing the sprung trap in the distance, knowing he had quarry. If he was lucky, it wasn't dead; he liked walking up on it, full frontal, knowing it saw him and could do nothing to escape.

He would stand over it, be it beaver, otter, mink or muskrat, and bend down to look at them for a bit, up close, right in the eyes, before he would kill them.

They would rarely struggle at that point, they would just lay quietly, or tremble, and look into his eyes, with pain, or fear, or helplessness. Most whimpered, or made some sort of noise, especially when he placed his hand gently upon them.

He wished he could somehow know their fear, their pain. He never felt pity, and he never let them go….never.

If his father or uncle were within earshot, he would shoot them with a rifle, *humanely*, as required by law. If they were afar, or if he was hunting alone, sometimes he would shoot them, but more often he would gut them slowly, with a Bowie knife, or kill them with his bare hands, watching them slowly die.

That elusive moment, when life is flickering at its very end and death is so close – that split second when the body and the mind finally give up and give in, vand consciousness, life as we know it, fades to black, was intoxicating to him – more so because he alone could control it, and his prey was at his mercy.

Whether they lived or died was in his hands – and they never lived. It was the ultimate rush.

That closet skeleton, however, Button kept to himself; no one saw it, and he shared it with no one, which made it all the more satisfying.

He didn't hate animals; to the contrary, Button believed he had respect for nature, and considered himself an avid outdoorsman, a conservationist. But he had no compassion for the animals he trapped; they were simply for sport, for his challenge and pleasure; the price they paid for being lesser creatures than him, coupled with simply being in the wrong place at the wrong time.

It's a bitch not being at the top of the food chain; he would repeat that favorite line to himself often, and always when he killed; he thought it was clever.

Button used hunting dogs, which he cared for and treated well, like one cares for the tools of his trade; they were not pets. Smoke was his favorite; he worked alongside Button for years....dependable, faithful. And Smoke loved Button, and was always at his side.

The day any of Button's dogs got too old or tired to hunt, the minute they got back to the farm from a day in the woods, Button would casually, with as much effort as one gives to a tired yawn, raise his muzzle and put a bullet in their brain, leaving them where they dropped. He wouldn't look back or even break stride; he would keep walking into the house. The lone gunshot was the bell to Rose to fetch the shovel; it was her job to bury them, without comment or complaint.

His dad kept his old, retired dogs; he had a kennel behind the second, smaller barn, away from the house, and told Button he would care for his old dogs too – especially Smoke, he deserved it, they all did; they were good and loyal, but someday, everyone gets old.

Button would ignore the offer and the advice, they were his dogs, he would say, and he would handle and dispose of them as he saw fit.

Rose and Button's dad knew Smoke was getting old, and they both tried to subtly interject, to steer him from the same fate as the rest. Rose in particular, loved Smoke, and constantly worried for him, knowing her brother. She would sit with him for hours out in the hay barn, scratching his head, rubbing his belly. He was a good dog. However, any attempt at a direct confrontation with Button on the issue would result in Smoke's immediate death, they both knew that; Button would do it simply to make the point. But Button seemed to have a genuine soft spot for Smoke, an affection he never showed for any of his other dogs, although they were good too. Smoke was just different; he did something to Button....he had an effect. And because of that, both Rose and her dad knew he had a chance, a real chance to live. A first for a Button-hunter.

Button and his dad were out on a particularly good day, a nice yield of game. Smoke missed a few, ones he would have never missed in the past; but it didn't matter, it was still a bountiful day; the two of them bagged more birds than they had in years. Button laughed with his dad and patted Smoke on the head, rubbing his belly hard for a job well done. As they piled out of the pickup, back at the farm, there was raucous talk amongst them, camaraderie recounting the hunt, their good fortune, the good day. Smoke's tongue wagged as he trotted alongside Button, glued to his leg, like he always was.

It was a good, good day....and Smoke was happy.

Button slipped behind the trio mid-stride, still in the middle of a laugh about something or another, and pulled the trigger.

The explosion startled Button's father; he spun and fell to one knee. Smoke crumpled in a heap before him, his skull crushed; the tilled soil slowly absorbed the pool of blood. Smoke never made a sound, never saw it coming....never had a chance. He was there, then he wasn't.

Thirteen years together, side by side, and it didn't mean a thing to him. He missed some birds he shouldn't have, simple as that. Button never broke stride, and never looked back.

At the crack of the gun, a flock of crows lit from a pin oak in the field and scattered in all directions, coalesced and slowly circled overhead, till they returned en mass to the same oak, and watched the sullen scene unfold, hidden amongst the green.

His father stayed on one knee beside his friend and quietly sobbed, rubbing the belly of his friend, the fur still warm from the autumn sun. He gently picked up the dog and buried him alone, in a place he never revealed.

He was gone for quite awhile.

And Smoke was never discussed again.

That was the last time Button and his father hunted together. It was an unspoken decision; it just ended. From that point, Button would go out alone, which he always preferred anyway. His dad just got in the way, and he never really liked him anyway. And as his father aged, and Button grew, his tolerance waned; he saw the old man as increasingly slow, soft and weak. Each day that passed made him despise the old fuck just a bit more. Seeing his face less was nothing but a good thing; he should have put a bullet in his brain too, for touching his fucking dog.

Button fished, hunted and trapped anything and everything that was legal to kill, not that he really paid much attention to the legal part.

As a kid, he started a list, the *Kill List* he called it, a chronology of kills he had, categorized by animal, along with the weapon and his age.

The first entry:

No. 1: Barn Cat - Age 6 - Slingshot

He remembered running into the barn like a storm-trooper, with his new slingshot in hand, hurling sharp driveway rocks at whatever target he could find. The bustle startled the mother, who bolted along with the rest of her litter, except one, the tiniest, who didn't know what to do, so she hesitated, just a second, but it was enough to find herself all alone. So she froze. But Button saw her. Without a second thought, he loaded another rock, pulled the elastic as taught as his strength allowed, his arms shaking against the tension, and hurtled the projectile. It hit the barn board with an awful crack, inches from her.

She still had a chance to run, to get away, and live; her mother eyed her from 20 yards, hiding quiet with the rest in a rot hole in the barn floorboards. But she was just two weeks old, and didn't know what to do, so she stayed still, hoping she'd be safe, unseen, as Button dug furious in his overall pocket for a second bullet. He got it, took a few steps closer to his quarry, took aim, closing one eye and unleashed.

The rock found its target, hitting her in the back leg, breaking it instantly, upon impact.

She fell and cried loudly, trying to drag herself away, but it was no use. He was on her immediately, smiling and digging, once again, into his pocket. She looked up at him with wide eyes, trembling, looking for her mother, looking for help. But he just stood over her, smiling, as he pulled the elastic back as far as his strength allowed; his little arms straining and shaking against the taut elastic. He watched her cry in pain, looking to him for help, but none was to come.

He unleashed the third rock and it hit her hard in the stomach, with a dull thud; a shot of blood exited her mouth, and then a slow trickled continued from the corner on her lips and her left nostril. Button laid his slingshot down and knelt beside her, putting his face right up to hers, listening as she mewed fainter and fainter still, her breaths getting shorter, till she stopped crying and her eyes went dead. That's when he smiled widest. It was also his first recollection, his first memory, of getting a hard-on, at six years old. He looked down and felt the little stick in his pants, his midsection was tingling in excitement.

And he liked it.

He dug into another pocket of his coveralls and pulled out his Swiss army knife. He proceeded to cut off the kitten's head; it wasn't easy and he made a mess of it, cursing at all the blood and tiring his arm trying to cut the tendons and break the bones. He kept the severed head in the rafters of the barn; he would sneak away and look at it all summer long, watching it dry, wrinkle and change - but he never told anyone about it, ever. It was his own little secret. He had the skull around for years; at some point, when he was teenager, he lost it.

During his life, Button must have killed a thousand animals, from black bear, eastern coyote, fox and white-tail deer, to jackrabbit, skunk, raccoon and weasel. He shot all types of fowl: turkey, pheasant, bobwhite quail, snow geese, brant, mallard, bufflehead, Canadian goose, rail, gallinule, ruffed grouse and others. Who would think such a menagerie of fauna lived, and died, in the woods of northwest Jersey?

He would shoot woodchucks, possums and squirrel on the farm for fun, sitting on the split-rail, leaving them for the dogs or turkey vultures to eat.

If the crows came down to scavenge an easy meal too fast, while he was still sitting there, he would shoot them too, just because. There didn't need to be a reason.

Crows are protective of their own, known to come to the aid and defense of other crows in distress; hunters know this well. If Button's shot didn't kill the crow, but just wounded it, it was a bonus; he would sit and pick off the followers blindly coming to its aid, and laugh about it — stupid crows.

It was an enabling feeling, having a gun across your lap, knowing you can kill, or let live, at will. For Button, there was no equal.

And because of it, the *Kill List* grew quickly.

That scrap of paper at age six eventually graduated to a black leather-covered mini-notebook, which went with him wherever he traveled, in his pocket.

It became a memento, one of Button's most valued possessions; his Bible.

Lilly didn't really know anything about all that; she obviously knew he was an avid hunter, but took no liking to it. It was a topic they didn't discuss, and she never looked at his little black book.

As she lay on Earl's bed, none of her thoughts about Button involved guns, or animals or death, it was about love.

Lilly drifted back; it was early December, 1981 and she was still sixteen, just about to turn seventeen.

1981 hadn't been good to Lilly.

Button was gone for two long years; he hadn't been home since leaving for boot camp as a nineteen-year old in '79 – Lilly, Rose and Carol saw him off on the bus at the depot across from *Luigis Rancho*. Lilly was several weeks from fifteen at the time Button went away, in her freshman year in high school. She remembered her mom quietly crying as he boarded the bus.

He joined the Marines; as if Button would be anything else, she thought, as she smiled to herself.

He was the most handsome young man in Warren County, and he was unpredictable and *wild*. She never understood how he would be able to handle the discipline and hierarchy in the military. Ultimately, he couldn't.

Button was extremely close to Carol growing up; she was like a second mom. He loved her as much as he loved Lilly, in some ways, maybe more.

It was a need.

She was beautiful, she was a respected adult in the community who paid attention to him, and she listened

to what he had to say, more than he got at home or anywhere else, unless he threatened to hurt someone.
Lilly remembered her mom took a shine to Button even when he was a kid; he was always on his best behavior when he was with Lilly within her ken – and he buttered Carol good with compliments and a bat of those deep blue eyes, with the long, dark eyelashes – women would kill for that boy's eyelashes.

Sometimes, even if Lilly wasn't home, Button would go over to the house and spend time with Carol, to feel what a real family, a happy family, must be like.

Lilly would come home and the two of them would have cooked dinner for her and Earl (Button never had any use for Earl, but he unfortunately came with the package), or the two of them would have made her some sort of present; goofy stuff Button and Carol found rooting around the house or on long walks in the woods, but those were always the gifts Lillian liked the best. Sometimes it was just a different-looking pine cone, sometimes it was a bunch of wildflowers picked from the side of the road; it was always different.

She still had her favorite *gift* in her room; a piece of a felled hemlock that Button had cut and sanded smooth, with a montage of pine needles, leaves, stones and other ephemera glued to it in a winding striation; they said it was like the breadcrumbs from a long walk through the woods – Button and Carol just picked stuff up as they went, thinking about how each piece reminded them of Lilly. Her mom went through each one, like stepping stones, weaving a story of where, why and how along their journey in the woods.

It was the last gift they made before Button went away in 1979, the day before he got on the bus. It was the last time her mom ever saw Button.

Button heard about Lilly's mom dying that past April, in '81, from just about everyone in Town he kept in touch with, but Lillian was the one to call him first; he was the first one she talked to about it, after Uncle Frank, who found the two of them in the house. Before Sam, or even Earl, she called Button.

Actually, she had never really talked about it with Earl to this day, not in any meaningful way. Earl never knew about the note nor what Carol said to Lilly right before she died; it was too hard and Earl wouldn't have really understood....Lilly didn't understand it herself.

But Button understood Lilly, at least in Lilly's mind. He helped her heal long distance in those early days and months; he was a true friend.

Button didn't come home for the funeral, it would be too hard on him, he told her – and he didn't want anyone, especially her, to see him that way.

Lilly stopped thinking about her mom.

Lillian heard rumors in Town that Button was coming home for the holiday, in December, '81, but he would repeatedly deny it when they talked on the phone. She had heard the same rumors many times before over the past two years, but it never panned out – weekends would come and go and he never made it back to Belvidere. Two years is a lifetime when your sixteen years old.

And this time was like the others; he had tried, but just couldn't swing the time off, he told her.

She always got so excited even thinking it may be true – she hadn't seen him for two years, and fourteen is very different than sixteen. She so wanted him to see firsthand what almost-seventeen looked like on her. It looked very good.

They had peck-kissed and flirted endlessly as kids, and they played *show and tell* once when she was almost eight and he had just turned twelve, but she suckered him into showing his little pecker, and he got no pussy-peak in return.

Vintage Lilly, she smiled to herself.

Button had gotten approval for leave a month earlier, in early November, but he wanted to surprise Lilly for her birthday the following month, in December. He got off the bus and walked into Town, stopping outside the Chinese Restaurant on Water Street, a half-block from Sam's, to call her from a pay phone.

She picked up and they talked briefly; he asked her what she was up to – she was just lying on her bed, reading. She told him the weather was beautiful, a powder-blue sky, not a lick of wind, and the temperature was in the 60's, in December! She wished he could see it.

He told her to pretend that if he could spend the day with her, what would she want to do. She smiled and stretched out on the bed as she answered – she said they would go for a walk over to the farm fields, just outside of Town, like they did as kids, and hold hands, and reminisce. He told her he would think the same thing, at the same time, and, in a way, maybe they could go for that walk together after all. She laughed and told him she missed him, and she loved him; she had told him that before, but since April, since her mom had died, she had been saying it more regularly. He said it too, but not nearly as often, and it was always reciprocal. He reciprocated again on this call, which made her warm, and happy.

He said he hated to hang up, but the long-distance charges were a killer and he had to go – he had an important meeting in about ten minutes he couldn't be late for, but he would talk to her again real soon.

She hung up and was happy and melancholy all rolled into one, like you feel whenever you end a phone call you hoped wouldn't ever end.

She curled up on the bed and cradled the phone, thinking about Button and wishing he would come home.

Ten minutes later she was awakened from her daydream by a knock at the front door; Earl wasn't home, neither was Frank. She got up and made her way downstairs. She just barely parted the front curtains to the right of the door, to peak at the knocker, like she always did, but the person was standing just out of eyesight; that was odd, she thought.

The knocker rapped again as she left the window.

She slowly opened the door, and before her stood a ruggedly handsome Marine, in full military cords. Her mouthed dropped, and both hands began to tingle with excitement, like they've fallen asleep, with the blood is just starting to rush back.

She didn't say a word - she couldn't.

Her face lit and her eyes welled; Lilly stepped through the door and walked right into his arms. It was the first time she *really* kissed him, amorously, on the lips, and they kissed long. She could feel his heart against her chest; it was the happiest she had felt in, she didn't know how long….maybe ever.

She pulled away and just stared at him; she couldn't believe he was actually standing in front of her, occupying the same space, for real. And she couldn't take her eyes off his face, his chest. He had filled out; he was thick, more muscular, and his posture arrow straight.

She was so proud of him.

"Am I late?"

He asked, as he smiled.

"No, you're right on time."

And she hugged and kissed him again.

Button took Lilly's hand and they slowly walked down to the sidewalk and made their way down Fourth Street, over to Knowlton and through the *new development*. Those houses were actually built in the 1950's, but were new compared to the Victorians in the middle of Town. The neighborhood had been called *new* for the last thirty years; it would probably always be called that.

They strolled hand-in-hand out past the edge of Town, to the open farm fields in what is now *Brookfield;* she would lean her head onto his shoulder from time to time, wanting to touch him and feel him more than just holding hands.

They made it past the last house at the edge of Town, and slipped between the skeletal corn stalks of the field they played in as kids. They came upon a tractor wagon still loaded with hay, climbed up top and lay there, side-by-side, looking at the warm, blue December sky.

They didn't talk, although they had so much to talk about. She never felt so content, so safe. Button rolled onto his side and just looked at Lilly as he ran his other hand gently through her hair.

"Hey, do you remember when we snuck out to the barn – it was the middle of the day, that Saturday after Thanksgiving? We climbed up in the loft, and hid in the hay bales, watching while my dad, the bastard, was calling for me to do chores and Smoke was sniffing around, trying to find us. He could smell us, but he didn't see us up there. And then my butt-ugly sister was snooping around, figuring she could find me and get some points with my dad by giving me up – laughing while he beat the snot out of me."

"Yeah, I remember."

Lilly knew *exactly* how this story was going to end.

"It was a day just like today; sunny, warm, the hay – I love that smell. I imagine no matter how long you live you never forget it. Whenever I smell hay, I think of that day."

She didn't answer; she just smiled and listened to the story unfold.

"What did we do up there that day? I can't remember."

Button said in a mock, puzzled tone.

Lilly swung her sixteen year old hair lazily to the side as she laid back in the hay on the wagon. Without a word, she pinched open the button on her jeans, and unzipped her fly, like she was slowly peeling a banana; Button could hear each metal zipper clip come undone – she worked that zipper down in a way that would have made most men finish right then and there, in their pants. He was in a trance, watching her undress.

She grabbed the sides of her jeans at the hips and slowly wiggled them down to just below her knees, exposing lean, sculpted legs that seemed to go on forever, till they vanished into her white panties, which hid a little, noticeable mound between the tops of her legs.

"You showed me."

Lilly whispered….

"And I was a little slow in showing you; I guess it's my turn."

And with that, Lilly ever-so-slightly lifted her butt off the hay and grabbed the cotton elastic of her panties, pulling them away from her body. Just as she did, he caught a glimpse through a gap in the side of the pantie leg – it was the first time he saw her crotch, covered in beautiful fur a few shades darker than the blonde hair on her head. Even though it was December, he could still see faint tan lines, remnant from the Indian summer.

"I hope waiting eight years was worth it; she's been anxious to meet you."

And with that, Lilly peeled her panties down. Even though it was sunny, the December air was cool; it felt good on her bare skin and exposed crotch. He could see some little goose bumps immediately form on the top of her thigh. He never knew goose bumps could look so good.

She pushed her panties and jeans down to her ankles, pulled one foot out completely and spread open her legs, giving Button a full view, to enjoy and do with as he wished. She ran her hand down her black wool sweater, which ended right above her navel, and continued over her exposed abdomen, flat as a board, to her vagina.

She fanned her fingers as they ran through the pubic hair, down to her lips. She let her middle finger slightly part the surface, barely touching them – he could see the hair move under her fingertip as she ran the length of her slit, out of sight, and then back up again, to the starting point, at her clit.

She pushed on the button gently, which caused her to involuntarily raise her hips; then she slowly buried her finger inside in one slow stroke; he watched it disappear, till it couldn't go in any further.

All the while, she never took her stare off his crotch. She slowly pulled out her finger; it was glistening – she put it to her mouth, and in the same slow motion, pushed it between her pursed lips, till it was again gone from view. She sucked on it a bit; he could tell by her cheeks and mouth she was working it with her tongue, then she pulled her finger out for him to look at; she had licked it clean.

He couldn't speak; his dick was so hard it hurt, which was not lost on Lilly.

He had jerked off a thousand times fantasizing about fucking her in every way imaginable; yet nothing he ever conjured in his head touched how good this was – and all she did was pull down her pants and finger herself....once.

He figured if he died right now, it would be okay.

He sat up and knelt next to her; she smelled good. He put his hand on her thigh and rubbed it back and forth, to wipe away the goose bumps.

She was still focused on his cock.

"He looks like he might be a bit bigger than the last time we met."

And with that, Lilly sat up, bending her legs but keeping them open in a V-shape, so he wouldn't lose his view. She beckoned him closer with her finger, leaned over and pressed her open lips on his trousers, breathing warm air through the crotch of his pants. She stayed there for a minute, just exhaling, never taking her mouth off his pants.

He was about to pass out.

She grabbed the buttons and slowly began to unhook his pants; his cock was straining to stay in his uniform – it wanted out. She slowly ran her fingernails up and down his shaft through the cloth as she unbuttoned him.

Everything she did was slow and deliberate, like she had written this script and committed it to memory.

He couldn't take his eyes off the prize between her legs, it was covered with arrow-straight, soft brown hair; it wasn't curly or extra thick – he could see her lips clearly through the hair, but it was thick enough to cover them. God he hoped he was first; he was pretty sure he was, based upon their talks over the months. He had figured she was waiting for him; he just hoped he wouldn't be the first while he was still inside his own pants.

Concentrate Button, just concentrate; don't blow it, literally he kept saying to himself as he felt the last button come free. Her cool hand pressed against his abdomen as she pulled on the elastic of his boxer briefs to find the prize. He was looking at the top of her head as she peeked inside to see how that twelve year old dick looked as an all-grown-up twenty-one year old.

She liked what she saw.

"This is what *I've* been waiting for the last eight years."

She whispered, as she slid her hand into his briefs and firmly wrapped her hand around his shaft.

She gently squeezed it and released, then squeezed again and released, on and off, while she held it; his eyes rolled back in his head.

How am I going to make it? I'm not going to make it Button kept saying to himself.

When he pulled down his pants as a twelve year old, she bent down beside him and looked at his little pecker close, studying it. She remembered him grabbing it and pulling it out straight, trying to make it look bigger.

That's when she first saw the dark arrowhead-shaped birthmark on the underside; it was tiny, but remarkable.

She never forgot it; she always knew she could pick that cock out of line up.

Now, with her hand wrapped firmly around that not-so-small, rock-hard pecker, she lifted it up to look.

And there it was, waiting for her all these years.

It had gotten bigger and faded a bit, but it was still there. She smiled and moved her face to his cock, sticking her tongue out to run it down the outside of his shaft, to kiss the arrowhead.

The tip of her tongue lightly touched his skin, while her hand half-cupped his dick, slowly jerking him off.

Her tongue made its way to his head; a pearl-sized bead of come leaked, waiting for her. She extended her tongue to taste it, then slid the whole head into her warm mouth and just held it there, without moving.

Her first taste of come; for some women, it's also their last taste.

Not for Lilly; she started jerking him off fast, wanting more.

"Lilly, stop, stop, stop, stop….STOP!"

He wasn't going to make it, he thought; no matter what he tried to think of, no matter how distasteful, even his homely sister naked, it wasn't going to work - too late - he was about to explode.

My God, how embarrassing.

Instinctively, he grabbed the back of her head and pushed her down on his cock; surprisingly, she didn't resist, she parted her lips and let his head and shaft slide into her mouth, right to the back of her throat; it slid all the way in, save the last half-inch at his balls.

And it was just in time.

He unloaded into the back of her throat, and it was heavy. God, it felt good.

Expecting her to gag and pull away, he let up on the back of her head, and just gently kept his hand in place. That much come would make any woman reflux, at least a bit.

Not Lilly.

Surprisingly, she didn't move at all; she let it all slide down her throat – she didn't give up a drop. Even when he was done, she kept his cock in her mouth, slowly running it in and out, keeping gentle pressure on his shaft with her lips.

There was no way this was her first time, he thought, no way. She was much too smooth, much too good.

"Where'd you learn to do that?"

He asked, breathing heavy.

She didn't answer. Obviously Button never heard of the *Kama Sutra;* Lilly silently thanked Earl.

He felt her tongue lick his shaft while his cock was still deep in her mouth – he never lost the hardness. Button could usually come twice without going soft, no problem. Knowing how he felt, he figured he was good for three, but he wasn't going to test that theory before he took the real prize.

As she worked on his cock, he dropped his hand down to her right knee, and, with the tip of his middle finger, he lighted scored a line down the inside of her thigh, just gently touching her skin, heading north. He was only halfway down the road when she started to moan, still

297

with his cock buried in her mouth. As he got closer, he moved his finger slower, making her wait.

She started to nudge herself closer to him, trying to speed him up – no luck. The more she started to squirm, the slower his finger progressed up her thigh.

He was just south of where her thigh met her crotch; he stopped the forward march a bit and just ran his finger in a small circle on her skin, barely making contact.

Now it was her turn to just about come, but she didn't; she felt like 6:59 with the alarm set at 7; almost there, but the clock just kept ticking – but God did it feel good, and he wasn't even in yet – he hadn't even touched her pussy.

She had been dreaming of this day for years; she could feel how wet she was - she wanted him to feel it too, right now.

This teasing is going to end quickly, she said to herself.

Lilly grabbed his shaft and slid it out of her mouth, then just ran her tongue up the underside, while she calmly spoke.

"You had better stop teasing and put something in me right now, or it is going to be another eight years, Oh!"

She didn't get to finish before expelling a loud moan as he thrust his finger in – one shot all the way to the end of his right middle finger. He started to rotate his finger in a clockwise circle inside her, running it along the walls hard, so she could feel the friction.

She slid his cock back into her mouth and worked it, while he worked her.

"That's number ten."

He said aloud, as he scribed ten revolutions inside her with a single finger, counting them down out loud, from ten to one, slowly, so she knew something was going to happen when the countdown ended.

"Three, two, one; now it's two - ten, nine…."

As he shoved a second finger in, again tracing clockwise. She was tight, his fingers barely fit, and she was going crazy.

The countdown to one resulted in a third finger, which he barely squeezed in; he could feel, and hear, and see, how wet she was.   She had never put three fingers in herself; the most ever were two, and they were her own, tiny fingers.

She could feel him stretching her.

He used his hand to cup her pubic bone, while he pressed his fingertips against the upper, inside of her pussy.   He just rubbed them back and forth as he squeezed her bone, which gave her a hard surface to grind on.   They rocked in motion together, his hand and her hip thrusts.   It was hard to concentrate on his dick in her mouth, so she let it fall out.   It stood at attention next to her face.

She was close, but she didn't want to come on his fingers.

"Put it in….now!"

She breathed.

He didn't need to be told twice.

In an instant he was between her legs; he straightened them out, rested them on his shoulders (*butterfly*, she thought to herself) and grabbed Lilly by the knees to hold her in place.   She quickly looked down to her crotch; she wanted to see him slide in for the very first thrust, ever.

She had plenty of time.

Button placed the tip of his cock just on the outside of her lips, barely touching her, and kept it there for a second, without moving it, waiting for a reaction.

She was just about to protest; as she opened her mouth to speak, he drilled her with one stroke, all the way in, till his balls rested on the hair of her lips. She let out a moan she had been holding for two long years, waiting for the day Button came home.

He was home.

"Grab my ankles and spread me open, in a V, and keep pumping me, hard."

She said as she watched his dick do her, like a machine. They were on the bed in the *Oui* photo spread, just like she always imagined.

"Spread them wider….wider!"

She said as she closed her eyes and listened to that beautiful sound; excess lubrication on the outside of her lips clicking every time his balls hit her.

It was as she always imagined, but better.

No quick come for Button the second time; he got down a rhythm and just pumped her like a piston – hard and deep. He closed his eyes and paced himself as he did her; she opened hers and just looked at his shaft as it slid out, was buried, and came out again; it was completely saturated with her. She loved watching and feeling his cock; it was thick, and it fit just right. And he had incredible stamina; thank God for the Marines. She couldn't take her eyes off the bulged veins on his shaft.

She told him to go faster, then slower, then faster again....then to stop completely and leave it all the way in.

"Don't move."

She would tell him.

"Just flex it inside, so I can feel your head."

Then, without warning, she would yell at him to pump fast and hard again.

All the time, Button would never open his eyes, but he would change his pace, just as she demanded. He never had a girl tell him what to do before, and he would have never listened anyway....except he was listening now, to Lilly.

She turned her head to the side and just let him pump her; she felt completely vulnerable and controlled, even though she was dictating the sex. That was the high; she was in control, but could feel as if she was being taken, against her will, at the same time.

What a ride....and she owned him.

As she laid there content, being pumped hard, like a rag doll, her eyes focused on a distant visitor. Someone had joined their dirty little party.

But it wasn't a *she* hiding in the closet to finish the *Oui* set; rather, it was a *him*; Joe Rydell, the tall gangly farmer who worked the cornfield, and owned the wagon, they were fucking on. Rydell and his brother had worked that field for a good part of the last twenty-plus years.

Joe had walked out of the hay barn to stretch, which was only about fifty yards away, maybe a bit less; he had been tinkering with some equipment, off-season repairs, as if there's an off-season for a farmer.

Something caught his attention; he stopped, took off his cap and was scanning the area by the hay wagon. He couldn't help but see Button, kneeling in his uniform, holding his arms in the air, attached to Lilly's ankles; there really was no way to miss it, if you happened to look in that direction. And that's what he happened to do.

He knew what he stumbled upon, but rather than turn, he just stood there and quietly watched, voyeur, his hands buried in his tan Carhartt pockets, broken in with years of rips and faded stains.

He quietly cleared his throat, walked a few steps closer and watched some more.

As if Lilly needed to be amped any more.

She wasn't embarrassed; to the contrary, she was juiced – she *wanted* the old man to watch. And she knew Joe Rydell knew it must was her; everyone knew Lillian, including Joe.

Just when she thought her pussy couldn't cream any more, it did. She had never been this wet.

Joe couldn't see anything but Lilly's legs, sticking vertical, flagpole. She started to moan, low at first, then louder, to the point that Button opened his eyes and took notice. He followed her stare, looked to the left, and spotted farmer Joe.

Instinctively, he started to pull out.

That wasn't going to do.

"Sweetie, just close your eyes, come on, don't worry about him, he isn't going to do anything but watch; he wants to watch."

Button wasn't convinced; he became distracted and lost his rhythm.

"Come on, sweetie, keep pumping, keep pumping, look at me, keep pumping, that's right, keep….ohh."

Button listened, refocused, did as he was told….and went back to work.

Lillian kept staring at Joe, who just stood still, staring back, never moving. She was moaning for him, for the show. She knew Joe wouldn't come closer; he was a shy man who spoke little and kept mostly to himself. She figured he felt as if he won the lottery; he wouldn't dare blow it by making a scene. And she wanted him to win the lottery too; to enjoy it for as long as he liked, her treat. She knew Joe casually, seeing him in Town time and again; the kind of person you exchange simple pleasantries with, but that's about all. She guessed after today's little performance, Joe knew her just a little bit better than pleasantries. This little coup wouldn't just make his day, it would make his life.

Lillian couldn't wait to greet him in Town; she would walk over and make small talk – standing real close when she did, to see if she got him flustered. Her bet was an easy yes.

My God, Lilly was juiced reliving that day, thinking about Button and farmer Joe; she wondered if Joe still remembered, twenty-five years later.

Guys forget lots of things, but they don't forget things like that. He was probably in his forties back then, around her age now. How strange to think of it in those terms; he seemed like an old man to her at the time.

She had completely forgotten about the key she was looking for, and Cord. Cord who?

She kicked off her shoes, pulled off her socks and unbuttoned her Capri's; she had Capri's in thirteen different colors, it was her favorite bottom. These were Navy blue; off they quickly came, along with black panties, the same way she did on the wagon, one leg out. She ran her hand down to her pussy and started to rub the sides her clit, straddling it with two fingers, as she finished reliving the story.

Lilly had suppressed coming when she was being fingered by Button; she wanted to wait and orgasm on his cock; but now, although it felt good, she just wasn't ready and he wasn't hitting her right. In the staccato throb between her legs, she was in a little valley. Bad timing; she could see by the contortions in Button's face he was ready – too ready.

Lilly was working herself hard on Earl's bed, legs spread out and open in a V. She strained to open them as far as she could, remembering how spread open she was for Button. She spun around to face Earl's headboard, so she could plant her bare feet against the wall and raise her ass off the bed while she masturbated, rubbing hard and furious. She planted and rocked her palm hard on her clit, while her finger worked just inside her lips. She wanted to come thinking of him inside her, like she planned back then.

And she did, loudly.

Cord had fallen asleep on the couch, till he got her wake-up call.

He sat up in a start and strained his neck to listen; did he just hear what he thought he heard? Was that a moan, a moan by Lilly? Was she getting off downstairs?

Cord was fourteen years old again, ready to plant his ear to the floorboards; he had no shame.

He rolled off the couch and ran into the bedroom and stopped to listen, like a bird-watcher waiting for the confirmatory call from the treetops. His cock turned to rock on the short trip from the living room to the bedroom. He slowly crouched down, like a hunter, then lay on the floor and listened, ear planted hard against the worn, wood planks.

Nothing. No moans, no noise. Did he dream that?

Lilly had finished, but she knew she couldn't stop at one orgasm, not when she was reliving the best sex she had in her life, bar none.

She had tried once to figure how many times she ever had sex, just with the guys. She actually did the math, grabbed a calculator, pencil and paper, guy by guy, how long they dated, how many times per week, or per day, they fucked, depending on the guy. Rough numbers for sure, but well thought numbers nonetheless. A serious homework project.

She was sure it was no less than seven hundred fifty times, and likely more than a thousand, that a guy unloaded in, or on, her; be it in her pussy, mouth or ass, or on her face, in her hair, shot across her stomach, in her pussy hair, on her legs, ass cheeks, lower back - they didn't discriminate as to where, and they always finished. *Jesus*, that was a lot of come, and pretty disgusting, thinking of it *en masse*.

She didn't need a calculator to tally her orgasms; she only needed the fingers on one hand; maybe four or five total, tops. Maybe.

Masturbation, on the other hand, back to early childhood, was probably twenty-thousand, and that was no joke. She did that math too.

Of all those sexual acts, with all those guys, the first one with Button in that cornfield on the outskirts of Town in December, 1981 was still the best she ever had, by far. Of the twenty thousand-odd masturbations, she probably relived that hay wagon romp thirty percent of the time, if not more. But she hadn't really used it that much in the last couple of years, since Button went away for the third, and most recent, time, which made this self-sex session all the more erotic. It was pent up, for sure, and needed a release.

She was going to use this Friday afternoon matinee for at least a few more climaxes on Earl's bed; little did she know, she wasn't the only one happy with that decision.

Less than fifteen feet away, Cord, whose ear was red and numb, pressed hard against the floor, wanted to think he was hearing something, but he wasn't.

Had she stopped?

He thought he heard the bed making noises, but was it just wishful thinking?

He looked around the room and saw the hot water radiator, with the water pipe running through the floor. He tried to stick his ear by the pipe, figuring he could get a better shot at hearing her, since the pipe probably tied into her radiators.

No better, nothing but dead air.

God damn!

He thought to himself. He wasn't going to waste this opportunity; he pulled out his hard cock and stroked it, waiting to something, anything, to happen.

He tried to picture her on the bed; she was probably lying on her stomach, hand in her pants, grinding on the duvet cover, thinking about him again. He guessed she got over being mad at him at the boat ramp.

Man, it would be so cool if he could hear her say his name out loud when she came, like Earl said she did. He figured she liked his story; she was getting it doggie-style again, just like he told her at *Nonpareil* last night.

He closed his eyes and pictured banging her like that; he figured they were fantasizing about the same story….that was pretty cool.

Lilly remembered notching a lot of firsts in that hay wagon romp with Button:

- first sex, obviously;
- first time she had seen a man's cock, in real life (not counting the Button peek at twelve). Growing up, she never saw Uncle Frank, thank God, and she never saw Earl as an adult; brothers and sisters inevitably see each other as little kids, and sometimes by accident as adults, especially if they live together for thirty-nine years, but she never saw Earl. Come to think of it, as far as she knew, Earl had never seen her either – *hearing* her was another matter entirely;
- first blowjob;
- first swallow;
- first outdoor sex;
- first combined public and voyeur sex – thanks to farmer Joe; and
- first anal sex.

Oh, right, she hadn't got to replay that part of the story yet.

She settled back in place, ass raised off the bed and feet planted firm against the wall above the headboard, and started to masturbate again.

Button was still pumping her, hard and fast. He opened his eyes and watched himself piston in and out; actually watching his prick disappear into Lilly's pussy as he stroked her was the straw that broke him.

Now Button used no protection, and obviously neither did Lilly, so it was up to him to pull out, which he did, but, like many guys, not quite quick enough. He wanted to get that last pump in, just one more stroke – it felt too good.

He never told her the first shot was not on her stomach, but deep inside her pussy. No harm, no foul, he thought, it couldn't have been that much; he held it while he was still in on that last stroke, didn't he? Yeah, sure he did; he tried to convince himself.

Not that Lilly would have noticed; he came all over her stomach, hips and the hair on her pussy; she couldn't believe how much come there was. Had she swallowed that much too?   Good God, that *can't* be calorie free.

He was exhausted; and fell beside her, breathing heavy.

Button never did ask her if she finished; maybe he figured she did, she thought, by all her moaning for the farmer's sideshow. Actually, the thought of whether Lilly came or not never even occurred to Button, but she never asked him, and gave him the benefit of the doubt.

She cuddled up against him; he just laid there like a slug. It didn't matter, she just wanted to feel him next to her.

She went to pull up her panties, but he put his foot in the way; apparently he wasn't done with her pussy just yet.

"I just want to look at it for awhile."

He said, staring at her crotch, at what he just had, and would have more of, as often as he wanted. Of what he now owned, his alone, for as long as he wanted. He thought of Carol and smiled satisfied to himself; mission accomplished, knowing how she'd feel that Lillian and him were finally together, just as they had discussed that last day they were together. He so wished she could somehow know what had happened. Then he stopped smiling, remembering he had one more box to check.

Lillian smiled and lay back in the hay, and closed her eyes, fully content.

Joe had retired to the barn; he too, apparently got more than his fill....way too much sex.

CHAPTER 23 - BUTTON? WHAT'S A BUTTON?

She felt Button tugging gently on her arm; she must have dozed off, half buried in loose hay. She didn't know how long she had napped, but it couldn't have been more than a half-hour.

He was trying to get her to roll over. Lilly opened her eyes and saw he was on his knees, his cock at attention; it looked even bigger and more swollen than the first romp. And his eyes were wild.

"Come on, get on your knees, bend over the bale. Come one, spread 'em open, wide. Open up."

She did as she was told, without a word. She got on all fours, like a dog, and leaned across a couple bales of hay he stacked, fashioned as if it was the end, or edge, of a bed. He shuffled behind her. She could see he took off his boots, military trousers and underwear; he was naked from the waist down, except his black socks, which looked kind of silly. But he didn't seem to be in a silly kind of mood.

Lilly felt him grab her ass cheeks rough, and pull them apart, letting in a lick of cool December air. She grew goosebumps instant from the chill. Then she felt Button breath warm air on her pussy lips and asshole. He ran his tongue up and down between her lips as he pulled her ass apart further; she felt so vulnerable, so aroused, more so than the first go-around. Whatever he was doing, he was doing it well, like he had done it many times before. And she liked it.

He licked the length of her pussy lips repeatedly, with each pass, he got closer to the fine hair around her ass; the last tongue stroke went right to her asshole, where he stayed and licked in a tight circle, like he did with his finger inside her cunt earlier.

Her first toss of the salad.

"Oh...."

Was all she said, over and again.

She felt him pull his face away and set up behind her, on his knees. She couldn't wait for that cock to pump her pussy again. Lillian's crotch throbbed, waiting for him to plow deep and pump her hard. She wanted that prick right now.

He took his right knee and knocked it hard against the inside of her legs, prompting her to spread doggie even wider, as wide as she could possibly go, completely exposed and defenseless. Even that was a turn-on - complete submission.

He pushed on her shoulders, prompting her to collapse her arms and rest her head on the hay, with her ass stuck high in the air.

He rubbed his abdomen across her ass, then grabbed her hips firm and pressed his head against her pussy, slowly giving her one steady stroke, sliding it in slow, till his balls rested against her lips, still swollen from their earlier fuck. He pulled it out at the same speed; it glistened wet, a mix of her and him.

He place his cock against her again, but this time a bit off-skew.

"A little lower."

She said.

He didn't listen; he just started to push.

"Button, little lower, little....low."

In a single, quick hard thrust, he buried the head of his cock deep into her ass.

She almost jumped from her skin, the pain of entry shot through her. Once he finished that first stroke, he didn't do anything; Button kept perfectly still, holding her hips tight.

"Ow, ow, ow, ow...."

Was all she said, over and over and he stayed statue. She was frozen in place and didn't move a muscle – she was afraid it would make it hurt more, and rip her apart.

"Shh, just relax."

He said, smiling. It felt so good, so dirty, and so right; the last punch of the trifecta. He looked to the sky and his smile widened, and looked to the ground, and smiled wider yet.

Lilly tried to relax, as she was told; she closed her eyes and slowly unclenched her butt muscles, which were rock hard. Her ass felt on fire.

Gradually, the pain subsided and it started to feel warm; she could feel him swelling his dick in her ass as he kept it still, as if on pause.

Then slowly, deliberately, he moved his cock in very short strokes, which got progressively longer. As he did, his shaft started sliding in and out easily; it was so tight, and his dick felt just as good to Lilly, maybe better, than it did in her pussy.

And as he pumped her steady, he whispered to the both of them.

"Do you like when I touch you? When I have you? When I take you? Do you? *Do you? Say it!*"

And as he fucked Lilly harder and harder up the ass, she repeated everything Button told her to, just as she was told. Yes, she liked to be touched by him, to be taken by him, as much and as often as he wanted. He owned her, she said, to do with whatever he wanted, without limits, without bounds. And with each word she recited, with each word of surrender, he fucked her more vicious, his cock throbbing like it never had before.

He pumped her ass savage for a full five minutes, non-stop; it was hard, violent sex, like a rape. And throughout the ordeal, he spewed dirty to her, constantly talking, debasing her. And she repeated everything he said, every vile word; she couldn't get enough.

She reached back, sliding her fingers furious over her clit as he pumped her. She wasn't going to let this one pass; she came once quick; she dragged it out as much as she could, announcing it to him loudly as she did, and then she came a second time, as she repeated his name over and over, asking him to please come in her ass.

He slid two fingers up her cunt while she was already in her second orgasm; he could feel Lilly's hand working her clit frantic on his way in.

Feeling his fingers inside her pussy heightened the sensation, extended her come. When she was done, he pulled his fingers out, grabbed her hair and roughly pulled her head back toward him, like a bitch.

And she liked it.

He told her to open her mouth wide, and she obliged. He shoved his fingers in, and she cleaned off her come with her tongue, as he continued to fuck her ass.

He started to pump even harder and faster now; she knew he was close. He told her he was going to unload in her ass. She begged again that she wanted it; he said he was giving it to her no matter what her answer.

Then Button said something a bit strange. It was the line he had been waiting eight long months to say to her; but now, he was talking to his cock, and to her, watching it piston in her tight can, as she moaned like a little whore. He was sweating profuse from the workout, and the words left his lips with bits of spittle, him pumping her like a maniac.

"Say hello Lilly."

He announced aloud, to all who were listening, as he shot his load deep inside her ass.

Lilly was gyrating her hips on Earl's bed, feet still planted hard on the wall, trying to push right through the plaster. She was lasered-in on sucking her come off his fingers while he pulled her hair hard, pumping her ass. She was so close, she was ready to come again.

"oh, oh, Oh, OH!"

Wake up call for Cord.

While laying on the bedroom floor, Cord had been fantasizing about pumping Lilly's pussy from behind, her bent over the couch; her pants were off, but her top was still on. She was gripping the top of the couch as he banged her hard. Cord couldn't believe he could hear her so easily, she must be literally yelling downstairs, no need to put his ear to the floor for that. Holy shit, she was out-of-control.

He started jerking off fast; he wanted to come at the same time she did. No problem; mission accomplished, in about thirteen seconds.

Just as he was finishing, Lillian was reaching a crescendo.

"Oh, Oh, fuck me, fuck me, fuck me! Oh, Do it! Button, Button, OH!"

Cord lay there on the bedroom floor, dick still in hand, already half-deflated. He had a puzzled look on his face. There was no *Cord* in that sentence.

Button? What's a button?

CHAPTER 24 – LOOKING FOR ME, GROCERY BOY?

Lilly lay for a bit on Earl's bed, catching her breath and running her hands gently through her pubic hair, a warm down period.

She reminisced about the rest of Button's first leave; that week was a blur of non-stop sex, multiple times a day, every day. They each had one-track minds; it was fantastic. She came a lot that week, but only when she helped it along by playing with herself, like she did the first time, on the wagon.

Did that count for coming when she was having sex with Button? Or was that really just masturbation?

She wanted to give him the credit. But even though he always felt good inside her ass or pussy, and she loved fucking him, she knew if she didn't play with herself, she wouldn't have come by him alone, so she figured it really wasn't him, but her.   And although she desperately wanted him to make her come, he apparently didn't have any thoughts on the subject, as far as she knew, since they never discussed the topic. He was finishing just fine, thank you, and when he heard her come, he was probably taking credit, she thought. Well let him think that, since it probably makes him feel good; it was her own little secret. She smiled thinking about it.

Truth be told, Button never gave the subject any thought at all. Truth be told, he didn't really give a shit whether she came or not.

The rest of their sex that first week was like the first, unprotected. Although Lilly insisted he wear a sheath after the wagon romp, Button protested, saying he couldn't *feel* anything and that he could control himself. As expected, he prevailed, and Lillian was almost three weeks late for her period, the first time in her life she was more than a day or two off a very regular schedule.

But by the time she became aware of that situation, Button had gone back to duty. She never told him about that little incident, or her lack of sleep for weeks of waiting, wondering what to do and who to tell. She ended up telling no one.

The day her period finally arrived was a happy day indeed. There hadn't been a better gift that she could recall. She just laid on her bed, smiling, rubbing her flat stomach and thanking no one, repeatedly, out loud. She took contraception into her own hands from that day forward. Never again was she going to endure another three weeks like that.

She only came to realize later that she was likely actually pregnant, for a short time anyway, and miscarried. That thought, surprisingly, made her happy, knowing, at least for a short time, that she was carrying Button's child, or some precursor, even though she never would have wanted it in the end. Not then, maybe not ever. But the thought, in the abstract, was fun, and enough.

Happy to have it and happy to lose it. To Lilly, it made perfect sense.

The next two years were probably the most stable, enjoyable time she had with Button; it wasn't mixed with the ever-increasing bad that eventually accompanied the ever-diminishing good. It was a tipping scale, in the wrong direction.

Yet even with all the baggage, she still loved him, even now, after three long years, with no explanation. And even though she certainly shouldn't, if he walked through her door right now, she knew, deep down, she would take him right back, without question.

It was pathetic, she knew, but she honestly couldn't help herself when it came to Button.

If you've never felt that way about someone, one simply can't understand how debilitating a feeling it is, the ability to constantly rationalize foolish decisions, to do things you know you shouldn't do.   It is simply overwhelming.

If Lilly continued fantasizing about that first week with Button, she would have been masturbating on Earl's bed right alongside of Earl, because she wouldn't have finished till morning. Instead, she sat up and looked for her pants, which had fallen on the floor. As she bent down, she heard a dull thud upstairs, like something dropped, followed by the sound of furniture moving across the wooden floor.

Holy shit, she completely forgot about Cord being upstairs.

She was pretty loud, but she tried to convince herself there was no way he could hear her getting off. If he did, that schmuck would probably think she was fantasizing about him again. But *never* again, she had too many Button stories to recycle; memory fades the rough spots.   Plus, she would never give Cord the satisfaction; his shit-eating grin in the Park when Earl spilled the beans this morning was just about all she could take. There would be no more of that. She was Button's girl no matter what, end of story. The guy upstairs was already passe, not worth another thought.

She slipped on her pants, fluffed the pillows and pulled the bed sheet tight to hide the evidence and carefully tucked the magazine into the back of the drawer, in the same spot she found it. While she was returning the magazine and resetting the stack, she inadvertently spied the third floor apartment key she originally went searching for.

She knew Earl would put it there, he was so predictable.

She smiled.

Lilly snagged it and put it in her pocket; she would decide later if she even cared enough to go snooping around upstairs. That box wording was a coincidence and nothing more. Besides, maybe fart-boy would be too embarrassed to show his face for a while, and would leave the two of them alone. One can only hope.

She went into the kitchen to start dinner.

Cord finished unpacking; the kitchen and bath accessories, the books, the clothes. Everything was set in its place, neatly, in order. He placed the herring gull feather on the dresser, adjacent to the bed. He also rearranged and straightened the rest of the existing apartment furniture, the dishes, the silverware, the spare light bulbs, the garbage bags – everything. He had promised himself he wouldn't do that, just keep it as-is, and put away his stuff like anyone else.

He tried to, but found himself thinking about it too much, and thinking led to obsessing, which never ends well. What was the harm, he figured, so he just did it. And he felt better about it. End of story.

It was after 4 pm; it had taken a couple hours, but it was done. Just to be sure, he reopened all the kitchen cabinets and drawers to see if he missed anything, to be sure nothing fell out of place. Nope.

He brought the ribbed aluminum ice cream scoop, the stainless steel vegetable strainer and two partial sets of the sterling silver place settings from the Estate, along with the shaving cream brush and the straight edge and the little white blanket. They were all put away in their place.

He smiled and was satisfied.

He fished the customer comment list he wrote out yesterday out of the kitchen garbage and put it in a drawer, along with Woody's welcome note. He could always throw it away again later. Then he figured it might be nice to put on a new set of clothes, since he was wearing yesterday's threads, stained with a dried mix of milk and blood.

New clothes, fresh start; at least it sounded good.

He grabbed the *DeMuth* cigar from Woody, the matches, and his unread local paper and headed for the door. There was a little daylight left, maybe a half-hours worth, he could possibly stretch it to an hour. Hopefully the second time around would be a charm, he thought.

And with that, Cord headed out, slamming the apartment door and trotting down the steps. He was going back to the Park, to read, relax, and smoke that hand-rolled cigar till the sun set and dark settled over Belvidere.

Button? What the heck did she mean by that?

He thought to himself as he passed the second floor apartment door. Maybe she meant her clit? Sometimes people call that a button; but why would she say that when she was coming? That was a bit odd, but she was an odd bird anyway.

Button on her pants? That made absolutely no sense.

Whatever.

Lilly heard him leave the apartment; she went to the front window and saw him cross Water Street and head up Greenwich, back toward the Park, the boat ramp, somewhere in that direction. She watched to be sure he kept walking, till he was out of sight.

Damn, she was not at a good stopping point for dinner preparation; otherwise, it would have been a good time to go upstairs and do a little investigatory work. Wait, hadn't she just decided she didn't care about all that?

True, but her curiosity about the box would ultimately get the better of her, of that she was reasonably certain. It had nothing to do with the clown upstairs.

When dinner is done, if he wasn't back, she figured she might take a quick reconnaissance, in and out, to get the goods on Cord Brin's box, or whatever his name really was.

C planted himself on the same bench in the middle of the Park; he couldn't believe he'd gone full circle. Less than six hours earlier, he didn't even know Earl; now it felt as if he knew him all his life.

He smiled as he unfolded the newspaper; he liked Earl, he really did. A pleasant surprise in what had so far been a shit-burger first few days.

He read the local rag, occasionally peering around his paper; more anonymous dog-walkers and bicycle-riders made the late afternoon rounds, looping the square.

Two large, middle-aged women with a portly little girl, about ten, slowly exited a shit-box station wagon, placed their hands on their hips and made an attempt to rotate their middles in a clockwise motion, some kind of obscene stretching exercise. All it did was further protrude their bellies in a cartoonish pose. After a couple swirls, they started a slow stroll around the green; judging by their banter, it was their first day of a new exercise program – they were certainly on the long-term plan.

"How many times we goin?"

The comment was followed by a smoker's hack and a reswallow of coughed-up cud. That was all Cord had to hear; good money bet on white trash, with a partial set of teeth and schooling all the way through the 10th grade for that one.

"It's three laps to the mile *[It was actually three and a third to the mile, but she rounded down]*."

A bit of silence, then the first one responded.

"Let's do one lap for now, my bones are *crackly*."

The larger of the two said, as she hobbled along. Pure poetry.

The second one didn't answer, she was already breathing heavy, after a half-block at best. The fat little girl jiggled ahead, spinning in circles and giggling because the two couldn't keep up with her; Cord could have crawled on his belly and kept up with those two.

'I'm goin' fast, I'm goin' fast, I'm goin' fast, I'm goin' fast."

The little cherubina cawed.

Cord looked for a rock to throw; if he was lucky, he could brain her with one shot. He had no tolerance for kids, he really didn't. And little fat ones were the worst.

Both women were two-hundred-fifty plus pounds, easy, and short, with bright white sneakers, just out of the box, and spandex biker pants. It would have been better for C if the sun had already set. How pathetic, he thought, as he raised his paper to block the view.

Then he looked down at his gut and saw the roll he owned. He pinched it with his fingers; he grabbed a bit more than he expected. Then C sunk his finger into his own gut – yikes, it kept going. Next he'd be complaining *his* bones were crackly.

'Fuck, I got to do something; at least the two cows and the dwarf were making the effort. And what am I going to do, stick a cigar in my mouth as I make fun of the thundering herd?'

Yes, yes he was.

That's it; starting tomorrow morning, he was going to start running around the Park. If he could find an excuse in this place not to make the time, he would be quite impressed with himself.

Tomorrow a.m. it is he scolded himself aloud, to be sure he was listening.

He picked up the paper and lost himself in the local headlines:

- Harmony Township man becomes centenarian - boring - skip;
- Continued squabble on Borough pool repairs in Alpha - skip;
- Redeveloper in Washington files suit against recalcitrant property owner while Town stands by developer and chides holdout for halting *progress* – Cord read that one;
- Sports section - skip;
- Business section - scanned quick - mainly abridged national AP runs - boring;
- Real estate section – C read it;
- Comics - read it, especially *Mutts*. My God, this shit newspaper actually had two of his favorites - *Mark Trail* and *Gil Thorp*. Things were looking up. Maybe Lilly was right, he was gay; no straight guy liked *Mark Trail* **and** *Gil Thorp*.

Cord scanned the silly rag for an hour or so, till it got too dark to read. He tossed it in the can and pulled out the *DeMuth*; it was getting a bit chilly, but not uncomfortable. He lit up and took a deep toke; right away he knew it was a fresh cigar; it drew easily and burned well.

A good cigar made all the difference; he would have to remember to thank Woody.

Cord would immediately produce a mouthful of saliva when he smoked a stale or inferior cigar; he didn't know why, but he would water like a Pavlov dog. He needed a side dish to spit in. But not with this smoke, completely dry; *tant mieux*.

The tanks ended up doing two labored laps, then piled in the low-rider wagon and left. He never saw them again.

Despite the day's events, he was still surprisingly content, enjoying the respite alone, with his cigar. The Park was empty; amber street lights around the perimeter had blinked to life without notice; they cast oblong glows along patches of sidewalk, separated by long links of darkness.

It was eerily quiet; no vehicles, no dogs, no people, just the light touch of a breeze rustling around last year's leaves, unseen, along the dark ground – stragglers under foot which made it through the Fall and Winter. With the Spring rain, they would soon melt into the Park lawn.

Although he didn't realize it, he had been staring, blankly, at the Lion House while he worked the DeMuth down. *L'antre du Lion* was cloaked in darkness, save a few filtered lights in scattered rooms, behind sheers and partly drawn curtains.

He wondered what Carol was doing in there, what her story was.

He inhaled and slowly released the smoke, smelling the burning tobacco as it enveloped his face. This was a good cigar.

He didn't tell Lilly he knew about cormorants. He had seen them all over the world, just about everywhere he went; they were ubiquitous.   But for some reason, he remembered the first time he ever saw them, or at least noticed them. Close to fifty of them were nesting under the Burrard Bridge – he knew because he counted; they would drop down from below the structure, like a plane dropping bombs, and fly like bats out of Hell down False Creek, out into English Bay to fish.

It was a non-stop medley of birds coming and going to big nests under the bridge, like bees to a hive. Most people who even took notice hated the birds; they were dirty, defecating over their own nests and on anything unfortunate enough to pass below, including boats plying the creek. But for some reason, Cord liked them, he always had. He liked them even more now, knowing about Aloysius, and Earl.

He would watch them while he sat along the park path behind Sunset Beach, eyeing the endless line of beautiful young women gliding by on roller blades, bikes or on foot. He never saw so many stunning women in one place; a fashion show runway, stunners, all of them.

He loved Vancouver, despite what happened there.

The cormorants would fish non-stop thirty to fifty yards off the beach, with the look of waterlogged muskrats when they resurfaced after a dive. He remembered them only staying down ten to twenty seconds though, never as long as Aloysius dove.   He also never saw one anywhere else in the world with the ear tuffs or the bright orange neck Al had; and never did he hear one grunt along with someone, like the Al and Earl duet. All that seemed something special, something just for Belvidere. So it seemed.

He thought Al was a pretty cool bird, then he thought about Earl. He was probably still down at the ramp, hanging till dark. He knew Al came back for Earl, and he knew Lilly was right; it had always been Al – regular cormorants don't look like Aloysius; he was clearly different....special.   Earl's life was filled with family and friends, and birds, who genuinely loved him. He was a lucky man.

Cord took a long toke of the cigar with that thought, and slowly exhaled. A thin beam of light caught Cord's attention.

Carol had opened one of the double doors, briefly letting the hallway light spill onto the porch. He faintly heard the door click shut, then nothing. He squinted his eyes toward the porch, but couldn't see a thing. Then, he saw the faintest twinkle on the far side of the porch, his right side – it looked like a candle.

She must be outside, sitting in the dark. What is she up to?

He got up, cigar in hand, and slowly walked the gravel wynd toward her house. He was cloaked in darkness himself, save the lit end of his cigar; but there was no way she could see that glow, he told himself. He tried to discern her outline on the porch – no luck. As he got close, he walked off the gravel path, onto the soft grass, directly toward the single candlelight flicking on the porch.

He crept along slowly, making as little noise as possible.

He stopped just short of the sidewalk; he was only a hundred feet or so away, but felt invisible, veiled in the dark. There was no one around, not a noise. He stood quietly and stared at the porch. He still couldn't see her, but every now and then the light would go black, then flicker again; she must be moving around, in front of the candle.

She was dead quiet.

Cord didn't realize his stand wasn't so secret; he had inadvertently emerged, partly so, from the safety of the shadows, his left flank clearly exposed within the outer lumens of the nearest streetlight. He couldn't see her, but she could see him, and did.

Cord was naked.

While he stared at the candle flicker on the porch, he felt the hair on the back of his neck bristle, for no apparent reason.

Welcome to the Hotel California he whispered aloud, and chuckled quietly to himself.

Just then, a seductive voice pierced the darkness. It threw a lasso and slowly dragged him out of the shadows; he was powerless to resist. And the message was simple.

"Looking for me, Grocery Boy?"

Earl pushed the door open and inhaled, absorbing the heavy aroma; flank steak, saffron rice and melted butter engulfed the apartment. He loved to eat, and Lilly was an excellent cook, as good as his mom was. His good mood got better.

"Bibby, Al went to sleep, at least I think he did; he flew in the big tree, the tire tree, and I couldn't see him anymore. No one came down the ramp; it was just us all afternoon!"

Earl smiled. No answer.

The table was set for two, in the large, open front room facing the road; half dining room, half living room. Earl saw the table down the hall, but turned left, toward the kitchen, to see Lilly, and the food. Lots of food, but no Lilly.

"Lilly?"

He said in a hesitant tone. No answer. Earl got a little nervous.

"Bibby?"

Earl heard the upstairs door click quietly shut, followed by the quick shuffle of bare footsteps down the hall stairs. He frowned and went into his bedroom to check the secret spot in the drawer.

She had spent too much time up there, she knew, but how couldn't she! She was lucky Cord didn't walk in on her. My God, did she have a load of news, with no one to tell!

Lilly quietly clicked open the door, saw the coast was clear, and quickly made her way into the kitchen.

The dinner was untouched on the counter, a sure sign Earl wasn't home. He could never wait till the food made it to the table, he would start eating standing up in the kitchen, no matter how much Lilly scolded him. He just couldn't wait. If he had been home, the food would already be half-gone.

She sighed to herself; good, no Earl to explain to. Now, how was she going to tell Earl about the news, without spilling the beans? This required some careful thought.

She went over to the sink to wash the stupid red ink off her left hand; however, as she was just about to start, she got nervous holding that key any longer than necessary.

And the bastard hadn't locked the door anyway; she didn't even need the damn key.

First things first; she had to get that key back in the armoire drawer. She opened the oven and checked the tray of rolls, warming until Earl got home. Just then, she heard the downstairs hallway door open; perfect timing – she tossed them in a wicker basket.

Rolls in hand, Lilly was preoccupied thinking of how to tell Earl about her find, talking to herself out loud, concocting a story, as she turned the corner and entered his dark bedroom.

She just caught a glimpse of the opened armoire, the top drawer askew, when the room erupted.

"AAHHHA!!"

Bellowed from the darkness.

Earl suddenly appeared from the side of the armoire, like the tilt of a Frankenstein, feet planted firm, leaning ominous from the dark of the shadows.

Lilly screamed; the rolls went flying through the darkness, the wicker basket followed, arcing through the air.

Somehow, Lilly held onto the key as she fell off balance, crashing into the wall. All her karate training, to fend off burglars hiding in the shadows, went out the window in a flash.

Lilly's heart was beating a mile a minute; it took her a moment to focus on the shape in the shadow and realize it was Earl. She didn't have time enough to recover and yell at him, he beat her to it.

"Where were **you**!"

He barked from the dark, as he wagged his oversized pointer at her.

Busted! The only defense was an indignant offense, a Lilly specialty.

"For God sakes Earl! You could have given me a heart attack! What is wrong with you?! I'm really getting tired of this."

Think Lilly, think.

"Where's the key?"

"What key?"

She purred in the mock of a clear conscience.

"You know what key, give it back!"

"Earl, do you know how long it takes to make dinner, and how much I like the little Portuguese rolls, heated just right, and now they're *all* over the room, because of *you*! Now help me pick them up! You are wiping off each one too, **every one of them!**"

Earl listened and did what he was told, because that's what Earl did, especially when it was Lilly barking the orders. And in the briefest of lapses, he forgot about the key, as he dropped to his knees, scuffling around like a kid, trying to recapture the scattered rolls in the dark. It was the all the break Lilly needed; she quickly stuffed the key back in the drawer as her brother's back was turned. That girl was quick.

"I can't see!"

Earl whined.

"Well, then why are you playing games, hiding in the dark trying to scare me, when all I was doing was trying to make your dinner, just like you asked, just like the best sister a brother could ever have would. Fine thanks I get for being so good to you."

"I'm sorry Lilly."

"That's okay, I forgive you, this time."

Lilly said as she turned to flip on the bedroom light. The tables had turned full, and Lilly stood silent, with the look of one now clearly having the upper hand, refusing to help retrieve the errant rolls.

As Earl crawled around on all fours, collecting the rolls, he remembered why he was hiding in the first place.

"Hey, where's the key Lilly? Give it back; I'm telling!"

"What key?"

She said again, this time with the utmost air of confidence.

She grabbed the wicker from Earl, a couple rolls were still missing; it didn't matter anymore - mission accomplished. They'd be found eventually, she figured, when she made Earl clean his room.

"Mr. Boeman's key; you took it and were snooping around upstairs – I'm telling Cord!"

"Where did you hide this key you're talking about Earl, the one you say is missing, that I took?"

"I'm not telling!"

And with that, Earl stood up and went over to the drawer, stood in front of it, and pushed some clothes around. As he did, he exposed the pile of nudie magazines, just a bit of the corners.

"It was in here, and now it's not. You took it!"

"Earl, I wouldn't go in your drawer without asking, that would be rude. Hey, what are those magazines; can I take a look?"

"NO!"

And with that, Earl stood straddling the dresser in a defensive position, eyes wide as saucers.

"Well, maybe if we both look, we can find this key. Are you sure it's not there? Why don't you look closer, maybe it's in that pile of magazines; here, let me help."

Lilly moved toward him in an exaggerated step.

"I, I'll look….it's okay."

And Earl turned quickly and tightly, keeping his big body between the stash and Lilly.

She smirked.

"Hey, here it is!"

Earl said, as he smiled. Then he quickly slammed shut the drawer and armoire doors, like locking a safe.

Lilly just stared at him.

"I'm sorry, I didn't hear you, what do you say again, Earl?"

As she tilted her head toward him a bit. He stood there, dumbfounded.

"Hey, here it is?"

He answered weakly parroting himself. But he knew that probably wasn't the right answer; it never was when Lilly talked to him like that.

"No, that's what I thought I heard, which is not what I was *supposed* to hear."

Lilly scolded. But Earl was confused, and a bit scared, so he just stood silent, waiting for her to tell him what he did wrong.

"What I should have heard, should have gone a little something like this: *I'm so sorry Lilly, for accusing you of taking my key, you're the best sister in the whole wide world.* Is that what I thought I heard you say? I think it is."

She folded her arms across her midsection as she said it, with an exaggerated lilt.

"Okay, I'm sorry, I think, but I'm hiding it again, so **you** don't know where it is."

"Fine, but why would I want the stupid key anyway? And I don't go in your room snooping around Earl."

And although that should have just about wrapped up the matter, it seemed Earl had lost interest in what she was saying. In fact, he wasn't even looking at her when she said it; he was looking at his bed, mouth agape, but no sound emerged.

Uh oh, she didn't like the look of that face; something was coming.

"What are **those!**"

And with that, Earl pointed peeved toward the wall above his headboard, where, plastered in the paint, right above the neatly made bed and tightly pulled bedspread, were the distinct shadows of two tiny footprints, spread very far apart, centered above Earl's perfectly fluffed pillow.

Guess she missed those; on the offense again.

"Earl, how many times have I told you about putting your feet on the wall *[Now, Lilly had never told Earl any such thing, ever, and the two footprints were the size of Earl's feet, when he was about three years old]*?!

With that, she indignantly turned and walked out of the room, with her rolls.

"Those aren't mine!"

He yelled to the back of her head.

"Were you on my bed *again*? Why do you hafta do *that thing* in *my* bed?"

"Do *what thing?*"

She said as she quickly spun to glare at him, holding the wicker in one hand, her other hand planted firm on her hip.

"You know what."

Earl started to turn red.

"No, I don't, explain it to me."

Earl harrumphed in exasperation, and sat on the bed.

"Just *forget* it."

"Okay, if you don't want to talk about it, Earl, that's fine with me, but be sure to wipe off the wall, it's bad manners to put your feet on the wall, even if it's your own room."

He just looked at her and frowned; he didn't say another word. She always won the arguments, always.

She walked over to him and kissed him gentle on the forehead.

"Come on Sweetie, dinner's ready."

With that, she walked out; Earl followed, head down, sliding his feet along the wood floor, like a sulking kid who was snookered yet again.

Lilly, on the other hand, was bursting, wanting to tell Earl all about her upstairs exploration. Earl quickly got over his mope, and was eating hearty.

Lilly casually spilled her segue.

"Hey, I went upstairs."

Earl immediately shot her a look.

"Calm down, I knocked first, but couldn't hear anything, and I was worried, you know, that he was okay, so I tried the knob, and it opened. He must not have locked the door. Anyway, I called around, to invite him to dinner, you know."

"You invited him to dinner?   I thought you told him today wasn't a good day."

"Well, I thought it would be a nice thing to do, don't ya think?"

She looked at him with eyes that could melt ice; Lilly was good.

Earl nodded eagerly.

"Anyway, he wasn't answering, so I wanted to make sure he was okay, in case he was home and maybe he was hurt, or something."

Earl looked at her with approval, waiting for more.

"Earl, you should have seen the place, it was creepy! Everything was stacked up extra neat, *too neat*, everything in the pantry was lined up, with all the labels facing the same way, and the silverware was all stacked in piles, and…."

"Why were you looking in his drawers?"

"Oh, I just looked in one or two to see if I could find paper to leave him a note, you know, inviting him to dinner, but I couldn't find any. Anyway, it was just like that movie we saw about the creepy guy who controlled his wife, didn't let her do anything, like a prisoner in her own house, and always called her *Princess*, remember? What was the name of that movie?"

"*Sleeping With the Enemy.*"

Earl said indifferent, chasing the last peas around his plate with a fork.

"Yeah, yeah, that's it! Creepy! Earl, everything, and I mean *everything*, was lined up, everywhere, even his underwear were folded and set in piles, exactly the same, each one, all folded exactly the same."

Earl just looked at her.

"Underwear? Why were you looking at his underwear?"

"I told you, I was looking for paper!"

Lilly yelled, exasperated that Earl wasn't as shocked and excited as she was at her reconnaissance.

"Anyway, in the cedar closet, you know, the one closer to the big front room, on the top shelf, was a pretty big box, all wrapped in packing tape, just like you were talking about."

Earl just sat there and listened.

"And it said just what you told me it said."

"Open When You Are Ready."

Earl recited again, pointing his finger in the air and bobbing it along as he said each word.

"Yeah, that's it; so I grabbed the box to take a look at it, you know, a little closer, to see why it was all taped up like that, and when I grabbed it, I realized it wasn't pushed back against the wall, so I slid it down the shelf, and behind it, you know what I saw? You won't believe it Earl!"

Earl didn't answer, but Lilly was so excited, that she sucked him into the story. Earl leaned forward in his chair, toward his sister, pulled in like a magnet; he stopped asking why she was looking for writing paper in all those weird places.

"There was a big packet covered in aluminum foil, this size *[Lilly drew the size in the air, redrawing it for emphasis]*. It was the size and shape of money, bills! Then I saw another, and then another, three big stacks! Earl, they were the same size, shape and weight of money! It had to be money! And that would be a *lot* of money, thousands, maybe tens of thousands, if it's money, and I bet it's all money!"

"Bibby, you better tell Cord you saw that; you better tell him."

Lilly ignored his advice, and continued her story.

"Anyway, the aluminum foil packs had fancy writing all over them, like some sort of graffiti, written with a red ink marker. It wrapped around on every face of the aluminum foil. They looked like a bunch of amoebas *[Lilly realized Earl wouldn't know what an amoeba looked like; she couldn't even believe she remembered what an amoeba looked* like], you know like puffy clouds in the sky, with smaller clouds drawn on the inside of the bigger clouds, with little dots in them too."

Earl was looking at her with a puzzled face; she lost him.

"Anyway, it's not important what the shapes looked like, but they were all over them, like it took a very long time to draw; why would someone do that? And the ink wasn't permanent; that was kinda dumb, don't you think? To not make it permanent?"

And with that, Lilly held up her left hand, showing large red ink stains on her thumb and forefinger; it was set in the skin but good.

Earl's eye grew wide, which in turn scared Lilly.

"What?!"

She said, startled at his contorted face.

"It was a trap Bibby, just like the bad guys do in the book, trying to fool Ken and Sandy, solving mysteries! But they're really smart about stuff like that - they would have *never* fallen for that amoeba cloud trick, but you did! Oh boy, you're in big trouble now!"

"Be quiet Earl, I didn't fall for anything; this isn't the *Hardy Boys.*"

Lilly was trying to convince herself it was no big deal, as she stared at her fingers. It wasn't working, and Earl's saucer eyes weren't helping. She grabbed the dinner napkin, dipped it in her water and tried to wipe it off her fingers. No luck; not a dent in it.

"Ken and Sandy would know what to do, and they're not the *Hardy Boys*, they're the *Holt* and *Allen* boys, just saying."

Earl leaned in and whispered to his sister, in case any bad guys were nearby, trying to listen.

"Stop talking about your stupid kiddie-book detectives, Earl, this is serious. He put that damn marker over every square inch of that fucking aluminum foil; every time I touched it to try and fix the smudge, I made it worse. Finally, I spun it around and just pushed it back against the wall and put the box in front of it....he'll never see it."

She looked at Earl to see if he agreed with that pipe dream; even Earl didn't buy it for a second.

"You should just tell him, Lilly; that's what mom would say to do. Cord would understand; I'd tell him your sorry too."

"**Are you crazy!** Who knows what those things are all about, let alone that stupid box; we gotta keep quiet, till I find out what's going on. *We* Earl, means *you too!* And stop talking about her."

"He's my friend; why can't you just leave him alone! Why can't he just come to dinner, like you said and we can tell him what you did, that you're sorry, and then it'll all be okay? Why can't we just do that?"

Earl put his hands over his ears and closed his eyes; he wouldn't look at her.

"I know you can hear me."

Lilly said as she tapped Earl lightly on the temple with her pointer.   Then she whispered at him.

"We can't be friends with a guy like that, Earl; we got to find out what he's up to. Besides, I couldn't find any paper to leave a note about dinner."

"You found everything else!"

Earl shouted at her, as he opened his eyes and took his hands from his ears.

Lilly ignored his little rant and got up from the table; she was going to get that red ink off her fingers even if she had to peel off her skin. Earl started to clear the plates, then he would do the dishes; that was his end of the bargain.

Lilly didn't tell Earl that before she got the red ink all over her fingers, before she even found the aluminum foil packs, when she thought Cord was just anal, she took one of the soup cans in the cabinet, above the refrigerator, and spun it around *just* a bit – a mere quarter turn off center with the others. It would be completely unnoticeable to someone normal, like her, but to this nutty guy, she figured he would *have* to notice and it would drive him crazy for not catching it the first time.

That was the experiment, anyway, just to fuck with him.

Well, when she got red ink all over her, she forgot about the soup can; she got nervous and scooted.

Now she wasn't so sure he was harmless, and that the can-spin was such a good idea; she would have to go back up and spin it back, till she found out more about this guy. She didn't want to end up with the knife she harpooned in his *Belvidere* note stuck in *her*. Who knows where that money came from, and who might come to Town, looking to get it back; maybe she should lay low a bit till she figured him out.

That was the plan.

She scrubbed her hand with every abrasive and chemical she could find under the sink; it dulled it, but you could still see a pink stain. She would have to hide that hand is all, no big deal.

Next stop, the Internet.

Lilly booted up and settled in front of the screen at the desk in her room. My God, she hoped she pushed that foil back the right way. In her excitement, she started looking at the those packs of dough, at least she thought they were money; they had to be money, before she really looked at how they were originally stacked. He might not notice the can, but if he checks the closet, he will *definitely* notice the foil packs if they are wrong, let alone all the smudges she made.

She tried to convince herself she put it back right and that the smudges were tiny; you would really have to look to see it. She wasn't doing such a good job on the convincing front. Well, it was too late anyway, she heard him come in earlier, when she thought it was Earl in the hallway. Funny, she didn't hear him moving around upstairs; she stopped and craned her neck to listen....nothing.

She anxiously typed *Cord Brin* into *Google*, to do a little stalking.

Your Search Did Not Match Any Documents.

Interesting, not a thing, not a *single* hit. That was odd; how often do you get a search a person's name and come up with absolutely nothing? *Not very often*, she answered to herself.

Then Lilly typed *Cord* and *Brin* separately, and got 89,100 hits; mainly about umbilical cords, spinal cords, and some doctor named Daniel Brin. Please, she thought to herself, if that guy is a doctor incognito, she'll eat her....something.

There was a science fiction writer, named David Brin; no way the guy upstairs is writing about monsters and distant solar systems. Plus, there was a picture of that guy – *definitely* not him.

How about Judith Brin, a Jewish ballet dancer? Now that she could believe; she was sure he had a pair of pink tights and a vagina hiding under those jeans.

The further she delved into the thousands of pages, the more off course she got. She killed over an hour plowing through the detritus, all seemingly dead ends.

She tried *Yahoo* next.

Did You Mean Cord Brain?

She laughed at that one; a brain this guy definitely wasn't.

But again, nothing, not a single entry for *Cord Brin*.

Typing *Cord* and *Brin* separately on *Yahoo* yielded a mere 35,300 hits; most looked the same as *Google*, except there seemed to be a lot more *vocal cord* entries than *Google*, whatever that meant.

All dead ends again; another half-hour of fruitless page scanning.

She leaned back in her chair, stretched her legs as she extended her arms in another stretch over her head and thought for a bit; in that *whole* apartment, and she went through almost all of it, she didn't find a wallet (maybe he took it with him when he left) or any papers with his name on it. No cell phone, no computer, no hand-helds (Blackberry, iPod, nothing). Not even a business card for anything, or anyone. No mail, no letters, no address book, no notes....nothing. Just some non-descript, old household stuff, clothes, a large white and gray bird feather, a taped-up box with that ominous, cryptic reminder and three packs of aluminum foil covered mystery, coated in non-permanent, red ink hieroglyphics.

She felt the hair on her arms rise.

Maybe, just maybe, she needed to be a bit less in-your-face with this guy till she found out more; he *really* could be a problem, or dangerous – no joke. She wished Button was around; he wasn't afraid of anything, or anyone, and no one, *no one*, ever got the better of him – he always came out on top. If he was around, this guy would be nothing but a joke. But Button wasn't around, and Earl was useless – Cord had him bamboozled but good – Earl would adopt Cord, if he had his way. And Sam seemed to like him too, so he was probably no help either. No, she had to figure this one out on her own, and be careful doing it. She would talk to Woody and Sam in the morning, discretely, without raising any flags, to see what they found out about him, his background, yesterday; Earl was obviously no help in that regard.

She logged onto her favorite porn site and surfed for a while; she quickly forgot about Cord and the red ink on her fingers.

After about fifteen minutes of scanning the free video sites, and finding nothing worth masturbating to, for no particular reason, she thought about Earl. She hadn't seen nor heard from him since dinner and the television wasn't on, at least as far as she could hear. It had to be almost two hours since they finished dinner.

Where is he? she whispered aloud to herself.

Then it hit her. In a start, she bolted from her chair and started to run, yelling out loud.

"Oh God….no, No, NO!"

CHAPTER 26 – A SLOW AMBLE BACK TO A PLACE CALLED HOME

"How'd you know I worked at Sams?"

He spoke casual as he crossed the street, heading for her porch.

"You didn't answer my question."

Carol replied monotone.

"Nor did you."

Cord deadpanned.

"Ah, so this is how it will be, interesting. You don't seem, at first blush, much like the rest. I wonder why that is? There has to be a reason; there's always a reason with that girl. Why don't you come take a seat, Mr. Brin; that is your name, isn't it?"

Cord still couldn't see her; he was walking toward a disconnect voice in the dark. He ascended the porch steps and turned to the right; now he could see her outline - it looked as if she had a bottle on a side table, a single candle and what looked like a miniature, a cigarillo – it was the wrong shape and color for a cigarette.

He walked into her exhale; a cigar it was, with a hearty aroma. It said a lot about a woman when she smoked a cigar, especially alone. He liked what it said.

"Care for a taste?"

With that, she handed the mini to Cord, who took a drag, looked at the brand in the candlelight, and passed it back – he recognized the white label, a *Davidoff*.

He hadn't sat, but rather leaned nonchalant against the porch rail, facing her.

Davidoff's were quality cigars, but it wasn't nearly as good as the *DeMuth*. But the offer and acceptance were pure posturing; it had nothing to do with the quality of the cigar, or any politeness in her offering same. What message was being conveyed? Power? Control? Equality? Supremacy? He suspected door numbers one, two and four. But why do that to a mere grocery boy? Because she somehow suspected he was something more; more than just another led-by-the-pussy Lilly squeeze; of that he was reasonably sure.

He chuckled under his breath; although there were a slew of *Davidoff* cigar shapes and styles out there, by fluke, the only ones he had ever smoked were a box of minis, at the *Biltmore* in Coral Gables, years ago.

That trip was a disaster, not that such an outcome was any surprise - they all turned that way in the end. But Carol's mini reminded him of that little cutie of a waitress in the courtyard grill, flirting with him and his date at the time....well, it was mutual. And throughout dinner; she was plying them both with bottles of Malbec, intermixed with Kir Royales, a booze kick combo they were on at the time.

She danced around a bisexual bent in their banter; she knew that's what C and friend were fishing for. And she was right.

When they hooked up with her in the bar after she got off shift, she proceeded to out drink the both of them, including C, which was a tall order indeed. The binge was followed by a drunken stroll back to the room for a threesome – that was the plan, so C thought.

Usually after a night of drinking, a girl gets better looking – not this one. Every drink he downed she matched, and with each bottom of the glass, he saw her face peel like an onion, getting more haggard as the night unfolded. But he still wanted to shag her, or watch while *she* did. That's the downfall of being a dog; although C certainly should have known better than get rolled like that, at some point, your cock takes over the thinking.

She was clearly an abuser; alcohol, drugs or both – she looked more the part with each swig, the costume sliding off, revealing the rot inside. He remembered her darting, nervous glance, the risk she took drinking in the place she worked, and working the customers in a grift. The bartender saw the gig and just watched, smiling wry as he dried glasses, having seen the play unfold more than once before.

Cord remembered lying face up on the bed, watching the ceiling slowly spin, while she went to the bathroom; his date was passed out, sprawled across the armchair, out of commission. C would still do her solo; his squeeze would have to get off on the story in the morning, as he fucked her; or not – at this point, he didn't care. All his cock wanted was that waitress pussy, bent over the end of the bed, right now.

He remembered the onion being in the can for an awfully long time.

He must have passed out with his mouth open; a moist drool blotch remained on the bedspread come sun-up. Last night's pants were still on, zipped and dry; damn – skunked. He found his date's full bottle of *Percoset* missing, along with the hophead. He shouldn't have told her about those damn pills at the bar; he remembered her interest piqued when he did. That's when she announced she was ready to do some 'exploring' and herded the two of them back to the room. C, the victim of a grift; what a joke.

Cord exhaled slowly, the smoke folded and swirled as it rose toward the porch roof, captured in the candlelight.

"So, how is it that you came to date Lillian? It's all a bit odd; I mean, you don't exactly fit the part. Although you do look, vaguely, remotely, like the last one, *he* was more rugged, handsome, and in much better shape….and without the tire, of course."

Carol glanced with utter distaste at Cord's midsection, as she took a long drag on the cigarillo.

Cord stood in silence; he didn't answer. He couldn't figure which one was worse, her or Lilly. No wonder they didn't get along - two peas in a fucking pod.

He extended his hand toward her, a silent request for another drag on the cigar. She was holding it loosely, her arm folded and resting on the wicker chair, letting it burn. When she saw his arm extended, requesting a toke, she raised her hand slowly and tracked the mini to her lips instead, taking an extra long drag as she looked out toward the darkened Park; then she lowered it again to the armrest, ignoring his request. She didn't even look at him.

He let out a short exhale from his nose and shook his head just ever so slightly in frustration; she didn't notice it in the dark. At least she's consistent; what a bitch.

"There's obviously bad blood between you and Lilly, but it doesn't seem to affect Earl – he seems to *really* like you."

It wasn't a question, but rather a hopeful segue into a revealing ramble by her. But he knew she was more sophisticated than the Belvidere yokels he stumbled across so far; she wasn't going to take that easy bait and babble like some self-absorbed idiot. He really knew that before he asked the question, but it was worth a try.

After an extended pause, she seemed to smile, at least a little, anyway, at his half-hearted effort. It was hard to really see her face, shrouded in the darkness.

She whispered in a pensive tone:

"Earl is a such a *nice* man; be sure to say hi for me when you see him."

With that, Carol stood up, carefully laid the remaining mini on the fish-shaped ashtray, grabbed the bottle – it was port, his favorite cigar partner – and blew the candlelight away.

"Goodnight; you can stay and finish the cigar, if you like."

A moment later, he heard the large double door open and creak shut; she was gone.

Cord sat there in the pitch dark, alone, save the glow of the tobacco. He picked up the remnant cigarillo, she only smoked half, lightly tapped it in the tray, and took it with him. He never looked back at her house as he crossed Hardwick Street. He shuffled through the darkened Park diagonal and made a slow amble back to a place called home.

He must have been up there the whole time; that was two hours, maybe more! Good God, what did he say! She ran up to the third floor door, and saw it ajar; she could hear them talking in the front room, down the long hall, but she couldn't see them.

"Earl, Earl, are you in here?"

She already knew the answer, but it was the flimsy pretense she felt she needed to gingerly pushd the door open and step inside, into the tiny kitchen.

There, staring at her, with a bulls eye drawn on it in pencil, was a notepad, stuck to the refrigerator by a magnet, with a little pencil attached. That *couldn't* have been there, she thought to herself.

The two either didn't hear her or ignored her; she figured either was likely.

She started to move toward the hallway, then she stopped dead in her tracks. She stepped lightly over to the cabinet right above the refrigerator, she was standing with her chin practically touching the notepad stuck to the fridge (that **couldn't** have been there, she said to herself again), and opened it slowly.

Every can was in its place and facing forward, *every* one, even the one she had quarter-turned to fuck with him.

She got another chill; the hair on her arms stood at attention – he *must* have checked all the cabinets right when he came in, because she never told Earl about the can. Why would he do that? Did he think someone was in his apartment? Did he think he forgot to fix them all, just right? Did he think they somehow moved on their own?

This guy was scary.

She was spooked and wanted to get out of there, right now, but she couldn't – she needed to fetch Earl. She slowly made her way down the hall, along the carpet runner, till she tentatively peeked her head into the front room.

"Earl?"

They were just standing up.

"He knows almost all the lines from *Neighbors – almost every one*! I had to help him a couple times, but he's really good!"

Earl squealed.

"We were doing them together; he was Vic and I was Earl – just like I really am, in real life, because I am!"

Cord smiled at how happy Earl was; he wished he was that happy. Was he ever that happy? He already knew the answer.

She frowned; as if Earl needed any more reason to like this guy. *Neighbors* was the key to the city, as far as Earl was concerned.

"Great."

Was all she said, resigned.

"Wow, the place looks, very neat, for a guy. Do you always keep things so neat?"

Cord ignored her comment; he didn't even look at her.

Then she looked at him and saw he was wearing an Oxford with a button down collar, just like Earl wore, how strange was that, and he was wearing tight black shorts. Wait, those weren't shorts, they were black boxer briefs, just like she saw in his dresser drawer; this guy was standing around, chatting in his *underwear*! And she was talking to him in his underwear!

"Excuse me, are you in your *underwear*?"

She said with disgust.

"Excuse me, are you in *my house*? *Uninvited?*"

He said with feigned disgust. Then he turned away from her.

"So, we're on then?"

As Cord put his hand on Earl's shoulder.

"Yep."

"Good, I'll give you that other thing later, the surprise, after dinner, okay?"

"Yep."

"Hey, what thing? What surprise? What dinner?"

Lilly jumped in, at the end of the conga line.

"I invited Cord to dinner tomorrow, but he…."

"Hey, **no way** Earl, you can't just go inviting people to dinner willy-nilly; you gotta tell me first, I need to give it…."

"Listen, its okay…."

Cord started to say, but she cut him off quick.

"**No, you listen**, when I want your two fucking cents, I'll ask; this is a discussion between me and **my** brother, it has nothing to do with you."

"*Actually*, it's a discussion between Earl and myself, and it has nothing to do with **you** *[C wagged an angry finger in her direction]*. Hey, Earl, I'll find a way to get it here and I'll surprise you; I'm sure you'll like it all, trust me."

"Okay!"

Then Earl thought about the other thing; actually, he never stopped thinking about the other thing.

"Did she really say that! *Really?*"

"Yes, really."

"Tell me again!"

Cord looked deliberately at Lilly, then leaned into Earl, put his hand on his shoulder, so he would bend a bit, and whispered in his ear, half-covering his face, so Lilly could neither see nor hear.

My God, those were killer eyes; daggers, pointed at Cord.

Earl was so excited, he didn't know what to do, so he bear-hugged Cord long and hard, in his underwear, picking him up a bit off the floor. He didn't say a word; he just squeezed and smiled.

Cord smirked at the gesture, feeling like a little kid being picked off the floor by a parent.

"It's true, and you deserve it. Oh, by the way, thanks for the heads-up on that *other* matter."

Cord said as he and Earl walked by Lillian, who just stood there, mouth open, eyes the size of the sun.

Earl just smiled as they both headed for the door. Lilly was left in the living room, alone.

"Hey, do you want to get out of my apartment, please; I'm thinking of doing some naked yoga, unless you want to join me."

"Yuck."

Was all she said as she walked by him and out the door; Earl was already nearing their apartment landing, whistling the *Neighbors* tune. Lillian started down the hall stairs, stopping halfway between Cord's apartment and her own as C leaned out his door, talking down to her.

"By the way, thanks for coming up and trying to invite me to dinner – that was so sweet of you; sorry I wasn't home, maybe next time. I'll probably just have something quick, you know, maybe some cold soup, out of the can."

With that he started to slowly shut the door.

"Oh, another thing, do I look like someone you used to know, intimately, that is? Someone, a mutual friend, just told me that; of course, they said I was more handsome."

He finished the sentence just as the door clicked shut. Earl shut their apartment door a split second later.

With that, Lilly was left standing solo in the hall; it was dead still. The *Twilight Zone* came to mind.

She heard the muffled sound of C's kitchen cabinet door swing open, followed by the clink of a soup can removed, opened slowly via the steady, metallic cadence of a hand-held crank.

What the fuck just happened?

She stood silent, with the eyes of a deer in headlights,
staring up at a stranger's door.

CHAPTER 28 – IT WAS DEFINITELY BEDTIME

Lilly charged into the apartment, looking for Earl; his bedroom door was shut. She didn't knock; he was lying on the bed, looking at the ceiling, smiling.

"What was that all about? What's going on? What were you talking about for the last **two hours**?"

"Cord told me not to tell, so I'm not telling."

"Earl, I'm your *sister*, you don't even know that guy; you can't keep secrets from *me*! What did he tell you about himself? Did you tell him I was in his apartment? Earl, you better not have, he could hurt me!"

Earl sat up and grimaced at her.

"Cord would never hurt you, ever! Not like *other* people!"

"What do you mean by that?"

Earl turned his head away from her in a quick jerk, staring silent at his wall.

"Earl, what does that mean?"

But Lilly knew *exactly* what, and whom, he meant. She let it drop.

She quietly sat on the corner of the bed, next to him, and tried a different tact.

"Did you tell him I was in his apartment?"

"NO!"

He shouted, like a kid, as he continued to look away.

"Does he know I have a key?"

"You DON'T; I do."

"Okay, does he know *you* have a key?"

"No, but I'm gonna tell him I do, from when I watched the cats. I'm telling him, and you can't stop me!"

"Okay, okay, you can tell him, but just not yet, okay? *Okay, Earl?*"

She said with emphasis.

He didn't answer and didn't move at first, then he slowly shook his head in the affirmative, but he did it begrudgingly, accompanied by an annoyed nostril-snort. He still refused to look at her.

She put her hand on his back and started to lightly scratch up and down his spine, just the way he liked. Into the breach for a second try.

"So, what do you want for dinner tomorrow night; you can bring your little friend, if you want."

"I'm having dinner with Cord by myself, and then were doing something special and I'm getting a surprise - he said so."

"A surprise?   That's great *[Christ, she could only imagine what that would be, and what new set of problems it would cause coming from this slippery guy – but Lilly had to stay focused, and would delve into that one later]*! What are you having to eat?"

"I don't know."

"We'll, how do you know if you'll even like it then? You know, you only like certain things, like, maybe, *homemade mini ravioli.*"

Now Lilly was pulling out all the stops; the only thing Earl liked more than flank steak and saffron rice was the handmade mini ravioli, stuffed with chopped meat, their mom used to make, along with over-buttered baby Brussels sprouts. Nothing topped that meal in Earl's book....nothing.

It would take Lilly a full day to make three or four hundred of those fucking miniature ravioli sides, place a thimble-sized bit of ground meat on one, and sandwich it with the other side, crimping the pasta edges with the very end of the tines of a fork; each ravioli was no bigger than a small postage stamp. She absolutely *hated* making them – her back would ache from bending over all day putting them together; Earl usually only got them once a year, for his birthday – and even then, Lilly would complain and play the martyr. But this was an emergency. After Earl caved on that, she figured, she could work him for the rest of the info he was hiding, including this stupid surprise she just found out about.

"It's not even my birthday! Not yet anyway; can we really have ravioli now? Really?"

"Sure, you name it."

Right when the words left her lips, Lilly realized she made a fatal mistake. But with Earl, there were no take-backs on such an important topic.

"I want them on Sunday! Oh boy, I can't wait! Thank you Lilly, you're so good to me! You are the best sister ever!"

He grabbed her in a bear-hug and squeezed hard, slowly forcing out her air.

"Wait, Earl...."

She said, beginning to wheeze as she lost her breath from his thank-you.

"I meant I was going to have them tomorrow for dinner, not Sunday."

As her voice squeaked to a whimper. Earl released her, and held her at arms length, talking to her like a doll, as she gulped for air.

"No, I already told you, I'm eating with Cord tomorrow; you can make them for Sunday – and since you couldn't find the note paper, which was stuck right on the frig, by the way, I invited him to dinner, so he can come on Sunday, so make enough for him too, make lots and lots of them, because he's a big eater like me!"

Earl bound off the bed, kissed her and went to the front room to watch an endless string of '80's music videos on the web.

She sat dumbfounded; she got taken again by that bastard, and he wasn't even in the room. She would have to make close to a *thousand* ravioli sides for Earl and *him*! She thought to herself, *could it get any worse?*

"Bibby, are you on the Internet? What the....? Hey! Can't you ever take a break from that....*stuff*!"

Interracial three-way; she forgot to log off before she ran upstairs. Earl was greeted by a black-and-black-on-white video loop of a blonde-haired nymphet, down and dirty on all fours, sporting a too-short cheerleader outfit and getting ass-fucked like a little dog, gagging while swallowing a ten-inch monster cock, over and over and over.

Lilly just shook her head; yes, it *can* indeed get worse. She didn't even answer Earl.

She brushed her teeth, skulked to her bedroom, shut the door and offed the light.

It was definitely bedtime.